ANY MAN SO DARING

ANY MAN SO DARING

SARAH A. HOYT

2003
50TH
ANNIVERSARY

ACE BOOKS, NEW YORK

An Ace Book
Published by The Berkley Publishing Group
A division of Penguin Group (USA) Inc.
375 Hudson Street
New York, New York 10014

First edition: November 2003

Library of Congress Cataloging-in-Publication Data

Hoyt, Sarah A.
    Any man so daring / Sarah A. Hoyt.— 1st ed.
        p. cm.
    ISBN 0-441-01092-X
    1. Shakespeare, William, 1564–1616—Fiction. 2. Great Britain—History—Elizabeth, 1558–1603—Fiction. 3. Stratford-upon-Avon (England)—Fiction. 4. Dramatists—Fiction.
I. Title.

PS3608.O96A59 2003
813'.6—dc22

2003057924

To my brother, Alvarim Marques de Almeida

"I my brother know Yet...in my glass; even such and so In favour was my brother, and he went Still in this fashion, colour, ornament, For him I imitate..."

Twelfth Night 3.4.379–83

Prologue

∞

SCENE: *A stage made of shadow and roiling cloud. In the backdrop a massive castle stands, built of rock so dark that it absorbs all light to itself and appears to radiate darkness in a halo.*

The stage faces a space vast enough to contain the universe and hide within it all the possible worlds. In that space, darkness deepens, a rich velvet darkness, alive like the secret dark of the womb, full of movement and expectation.

An uncertain flicker of what can scarce be called light glimmers, then disappears again, as if it had never been.

Vague rustles echo, the sound of beings—men?—turning and shifting. Myriad small noises merge into a silence louder than any sound.

It is a silence that makes one hold one's breath, as one's ear strains to listen to that which can't be heard: the scurrying of thoughts, the gliding of time.

Out of the dark castle, a being strides. He looks like a man, with short curly black hair and classical features. Taller and more beautiful than human ever was, perfect as unmarred crystal and twice as cold, he looks immortal as a stone or a cliff is immortal—immune to death and life, both, and permanent in its indifference.

He wears a velvet suit, after the Elizabethan fashion—doublet with broad shoulders that narrows to cinch his waist, and hose that outline the muscular contours of his legs. Beneath the hose, stockings and well-cut slippers show. All of it is the dark red of old blood, almost black as it shimmers under diffuse stage lights.

In the middle of his chest, where his heart should be, a black, gaping nothingness throbs and roils, as if all the nights of the world were there collected and from there reached to haunt the mortal mind.

Tendrils of something rise from him. Were they visible, they might resemble vapor rising from ice exposed to the sun.

But these tendrils are invisible. They can only be felt. Their expanding reach, beyond the creature's presence, is the searching out of fear, the spreading of dread.

For in this something—the creature's trail—mingle both the divine cold of godlike indifference and that assured, immutable immortality which mere humans fear more than death.

In his hand, he carries a hunting horn. He steps softly to center stage, his steps small, controlled, as though he fears someone or something. But what can a creature such as this fear?

The posture becomes him ill. It is too human for such a thing as he.

"There's no harm done," he says, and looks furtively toward where the audience sits, like a schoolchild in a crowded room, striving to remember his lessons for strangers. He looks from beneath a straggle of dark hair that almost covers his eyes, a gaze all too human, all too frightened.

"No harm." He looks over his shoulder as his hand clenches, white knuckled, upon his hunting horn. "Have I done harm? Can one like me do harm and make the mistakes to which human clay is subject?"

He shakes his head and looks bewildered. "It is not possible. No. I've done nothing but in care of her. Of her, my dear one, my . . . daughter."

A smile softens his expression, but he lifts his fingers to touch his own lips as though perplexed that such a human expression should dwell there.

He lowers his head, so that his hair again obscures his eyes. A furtive look veils his features, a furtive expression returns to cloud them, like a tenderness afraid of owning itself.

He frowns at his dark red boots for a breath, then looks up and audibly inhales.

As if he cannot believe the words his own lips form, he speaks again.

"She is ignorant of who she is, nought knowing of whence she comes. She thinks I am her father and nothing more. She thinks she is my daughter, nothing else." He shakes his head again. "More to know never meddled with her thoughts.

"Her mother was a piece of virtue and her true father was the King of Fairyland. She was his only heir, no worse issued. Her father, though, a wretch, scarcely deserving of the name, sold kingdom and soul to the dark forces that ever lurk at the edge of magic—and gave himself, indeed, to me, to my immortal, dark power." He looks at the audience as he gestures with his free hand toward the space where his human heart would be, if he had one. It is a gesture of explanation and exculpation both—explaining that he is what he is and apologizing for it in one. He clears his throat, a sound like thunder. He shuffles his feet upon the stage, and from his soles issues sustained howling, like the winds upon distant mountain fastnesses.

"I, myself, am the Hunter, the justicer everlasting, the punisher, the avenger, the supernatural sword that cuts through the heart of malice and slices off the head of ill-intent." He shrugs and opens both his arms this time, as though to signify 'tis not his fault that he is what he is.

"And thus I collected Sylvanus, King of Fairyland, whose several crimes cried to the heavens for vengeance.

"But with him he brought the child, a small babe, untouched by evil,

3

innocent of envy. What was she to me? Or I to her? What could I do with such a flower that even the exhalations of ancient evil could not touch?

"And she . . . oh, a cherubim. She did smile, infused with a fortitude from heaven. What could I have done? I took her as my own, and here I raised her." With a gesture, he shines a light on the tall, impossibly perfect castle, rising atop a black mountain. *"Here on the far borders of Fairyland, where neither elf nor man would seek her out nor disturb the perfect innocence of her childhood. Here, where no one would touch or hurt her, here I guided her first steps, comforted her crying, and harvested her smiles, greedily, as the patient fisherman who waits beside the treasure-bearing oyster to steal the shining pearl. Thus I've learned the gentle heart of a human parent and been father and mother to a frail elf child.*

"But living creatures cannot long dwell in my sphere of justice and vengeance. Without even knowing of them, she longs for her own kind.

"And I myself—" Again, he looks unnaturally bashful. *"I feel a sadness, a desire to be again the unburdened beast I once was, who knew nothing but swift revenge and swifter cutting, and feared for no one, not even himself."* His immortal hand shakes as he lifts the horn. *"Now I do fear for her, as I've never feared for whole countries, entire worlds, for rich civilizations or sparkling cities. I fear the blade that might sever a single one of her shining hairs, and more, I fear the evil—my own and others—that can tempt her to immortality darker and deeper than any death.*

"For the sake of her frailty am I made frail and for the sake of her fear do I tremble.

"Months on end have I put off the evil hour when I must perforce part with her, but the evil hour is now upon me. It will not pass without a pang, a pain, and a rebirth.

"Like any enchanted princess, my own Miranda must awaken from her dream of innocence and relearn the ways of her kind, and in their world risk virtue and life in that struggle from which no warrior emerges unscathed.

"Yet the Fairyland to which I must send her back roils in blood and tosses in strife, in the jaws of civil war, where civil blood makes civil hands unclean.

"And still it is her hour and she must go, to happiness or doom as chance may fall. For she is grown and within her stirs the need for a companion to her life, the need for her own path in the changing world.

"As within me stirs the hunger to forget who I was these fourteen years and return to my simple, brutish, clean ways. My rounds of vengeance have long softened their visitation upon the troubled world. And that, as all perverting of the natural order, brings flourishing of evil in its trail."

He turns to the audience. From the amorphous dark comes not a sound: rather an amplification of hard-held silence—a composition of held breaths, of fast-beating hearts, of pulses rushing, rushing, in mad expectation.

To them, the Hunter speaks, softly, in a confidential stage whisper. *"Something I must contrive—a way to help my princess to happiness and ease."* He nods at his own words. *"Yes, this much I will do. The hour's now come; the very minute bids thee open thine ear. Obey and be attentive. For here will unfold events to amaze your eye, astound your mind, and stun your reason.*

"Listen. Watch. It is a story as old as the world and as new as the womb of tomorrow."

He lifts his horn to his mouth and blows. What emerges is not sound, but sudden wind, a flash of blinding light.

The audience sighs, an expectant sigh. Its sigh trembles and transmutes, flutters and changes, till it becomes the sounds of a bustling city waking up.

Hunter and castle vanish. The stage light grows brighter and a different scene emerges from the darkness.

Scene 1

ꙮ

Early morning, in Elizabethan London. Down the myriad narrow streets, bordered by five-story-tall, wooden houses, foot traffic scurries and carriage traffic lumbers. Oxcarts, laden with the produce and goods needed for the daily life of the teeming city, creep at an almost imperceptible pace. The occasional messenger on horseback, impatient of obstruction in his way, shouts and lays about him with his whip. From busy workshops, the clang of metal, the knocking of wood, the untiring noise of work reverberates, an unnoticed background to daily life. Though it be early, taverns are full and from them emerges the clacking of cups, the unruly noise of drinking songs. The gleeful shrieks of children at play, the admonitions of their vigilant mothers weave joyful notes through this tapestry of sound. All is busy, all resounds with life in London—save, it seems, a soberly dressed man who sits upon a narrow stool in a second-floor rented room. The room itself looks like a hundred other rooms let to respectable burghers throughout London: its furnishings compass bed and chair, clothes-storing trunk with ceramic basin and ewer atop. The only added thing is the narrow table at which the man sits, with paper and inkstone and newly sharpened quill. He is a middle-aged man, but yet good-looking, his hair receding in front but curling over his collar in the back. His face is oval, his lips small, his nose well shaped. He wears a dark wool suit, well cut but no more so than the suits of any middle-class man. From his sleeves and collar a correct amount of white lace peeks, and the single golden ring in his left ear is no ostentatious jewel. But it is his eyes—golden and as intent as the eyes of a falcon intent on the prey—that give him distinction and make him memorable. Those eyes, surrounded by the dark circles of a sleepless night, glare at a blank piece of paper. His name is William Shakespeare and he is the best-loved playwright in London.

W ill glowered at the paper and at his hands resting on either side of it, with something between impatience and dread.

Never had Will felt such fear of a blank page and the words he should pour upon it. Nightlong, he'd tried to write, yet the page remained virgin of any ink.

Taking up the pen, he subdued the treacherous tremor in his right hand. He dipped the pen into the inkwell, which he had earlier filled with the grindings of his inkstone and water.

Vortigern and Rowena, he wrote upon the virgin page.

He knew what he *should* write next. This was the grave and most piteous story of the King of the Angles in northern Britain, who, for a woman's love, sold his kingdom to the Saxons.

Will put his pen to his mouth and nibbled upon the feather end.

Words poured into his mind. He could picture noble Vortigern beholding Rowena's beauty and struck with awe, speaking, "But what may I, fair virgin, call your name, whose looks set forth no mortal form to view, nor speech betrays aught human in thy birth."

He closed his eyes and allowed his hand that held the pen to trace the letters of these words upon the willing paper. "Thou art a goddess that delud'st our eyes and shrouds't thy beauty in this borrowed shape."

The movement of his pen stopped.

The words were familiar, and yet . . .

As many times before, in the night, Will was sure that someone stood behind him. Without turning, Will could feel someone there, a suggestion of laughter, a hint of amusement.

A soundless voice played in Will's mind the next line of what he had been writing. *But whether thou the sun's bright sister be.*

Will stopped as the hair at the back of his neck prickled up, for the words had the manner, tone, and voice of the late Christopher Marlowe, once a greatly admired poet, but dead now for three years. Dead and buried.

Yet the feeling of his voice, if not its sound, ran through Will's mind. *It is Dido, Queen of Carthage, Will. My Dido, Queen of Carthage. Those lines are spoken by Aeneas to Venus.*

Can't you wait till a man turns to dust in his grave before stealing his words?

The mockery, the feeling of disdain, was as much Marlowe's as the tone of voice. When alive, Marlowe had been the play fellow of nobility, the best-dressed dandy of sparkling London.

Will could swear that if he turned, dead Marlowe would stand there, behind Will, in all of Marlowe's marred elegance, his brittle grace.

He would smile at Will, a mild, ironic smile made horrible by the wound in Marlowe's right eye, and the blood trickling down Marlowe's small, neat features to stain the white lawn collar of his well-cut velvet suit.

Cold sweat dripped down Will's spine. He shivered.

He should turn. Turn and dispel this irrational fear.

Turn, he told himself, *turn. The sleeping and the dead are but as pictures; 't is the eye of childhood that fears a painted devil.*

But his body would not obey, and he remained sitting, his hands on his table, his quill pen beside them—slowly seeping black ink onto the blond oak wood.

Between his hands, the paper sat, with Marlowe's words shining upon it.

This was the first time that, unknowing, Will had written Marlowe's words in his own hand. But he'd long suspected that every word that trickled from his pen was indeed Marlowe's.

The words came through him as though originating in some unknown fountain, not within Will's brain. And they had the cadence, the effect of Marlowe's own plays.

There hung the problem.

For if the words were Marlowe's that made Will a success, it was not Will's success, but rather Marlowe's. If Marlowe's words had earned the gold that, accumulating, would soon allow Will to buy the best house in Stratford-upon-Avon; if Marlowe's were the words that had created Will's newfound wealth, what right did Will have to use them to buy a coat of arms that his only son, Hamnet, might proudly display?

Marlowe was dead. After life's fitful fever, he slept well.

But then, whence came his words, like pieces of himself, evading his pauper's grave, at Trinity Church in Deptford, and filling Will's brain and his plays and his purse?

What a horrible form of grave robbing this was, were it true.

But Will meant to steal from no man. Yet each of his words echoed the words of Christopher Marlowe, the greatest playwright the world had ever known.

Warm air drifted through Will's open window, stale and smelling of the city's odd mingle of spices and refuse.

Despite it, Will felt cold, with the cold of the grave.

If Kit Marlowe haunted Shakespeare, why did he do it?

Will had been but an acquaintance of Kit's, not close at all.

Spirits walked for many reasons: for injury done to them—aye, and Marlowe had been murdered. Yet Will was not one of the murderers. For something left behind—and who knew what Marlowe might not have left. Yet force, Will did not know it, nor did he have the object or the riches. For the craving of grace and forgiveness—and Marlowe, who in life had blazed forth atheistic opinions, might well need that. But Will neither judged Marlowe nor condemned him, understanding the man's brittle genius and the doomed love that had led him astray.

But maybe this was different. Maybe the reason Will felt Marlowe so close to him was that Will, and Will alone among mortal men, knew the truth of Marlowe's death.

Most people believed—and not a few averred as though they'd been there—that Marlowe had been killed in a tavern brawl over a bawdy, disreputable love, variously given as male or female, as best suited the speaker's indignation.

Moralists and Puritans had rushed to see in Marlowe's death a judgment on Marlowe's mad, carousing life, on Marlowe's too free opinions, his too analytical mind.

Yet Will would wager that the divine weighed men upon different scales than those of sour-lipped envy.

If those who spoke could but guess, if they could but know that Christopher Marlowe had died in a brawl over the throne of Fairyland, in a fight to preserve the world from the grasp of a dark power! Oh, if they knew that Kit's death, his sacrifice, had earned freedom for them and their children, aye, and their great-grandchildren, too, how they would revere Kit Marlowe, how his cynicism and mocking would be forgotten.

And remembering Kit Marlowe, how they would recognize, in each of Will's words, the tone, the cadence, the fall of Marlowe's words. Will had written the *Merchant of Venice*. Aye, and it was like Marlowe's *Jew of Malta*.

And in Shakespeare's *Titus Andronicus* there echoed the power-and-blood feel of *Tamburlaine the Great*, with which Marlowe had stormed and conquered the London stage.

And there, upon his *Venus and Adonis,* and his *Rape of Lucrece,* the long poems that had settled his literary fame, how come no one saw the rhyme and word, the very turn of phrase, that Kit Marlowe would have used?

For here was the puzzle, here the coincidence that haunted Will's mind like a bad dream standing in wait through a sleepless night.

Will Shakespeare had never written much worthy of note up to the night of Kit's Marlowe's death. And then, as though through a transference of power, a magical transfusion of the poetical vein, he'd found himself able to write: to write words like Marlowe's.

But were these Marlowe's words, grafted on to Will Shakespeare like an alien strain on to the homely vine? And if so, did Will deserve one coin of the money he'd earned? Or should he cease writing and let Marlowe rest in peace in his unmarked grave in Trinity churchyard in Deptford?

The need to write, the need *not* to write, the words trying to emerge, the fear that these were not his words, blazed behind Will's eyes in a pounding headache. Impulses dwelt within him, locked in close fight like relentless duelers, with his writing as a prize.

He was late with his writing. It had been more than a month since he'd promised Ned Alleyn, the chief investor and share holder in Lord Chamberlain's men, that he'd have a play for him. More than a month since that play had been expected to open on the boards of the theater.

But no more of the play was written than that one sentence upon the page and now, thinking about it, Will knew—knew—that he could never write it. For this play would be about a man betrayed by a woman into giving up his power.

Even the theme was Marlowe's and not Will's. Marlowe had written about war and masculine courage and the danger of love and feminine gentleness. Women were either near onto inanimate objects in Marlowe's plays—bargaining chips in the games of male power—or vile seductresses.

And here Will was, Will, who'd been married since he was nineteen and who loved his absent Nan as tenderly as man could love woman. Why should he echo Marlowe's themes and Marlowe's philosophy, save that Marlowe's ghost was in his brain and infected his thought?

Will put his hands over his eyes, and groaned. It seemed to him, for just a second, that his groan was echoed, in Marlowe's tones, from just behind him and to his left.

If he opened his eyes and turned, would he see Marlowe standing there? Russet hair pulled back into a ponytail, one large, almond-shaped grey eye watching Will with weary amusement, while his other eye trickled the blood and brains extracted from it at dagger point?

Instead of turning, Will closed his eyes and called to the still room behind him, to the mundane sounds of the wakening streets outside. "Stay, illusion," he said. "If you have any sound or use of voice, speak to me. If there be any good thing to be done, that might do you ease and grace to me, speak to me. If you are privy to fate which, happily, foreknowing may avoid, oh, speak! Or if you have uphoarded in your life, extorted treasure in the womb of earth, for which, they say, you spirits oft walk in death, speak of it. Stay and speak." And hearing a slithering and a sound like the door opening, he called out, "Stay, Marlowe."

"Will?" a voice asked.

Will jumped, overturning both the stool upon which he'd perched and the inkwell.

The inkwell bled upon his sleeve and poured its rich black liquid on paper and table, dripping its excess onto the floorboards.

Will, his heart at his throat, the lace of his sleeve dripping with ink, realized all too late that the voice he'd heard was the uncertain, shy voice of Ned Alleyn, theater entrepreneur, insecure financier of plays and poets.

"Will, to whom talk you?" he asked again. "And why did you call Marlowe? I knocked upon your door, but you answered not, and so I came."

Feeling like a fool, Will turned and lifted his hand to pull back his hair.

He felt the moisture on his hand too late, and realized that he'd painted a black streak onto his forehead.

"Er . . ." Will said, and once more, nervously, he ran his hand back upon his forehead and hair. "Er."

"All you playwrights are mad," Ned said.

Ned Alleyn was a medium-sized man, with medium-colored hair and medium-colored skin. He wore his suit shabby and much rubbed, the green velvet faded in spots and, in other spots, showing the weave beneath.

Ned could have walked unremarked into any assembly in this town. In fact, the only thing at all remarkable about him was his brown eyes. Not for their color which, like the rest of Ned's person, showed that eagerness not to be noticed, that urge to blend in that made Ned Alleyn so commonplace. But in those normal, unremarkable eyes something burned, something urgent and immediate, so urgent and immediate that it seemed to hold in itself the flickering flame of madness.

When Will had first met Alleyn, when Will had first started writing plays for Lord Chamberlain's men, Will had flattered himself that the keen expression in Alleyn's face was genius and passion for theater.

But over the next couple of years, Will had identified the true cause of Alleyn's expression: it was fear.

The financier had convinced Ned's father-in-law, Phillip Henslowe, to allow Ned to finance the start of this new theater company. Perhaps Ned truly loved theater and what went with it. But Ned hadn't realized, perhaps still didn't realize, what it took to make money in theater. Phillip Henslowe's own forays into the theater had been well financed, by brothels and gambling businesses.

But Ned was an honest man, and he was going at it with clean hands. Often the funds felt short, and on occasion, the actors had to storm his office and demand payment before their shares were disbursed.

The look in Ned's eyes was sheer, manic fear that his acting company would fail and that he'd be ruined. And today it seemed to Will it burned with heightened strength.

He stepped further into Will's room, on tiptoe, as though he were afraid of waking someone. His face looked pale enough to be that of a ghostly apparition.

Will cleared his throat. "Morrow, Ned," he said. "What brings you to my abode so early?"

Because it was not normal for Ned to be here, it was not normal for Ned to come into his employees' rented rooms thus, without a knock, without a by-your-leave.

The entrepreneur's eyes widened, as though he were an intruder caught in an unlawful incursion, and his hand went to his throat, as though feeling the noose with which thieves were hanged. The voice that issued from his lips was small and frighted.

"Er . . ." he said. "Your play. You said you'd have a play for us in a week. That was three weeks ago. Where is your play, Will? Can I look at it, can we have it, in foul papers if it needs be? For the rehearsal." His brown eyes rolled madly about the room as though trying to find, in the spare, carefully made bed, in the neat trunk, in the desk with its piles of clean paper, a hidden play, a stowed-away manuscript.

Finding none, his gaze returned to Will and bore with mad panic into Will's own eyes. "Will, the receipts are down. Everyone has seen your *Merchant of Venice.*" Ned wrung his hands together, as though one of them were a wet rag and the other one the washerwoman's hand. "An excellent play, Will," he assured confidentially. "But all the other companies are presenting it now, and we have nothing new for to bring in the people, and our coffers are empty. Winter will come soon, Will, and I don't know how we'll survive through winter." His gaze dwelt, amazed, on Will's lace, peeking at sleeve and collar. "I know your long poems, *Venus and Adonis,* and the other, the one about the rape, give you some protection from the miserable conditions of the theater. And at any rate, your plays are worth all we pay for them. Only we need another one, Will. Is it ready?"

The panicked cascade of his words having finished tumbling from his lips, Ned stared at Will, the intelligence of his gaze sharpened by galloping fears. Behind his ordinary brown eyes marched armies of despair, brandishing flags of hunger and privation.

Will felt color climb to his cheeks, for the play should have been ready, could have been ready, more than a week ago, but he'd delayed, because he felt Marlowe's words trickle through his incapable fingers onto the waiting paper.

Will felt himself nothing but a vessel for the doomed genius of the late Kit Marlowe, and he wanted to be more. He wanted to write his own plays. He wanted to be applauded for his own work.

Yet how to explain this to Ned, whose very blood ran with ciphers and figures, whose fear was fueled by a tide of red ink upon the company books, whose very life depended on the take of the theater on any given afternoon.

"The play will be done . . . er . . . very soon," he said. He would have to write it. He would have to write it no matter whose it turned out to be, he thought, staring at Alleyn's eyes and feeling Ned's fear like a palpable thing, like a living creature, sniffing about the room and looking for an escape route. "The play will be done."

"Do you have part of it?" Ned asked. He stood on one leg, an anxious stork. "Do you have part of it, some papers I can give the men to rehearse? They are as dispirited as . . . someone much dispirited. They see no end in sight to empty theaters. You may well imagine. If you can give me a little, a few words . . ."

Will swallowed and shook his head. "Not yet, but I will. I promise you I'll have it ready soon. It's called *Vortigern and Rowena,* and I have all the scenes laid here." He tapped his head. "I have all the scenes, and I know what to do. I just have to write it. A simple matter."

Ned's eyes widened again, surprise and confusion in them. "But you've had two extra weeks," he said. "And you wrote nary a word? What is wrong?" Ned's small, sensitive nose sniffed at the stale air of the room, as though looking for something—alcohol? Or vestiges of madness? He advanced into the room, approached Will, with every step drawing closer and yet giving the impression of cringing away, as if afraid of giving offense or causing harm. "What is wrong?"

Will shook his head and shrugged.

"Oh, it scares me. Much does it scare me," Ned said, and his hand again went to his throat, as though feeling the constriction of a noose. "Your face just now, your expression. Oh, it misgave me and made my heart turn on itself, for it was Marlowe's expression that last month before he was killed—it was the look of a man with a devil at his heels and burning fire before him. Are you in trouble, Will? Trouble like Marlowe's?"

Now the frighted rabbit that Ned normally personated became something other, something different—an eagle, impassive of eye, undeniable of voice—his gaze narrowing upon Will like the gaze of an angel seeking out sin, his voice the voice of an avenging preacher demanding confession.

Will drew back. Did Ned have to mention Marlowe? Did he have to pronounce Marlowe's name? Did he have to compare Will's expression to Marlowe's?

"If you mean I've gone all fond of boys and tobacco, as Marlowe claimed to be, then no. I suffer from no such ill." But as he said it, it seemed to Will he heard Marlowe's light laughter, Marlowe's careless voice declaiming, *All that don't like boys and tobacco are fools.*

And Will knew, knew with a deep certainty as never before, that Marlowe's outrageous statement was foolishness, designed to get attention and little else. Designed to put a soothing balm in Marlowe's aching soul, Marlowe's aching heart, by shocking other people.

Because Marlowe had loved neither boys nor tobacco. Marlowe had loved the King of Fairyland. Or at least the King of Fairyland in his female aspect as Lady Silver. Will had never wished to know how Marlowe felt about Silver's male aspect, the king proper, King Quicksilver of the Elven Realms Above the Air and Beneath the Hills of Avalon.

Just thinking on Silver, it seemed to Will that he saw her white skin, her jet-black hair, felt her silk-soft skin upon his weathered cheek, the petal-tender touch of her lips on his lips.

He jumped, startled.

Oh, he hated Fairyland and all that went with it.

Marlowe had died because of his love for the cursed elf. But Will had other loves—his wife, his daughters, his only son—he would not be caught unawares. He would not die for such a foolish thing as a bit of magic, a twist of glamour, the illusory love of elves, those creatures colder than moonlight, eternal as time, and more insensitive to human suffering than impenetrable granite.

Did Marlowe follow him, did Marlowe's words echo through him, because Will alone knew that Marlowe had died as a hero, not as a debauch?

Will touched the tips of his fingers to his lips, where he'd felt the shadow of the elf's touch, and looked guiltily at Ned Alleyn.

"And there you go," Ned Alleyn said. "There you go, jumping at shadows and blushing at nothing. Thus did Marlowe act too, and then, the next thing we heard, he had died of the plague, and then this was not true, and he'd died in a duel in a bawdy house. And then again, there are rumors, rumors that go afoot in the night and hide themselves in daytime—rumors that Marlowe worked for the privy council and it was by them that he was killed." Ned, this new Ned that was more father than cowering entrepreneur, fixed Will with a cold eye, and put his hands on his hips and asked, "Are you involved in secret work, Will? Do you plot?"

At this, Will laughed. He laughed before he could contain himself. Did he plot?

Oh, what were plots? He'd been involved in plots and counterplots, in the warp and warf of Fairyland politics and murderous intrigues.

Fourteen years ago—was it that long?—when his Susannah was a new-born babe and Nan but a new bride, they'd both been stolen by the then King of Fairyland.

To reclaim them, Will had waded into Fairyland politics and drunk deep from the fountain of intrigue.

Did he plot?

Three years ago, with Marlowe, he'd rescued the King and Queen of Fairyland—and the whole mortal world with them—from a power darker than any dreamed by cloistered monks in their worst nightmares, or the darkest visions of mystics who saw apocalypse and destruction in the shadowed years ahead.

Oh, Will plotted, had plotted, and now he wanted to plot no more. He wanted to remain a mortal among mortals and to know no more of Fairyland and its dark corners.

His laugh halted abruptly, on something like a hiccup, and Will read alarm in Ned Alleyn's scared face.

Ned's eyes looked as if they'd drop out of his face, and their panicked look had become something else, a stare of great cunning, an examining glare, like that of a physician with a very ill patient. "If it's not plots," he said. "If it's not plots, then perhaps it's witchcraft, friend Will." Ned's hands grabbed Will's sleeves and held tight—white, thin fingers grasping the black velvet, like spiders clinging to the sides of a gallows. "Perhaps it's witchcraft. Perhaps you've been charmed."

Will felt blood respond to his cheeks, though his lips remained mute. Had he been charmed? Who knew? Once you'd been touched by the fairyworld, would you ever be clean again? Had not the fairy world sought Marlowe out, thirteen years after Marlowe's last involvement with them?

Will shook his head to Ned Alleyn's question, deferring answer.

Ned sighed impatiently. "You actors and playwrights are all the same— those of you who keep your wives far away. Looking for young ladies to still your pain and idle away your solitude, you scant notice if the lady is good or means you evil. And most such bawds, perforce, mean you evil. I, myself, always thought that was what brought Marlowe down—an evil word pronounced by some hag in some black midnight." Now Ned pushed his face close to Will's and asked in a confidential whisper, "Did you, perhaps, Will, disappoint some woman, lie to some bawd, and bring on yourself the cooking of bats and dead man's fingers in a spell that makes your blood boil and your mind race?"

Will tried to shake his head, but what if his problem were truly enchantment? For Marlowe had died in a horrible manner, killed by a supernatural being. Perhaps Marlowe walked the earth, full of hatred or need for revenge. Perhaps Marlowe . . .

Again, Will felt as though Marlowe stood just behind him, Marlowe's grave-cold breath brushing his neck and making the hair there stand on end.

Should Will turn, he would see Marlowe standing there, staring at Will with amused pity in his one remaining eye.

The feeling was so intense that Will did not dare turn and instead stared at Ned's face and remained still, feeling like a hunted animal brought to ground and unable to move.

"That is the problem, is it not?" Ned said softly. And without waiting for an answer, added, "Get yourself to Shoreditch. There, in Hog's lane beside the sign of the snake, you shall find a small brown door, which, when knocked upon, will reveal a Mistress Delilah. Mistress Delilah will remove the ill that's been done to you quickly enough and then can you write my play." Ned smiled, the sweet smile of the completely deranged who, having obsessed on something, cared for nothing else. "And have it ready a week hence."

Will swallowed and made a sound that might be interpreted as assent. Was Marlowe's ghost truly standing behind him? And if he were, would Ned Alleyn see Marlowe?

Ned looked only at Will, and spared no look at the shadows behind Will. "Good. Get you to Mistress Delilah. She will not disappoint." Thus, with a tap on Will's shoulder, he turned on his heel and left the room, never turning back.

Will wanted to scream for him to turn back, wanted to yell that Ned should turn back and look—look behind Will and see if Marlowe's ghost stood there.

Mistress Delilah, Will thought. *Beside the sign of the snake in Hog's Lane.*

Well did Will know Hog's Lane, having lived there, hard by Hollywell, in Shoreditch, where the Rose Theater had been located in which Marlowe's plays had found abode and applause.

It was a hard scrabble district, full of raw, shoddy construction and the people who could afford nothing better: recent migrants to the city, lost souls, vagabonds, and those living just outside the law. A fit place for a witch.

Going to see a witch was against the law, a minor act of sacrilege and heresy that, depending upon the law's mood, could warrant either penance and a fine or jail, or even death.

Will was a good Protestant, forever just within the pall of the Church of England, its blessings and its munificence.

He had willed it so, despite his contact with Fairyland. He had willed himself to be a churchman. He wanted the respectability that came with it for his children and their children.

Not for them to run from the law that outlawed their beliefs. No. They would believe what most believed and be accepted by all.

If Will went to see Mistress Delilah, she could tell him whether Marlowe's ghost truly followed him or whether it all was but the spinning delusion of an overheated brain.

Will bit at his moustache, which, following the contours of his upper lip, outlined his mouth in a thin, dark line, merging with his beard on the sides. He chewed the corner of his mouth and his moustache.

Turn and look, he thought to himself. *Turn and look, you fool! You don't need a witch to confirm the lie of what you know is an illusion. Turn and look.*

Slowly, with infinite caution, he turned his head, to look behind himself.

But before his head was turned and while only the corner of his eye looked onto that dark space behind himself where he felt sure that Marlowe's ghost stood, he caught a glimpse of blue, like the blue velvet in which Marlowe had gone to his moldy grave.

Just that, a glimpse of blue, by the corner of the eye, a hint of movement, a shape that might have been a man and a sound—so light that it would be drowned by the lightest whisper—no louder than the fall of a feather, the rustle of paper in a far-off room.

But that sound, Will would swear, was Marlowe's laughter.

Marlowe's cursed laughter, which should long ago have been stilled by the dirt that filled Marlowe's long-dead mouth.

Will jumped, stifled a scream.

He grabbed his cloak from the peg on the wall next to his bedroom's door and, without turning, without looking, rushed out the door, out of this respectable rooming house, and toward Hog's Lane and Mistress Delilah.

As he walked the narrow streets, elbowing apprentices and squeezing his way between slow, fat matrons burdened with shopping, Will could hear behind him the immaterial but ever-present steps of Kit Marlowe following him.

Scene 2

☙❧

A clearing in Arden Woods, hard by Stratford-upon-Avon. To mortal eyes, it is but a sprawl of rank weeds and straggling bushes, in the gloom beneath the overspreading shade of larger trees. Those with second sight, though, see a castle rising there, a noble palace, the capital of Fairyland in the British Isles—the reign of elven Avalon. The building is a white palace, a thing of beauty, with walls so perfect and smooth, towers so high and thin, as to defy the imagination of humans and the reach of mortal artistry. In front of the palace, a clumsy structure of uneven boards rises, under the ceaseless hammers, the untiring work of many winged fairies. These winged servants of Fairyland, small and dainty, flying hither and tither in flashes of light, work at building the platform for an execution block. The sound of their hammering penetrates the innermost confines of the palace, the royal chamber. There King Quicksilver stands before his full-length mirror. He looks like a young man of twenty, with long blond hair combed over his shoulder. Around him, his room lies neatly ordered, with a large bed, curtained in green, a painted trunk, a well-worn golden suit of armor in the corner, and—on the wall—a portrait of himself which, when viewed from a different angle, shows a dark-haired woman—Quicksilver's other aspect.

Quicksilver looks only at his mirror, never at his portrait, as he raises his hand to adjust the lace collar that shows over his jacket.

When the knocking first sounded, Quicksilver wasn't sure it was more than an echo of the hammering without the walls.

How much noise the servants made in building the execution block.

He flinched from the thought of the block and the purpose it would serve, from the execution to come and the inevitable spilling of noble elven blood.

"Am I a butcher?" Quicksilver asked his own image in the mirror. "A tyrant?"

His image stared back at him, bland and blond, looking as it had since Quicksilver had reached adult stature at twenty. It presented a fair prospect, slim and elegant, in the black velvet suit that molded Quicksilver's long legs, and displayed to advantage his broad shoulders and his svelte body. Though Quicksilver neared sixty-five years of age, yet he looked like a youth of twenty, his moss-green eyes full of sparkle, his perfect features unmarked by wrinkles, his pale blond hair shining like liquid moonlight, combed over his shoulder.

As his own people reckoned their life spans, Quicksilver had barely grown out of adolescence and was a very young elf indeed.

But looking at his own reflection, staring at his own dazed, tired eyes, Quicksilver felt old. The last three years, he had spent commanding armies and putting down rebellion.

Had those three years of fire and blood, of fear and fighting, left no mark? No mark but the look in his eyes, and this tired, careworn feeling in his soul?

How strange nature. How strange that such resounding evil, such suffering, so much blood spilled, left the King of Fairyland looking young and untouched.

Something sounded again—a knock that seemed different from the clamor of the hammer upon the wood of the block.

Quicksilver glanced away from the mirror toward the thick oak door of his room and called out, "Come in."

The door opened to reveal the slim, pale loveliness of Ariel, Queen of Fairyland, Quicksilver's wife.

She slid into the room furtively, and cast a worried glance at Quicksilver, like a child afraid of scolding.

Quicksilver smoothed his lace collar.

His hands felt rough against the lace and Quicksilver's knuckles had thickened.

For three years, those hands had held charmed swords and thrown magic-spelled lances, and taken elven life, with no remorse—or almost no remorse.

Could they now return to the smoothing of lace, the holding of game pieces, the signing of documents, the caressing of his wife, the quiet tasks of a king in peacetime?

They must, Quicksilver thought. After this day, this awful final day of killing, his hands and he himself must learn to live in peace.

The civil war that had rent Fairyland in two was finished. Rebellious subjects, enemies to peace, profaners of neighbor-stained weapon were reformed, and their leaders dead, or soon would be.

Quicksilver had won and today the main leader of those who had challenged Quicksilver's rule would meet his swift and merciless end upon the block.

Quicksilver tried not to think of it, even as hammer blows sounded from outside. The worst horror of civil war had been visited upon him.

His enemy, whom he had defeated, was his near relation, almost the last surviving branch of Quicksilver's own blood.

Quicksilver's own Uncle Vargmar, elder brother of that Oberon who had sired Quicksilver, had led the rebel troops in their treasonous bloodshed.

Ariel's reflection upon the mirror—half obscured by Quicksilver's own—showed as an intent oval face, staring out at Quicksilver with light blue eyes as though she could read Quicksilver's grief and worry. Her expression wavered as Ariel took a deep breath.

"Milord," the Queen of Fairyland said. She came forward, closing the door behind her. Her hand, soft and small on Quicksilver's arm, might have been a sparrow that, alighting timidly upon a branch, fears the snare that will snag him should he delay. "Milord."

Queen Ariel's voice was a mere whisper. Yet Quicksilver remembered how his queen, small and slight and seemingly fragile as she was, had stood by him through the years of this awful war—how she'd nursed the wounded and—being the seer of Fairyland—had endured troubling dreams of blood and upheaval, as she governed the hill in his absence.

He turned to her and gave her his attention with a respect he'd have thought impossible when he'd, blithely, unthinkingly, married her fourteen years ago.

"Milady," he said, and attempted to smile.

"Milord, I dare speak only because I fear if I do not, I shall lose you." She looked at him, her blue eyes veiled, disturbed, as by a dream that refused to dissipate in the light of waking reality. She put her hand on Quicksilver's sleeve, and spoke in a way made graver for his knowing that she was the seer of this hill, endowed with the power to pierce the future and give warning of it. "Aye, me," she said. "I have an ill-divining soul." Her eyes opened wide, unnaturally wide the way they did when she gazed upon her inner visions. "Methinks I see you, now thou art so low, as one dead in the bottom of a tomb. Either my eyesight fails, or you look pale." She looked at him, a look of enquiry.

He sighed, and touched her face with his fingers, gently. "And trust me, love, in my eye so do you. Dry sorrow drinks our blood."

Her large, blue eyes shone unnaturally, as though washed by tears, and her skin looked almost as pale as the white lace upon her black dress.

"Forgive my daring," she said. "I know you've won a great war, and that upon you and you alone weighs this decision and this thought. So forgive your foolish wife for speaking."

Quicksilver managed a smile, though it seemed to him his lips would crack with it. "Ariel is not foolish," he said. "And my queen may dare what she well wishes." He put his hand out to cover her own hand.

The hammering went on, like mad music.

Quicksilver gritted his teeth. He ran a finger down his wife's cheek and cursed the rebels who had put fear and horror in Ariel's gaze and etched Quicksilver's soul with the acid of war. Curse them.

Today their leader would die. Was justice not served?

What else could menace Quicksilver? What else could put such fear in Ariel's eyes, such pained discourse upon her tongue?

"Milord," Ariel said, her voice trembling. "You are not well. Your spirit like mine fears something that the mouth knows not how to utter nor the sense how to understand. Yesternight you urgently stole from my bed. And yesternight at supper, you suddenly arose and walked about, musing and sighing with your arms across, and when I asked you what the matter was, you stared upon me with ungentle looks: I urged you further, then you scratched your head and impatiently stamped with your foot. Yet I insisted. Yet you answered not, but with an angry wafture of your hand gave sign for me to leave you: so I did. This humor will not let you eat, nor talk, nor sleep, and it could work so much upon your shape as it has much prevailed on your condition. Quicksilver, is it Vargmar's execution that so weighs on you? And if so, is it really needed?" With her free hand, she waved toward the front of the palace, where the block was being built. "Might mercy not serve here?"

Mercy? Quicksilver frowned as he felt his features harden and his eyes widen in horror.

Vargmar, who'd die today, had blighted Fairyland for all too many years.

The revolt that today would end in blood and ordered pomp upon the block had started with the murder of Quicksilver's own guards upon a silent midnight.

These murders had served the greater plan of murdering Quicksilver himself, as he innocently slept by fair Ariel's side.

Quicksilver shuddered, remembering his guards' bloodied corpses, crumpled in a heap outside his door and then vanishing into nothing, as did the corpses of slain elvenkind.

Only the guards' valor in that final test had saved Quicksilver. They'd stayed alive long enough and called for help loud enough to rouse the household—against the greater numbers of magically powerful foes.

Their blood had purchased Quicksilver's own life.

Only then had Vargmar and his accomplices, caught at their attempt, called to them the malcontents and dregs of Fairyland and with them taken to the hinterlands of the fairy realm.

Those dregs had scourged the hills long enough.

Quicksilver let Vargmar live? What for? That he might call to himself another such coalition and think of new ways to amaze the cowering world?

Quicksilver stared at his wife's face, uncomprehending.

Mercy?

Quicksilver sighed. "I've won the war, milady, and this much I know. I cannot have lasting peace if I show mercy. I showed mercy to my brother once, showed him mercy despite his evil acts, and that was only the beginning of a worse strife."

"But your brother—" Ariel started.

Quicksilver patted her hand, and let it go. "Milady, you were not there when, on the fields of Mars, I stood surrounded by enemies and must slash my way out or die. Nor were you there on that awful night when I woke to feel a blade at my throat and see an enemy crouched beside my bed. Malachite saved my life then, by killing my foe. Think of all the valiant elves who died as I would have, by stealth and dishonorable attack. The fine flower of this hill was squandered upon the hills and marshes. The harsh, wild ground drank up their blood. Now you would that I show mercy to the man whose ambition murdered them. Arrest such thought, my Queen. Mercy would not serve. It is unworthy."

Ariel gasped and her face hardened. Determination erased the normal, gentle cast of her features. "You wrong me, my lord. If I went not to war, it is that you left me behind to rule your kingdom against your return. And if I speak now, if I speak, oh, lord, it is that I fear for you. For I've had dreams such as never before, dreams that stain my nights with blood and make my sleep rank.

"I dreamed tonight that I saw you as a statue which like a fountain with a hundred spouts did run pure blood, and many lusty elves came smiling and did bathe their hands in it.

"Do not go on with this, milord. For I fear for your life if you should."

Quicksilver narrowed his eyes.

Ariel's dreams were normally true, but this one smelt not of truth. Rather, the dream, like a frighted, wild thing, knocked its teeth and ran wild with terror. The war that had, for so long, held fear over all of their heads now, being ended, allowed Ariel to give voice to that fear.

Knowing she was affrighted, he spoke softly. "From whom should I fear?" he asked. "Who would harm me, once Vargmar is dead? For his own son has deserted his cause, and those centaurs whom he, with great pride, accounted his closest allies, have sworn fealty to me." Again he raised his hand, pulling back strands of Ariel's disarrayed pale blond hair. "Be of good cheer, for once Vargmar is dead, you'll have nothing to fear."

Ariel held her hand over her heart. "And yet I misgive me. Can this not be delayed?"

"What? And I shall ask the executioner to stay his ax till Quicksilver's wife shall meet with better dreams?

"Your fears are foolish, wife, and if I stay my hand because of them, I will all the more encourage that violence you fear against my person."

Ariel blushed. Red splashes stained both cheeks and the bridge of her nose. "Woe is me. For once were my dreams accounted of service to my lord."

She drew herself up to her full height, which yet came no higher than Quicksilver's chest.

Her face strained and white, she looked like the miniature of a warrior queen, as endearing as disconcerting.

He wanted to hold her and knew he mustn't. He must stand firm.

This time her hand gripped his arm tightly. "The violence of the last three years has wounded you, milord, maybe more so than it wounded your enemies. Now you have won and maybe it's time to exert kind mercy and with it balance the scales of retribution that threaten to crush your joy and peace. I do not know what my dreams divine, but I do much fear that in killing the traitors, milord, you'll kill part of yourself also."

Quicksilver shook his head. If any part of him there was which harshness could kill, then it was dead already. "Trouble you not, my lady," he said, offering her his arm. "Trouble you not. The villain will die and I shall be none the worse for it."

Speaking thus, he led her to the door and out of it, to the broad, marble-paved corridor outside the bedroom.

There, courtiers waited for their sovereign to lead his court out of the palace, to where the traitor would die.

Amid the courtiers, Quicksilver marked Proteus, Vargmar's only son, a pale, golden-haired youth in a dark blue velvet suit that made him appear even paler and frailer. Looking on him, Quicksilver wished Proteus strength.

Quicksilver himself had been little older than Proteus—in his twenties and a child in Elvenland—when Oberon had died, leaving Quicksilver orphaned. And oh, with what heat had Quicksilver sought vengeance for his father's spirit.

Would Proteus?

Quicksilver took a deep breath and looked away from the youth, who bowed to him while attempting to smile with bloodless, ghastly pale lips.

It was not the same situation at all.

Oberon had been cut down stealthily by an assassin's knife, while Vargmar would be executed after inciting half of Elvenland into a war against its rightful sovereign—after killing half the youth of Elvenland.

How many elves, fairies, how many trolls and centaurs even, had died in those three years in which Vargmar had rained blood and destruction on those outposts that had remained loyal to Quicksilver and by stealth and dishonor killed all those whom he dared not face upon the open field?

And for what? For what but Vargmar's ambition and his desire to be king?

Vargmar's peasant troops—servant fairies, changelings, small elf lords, ignorant trolls, the little band of transplanted centaurs who'd come with the legions to the south of Avalon and, ever since, been torment and strife to Fairyland—all those had been forgiven. They'd been allowed to say they'd been Vargmar's dupes and had believed that Quicksilver meant to destroy Fairyland.

But Vargmar had knowingly betrayed his sovereign.

Knowingly, he must bleed for it.

The sound of hammering stopped.

The block was ready.

Quicksilver led Ariel across the throne room, to the broad stairway at the entrance of the palace, and down it, toward the crude execution block.

The palace guards would now be getting the prisoner, while the executioner troll—a creature three times as large as any elf and covered all over in golden fur—stood patiently upon the stand that supported the execution block, holding his large, magical ax—a contraption of black crystal created by dwarves in the bowels of the earth.

But none would die by that ax till Quicksilver raised his hand and let it fall, in the signal for the execution.

Quicksilver took a deep breath. He could stop it all with one gesture.

The day was bright, but its brightness muffled, like sunlight shining through cheesecloth, as though the sun itself mourned and felt reluctant to watch such spectacle.

But why reluctant?

Quicksilver smarted at his own hesitancy, at his cringing heart. For was not what he did honorable? Did he not have law, tradition, and right on his side?

His lieutenant in the war past, his erstwhile page, his faithful friend Malachite, emerged from amid the ranks and knelt at Quicksilver's foot, signaling need to speak to his master.

With a wave Quicksilver bid Malachite stand.

Malachite had ever been Quicksilver's companion and almost always Quicksilver's closest friend. A changeling—kidnaped from nearby Stratford-upon-Avon sixty-four years past—in the course of normal human life, he should have been an old man tottering at the brink of that second childhood from which none grow up.

Instead, he looked vital and young, a human youth aged twenty, with dark hair and dark jade-green eyes that nonetheless looked as tired as Quicksilver felt—and red-rimmed besides—as from fretting, sleepless nights.

Standing up, he stepped very close to Quicksilver, and leaned closer. "Milord," he said. "Milord. I would fain not speak, but speak I must, for your own safety is imperiled, which is that much dearer to me than my own."

He stopped again. When he spoke, his voice echoed as little more than a whisper, barely audible to anyone other than Quicksilver and perhaps Ariel.

He glanced toward the mourning-clad Proteus, surrounded by centaurs—high-ranking centaurs who, through the war, had been Proteus's friends and his own council of war. Like him, they'd been pardoned and now Chiron, Hylas, and Eurytion ringed Proteus about with their sturdy equine bodies.

Hylas had the horse body of a black stallion, surmounted by a powerful human torso. Chiron was a dappled white and black, and Eurytion a fair brown. All of their human bodies were golden-skinned, and their features and their dark curls bespoke their ancestors' origins in far-off Greece, where some of their kin still lived in hiding, away from the humans who'd almost destroyed them.

Today their equine bodies were well brushed, their human halves oiled to glistening and ornamented with splendorously barbaric bronze jewelry. They had bound their curly black hair back with leather. Their faces . . . Was

Quicksilver imagining in their faces the closed-mouthed, downcast look of
those who plotted still?

Yes, he must be. It was hard to forget that ever since they'd come to this
island, the centaurs had worked treasons and plots against the rightful Kings
of Fairyland. Or else, once having caught a whiff of alcoholic brew, would
they run mad through the countryside, a danger to human maid and elf maid
alike, a danger to themselves and that separation that must exist between
human and elven spheres.

Twice before, to prevent wars between human and supernatural realms,
had Quicksilver needed to make use of all his power to make injured mortals
forget the grave outrages of these centaurs. Twice.

And then the centaurs had joined Vargmar in the war.

"I misgive myself, Lord, over your cousin, Lord Proteus," Malachite said.
"The son of the traitor. He looks with such ferret and such fiery eyes. Let me
have men about me that are fat. Sleek-headed men, and such as sleep of
nights. Yond Proteus has a lean and hungry look." Malachite stopped. He
spoke again, clearer. "He thinks too much: such men are dangerous."

Quicksilver's eye followed Malachite's indication, but where Malachite
saw thought and maybe treason, he saw only a youth, painfully thin and
painfully drawn, his eyes burning with grief and perhaps shame.

What shame must this not inflict upon the young, already too prepared,
by nature, to be shamed by everything?

Quicksilver shook his head and, with more pity than condemnation,
sighed. "Would that he were fatter! But I fear him not. Come, speak softly and
tell me, is his leanness your only reason to fear him? Or have you detected in
my good kinsman any mark of treason? For truth, he foreswore his father's
ambition in front of my throne, publicly, after the last battle in the fields of
the Avon.

"Did he forswear false?"

Malachite looked up. His odd, dark green eyes met Quicksilver's look,
unflinching.

There were depths to Malachite that Quicksilver couldn't quite fathom. He had taken Malachite for granted, as a changeling and a servant when they were both children, playing together at the feet of Great Titania.

But little by little, in the twenty years since Titania's death, pain and strife and strange events had shaken the fairy kingdom to the root, and revealed in Malachite that sort of strange intelligence that moves in the depths of the brain like deep-buried water. And like such water, it seldom found an outlet that allowed it to bubble to the surface. Malachite thought deep and spoke little, not because he was secretive or kept his own counsel but because the workings of his brain, the machinery of his thought, had little commerce with words and found them hard purchase for his tongue.

Perhaps, Quicksilver thought, it was the peasant, human blood that ran in Malachite's veins—little altered by Great Titania's suckle that had purchased for Malachite the golden life-span of elf—the blood of men and women wedded to their land and knowing little, needing little, of speech or fancy words.

While Malachite's wide-open eyes stared at Quicksilver, as though seeking to speak as Malachite's mouth couldn't, Quicksilver looked at his subordinate's hands—those large hands with their broad, flat fingertips, so adept with the sword, so slow in the cleverness of card games, so halting to play any instrument.

Malachite's hands knit together, clutching one upon the other as if in struggle. And his mouth opened, and let out a single syllable, a sound of frustration and despair. "Oh," he said, and took a deep breath. "Oh, I can tell you nothing, point at nothing, that Proteus has done that is treasonous. I can do nothing, nothing, to make you understand the danger you face. I only know I like not his looks and trust not his words, nor his false meekness, nor his scraping bows. There is a quick intelligence in him, something that hides beneath his complaisance and spies through his bright eyes, like an assassin's dagger seeking a place to strike." Malachite shook his head. "I think it is not meet that Proteus, so well beloved of his father, Vargmar, should outlive him. We shall find him a shrewd contriver, and you know, his means, if he improve them, may well stretch so far as to annoy us all, which to prevent, let Proteus and Vargmar fall together."

Quicksilver looked on Proteus again, then on the brand new block, which Vargmar was to ascend and stain with the noblest blood in Fairyland.

He marked with unease that Proteus had surrounded himself with centaurs, that is, with others who'd think they had reason to avenge themselves on the king. Yet Quicksilver could not bring himself to punish treason and potential treason in the same stroke.

And the centaurs . . . Oh, the other Kings of Fairyland had survived them well enough. Quicksilver would yet.

Thoughts were not crimes and until they became action they must not be punished.

No. Steeling his voice to gentleness, to soothe Malachite and not inflame him, Quicksilver said, "Our course will seem too bloody, Malachite," he said. "To cut the head off, and then hack the limbs, like wrath in death and envy afterwards. For Proteus, even if treasonous, is but a limb of Vargmar. Let's be sacrificers but not butchers, Malachite. We all stand up against the spirit of Vargmar, and in men's spirit there is no blood. Oh, that we, then, could come by Vargmar's spirit and not dismember Vargmar. But alas, Vargmar must bleed for it. As for Proteus, think not of him. For he can do no more than Vargmar's arm when Vargmar's head is off."

Malachite looked his misgiving and shook his head, but he could not or did not speak.

"Come, Malachite, for this our needful bloodletting must be done with, that the hill, that feverish patient, can rest," Quicksilver said, and thus speaking, led Malachite and Ariel both out of the door, to watch the dread spectacle.

The guards of Fairyland waited, two enormous giants in diamond armor, standing one on each side of Vargmar, who, shorter than Quicksilver's father, yet bore some resemblance to Oberon in his lean, spare stature, his aquiline nose, the dark curls now gathered by a strap, to make the ax's work easier.

Like Quicksilver, he wore a dark suit and he gave the King of Fairyland a look of such withering disdain that it was Quicksilver who must look away, like a child caught at fault, a sneaking waif.

Vargmar climbed the steps to his last destination.

As Vargmar's head rested on the place where the ax was to strike and the executioner stood over him, waiting only Quicksilver's order, Ariel said, "Milord, think. Consider. Maybe this need not be done."

From Quicksilver's other side, Malachite whispered, "Milord, what's another stroke of the ax? A single day could rid you of all traitors."

Poised between foolish mercy and wholesale massacre, where ideas were made crimes and suspicions fact, Quicksilver shook his head.

No.

He raised his hand, and as his hand fell, so did the ax, suspended above the head of noble Vargmar. The charmed ax fell, cleaving head from body. The head rolled and the blood poured from the severed neck like water from a fountain, bathing the new boards and filling their pores with the glistening, glimmering, magical blood of Fairyland.

Quicksilver felt as though something—some gigantic hand, all claws and talons—had reached within his soul and wrenched.

"Oh," he said, and stood. Pale, he stood, trembling, while the gazes of his court converged on him, half appalled, half anxious.

For a moment, it seemed to him he saw his own female aspect, the lady Silver, stand in front of him, like in a mirror. But she faded so fast into the hazy air he wasn't sure he'd seen it.

He gasped for breath, feeling cleft in twain, feeling blood leave his cheeks. For a moment something like a fog intervened between the king's eyes and the scene before him, and it seemed to Quicksilver that he had died and—dead—viewed himself among the living.

"Milord," Ariel said, standing and wrapping her arm around his, her hand small and restless and anxious like a small, frighted creature that seeks shelter in a storm. "Milord."

Quicksilver tried to answer, but only "oh" would cross his lips again, for he'd realized his affliction and the cause of his distress.

He'd been born a dual creature, male and female entwined and able to shift between the two aspects as the mood served, as the time demanded and sometimes—without meaning—as the unseen currents of events moved him.

Through the war he'd kept his female half—the dark-haired Lady Silver—in tight check. Her mad humor, her emotional nature, would have thrown victory to the jaws of defeat. Besides, Malachite and, indeed, all of Quicksilver's army, felt uncomfortable with and leery of their leader's capacity of being two in one.

But even then, through the war's dark days, had Quicksilver felt the lady Silver within him, like a twining beat echoing his own heart.

Twins they were—joined at the soul and born in one instant, one sundering breath serving both. Like twins and like one single person, who with his soul confides in secrecy, they'd ever been each other's closest company.

Flesh of one flesh, blood of one blood, one creature in two and two in one.

Even when being Quicksilver, Quicksilver had known that he could change and that the lady Silver lay dormant, not dead, just beneath the stern masculine shell that he must keep around himself.

Now, on that ax stroke, something had broken. Like fabric tearing, like a tether loosened, something had let go.

And try as he might, look as he might, Quicksilver knew that the lady Silver no longer lived within him, twining his heart and soul.

He'd become Quicksilver—Quicksilver alone and immutable.

Quicksilver, King and ruler of Fairyland, whose heart had much duty and no joy.

Much as he'd cursed his capacity to change in the past, he now lamented its loss.

How could half a king rule this war-torn kingdom?

Scene 3

✦

A fierce landscape, where ancient forest meets sharp black cliffs, raised high and jagged. From a certain quality of the light—a filtering, a dimming, an ever-present glow that comes from nowhere in particular—it is plain that we are watching Fairyland. From the forbidding, cold quality of the landscape, it is plain that this is the remotest confine of Fairyland, where the supernatural world of fairies, of elves, of gnomes and trolls comes up against unyielding reality and there arrests, neither world giving way and nothing prevailing. Even the forest looks dead and still, the immense trees piercing the sky with their tops upon which no creature chatters and which no breeze ever bends. On the topmost cliff, a prominence of jagged black rock that curves like a frozen wave, a castle rises, as black as its surroundings and yet blacker, a broad construction with four towers, a central hold, thick walls, all so dark that they seem to drink up any light that approaches them, so that near them semidarkness reigns. The castle's front gate is closed and nothing at all moves at tower or window. Even the pennant flying above the central hold—a dark blood-red flag embossed with the dark shape of a rider blowing a hunting horn—droops, still in the motionless air. But deep within the palace, past brocaded rooms and well-furnished salons, creatures move and breathe. In a library twice again as large as many palaces—where the walls are covered in shelves that groan beneath the weight of ancient volumes—two young creatures scurry. One is a debased brute that gives the impression of being half human and half canine except for traits more menacing than those appertaining to either species—long, sharp incisors and a thick, powerful body. The other is a girl, fifteen or so, whose very perfection bespeaks her elven origin. Her long blond hair, her shining green eyes, her graceful countenance lend distinction to her simple green dress.

"Ush, Caliban," Miranda said over her shoulder, directing a stern gaze at her brutish companion. "My father is yet by."

"Why must we come here now?" Caliban asked, fixing her with a pleading gaze. He shuffled his great hairy feet, making his uncut toenails shriek against the mosaic floor. "Why now? Why not wait till the master is gone? Why come at all? When the master finds out . . ."

"We must get the book in time for my lord Proteus to—" Miranda stopped, took her finger to her lips, and glowered at Caliban.

From the bowels of the palace came the sound of heavy striding boots as the Hunter's decisive steps fell upon the polished marble floor of this, his palace.

The Hunter's voice rumbled like thunder, calling to the cursed dogs that nightly he led on their hunt for lost souls. "On Malice, on Envy, on All Unkindness," the Hunter called.

His voice reverberated from the high ceilings, echoing on the walls of the vast building, like the sounds of an approaching storm.

In response, whines and barks sounded. They might have been the answer of any dog when called by his master. Only these were louder and, withal, more cutting, the sounds of damned souls baying and whimpering at their captivity and torment.

The Hunter laughed and more dogs bayed. The Hunter's heavy steps sounded overhead, and Miranda's heart sped up.

She closed her eyes and she swallowed hard. What would her father, immortal Lord of Justice, do if he found her here in his library, where he'd often forbid her to go alone?

She tried to still the scared flutter of her heartbeat. Nothing would happen. Nothing. She prayed to the gods of the night to make it so.

She heard the front gate open and the sound of horse's hooves upon the hard rock path outside. The gate closed. Her father was leaving on his nightly rounds.

What kind of a daughter was she, that so disobeyed her father? That she must hide and fear her discovery? She shook her head.

The Hunter was not her father, but her adopted father. A minor difference, but a real one, for the duty she owed him, for her upbringing, was dwarfed by her duty to her real blood and to those over whom she should have ruled as queen.

And yet how hard it was to think she was disobeying the Hunter, for he was the only father she had ever known.

For most of her life, she'd thought herself the daughter of this striding, immortal giant, this creature of primeval cold, this justicer that had existed before mankind and would go on living long after mankind had ceased its vain striving upon their circle of mud.

For years, while he'd stooped to her small size, and watched with proud smile her hesitant first steps, and taught her to form the words of men, and schooled her to play the music of elves, and held her fiercely to his inhuman heart, she'd thought he was her father and she his daughter and that this solitude of hers, here, at the far ends of Elvenland, was no more than the result of her immortal, exalted parentage. Oh, sometimes she minded the solitude and sometimes she cried for the company of others like herself, or sat at the window looking down upon the ground frozen in black waves, or at the distant tops of the immutable forest, and it seemed to her as though her heart would break.

But she believed this was her destiny, as the daughter of the dread Hunter.

But then one day—oh, happy day—two months ago while the Hunter was gone, she'd heard a song from outside the palace, a heavenly song.

Nothing, beyond her own voice, her own playing of the virginals, had ever delighted her ear in any way close to those sounds.

She'd gone to a high window, transported, wishing to see more, to hear more of this miracle, this eruption of joy in the dark fabric of her days.

And there she'd seen him. Proteus. Ah, Proteus.

On first seeing him, she was overcome. She'd thought him a spirit, a thing divine, for nothing natural had she ever seen that was so noble.

He was the first elf that she ever saw, the first male besides the Hunter or her troll serf, Caliban. The first that she ever sighed for. What a piece of work was elf. In understanding, how like the gods. In look, how like the angels.

On seeing him—his noble features, his light-spun hair, his luminous black eyes, she knew that nothing ill could dwell in such a temple, for if the ill spirit had so fair a house, good things would strive to dwell with it.

She'd come to the window and listened to him. He'd sung to her beauty. She'd gone to the door at his behest and, for his sake, opened the back gate of the castle, ever kept locked.

In the wood outside, which had always seemed to her forbidding and shifting, like dreams remembered in the waking morning, she'd talked to Proteus.

They'd met, they'd wooed, they'd made exchange of vows.

What Proteus had told her had shattered her heart, then built her a new one.

To vows of love—and of those there were plenty—there had joined other, more substantial information. Stories of the fairy kingdom, the resplendent court that gathered around a tyrant king: Quicksilver. And more, he'd told her in that long night. So much that she feared that her reason and her understanding would sink under it all, like an overburdened bark.

For how could what he'd told her be true?

He'd told her she was not the daughter of the Hunter. She was no kin of the cold immortal creature. Instead, she was the daughter of the late and virtuous King of Fairyland. Her father was Sylvanus, whom his brother, Quicksilver, had tricked into deposition and shameful death.

Here, Proteus had rushed his narration and refused to give her the details of it.

Miranda credited it to his kind heart that avoided giving her pain.

And though his news be strange, like a window opening to an unknown world, she'd looked at his face and read there the volumes of truth and the chapters of love.

He'd left her before the rosy morn of humans that looked like dim sunset in Fairyland. He'd left her when the horse of her adopted father loomed in the horizon and the barking of his dogs could be heard over the eery, still landscape of frozen waves of rock and millenary trees.

Proteus had come again the next elf-day and the next and the next.

His beauty assured Miranda of his truth when he spoke to Miranda of his love for her and of the just war he and his father, Vargmar, waged against the evil tyrant, Miranda's uncle.

For Miranda knew, from legend and tale—all that had kept her company through her lonely childhood—that the good were always beautiful, while the evil carried some obvious deformity upon themselves.

There was nothing deformed in Proteus, and so he was her true and gallant knight.

When they won the war—Proteus had told her—Miranda would be Queen of Fairyland, and Proteus her trusty husband.

At such prospect, Miranda grew giddy, even as, in the Hunter's library, she waited for the hoofbeats of her adopted father's horse to vanish into the thunderclouds that announced the sunset of mortals, the dawn of fairykind.

She wished her errand could have waited longer, till she was sure he was gone for the night and would not return.

But outside the wood, Proteus would already be awaiting her, and he'd told her their errand was likely to need all the time in the day of fairy, the night of mortals.

Proteus had asked Miranda to search for one of the Hunter's books from these shelves. He'd shown her the symbols that should be on the cover, and he'd told her it was a book of arcane and powerful spells.

For Proteus's side had lost the war and his father would soon be executed by the tyrant, Quicksilver.

Nothing remained for Proteus but one more desperate spell, one last magical attempt.

At which Miranda must help, for his magic was tied to the hill and any magic he used would be noticed by the evil king, Quicksilver, or his spies.

She felt her heart hammer within her chest, part excitement and part fear, for what if Proteus failed, what if he died?

But no, she would not think on it. Nay, she would refuse.

On such decision, she shook her head and drew a deep breath, and hearing Caliban moan a complaint behind her, she snapped, "To it, Caliban. Here, here's the symbols that will be on the cover." She withdrew from her bosom and displayed to him the piece of paper upon which Proteus had traced the figures. "This is what it will look like, and you'll help me look."

"But mistress—" Caliban started.

"Don't mistress me. Just search for it."

Well she understood his reluctance, for Miranda knew in her inner heart that the Hunter would not be pleased if he caught her here. And he would punish Caliban doubly were he to find the brute here.

The Hunter had taught her magic—some magic—and he'd told her that barring the eternal creatures, creatures like the Hunter himself, she had more power than any man or elf.

But he'd never told her to look into the arcane books, never taught her to read the strange language they spoke. He'd forbid it, indeed, professing himself afraid for her safety, her sanity.

43

A treacherous thought crossed Miranda's mind, that perhaps the Hunter had kept her from the books to thus seal her away from discovering her true origin.

She stamped down the thought.

The truth was that her adopted father had never been less than kind to her. The innocent deviltry of her childhood, the temper tantrums of adolescence, all had met with a bemused affection, a gentle joy in her presence.

She thought, as she looked through the volumes, and climbed a ladder to reach the upper ones, that the Hunter might be hurt. Just that. He wouldn't blame her and he wouldn't turn on her. But his eyes might acquire a wounded look and she might know that she'd hurt this immortal creature who'd never done her aught but good.

She would know she had returned kindness with ill-will.

Could she bear it?

She gritted her teeth, thinking of her adopted father's wounded expression. Force, her heart would break. She felt the sting of tears behind her eyes, like the swelling of rain-laden clouds, that must burst in water or else break in storm.

Then she thought of Proteus, poor Proteus, whose father had been defeated in battle, whose last hope had been dashed.

She swallowed back the pressure of her tears and told herself that she must hurt the Hunter to save Proteus, and that Proteus, the weaker, needed her more.

On this resolution, she reached for the shelf, and found her fingers brushing the symbols Proteus had drawn on the spine of a blood-red leather-bound book.

"I've found it, Caliban," she said, and holding her green dress up away from her rushing feet, she climbed down the ladder.

Caliban hadn't been making much effort to look at books. He'd been standing by the bookcase, glaring at Miranda with an air of aggrieved dignity. Now, he followed her out of the library with dragging step.

"Mistress, I don't think you should trust—"

A look quelled him. When Proteus had first appeared near the castle, Caliban had made such comments, and indeed, enlarged himself upon the theme that Miranda shouldn't trust the stranger, that the stranger was just that, and might bring danger and treason to her life and him and even the Hunter.

Miranda had answered his doubts then, and clearly enough. By accusing him of jealousy of Proteus's clean beauty, she'd reduced the beast to sputtering tears.

Since then, Caliban had been quiet on the subject till now.

What did he sense now, that pulled such words from him?

Miranda gave her beastly servant a searching look but saw no more than his normal, surly, red-eyed boorishness.

He'd been taken from his parents as a cub by the Hunter, who'd wanted him to be a serf to Miranda.

Did Caliban miss his parents' smelly cave in the far northern mountains?

Did he crave the companionship of his litter mates?

"What, mistress, what?" Caliban asked.

Miranda realized that she'd been staring, thinking odd thoughts indeed. Trolls were brutes with no feelings nor memories.

Yet why did Caliban look ever so mournful?

Oh, nothing, it is nothing, Miranda told herself. *No thoughts, no feelings does he have that are worth my concern.*

She held the magical book to her chest, and tried to think only of Proteus as she climbed the spiral staircase that led to the back door of the tower.

Outside the tower extended a vast garden, a thing of marvel built by the Hunter for Miranda's delight.

On this expanse, flowers grew together that had never, in either geography or season, known each other's company. Lilies intertwined with roses and those with tulips, and those yet with the exotic orchid that grew in colors so perfect and absolute that they would have been worth a king's ransom in the world of men, where none knew the kind.

Miranda paid no attention to the flowers, nor to the singing of myriad multicolored birds, nor to the smell of warmth and life that diffused into the crisp morning air. All of it had amused her when she was a child, but now she was a woman and she must put her childish toys by.

She walked along the path between the tower door and the gate that opened in the encircling wall, the gate that led to the forest and to Proteus.

The book in her arms felt very heavy and cold, and she couldn't help but hear, in Caliban's shuffle behind her, an ominous question.

Why did Proteus want this book?

Thinking about it now, Miranda realized she did not know. She'd been lulled by Proteus's talk of love, of proving her love and of righting the great wrongs done to both their families.

And yet a book of spells was for spelling—and what spell would change the outcome of the elven civil war? What spell would restore Miranda to the throne? What spell could bring back the brave rebels who'd lost their lives in the war? What spell could give Proteus back his father?

Spells—Miranda had learned—rarely could perform even one such miracle, much less all of them.

Miranda doubted not that Proteus meant well. It would be going against her very soul to doubt it. But what if Proteus overextended his power? What if he misjudged some spell's power?

How did he expect Miranda—Miranda, who had scant training in magic and whom her fath . . . the immortal Hunter had forbidden from meddling with the higher books and spells in his library—to perform such a spell?

The spells in the Hunter's library were, after all, designed for the Hunter himself, with his immense, cold, immortal power.

What would they do to a mere elf?

She tried to push her fears to the back of her mind, and yet they returned, sped thence by her aching heart.

She couldn't do this, she thought. But neither could she bear the thought of losing Proteus.

Opening the gate and leaving it open, she slipped out of the castle, with Caliban, onto the black waves of rock outside.

Across an expanse of broken rock, the forest stood, wreathed in misty twilight.

Miranda tried to see Proteus amid the trees, but she could discern neither his look, nor his golden hair, nor any limb of him, and when she got to the forest, she found their usual meeting place empty.

Oh, had her evil uncle, the dark king of elves, found out where Proteus was headed? Had the tyrant stopped him?

Scene 4

ᗧᎧᎧ

The inside of a peasant's kitchen. A broad fireplace, overhung by an even broader chimney, holds a brightly burning fire. Over the fire a pot of something bubbles with a merry sound. By the fireplace itself cooking implements sit—pots and pans of iron and of clay. In a corner, not too far from the fire, a cradle hangs upon a stand, and moves slightly, now and then, giving the impression of a child or babe turning within it. To the left, at a bench pushed near a scrubbed pine table, a woman sits. She wears plain peasant clothes, kirtle and shirt, with neither lace nor embroidery. Over them, a plain apron. She scowls at Will, who sits across from her.

"Speak," the woman said. "Or go. I have no time for this."

She was young, with a rounded face. A white cap covered her brown hair. Her dark eyes, surrounded by bruised circles, gazed with the intent wisdom of a much older woman.

Will, sitting across the table from her, felt the power of that glare. He shouldn't have come here. He shouldn't *be* here.

What did he, Will Shakespeare, master playwright, the toast of the London stage, have to do with witches, with fortune tellers, with those who had commerce with dark forces and other worlds?

Oh, playwrights of the past had been involved in such things. Kit Marlowe had been the rumored member of the School of the Night—that group of dark seekers—the disciple of magic, involved with things beyond the ken or interest of mortal men.

Marlowe. Will felt as though Marlowe stood behind him, fixing him with an intent gaze. Will shivered. In this homey kitchen, redolent of herbs and cooking, Will felt cold. Yet sweat beaded on his upper lip. He found words. Innocuous ones . . . "I came, good woman, in search of help in my trouble."

The woman's dark eyebrows rose, above her young-old eyes.

She flung up from the bench suddenly, with an impatient quickness that reminded Will of his own wife, his Nan, back in Stratford-upon-Avon.

Approaching the fire, she stirred her pot with a long-handled wooden spoon. "Bubble, bubble, toil and trouble," she said, then turned and grinned at him, displaying white, even teeth. "Indeed. Much you tell me. Do you think people come to see me when they're not in trouble? Nay, I tell you. When the thread of their life runs smooth, they stay in their homes, by their snug hearths away from the likes of me. Which trouble brings you to me, Master Shakespeare?"

Will's heart skipped a beat.

She'd called him by name. And he'd not given her his name. It was the first sign, the first display, of power from this woman. Will had come here blindly, on Ned's word. He'd not known what to expect, save cobwebs, exotic animals in jars, and the hands and fingers of long-dead criminals on display or bubbling over the fire in noxious potions. He expected a crone, muttering curses and glaring at him with half-mad eyes.

Instead, he'd found a kitchen not so different from his own kitchen at home, and a young woman not so different from how his own wife back home had looked ten years ago.

But now, at last, she showed her otherworldly power, her true nature.

Trembling, Will repressed an urge to leave while he could. If she had such power to look into his mind and heart, he shouldn't be here, shouldn't meddle with her. Yet if he meddled not with her, the ghost would stay with him. If there was a ghost.

"You called me by name," he said. "How did you know it?" Because, if she could read his thoughts, she already knew his fears. Why did she not calm them?

She turned around and laughed, an easy, young laughter that vibrated in the homey, food-scented air of the kitchen. "Not through my powers, Master Shakespeare, which, at any rate, I would disdain to use for such a purpose." She reached to the shelf over the chimney and, from it, pulled a much-thumbed booklet, which she held up.

On the cover was an awful woodcut of Shakespeare himself. Beneath it, faded words proclaimed: *The Poems of William Shakespeare, the sweet swan of the Avon, his Venus and Adonis & the Rape of Lucrece.*

It was not any edition that Will himself had authorized. Likely a print laboriously copied from the first editions and full of errors. Doubtless, sold more cheaply than the original print, though. As for the likeness, the best that could be said was that it was enough like him. Enough to recognize him.

"But if you have no great powers . . ." Will said.

The woman set her hands one on each side of her waist and grinned at him. "I did not say that. But I have more respect for my powers than to do tricks for you, like a pet witch, a tame witch, a juggler on the street corner.

"Those who do tricks, mind, are tricksters and swindlers and no-accounts, trying to get pennies from your pocket, nothing more." She paused and looked wistful. "As for me, for years, I denied what I was. I would have no commerce with the supernatural, no part in witchcraft. I denied and resisted till the forces beyond took me and held me in their palms, and made a mockery of my reason and senses. I denied till I ran about, with my hair unbound, insane and pursued by things none other could see.

"Then did I come to heel and break to saddle, and take on the duties that must be mine. For that I work. Not for money, but for the peace that comes with doing what I'm meant to do. I do not show off. I am no juggler." Turning her back on Will, she resumed stirring the pot. "And therefore you'll tell me what troubles you have, or you'll be gone. There's the door and yonder the road, and I'll wager you know your way well enough to your cozy quarters, your respectable rooms."

As she spoke, Will pictured the street outside: Shoreditch at its worst, with winding, narrow streets from which the hastily built five-story buildings on either side excluded all sunlight and all fresh air.

The streets he'd walked to get here were unaccustomed for the respectable burgher he'd become.

He shouldn't even have been in this part of town. And yet he knew it well enough. It was but three years since he'd lived here, as had Marlowe, as still did many of the poorer actors.

The thought of Marlowe again brought a chill, again the feeling of being watched, and Will imagined walking that street, alone, back to his quarters.

And step on step, Marlowe's steps would dog his, and thought on thought, Marlowe's voice would echo in his mind, mocking Will's worries, smiling derisively at Will's wit.

Marlowe had been dead for three years. To Will, he was more alive than ever.

And Marlowe would write his plays through Will or—barring that— prevent Will from writing plays altogether.

What, then, would Ned Alleyn do, having lost his investment? And what of the other actors of Lord Chamberlain's men, good men all, some with large families?

How would they attract an audience away from so many rival companies, but for plays and words that stood above the rest?

"It is a ghost," he said, half expecting the woman to laugh. "I'm prosperous enough, happy enough, but there's a ghost that haunts me and stands by me and, day and night, will ne'er let me be."

She didn't say anything. She didn't even turn to look on him. Her arm moved steadily, the spoon in her hand stirring the cauldron.

And that silence, more than any entreaty, called Will's response. "It is Kit Marlowe," he said, and having said it, felt like a bladder that, pricked, spilled its substance into the air and was left empty, purposeless.

Now the woman spoke, now she turned, now she let go of the spoon. Her dark eyes, serious, fixed on his. "And was he a friend of yours?"

"Nay," Will said, then misgave, as in his mind Kit Marlowe's look reproached him. "Or maybe yes. He was such a multifolded creature, so . . ." He sighed, words failing him. "Too good to be so and too bad to live. He . . . I believe he meant me well, but he died before I truly knew him."

She sat at the table, moving slowly, like a cat afraid of disturbing a skittish bird.

"How did he die?" she asked when Will remained silent. "I've heard such various accounts," she said. "That he died of the plague, or that he died in a tavern brawl over a lewd love."

"He died of his love," Will said, surprising himself with it. Strangely, it seemed to him as though Marlowe now spoke through his lips. He remembered Marlowe giving just such a discourse on love three years ago, over a meal at the Mermaid. "Love is a lethal disease and it claims more victims than are accounted."

Now she smiled, a smile as cynical as any of Marlowe's own. "No. Faith. The poor world is almost six thousand years old, and in all this time there was not any man died in his own person in a love-cause. Troilus had his brains dashed out with a Grecian club; yet he did what he could to die before, and he is one of the patterns of love. Leander, he would have lived many a fair year, though Hero had turned nun if it had not been for a hot midsummer night; for he went but forth to wash him in the Hellespont, and being taken with the cramp was drowned and foolish chroniclers of that age found it was—Hero of Sestos. But these are all lies; men have died from time to time, and worms have eaten them but not for love." She paused and looked at Will, and her smile turned to a slow, puzzled frown. "And yet believe you this of Marlowe? Mean you to tell me that, like a lovesick maiden in a chivalric tale, he sat like patience upon a monument, staring upon grief, and, from this green and yellow melancholy, he thus sickened and died?"

Will shook his head. He'd never spoken of this before, but he felt as though Marlowe stood behind him now, and smiled upon his speech.

Had this woman been the witch of his suspicions, in a smoke-filled den filled with despicable relics, would Will have spoken?

She looked like Will's Nan, and she mocked his turn of phrase and spoke with such familiar, gentle persuasion, that he couldn't help but confide in her.

"Wish that he had died thus, of such green and yellow melancholy," he said. "By God, I wish that he had. Then would my mind be easier. But he was a sanguine man and his love, like everything else about him, was a mad blaze of the fire that ran too hot and dry through his veins. He could not love mortal, could not be contented with that. It was too easy that, and too clean. Too meek and small, such joy, for Marlowe, the great poet." Will paused. He shook his head and for the first time looked upon Marlowe's memory as upon that of a young man, too young, too rash, too foolish, who'd really never known anything about the world.

"The great fool," he said. "He loved a creature who was . . ." And there he misgave, and there he stopped, his mind turning upon this point of much import: the woman to whom he spoke had been so curt, so perfectly possessed in her practical view of the world, so much like his Nan, that Will feared to mention the fairy kingdom and its denizens.

Would she not throw it back on his face? Would she not laugh, as an adult laughed at a child's fantasy? Did she know of the elven kingdoms which twined mortal realms, existing side by side, and yet not touching, like two sides of a single paper?

"If you mean to speak of the good neighbors," the woman said, startling him, "I already know you've been among them. There's the mark of their magic in you." She stared at him, her eyes squinting like the eyes of an old woman who tried to discern some exceedingly small object in a dark midnight. "I would say the mark of their love, if I didn't know better. For the love-protection upon you is a hot love, a burning flame of passion and selflessness, and they do not love so. Their love is a cold thing, meager and small, like their gold that, once spent, changes once more to leaves and dirt, like their food that only makes one hunger for more."

"It is love," Will said, and felt a great anger grow within him, his gorge rising at the thought of this love, unrequited, as insulting, as hurtful as hate unprovoked. Had he truly, still, the fingermarks of the creature upon himself? "It is love and he who loved me—"

"He?" the woman's eyebrows rose, startled, above her dark eyes.

"The lord Quicksilver, the king of elvenland. He is a dual creature, able to assume now the aspect of a man, now that of a woman, and man and woman, both truly. The lady Silver, his female aspect, she once loved me well, and maybe Quicksilver loved—loves me too. I much fear he did, maybe does."

"You fear? You have her love? His love? And you come to me? What can I do for you?" The woman looked outraged, vaguely insulted. She set her hand on the table, and made as if to rise. "As the good book would say, whence am I worthy to receive my Lord?"

And now Will's anger rose, red-hot, and he trembled as he clenched his fists and stood from the table, facing the woman no longer ashamed, no longer embarrassed, no longer fearing her strange and antic powers. "Oh, curse that love and the one that gave it. Curse his interference in my life. Curse that twisted, strange affection that took Marlowe and, in a fight for the kingdom of Fairyland, like a flame consumes a candle thus consumed him.

"King Quicksilver used Marlowe, nay, used all of us like a puppeteer uses the puppets he holds. When his brother, his deposed brother, the past King of Fairyland, tried to recover the throne, Quicksilver used us, his mortal slaves, to defend him. And like slaves, nay, like sticks and stones that children play with in a counting game, he threw us into the fray, caring not who wielded the fatal blade and who was cut—dead with the blade through his left eye, the blood tingeing his well-cut doublet and that collar of the finest linen of which he was so proud." Will pounded his fists together upon the table, a violent slam that made the table shake. "Thus died Marlowe, the Muses' darling, the best poet ever to bestride a stage and reach for the stars." He swallowed. "Thus died all the countless poems he would have penned in the remaining years of his natural cycle, the children of his genius—all perfect, all fire and air—so died they with him, broken, throttled, buried in a pauper's grave in Deptford and forgotten by all. All this—all—for the cursed elf's love."

There were tears in his eyes and through them the cottage looked weird and distorted like a drowned landscape, like a scene observed from far off and only half understood. A sob cut his speech, unexpected, like a visitation from outside himself. "And thus I got to live, I—unworthy. But my life is shadowed by Marlowe's ghost, and when I try to write, it is his words, those great, echoing words that made the stage tremble, that drip upon my page like echoes of his blood. And thus, miserable, I have sold my friend's blood to make a living." He realized tears were falling down his face, unashamed, like the great crying of a woman or a child. He turned his face away from the woman and sat down.

Anger had left him. Fear had abandoned him. Nothing remained to him but this feeling of having run far and long and now having come to some sort of wall, some sort of end. He could go no further.

A great sob tore through his lips, shaking him.

When he looked back at the woman, he couldn't read her expression.

She was looking on him, frowningly, not as though she disapproved of what he'd said. More like someone evaluating a piece of work.

Thus had Will's father looked, when staring at a newly sewn glove. Thus did Nan look after planting flowers in a row, when looking at their arrangement.

Thus this woman now looked on Will, her eyes squinting down, her gaze fixed.

She was going to tell him that there was no ghost. She was going to tell him that Marlowe had died and did not walk the land as did shades that had some work to do, some wrong to right.

She was going to tell him this and mock him and send him on his way like a truant child.

Will found himself longing for such mocking. It was a consummation devoutly to be hoped for. Then could he believe that his work was his own and no one else's. Then could he shrug that feeling of steps that doubled his own and actions that shaded his every movement—that feeling of words not his own falling in burning sentences upon his page.

"You've done well enough from his words, have you not?" the witch asked. "He wanted to give you his words, and you've profited from them. Why would you wish it otherwise?"

"It is his words, then?" Will asked as his heart sank and his blood, seemingly, lost all heat and force. "It is his words I have?"

"His words were a gift, magical, come to him from Merlin, his ancestor. Marlowe willed them to you with his dying breath. They are yours now. Go home and live contented." The woman looked at Will, the marks of her former outrage still upon her.

It was, Will thought, as if she believed he was refusing a gift other men would kill to have.

He felt his gorge rise. "Be contented? How can I? When I can't write my own words? When the sentences that come from my brain and trickle upon the page through my hand are not my own?

"Be contented, you say. I might as well be dead, then, and Marlowe alive, for when a man's good words cannot be heard nor a man's good wit understood it strikes a man more dead than great reckoning in a small room."

The woman shook her head. "The gift has cost him dearly, for his ghost has been chained by his words and thus banned from the heaven or hell his actions merited. The kindest thing you can do is to accept gracefully what was so dearly purchased."

"It is his ghost?" Will said. "It is then truly his ghost that dogs my steps? That breathes down my neck? That writes through my pen?"

"His ghost, aye," the woman said. "And his ghost craves a word with you."

She waved a hand, and lifted it, the little finger wiggling, and set it down again, the edge of it outward, like a knife cutting the still, warm, homey air.

There beside the great bench at which Will sat, Marlowe stood.

Marlowe, still well attired and carefully combed, his auburn hair pulled back and tied with a blue satin ribbon.

One almond-shaped grey eye looked at Will in great amusement, the other dripped gore and blood, to which Marlowe paid no more mind than if it were tears.

Will felt horror grip him, expelling air from his lungs.

Marlowe might have been alive, there, beside Will.

The ghost got a lace kerchief from his ghostly sleeve and with it dabbed at the blood upon his ghostly cheek.

It smiled, a ghastly, bloodstained smile, and said softly, "Good morrow, Will."

Scene 5

ᔥ

The palace of Fairyland as people disperse, yet celebrating the conclu-
sion of the long civil war. After the horrendous spectacle just witnessed,
friend leans on friend and one holds the other's arm, each congratulat-
ing the other. Girls and youths whirl in mad cavalcade amid the trees
and around the execution block, dancing as though to unheard music.
A young male elf declaims a war poem about Quicksilver's feats. Quick-
silver stands atop the marble stairs of his palace, and watches Proteus
vanish amid the trees. Malachite approaches.

"Let me follow him, milord," Malachite whispered, his hot breath tickling
Quicksilver's ear, his gaze fixed on Proteus's golden hair, Proteus's
retreating back. "Let me follow him for you."

"Whom would you follow?" Quicksilver asked, startled, called back from
his contemplation of Proteus and of the great ill he could be thought to have
done to Proteus.

What did Proteus think of Quicksilver?

He'd killed Proteus's father, and he could give no man back his life. No elf
either. All of Quicksilver's magic, all of the hill's might, could not restore the

life of an insect that had once buzzed through a long summer afternoon, much less the life of a being with thought, like a man or an elf.

Whence, then, should Quicksilver take the life he could not give? Whence came his right to do so?

Yet Vargmar was a traitor, and as a traitor he'd deserved to die.

Yet Vargmar was his uncle, and as his uncle, Quicksilver had owed him respect.

Yet Vargmar had done war on Quicksilver.

Yet had Quicksilver brought the war about through his own immense failings? Through his divided self that failed to attach the loyalty of the warrior male elves?

He was lost in this thought and feeling still the discomfort he'd felt when the ax had severed Vargmar's neck and spilled the noble blood to seep into the raw wood of the block.

Quicksilver felt a great sadness, as though he'd lost something, as irretrievable as life itself. His innocence? His peace of mind?

He thought of that image of Silver he'd seen before his eyes. Silver fleeing him? But why should he lament that? Had he not, always, wished he could cease being a double being, at war with himself?

Out on the block, the body had already twinkled away into the nothing of a noble elf who'd been condemned to eternal death and barred from the wheel of reincarnation that was elves' recompense for their exclusion from the paradise of mortals.

But the thoughts, the unease, lingered in Quicksilver's heart and mind.

And then, Malachite's suggestive whisper, his offer to follow—

"Whom? Whom do you wish to follow?" Quicksilver asked, turning to look into Malachite's dark green eyes.

Malachite narrowed his eyes. "Proteus, milord."

"Proteus?"

"He's gone away from this festive gathering," Malachite said.

Quicksilver looked around, at the swirling, festive mass of elves, who celebrated the end of the war.

Girls sang and smiled and twirled with youths in improvised dance. They were relieved peace had come and that they'd survived the strife. But Proteus might think else.

"He's taken himself way from the scene of his father's death," Quicksilver said. "To mourn in peace. Can you blame him?"

"Aye, I can blame him for mourning a traitor," Malachite said, his voice cutting.

And what could Quicksilver retort to that? For it was true, as it was true that Proteus's wounded pride, injured spirit, might lead him wrong.

But Quicksilver was not wholly ready to burn the branch where he'd cut the root.

The last glimmer of Proteus's pale hair, the last movement of his dark velvet suit, vanished amid the trees not so far away, and Quicksilver sighed.

Maybe Proteus should be followed, and saved from any passing thought, any folly, any youthful mistake.

But if Malachite followed Proteus and caught him at fault, if Malachite knew that Proteus had even weighed treason in the scales of his mind, how could Quicksilver forgive Proteus's straying and consider it normal of a youth so wronged by fate?

No. If Malachite knew, if anyone in the kingdom knew that Proteus contemplated treason, then Quicksilver must have Proteus executed.

For did not, even now, Quicksilver's enemies say that Quicksilver was too soft and yielding, the female half of his nature making him less than a warrior king should be?

"I will follow him," Quicksilver said. "I will."

Malachite stepped back, startled. "Milord—"

"No, Malachite. Cease your strife, for you cannot win. The war is over and we must return to family and hearth and the burdens of peace. I will go. He is my relative and my responsibility."

And before loyal Malachite could protest, Quicksilver slipped away, amid the crowd, following the magical trail of Proteus's presence—away to the depths of Arden Forest, where the sounds of celebration and joy echoed only distant and diminished.

Behind him, Quicksilver thought he heard the slow and steady hoofbeats of centaurs.

But he turned back once, twice, and he saw no one following him.

Scene 6

ᘓᖜᘐ

The witch's homey kitchen, where Will stares, horror-stricken, at Marlowe's ghost. Marlowe smiles, sits down.

There Marlowe stood, there, beside Will, to his left—wearing the blue suit in which he had died. The knife that had pierced his left eye had left it bloody and gory. Blood trickled from it like tears, dripping upon Marlowe's fine clothes.

Yet withal, Kit's remaining grey eye stared mockingly from beneath a perfectly arched russet eyebrow, and his small mouth, with its protruding lower lip that gave Kit the look of a permanent pout, twisted in a wry smile between his thin moustache and his sculpted beard. "Hallo, Will," he said and stepped mincingly toward the table. "And hello, good mother." He bowed to the woman.

How young he looked, Will thought. Dead but three years and yet, how young he already looked to Will's older eyes.

Oh, truth be told, Marlowe had always looked younger than Will.

Though they'd been born in the same year, and Will was the younger by a few months, they were spun of very different stuff.

Marlowe's delicate features and pale coloring had always lent themselves

better to the displays of beauty and the folly of youth than Will's ruddy complexion, Will's receding hair.

But now Kit looked even younger. Like a flower, when cut and pressed,
shall forever remain as it was, so had death preserved Marlowe and kept in
him the smile of the twenty-nine-year-old and the ready wit of the successful
playwright.

His single eye gazed upon Will, amused. "You have grown old, Will," he
said. "And you have waxed prosperous."

Will said nothing. Now, here, facing Marlowe's ghost, he didn't know what
to say. So long, he'd wanted to be rid of Kit, so long he'd not been sure
whether Kit's specter really existed or whether it was a figment of his imagination, a burden imagined.

Looking at Marlowe gave Will the first certainty that the words he'd written, the words that had made him famous and that caused everyone to
acclaim him, were in fact Marlowe's.

And the first doubt about wanting the ghost exorcized.

There was not, there had never been, a Sweet Swan of the Avon. There
was, instead, a doomed shoemaker's son from Canterbury, dead three years
and yet attracting London's attention and adoration with the words of his
dead, immortal pen.

Will eyed Marlowe's ghost narrowly and Marlowe smiled back, a strange
smile, like a child who's done something he knows he'll be punished for.

"Why do you haunt me?" Will asked. "What do you want of me?"

"I never meant to haunt you," Marlowe said. "I was foolish. I gave you my
words," he said. "But no one told me the price to pay and the penalty of my
good deed. In the final judgment, because of that one good deed, when the
judge weighed my follies in the scale against my worth, the two plates of the
scale came dead even and did not move.

"Thus was my fate weighed, thus was I judged too good for hell, too ill for
heaven, and then did my words like a golden filament, an unforgiving tether,
call to me and hold me here." His one eye filled with tears, while his mouth

yet twisted in a smile. "It wouldn't matter to me, nor would I care, but for Imp, that son I fathered without meaning and killed without intent. He waits for me heavenward. I disappointed the boy too much when living to disappoint him again now."

Will raised his eyebrows. He didn't know what Kit meant. Oh, he knew well enough—or at least suspected—that Kit had fathered a son by his erstwhile landlady and that the boy—nicknamed Imp—aged six or seven, had died in the awful struggle for the elf throne that had claimed his own father's life. But what Kit meant otherwise, Will could not tell.

Will's imagination had never run to matters of final judgment nor of glory ever after, and what Kit spoke of seemed too legalistic, too exacting, to be real.

Yet what did Will know of reality, he who had meddled with the fairy realms? Other people thought that an illusion and yet Will knew it was real. How dared he doubt the reality Marlowe averred? For Marlowe was dead and, therefore, should know of judgment and heaven and hell. More than Will, who had not yet shuffled off his mortal coil.

"I know you do not understand, yet hear this—one good deed would put me over the threshold of heaven, one good deed alone would catapult me to glory with angel wings and harp song." Kit tried to look innocent, but his small, expressive mouth twisted in wry amusement at such an image. Then his features sobered and softened, and his gaze seemed to look on something inexpressively dear. "And Imp's company forevermore. So you must hear, for this is my good deed, and I wish it accounted to me as it should be. I came to pay you warning.

"In the fairy realm, anew, does trouble boil like pus out of an ill-healed wound. There's conspiracy afoot and disaster beyond it. A trap for Quicksilver is being laid, with your undistinguished self as the cheese that shall lure the royal mouse."

"Myself? As bait for Quicksilver?" Will asked. It passed his understanding. He'd not seen Quicksilver for three years, nor did he know what Quicksilver thought of him now. They'd not parted so amicably three years ago. Could Quicksilver still love him? Could the lady Silver still love him?

At the thought of Lady Silver, he grew dizzy and shook his head to clear it. "But what will they use to draw me into their quarrels who am so well schooled in their effects? How will they tempt me into their death-dealing duels, their magical arguments?"

Kit's ghost appeared to hesitate. His gaze wavered, and his hand moved, midair, as though attempting to clutch aught that wasn't there. His whole form seemed to wink out of sight for a moment, only to firm up again.

"This is my warning. Pay heed, Will, do not go rushing where your heart leads, for it will only lead you tripping into nothingness."

"Speak plainly," Will said. "I tire of riddles." What a nimble tongue this ghost had, which defied Will's understanding.

"You, too, have a son, an eleven-year-old boy."

"Hamnet?" Will heard his own voice, raspy and menacing, erupt from his throat as though it would scratch it on emerging. "What of Hamnet?" In speaking, he half rose from his bench and stood, trembling.

He had that one son, aye, that one light and hope for this days. His two daughters—fourteen-year-old Susannah and Judith, Hamnet's twin—he loved well enough. But Hamnet would carry his name. As a man, he would be all that Will had failed to be, better educated and better trained and therefore more accomplished and better received in polite society than his father.

Hamnet would be the first of a Shakespeare family of scholars and gentlemen.

The coat of arms for which Will's father had first applied and which had been forgotten when John Shakespeare's fortunes had dimmed would now be resurrected, with added luster from Will's toiling with the unyielding quill. From it, Hamnet would receive that status and grace which Will lacked, the name of gentleman, the right to wear a sword, the reverence and respect of humbler men.

Hamnet would attend university. He would know the Latin and Greek that often evaded his father's rude tongue. He would . . .

Kit remained silent, staring at Will, as though studying Will's changes of expression like a recondite book.

"What of Hamnet?" Will said again, and put a hand forward and drew it back, knowing he would touch nothing there, and fearing yet. What would his hand feel, where Marlowe's ghost sat, immaterial? Nothing? Or if it felt something, what would it be? The cold of death? The dustiness of the tomb?

"Hamnet even now and as we speak," Kit said, "is being lured into the forest by fairy power. And from the forest will he be taken elsewhere, to a place beyond the real world, where magic reigns supreme."

Will stood. He forgot his problem with his plays. What cared he now whose plays those truly were? He'd written naught but for Hamnet's sake, for the sake of Hamnet's future.

He forgot that he wanted to be rid of Kit Marlowe. He forgot all save that his son would be kidnaped into Fairyland, that land of treachery and wonders, of danger and eery terror.

For—once in Fairyland—who knew what might befall Hamnet?

Hamnet was but a child, easily dazed. The glitter of fairy would deceive him, and those hollow riches that magic could spin would confuse him.

Taken to the cloud-piercing castle of the hill, shown the power of effortless magic, the joy of elven dances, could Hamnet resist?

Or would Hamnet, with ready, eager joy, eat of the fairy food and thus become a changeling, one of them who, under the hill, compassed their immortal lives, never knowing the greater joy of brief human lives?

Would Hamnet thus become a brittle thing, frail and beautiful as spun glass? Know the joy of hate and the pain of lust, but not the greater, mellower fire of human love?

No. Curse the thought. Hamnet would not be of them.

They could not have him.

Marlowe had brought Will news of this, hence Marlowe must, by heaven and hell and the dust beyond, help Will save Hamnet from this fate.

Once before had something like this happened. Once before had Will's family been taken into Elvenland.

With Susannah but an infant in arms, his Nan had been stolen, and his daughter too, to serve the perverse King of Fairyland. Then, ten years later, Kit Marlowe had succumbed to conspiracies engendered by elves.

Now Hamnet, his father's darling, the hope of Will's old age, would be taken also? Taken to that world of passing promise and empty joys?

Will dared Fairyland to rip his child from his arms.

Will trembled as he stood and, standing, felt blood drain from his face and leave him as pale, as colorless, as immaterial as the ghost beside him.

He reached for the woman, who still sat at the head of the table.

She looked from man to ghost and ghost to man, puzzled, like a child laboring at a difficult problem.

"Good woman," he said. "You must send me hence. If there's a way you can make me travel with magic, like the fairy bridge of air, between two points without touching the gross material world between, then send me to Hamnet now, for I must rescue my son."

"No!" Kit reached for Will's arm. Strangely, Kit's hand had weight and could be felt, heavy as the tomb and cold as ice as it touched Will's arm and burned with chill through Will's sleeve. "No, you fool. That is what I came to tell you. You must not go. Not you. You must—"

He had no time to say more.

The woman screamed at Will, her eyes rolling, wide open, terrified, the eyes of a horse about to bolt. "You must not do it, Master Shakespeare. I sense dangers—"

Will had never in his life pulled the dagger in his belt against man or beast. That humble weapon he used to cut bread, to slice his mutton, to pare his nibs, and to crumble his inkstone.

He found his hand on the dagger, the dagger in his hand, pressed against the witch's neck. "Now, good woman," he said. "Now. Send me to my son."

Scene 7

ᔰᕧᔮ

The same odd landscape of broken ground, amid which the black castle rises, dark against the sky of Fairyland. Past it, in the forest, where each tree seems to reach upward to touch the indifferent sky, Miranda paces, while Caliban watches her, his canine eyes fixed in abject and mute misery.

"Why comes he not?" Miranda asked, and in asking, she paced as though, by walking, she could arrive at an answer. "Why tarries my lord so?"

She held the book to her chest, and walked back and forth in a narrow space, circumscribed by the rough trunk of a broad, sprawling oak, and the towering height of an ancient pine tree.

"He comes not. Has he forgotten me? No, I am foolish. How could he forget me? Yet I shall go distracted, for he comes not." Holding the book precariously with just one hand, she traced, upon the pine tree's scaly trunk, Proteus's marks made by his dagger. M and P. Their initials entwined, as their hearts already were, as their lives would be forevermore. "No. My poor lord. What tongue shall smooth his name when I, his intended wife, so abuse him? No. He would come if he could. Therefore, he cannot. But why can he not?

Why, Caliban? Has the tyrant stopped him on his way? Has the fiend had my love executed?" Thus speaking, in great anguish, Miranda turned her anxious gaze to Caliban and sighed. "Speak, Caliban? Why are thou mute? Think you that he was stopped? Think you my lord is . . . dead?"

Caliban only looked, his eyes mute and immense.

Throughout childhood, Miranda had thought that Caliban's eyes were like her own, her own eyes never glimpsed except hazily in polished bits of tin and the ice upon a pond's face on a cold winter's morn.

She'd thought Caliban's eyes were like her own, or at least closer to her own than the cold fire of the Hunter's eyes.

But now she knew better. She'd seen her kind and her like in Proteus, and compared to him, Caliban was a nothing, a creature of strange, primeval forests, a creature like a dream unformed, like a nightmare unfinished.

And his eyes, how dull his eyes were. How they made Miranda long all the more for company of her own kind.

"Speak, Caliban," she said, her voice full of impatience. Her anxiety for Proteus, her wondering about him, screamed through her lips, unmeant, turning itself into anger and lashing out at the ever-present Caliban. "Speak, Caliban, or I shall go insane. What thinkst thou happened to my lord?"

Caliban raised his morose gaze to meet hers, and his eyes were full of patient misery, as though he'd made misfortune a friend and lay down companionably beside grief. "How should I know, mistress, what has happened to the elf you wait for? My opinion of him, you do not wish to know, and beyond that I know nothing, nor can I divine how to steady the mad rushing of your heart."

Miranda clicked her tongue impatiently. "Such beautiful words to hide such rude meaning. You would not comfort me."

"It is to me that such comforting should fall," Proteus's voice said.

Miranda turned to see him approach through the broken landscape behind her. He looked tired, his hair matted and wild, his eyes sunk within dark circles, his face so pale that lips and skin and all seemed to melt in uniform grey-white sadness—like curdled milk or dingy sheets.

Yet he attempted a smile for her and through his colorless lips his voice came, if not as spirited as usual, making a brave attempt at spirit. "If comforting you need, lady, it should fall to me. Why ask you this of such a creature as Caliban?"

She turned fully and smiled on him. "You were late, milord."

He tried to smile, but his mouth seemed to lack the strength to turn upward and, instead, hovered in indecisive sadness, halfway between smile and frown. He sighed. "I had heavy business to attend to. Heavy business." His black eyes, like shiny pebbles long polished by the patient sea upon a familiar shore, turned to her. Today they looked opaque and remote, as if the sea that rolled them were a cold sea, on whose shores no one lived and whose depths harbored no creature. "Today I saw the noblest blood of Fairyland spilled wantonly like so much water. Today I saw my father—My father—" Here he stopped. His lips trembled, and his eyes blinked rapidly, a tear drop caught upon his blond lashes looking like a dew drop that the morning has forgotten upon the flower.

"My lord," she said, and put her hand on his wrist, struggling to hold the heavy volume with the other hand.

"You've got the book," Proteus said, with such effusive joy that one would think she'd gone away to war and brought back the bounty of a thousand captured cities. "You've got the book, Miranda. Lady. My queen."

She was gratified as ever to be called his queen and smiled upon him, a smile that was part pity for his sorrow and part pleasure at his company. "It didn't take that much work, Proteus. It is not as though it were on the bottom of the sea or upon high cloud. It was in the library, and there I found it."

He looked at her, and his eyes were suddenly animated. Pebbles upon which a ray of sun played, making them shinier than jewels. "Ah, no. You'll not play down your value, for did you not brave the wrath of the immortal Hunter to get me this?"

He took the book from her and, setting it atop a taller shrub, opened it eagerly, searching through its time-yellowed pages. "Did you not go so far, indeed, for my cause? When we shall be married, you shall reap the full immortal joy of true love and true queenship."

Miranda squirmed and felt her cheeks warm, pleased at his praise and yet finding it difficult to believe she'd been in any danger from the Hunter.

Oh, perhaps the Hunter wasn't her true father. And perhaps he and his dogs roamed the night punishing evildoers.

Yet she'd been his joy and his happiness for years now. She'd seen him smile at her smiles and come as near to crying at her griefs as such a being could.

The Hunter hurt her? She'd sooner believe Proteus might.

It seemed to her, also, that at Proteus's praise of her, Caliban made a sound in the background. The sound was too faint to be sure of its quality, but Miranda would have sworn it was a snort of doubt and derision.

To abstract herself from her sense of discomfort at this praise, Miranda looked at Proteus's hands as he turned the pages of the book.

Such long, white fingers. How could Proteus ever have held a sword or discharged himself honorably in battle? It seemed to Miranda as though her own hands, trained as they were to do nothing except the labor of the pen and the working of her needle upon the pliant embroidery fabric, were stronger and more purposeful.

Proteus's hands shook as he turned the pages, and rushed eagerly, like lizards darting upon a patch of sun, following the first line of every page, as though he couldn't read it with his eyes and must trust his hands to guide him upon the meaning of the letters.

Proteus's index finger darted out, eager and curious, tracing the cryptic symbols upon the yellowed paper, then slowed, on tracing the second line of symbols, and finally, stopped altogether.

He would turn the page and then trace the mystic symbols again.

The symbols were like no alphabet Miranda had ever seen before—strong and coiled like serpents about to strike. It seemed to Miranda, as she stared, that they writhed and moved upon the page, living letters—predators lying in wait for . . . whom? A reader? An enchanter?

Their strangeness, the sense that they were alive, made her eyes strive to focus, caused her head to ache.

And yet, the more she looked on them, the more she thought that she could almost understand them. Almost.

Those letters that twisted and writhed were like a phrase, hovering at the edge of her tongue, like a recollection of a dream, almost grasped and on the edge of vanishing forever into the nothingness that engendered them.

As Proteus turned pages, Miranda's gaze traced the letters. There, that was a spell for . . . finding what's been lost. And there, that was a spell for restoring hair that had fallen.

Yet farther on, she thought she saw a spell for mending a broken love, and for finding gold.

Proteus's finger moved on, restless, seeking.

"Milord, what words are this?" Miranda asked, fearing to interrupt him, fearing that he might upbraid her if she did, yet too puzzled to hold her tongue. "Milord, how is it possible that I can almost understand such strange symbols? What symbols are they?"

For a moment she thought that Proteus had not heard her, as his finger rushed on upon the page. But he spoke, as from a distant place, without turning, without so much as lifting his gaze from the page. "Those letters, Miranda, are the writing of our kind."

"But I've never learned it, why should I understand it?"

"Because the language of elves is born with elves," he said as his finger moved upon the yellowed page like a creature distinct from himself. "Such is the virtue of our tongue that, unlike man, who must be taught his language and learn to speak it, haltingly, as we learn to walk, step by step, elves are born knowing how to read and write their language." Now he looked up, his dark eyes amused, a slight curl to his pale lips indicating, if not a smile, then a willingness to smile. "It might not be conscious language, and an elf raised away from her kind might not know she has such knowledge, but it will come to the mind when she hears or reads it, like water, long buried, finding an opening in the ground will bubble to the surface."

Miranda blinked. The symbols still seemed vaguely disquieting to her. Something in her heart, some certain part of her soul, thought that letters should not be alive nor should they insinuate into her mind with language she'd never known she possessed.

Still, she squinted and made an effort at reading the book as Proteus turned the page.

And there, on the page next to last, she found she could read a row of symbols that translated as a spell to start a fire.

Proteus turned the page with a peevish gesture, and upon the next page—the last one in the ponderous leather-bound volume, Miranda read, *Spell for transporting of humans to various parts of Fairyland.*

She sighed and shaped her lips for an apology, sure that now Proteus would close the book and turn on her in just indignation, asking why she'd brought the wrong book and accusing her of some childish mistake.

But Proteus moved not. His finger had stopped upon that first line of text, his eyes wide and intent on the words.

Curiosity warred in Miranda's heart with a strange, undefined dread.

Transporting humans to Fairyland? Why would one do so? What would justify it? She'd read enough tales, sang enough ballads—furnished to her by her loving adopted father—to know that by ancient law, by millenary decree, the two worlds should be kept separate, else tragedy resulted.

And why would Proteus want to transport a human to Fairyland?

The thought warred in her heart with her desire to keep still and not bother Proteus at his reading. Her restraint finally overpowered, the question flew through her lips, like a sigh. "Milord," she said. "Milord—I thought you needed a spell to fight the wicked tyrant. What can a mortal have with our spells? Why? And which mortal?"

"A child," Proteus said. Without looking up, he spoke, while his long finger ran along the lines of characters. "Quicksilver, the tyrant, loved once, you see."

"He loved a child?" Miranda asked, startled, as her opinions of the creature shifted. She couldn't imagine seeing him as she saw the Hunter—a fearsome creature of darkness, but one who could love and care for something as helpless as a child. Maybe her uncle wasn't as bad as Proteus said. And yet, he'd killed her father, had he not? He'd killed Proteus's father, had he not?

How could such a creature be anything less than a monster?

Proteus shook his head at her question. "No, not loved a child, but he loved the child's father." Proteus looked up, and for just a moment, a sneer disfigured his beautiful features. "When Quicksilver gave his heart, it was not, as befits immortal elf, to honor or truth, to the hill, or even to another elf, his equal, but to a gross mortal, a creature base and fleeting."

A strange, feral smile distorted Proteus's face. "While this man is too wily to fall into our traps, the creature has three children, one of them a son and prized higher than both the other two." He looked not at Miranda but at the air above her left shoulder, as though there he saw, arrayed, an army disposed for his command. "If we take the human's child, the human shall go, mewling and complaining, to your uncle's throne. And your uncle, who still can deny him nothing, will come after the child. Here, in this isolated place, we can then kill him. Then will you be the Queen of Fairyland and rule by my side over the glittering hill."

All of a sudden, as though only then noticing her, Proteus extended hands to Miranda. "Oh, Miranda, how fair you'll look, wearing the jewels of the ancient hill and leading the dance by my side."

The prospect was so dear to Miranda's heart, the shine in Proteus's eyes so strong, so full of that soft redolence of love and hearth and home, that for a moment, as though entranced by it—as though she, an elf, were pixie-led—she gave her hands to Proteus and allowed his dream of a large court, of her own majesty at the head of it, to keep her from thinking of what they'd be doing to get there.

But little by little thought intruded. The sovereign of Fairyland had more than his share of power with which he'd been born, that share of power that Proteus told her was so large in her also.

The King of Fairyland, by ancient law, held in him the power and strength of all his subjects. With such power and such strength, he was stronger, more vital, better protected than any of his subjects—stronger than Proteus. Perhaps, even stronger than Miranda.

Miranda felt a shiver of cold up her spine. "Milord, you say you'll bring the king here and we'll overpower him. But he is king. So how will we do that?"

A smile, more beautiful than an angel's, gilded Proteus's features as he let go of Miranda's hands and reached into his black velvet doublet, pulling out . . . something.

It was a net, but to say so would only be to prove the inadequacy of words for their purpose. It was a golden net, spun of air and magic, a thing glittering and perfect, like distant stars in a summer sky.

"Oh," Miranda said. She reached for it.

Proteus pulled it back, held it away.

"Touch it not," he said. "Touch it not for it is a magic net. I have bespelled myself to endure its touch. With this net Circe caught the spirit of the hero, Ulysses, and kept him in her thrall for years. With this net did Medea bespel Jason and lead him to marry her. With this net shall we catch the tyrant's magic. And when he's thus, unable to defend himself, we shall have revenge. Your power is enough to protect us if he's immobilized."

Relief flowed over Miranda and, for a moment, masked something else—a twinge of worry, a fear—no, not fear. She realized that she felt guilty, scared of what they were going to do and of how it might stain her mind. "But killing him by stealth is dishonorable," she said. She remembered her father—her adopted father—explaining to her the crimes he punished, and this sounded like base murder, which was one of them.

Proteus's eyes widened in surprise, as though he'd never expected her to protest any of his decisions. Then he shrugged.

"The king of the hill is such a creature, with such magical power at his disposal, that we kill him by stealth or not at all." He shook his head. "I knew we'd need this from the beginning. We'd heard of it, my father and I, from the centaurs of the south that serve us. There were tales of their ancestors that told of this net. Yet my father thought that he could win by mere force. I searched for the net alone, but it lay near the base of Vesuvius, covered in so many spells and incantations that it took me all my magic, all my effort, to find it, to penetrate its shields, to acquire it." He looked into the middle distance again, and his eyes slowly filled with glittering tears. "While I was thus occupied, Quicksilver won the war and imprisoned my father. He had my father condemned to death. To save my own life, I had to forswear my father and my claim on the kingship of the hill. I did it so I could live to avenge my father's death. Lady, I promised then that, if it took my last breath, I would ensure that the net would be used and would help me slay the tyrant." His eyes filled with tears and he looked at her, a picture of resolute tragedy, a picture of grief and courage so mated that one could not be pulled from the other.

Miranda knew not what to say. For once her quick wit fed no words to her still tongue.

But then she thought on the child they would kidnap, steal from his mother and the safety of his hearth. The child's father might be the beloved of Quicksilver, but what had the child done to deserve being enmeshed in the battles of immortal elves?

Yet the father of this boy had been loved by the tyrant. How good could a mortal be whose heart knit such an evil creature as Quicksilver to him?

No. No. The boy might well be evil, a dark thing.

"Show me the child," she said. "The child we would steal."

Proteus looked oddly at her. "The child? Why, my lady? He is a mere mortal."

His words failed to reassure her, rather spurred her sense of guilt to frantic exasperation. Proteus cared not for the innocent creature.

Why felt it she so keenly?

Mayhap because she herself had been raised as a foundling, far from her own people and those to whom she belonged.

Imagining removing a child from his parents made her head pound and her heart clench in shame.

"Show me the child," she said.

Proteus sighed and rolled his eyes, as though signifying that the madness of elf princesses must be indulged.

Absently, he traced cabalistic symbols midair.

Something like a window opened in the clear air, in front of Miranda's eyes.

Through that window, she beheld a forest, but not a forest as this one that she knew so well.

These trees were smaller, their trunks more embraceable, their tops not reaching so far into the distant sky.

Amid the trees, a boy scrambled.

He was a mortal boy, with brown hair, roughly cut, in a round cut short about his ears. His rough suit of once-good cut and material showed wear at knees and elbows, as if he'd scraped it against too many trees.

His eyes, as wide and golden as those of a falcon intent upon the chase, looked fixedly and feverishly ahead of him, as he rushed, tripping, into the forest.

It was as though the boy followed an alluring phantom or a glittering vision that would not tarry for him, and that rushed deep amid the trees, ever out of reach.

Pixie-led, Miranda thought, remembering legends she had heard of mortals lured by illusions into Fairyland snares.

She looked at the boy's wide, golden eyes and felt an odd sense of identity—as if the boy were a part of her and she, herself, were thus being tricked into some unimaginable trap.

A shiver ran up her spine.

Pixie-led.

Scene 8

∞

The witch's cottage, where Shakespeare stands, his hand—which trembles—holding his knife at the witch's throat. Nearby stands Marlowe's ghost looking like a live man, save for the gore and blood that drip, continuous and seemingly unnoticed, from his eye.

Could Will cut the woman? Kill the woman?

He looked to the cradle in the corner, moving still in tiny movements. From it a mewling sound emerged, as of a young baby starting to waken.

Could Will kill the baby's mother?

Faith, Will did not know and hence his hand trembled. But he commanded his voice to be firm and in as false a firm voice as had ever rung across stage, he said, "Give me some potion, woman. Or perform some spell, as will from hence take me to my son's side, not passing mortal land nor ever covering the lengthy distance weary mortal feet must walk. For I must go to him, in all haste."

"You fool," Marlowe's ghost wailed. "You poor wretched fool. You know not what you do. Put up your knife."

But Will shook his head. "What know you, Marlowe? What know you, spirit that was Marlowe's soul? What know you of a father's care?

"Your fathering of a boy was only of such kind as any may do, late one night, gorged with drink, at a tavern.

"What know you of a father's heart?"

The ghost of Marlowe wavered, going grey and dim, then reappearing in full firmness. The effect was that of a mortal staggering under a harsh blow and then recovered. "I know I saw my son grow through the whole seven years of his life, and held him in my lap and told him stories, and marked daily the changes in his countenance as he waxed in wisdom and size," he said, and smiled. "When last did you hold your son upon your knee, Will? You, who labor in London, so far from your family—what do you know of that son so far away? Know you that often, tired of his house where women prevail, he runs into the forest and there finds solace in solitude? Know you how much he misses you? How he pines for you? And yet you live in London and there pursue your fame. How dare you compare your fatherly love to mine?"

"All I do is in care of him," Will said. Marlowe's comparison hurt him more than he dare acknowledge, even to himself. When had he last held Hamnet upon his knee? "I make money that he might wax prosperous. I labor far from him, that he might lack for nothing. He is my only son."

Marlowe raised skeptical eyebrows, made all the more ironical for one being raised above a wounded orbit. "Faith, you have two daughters." His voice dripped with something like envy. "You have two daughters that, yet, were your son taken up, would remain behind to light your days. How can you say, *He is my only son,* and thus make it sound like he is your only child?"

"Daughters," Will said. His hand that held the knife trembled. "Daughters are their mother's mirror, her rightful company. My son, him I can guide in the way of men, in the road of learning, in a profession worthy of the name.

"My son wears my surname, and he shall crown with pride my waning years. The fairyhill shall not have him." He turned his attention to the witch once more. "You will transport me wherever he is, that I might protect him."

"Your heir and not your son you love," Marlowe said.

"The both are one," Will said. "The two of them are one, conjoined. My only son is my only true heir." Will's head hurt and his eyes stung with tears that he refused to shed before Marlowe's dead and mocking eye. He pushed the knife closer to the woman's neck. "Therefore, send me to him."

He did not see the woman move, but felt as though the air trembled all around him. His eyes stung, as though a cobweb had fallen upon them.

He blinked and the homey cottage changed. Light dimmed.

It seemed to Will that he stood in a rocky cave, the walls rough and moist, covered in green and crawling things and dripping with moss from which ran foul, stinking liquid.

The ground underneath his feet, instead of scrubbed oak and clean rushes, turned to bubbling foul mud, from which greyish stench climbed to his nose in stinging vapors.

He felt his feet sink slowly into the mud and the cold, slime seep into his shoes.

Within the mud, creatures crawled, their horror visible only now and then, in a claw surfacing, a many-toothed snout emerging above the ooze, dripping venom from sharp fangs, only to vanish again beneath the mud.

Here a rolling yellow eye, with a vertical slit for a pupil, peeked in deranged hatred at Will.

There a forked tongue emerged from the mud and lashed itself around Will's ankle.

Teeth fastened on his foot and pulled him down.

Will screamed, feeling his flesh pierced.

The witch was evil, after all. This was a demonstration of her true powers.

As he thought this, the witch in his arms also appeared to change and writhe into a monstrous black serpent coiling madly against him, her forked tongue licking at his cheek.

This was her mistake.

Will saw the change and the horrid, coiled serpent in his arms. But those same arms felt, against them, the heave of a human bosom. His hand, splayed beneath her chest, felt the rough weave of her apron.

He tightened his grip on her.

"Be still, woman," he said. "Would you fool me with your childish tricks? I've seen better tricks, long ago, in Fairyland."

The witch whimpered and, in a moment, was matronly and soft and human in his arms again.

The space around became again a cozy kitchen.

And Will held his knife to the woman's white throat. "I know you have some potion or some magic which you can give me that will serve my purpose."

"Do not do it, for it will serve only his death," Marlowe said. And with tolling, unmistakable fear. "And Quicksilver's also."

So the ghost sought yet to preserve Marlowe's erstwhile beloved, Quicksilver.

With a disdainful smile, Will dismissed all of Marlowe's prior argument, which he now knew served only to protect Quicksilver.

Quicksilver be damned. Will would save Hamnet. "Let me have the cure for my ill, woman. And I will make it well worth your while." At the mention of gain, he felt her tremble, and he pushed his knife toward her throat. "Else, tempt you a desperate man."

"Such potions have I," the woman said, her voice fluttering. "But the law, of human and fairy kind both, is death to any that sells them."

Will cast an eye at the child in the crib. "You have a child who deserves better than an hovel in Shoreditch. A child, I guess, who knows not his father. Who, but you, should provide for your whelp? Art thou so bare and full of wretchedness and fearest to die? Famine is in thy cheeks, need and oppression starve in thy eyes, contempt and beggary hang upon your back. The world is not your friend, nor the world's law. Then be not poor, but break it, and take this."

He put his knife away and, from his sleeve, pulled out the small but heavy leather purse full of golden coin he'd meant to send to Nan when next he found a trusty messenger.

The woman looked at the purse, her eyes wide, cupidity plainly written in large letters upon her pupils. "But master," she still protested, though her voice came fainter. "Master, I cannot send you anywhere before your son will be transported. Even now I sense him being taken, not to Fairyland but to another place—a place of greater magic and stronger danger.

"Three days in that land and you'll forever be captive there. And though there even mortal men can perform magic, yet is the magic there so strong that you will not be able to control it. And having used it will you—even if you return—forever be magic in the land of men."

Normally Will, who mistrusted magic so, would have shrunk from such a menace. But now he could think only of Hamnet alone in a threatening place. "What is this place, if not Fairyland? And why would Hamnet be transported there?" He held the purse in his hand before her gaze.

She stared hungrily at the purse but did not reach for it. "This place is the beating heart of Fairyland, the burning ember of magic. It is called the crux. He will go there for the trap has been so disposed."

"And after three days in the crux one cannot return?" Will asked. He imagined his son, small and inexperienced in dealing with elves, and with humans at that, trying to find his way out of this strange trap.

"That, and more. If you go in there, when you leave, for which you'll have to attempt to use magic, you will have to leave behind a part of you—something dear—in sacrifice in order to return. I am poor," she said, and sighed, looking at his purse. "But not so poor that I would do you such wrong. Put the purse away, Master Shakespeare. The specter of Marlowe is right. Stay you here and rejoice in the daughters you have left."

"No," Will screamed. They spoke as though Hamnet were lost forever. "No. Give me the potion that will take me to Hamnet. Sell it to me. This money and whatever sacrifice I must make, I count of little importance to recover my son."

The woman sighed. She stretched her fingers till the tips touched the leather of the purse.

"Do not listen to him," Marlowe said. "It is his sure death and the death of the king of elves besides."

Both Will and the witch ignored him.

The witch slowly opened her hand and closed it around the purse. "I'll sell you the potion." She sighed. "My poverty, but not my will, consents."

She put the purse in her own sleeve.

Marlowe screamed.

"I pay your poverty, not your will," Will said.

The woman went to a high shelf by the cradle. Looking into the cradle, she cooed at its occupant. Then she reached for the shelf and got a bottle and, returning to Will, proffered it.

"Drink this, and you shall be transported."

Marlowe's ghost cursed them, and belabored them both with his heavy cold hands. "Stop," he shouted, but they regarded him not.

Will took the bottle to his lips and drank while the woman felt within her sleeve the golden coin.

No more had Will swallowed the bitter blue brew than a roaring started in his head—a roar like the sea at its fullest tide, like a storm approaching over the waiting land.

His throat closed and his hands clenched in on themselves.

"Woman, you have poisoned me," he gasped.

She looked at him, mute with terror, her eyes big and blind with fright.

A whirlwind blew all around, cold and howling, carrying him away from present reality. Sounds and sights receded till they were dim and distant like an ill-remembered dream.

The feeling of the bottle in his hand receded too, and from very far, he heard the bottle break.

He had a moment of panic and wondered whether the witch's cunning potion had sent him bodily to hell.

As darkness closed in on all sides and his vision darkened like falling night, he took with him one last glimpse of Marlowe's ghostly face, amazed and pale, of Marlowe's single eye staring in horror.

What potion was this, whose effects horrified the dead?

Scene 9

∽∾

The forest by the Hunter's castle, where Proteus and Miranda stand, side by side, and watch through a magical window as Hamnet clambers into Arden Forest, tripping over branches and roots, as a mortal will who chases elf illusion.

"Why is the child rushing into the forest?" Miranda asked, watching the boy in fascination.

Pixie-led, her mind whispered. Yet a charm was magic and had Proteus not said that he could not use magic without the tyrant knowing of it? Was that not the only reason to have Miranda perform the transport spell in the Hunter's great book?

She lay her hand upon the cold page of her adopted father's spell book, as though through that hand, from the page, through her cold fingers, she could drink up the Hunter's eternal strength.

Pixie-led.

Proteus looked at her and smiled, the fond smile of an adult looking at a child. "We've set a charm on him," he said. "To go into the forest." He shrugged at what must have been her shocked expression. "It is easiest to spell him from Arden Forest, the land that has been magical to our kind from time immemorial."

Miranda felt cold at his words. "We've laid a charm?" she asked. "We?"

Since the war had ended, there had never been mention of anyone helping Proteus but Miranda.

Was he indeed a liar?

She looked at his golden hair, his perfect features, his dark eyes. Perhaps he had lied with good intentions, for no one who looked so beautiful could be evil.

And yet, if he had lied, how could she trust him?

Seemingly unaware of her moral struggle, Proteus chuckled. "Some friends there remain to me, from my father's coalition." He looked at Miranda and smiled and, reaching for her hand that rested upon the book, petted it reassuringly. "They are, to be truthful, immigrants in our land and therefore they feel not the pull of the hill. Though their magic, like mine, is Quicksilver's tribute, his to unjustly control, yet have they some arcane powers that the king cannot compass.

"But nominally they are Quicksilver's subjects, and like me, they pretended to submit. But they're still on our side, and they will help us."

"Who are they?" Miranda asked. "These, our allies, of whom I've never heard before?"

"Princes and nobles all," Proteus said.

"Of elvenkind?"

Proteus shrugged. "Of a great magical race, no worse issued than ours, nor no less ancient. Some would say more."

It was clear Proteus wished to say no more about it and—knowing that when he avoided to speak of something, it was to protect her—Miranda forbore to ask.

Just in such a way had he avoided speaking of her father's deposition—seeking to give her no pain.

Perhaps, from what he had already said about these allies, a better-brought-up elf, cognizant of her own kind, would have guessed the race he alluded to.

And there was the reason for his not telling her of these allies before. He suspected her ignorance and wanted to protect her from humiliation.

She looked at him through moist eyes.

Kind, kind Proteus.

Proteus made a gesture in the air that closed the window through which Miranda had seen the mortal boy rushing into Arden Woods, magic-led.

But in Miranda's mind, she could still see the boy rushing forth.

She looked at Proteus and, anxious, set her hand firmly about his wrist in warm entreaty. "The boy will not be harmed," she said.

Proteus looked back at her, surprised, as though she'd spoken a different language, so arcane that he could barely divine its meaning. "The boy?"

"This boy." She pointed toward the place where the magical window had hung suspended, the place where she'd seen the boy. "This mortal boy. He is no enemy of ours, no part of our injury. He will not be harmed but will, never knowing what happened, be returned to the safety of his mother's arms."

"Oh, we can return the boy to his mother," Proteus said. "I confess to you I scarce thought on him. He's but a tool and mortals are such beings who live such ephemeral and inconsequential lives that sometimes I count them as no more than flies on a summer's day and give them not a thought." His hand closed over her hand, though, and he smiled. "But if fair Miranda wants the human boy returned to kith and kin, to kith and kin shall the child return." He smiled, his smile that made all thought vanish from Miranda's mind, her heart radiate with warmth, as her knees went weak.

She nodded, but sighed as she thought of what they would do. "And yet," she said. "It is wrong to kidnap the boy, is it not? It is murder to kill even a tyrant when he cannot defend himself. And I fear me on this, and on my adopted father's judgment. Only . . . Hear me not. Do as you will."

Proteus looked away from her and down on the book again. His smile of indulgent amusement slowly changed to a frown that knit his brows together over his dark eyes.

"Is anything wrong?" Miranda asked.

He looked up. In his gaze there was an exasperation that Miranda had rarely seen—or rarely seen displayed toward her.

"Nothing is wrong," he said, but his mouth twisted in wry contradiction of his words. "Nothing is wrong, save only that everything is. For my efforts I am rewarded with this, a book I cannot use."

"You cannot use?" Miranda asked and, with quick, reprimanding tongue, "Woe is me, then, that brought you the wrong book."

Behind her, Caliban snorted and Miranda shot him one quelling glance over her shoulder.

Proteus's hands closed around hers. "Woe rather to me, Miranda," he said. His voice was slow and doleful, full of quiet acceptance, of tolling defeat like a bell echoing over a dark night and an open grave. "Woe to me, who wanted with this to achieve revenge, to cleanse my father's blood from the kingdom of elf. Woe to me, who wanted to defeat the tyrant and set you, milady, on Fairyland's throne. Woe to me who—" He let go of her hands and, with a final sounding bang, closed the heavy cover of the ancient book.

"But no, milord, no," Miranda said, nettled by his passivity and grieved by the grief she read in his eyes. "No. Look at me. There is still hope. If this is not the right book, I'll get you another. If this is wrong, I—"

"But it is the right book, Miranda," Proteus said. "It is just that within the compass of my ability and the measure of your power, I believe even you lack the strength and magic to make this spell work."

Again he opened the book to the last page, and looked longingly at the spell, as though it contained all his dreams and as though all of them were set upon an unsteady bark in a deep sea. "I cannot use the power and you lack it. My father would have been able to do it, but alas, my father is dead."

Miranda looked at Proteus's hand, poised atop the cover of the book. She remembered how the letters of the spell seemed, alive, to contort and writhe with their power.

She had not enough power?

But Proteus had once told her that she, of all those born of elf, had the greatest power, the strongest natural magic.

More, the Hunter had told her that she did.

She grabbed Proteus's wrist again, where his sleeve ended and before his glove began. His skin felt icy cold. "Milord, what will happen if I have not enough power to actuate this spell?"

He looked at her, his dark eyes shining with moistness. "It is dangerous to you, Miranda. If you lost control of the spell miduse, it could kill you. I cannot allow it."

"I ask you not to allow it," Miranda said, and opened the book. "I tell you I will do it."

Proteus opened his mouth, closed it, then opened it again, as though surprise had stolen his power of speech. "You've never done the magic, have you? Never done such magic, never used such power. How can I trust you now?"

"How can you not trust me?" she asked as she felt her enthusiasm rise and heard her voice high, excited, ringing like merry bells over the desolate landscape. "How can you afford not to trust me when I am the only one who can do it? I am the only one who can rescue your plans for revenge, aye, and buy the kingdom for both of us, withal. I can set the crown upon our brows. I can. Only let me try this spell."

Impatiently she tore at his hands, pulling the book from his grasp.

"Then you no longer feel ill at ease about the trap? Your conscience will allow you to do this?"

She thought on it. She didn't like the thought of murdering Quicksilver by ambush, but then how else should tyrants die?

And as for the child, she would ensure that he returned, unharmed, to his mother. "If it is to be done," she said. "It is better it were done quickly."

And touching the spell with eager finger, she thought how she would be the one to rescue Proteus's cause. In years to come, the kingdom of the hill would make songs to her courage, her bravery, her magic use, as well as to that beauty that Proteus never tired of praising.

Proteus would thank her. He would be forever in her debt.

She looked at the words upon the page as they twisted and writhed—symbols of fire and air and water entwining, now forming this, now that compound, eternally mutable and forever themselves.

How could one read a language that changed? How could any book mutate thus, the words imprisoned upon the paper, yet free to twist and acquire new forms?

She blinked at the words as they wended and writhed, like worms crawling one upon the other, so that a symbol became the other and it was hard to see where one ended and the next began.

She stared and her eyes burned with the sight of it, and a headache pounded at the back of her head.

She could never read this, let alone perform the spell.

But even as she thought it, as she felt the dull, aching misery of defeat, the horror of failing fair Proteus, a realization formed from the mutable words and her mind.

She could read it.

Aye, and she could magic it, too.

Or rather, while the words changed and transformed, while the very trappings of the spell seemed to hesitate and dissolve into another form, yet the essence of it remained untouched—and in that being untouched showed something—the instructions for the spell.

It was, she thought, as though the page displayed a changing front, a mutable facade to the world. Beneath the facade, the real spell lurked, immutable and unvarying like the stars affixed to the dark sky.

Reading the words as a man that treads upon debris on the surface of a river to reach the safety of the other bank, she focused her mind on the unchanging—on that which, at the back of the spell, appeared to be constant and eternal.

"Miranda, wait," Proteus said. "You must remember the boy you saw. You must call him and none other. You must bring him here."

He touched her hand, and from his mind to hers, an image fluttered like a leaf dropping from a high tree: the boy with curly hair and golden eyes forging his way into the forest.

Part of Miranda's mind received the image and thought on it, and how odd it was that the boy felt like part of her very soul.

She gave it not much thought, though, not much attention: the boy was a means to an end and their presence in his life would be but a brief hindrance.

He would be there and gone, and his life would change but little if at all.

He would perhaps imagine that he'd slumbered in the woods and there had a dream of magical creatures. Then he'd dust himself and go home to his mother.

But Miranda's life, and Proteus's would be changed forever. She would be free of this life of shadows and solitude. And Proteus would . . . Proteus would have his revenge and her hand.

Reaching for the boy in the woods with a part of her magic, keeping her ultimate objective in mind, Miranda lifted her small soft hands, so unaccustomed to this work, and traced high the cabalistic spells that she could perceive through the mutable surface of the changeable words.

There, there, there—she traced symbols of fire upon the still air of this forgotten place.

There, there, there—the symbols glowed and shone and twined—fire and air and earth and water. The elements in conjoined upheaval wrought what they'd never thought to form.

From the stillness of the air, the accustomed certainty of this place outside time and space, something emerged—a tunnel, a black howling vortex.

It opened in front of Miranda and she, startled, hoped it was the means to bring the boy here, nothing more.

Caliban whimpered, a high, animal sound.

Miranda felt as though her hair, her clothes, all had been caught in a storm of light, in a haze of energy, in a glow of magic. Her hair, her clothes flowed around her as though immersed in water, or rather, like living things swimming in water.

She set up the spell and caught the boy in it—a wriggling silver fish in a sturdy net—and opened the howling tunnel to this dark corner of Fairyland, and she raised her arms to the heavens, and with sure voice she called, "So be it."

At that very moment, she felt two minds touch her own—two other minds, their thoughts alien to her inner voice.

One had the familiar feel of her adopted father's thoughts and words, his protective gentleness, his eager affection. This mind voice echoed, fear laden, *Child, child, what have you done?* it asked. And added, *Be careful, for there are traps ahead.*

The other mind was unknown to Miranda. It gave the impression of a cold, glimmering crystal, hard but brittle.

It screamed in her mind, *You can't do this.*

The moment froze, like an animal caught in ice, slowly ceassing struggle, slowly dying, everything guttering through time like a dying candle, the slowness excruciatingly painful to the unsure heart.

The tunnel stopped howling and screaming, and through it, pulled by magic, a boy shot, yelling who knew what.

But he did not land in the clearing near the castle of the Hunter. Rather, he gained altitude, and like a bird flying high above the black turrets, he passed. In a moment he was gone.

Then something else, someone else—more than one person, if the feeling served—hurtled after him.

Were those the voices in Miranda's mind? Had the Hunter pursued the child? Why?

The tunnel closed and all was still.

"Miranda, what have you done?" Proteus asked.

Miranda did not know.

She tasted blood in her mouth, and felt as though she'd been hurled, screaming, into another reality. Her arms and legs hurt as though bruised and her throat felt scratched, as if from screaming.

She'd got it wrong? How could she have got it wrong? Where was the boy? And who else had gone with him?

Scene 10

ᘯᘓᘒ

The bridge of air, a structure woven of light and magic power, suspended—one end of it near the hill in Arden Woods, the other hovering over the strange terrain near the Hunter's castle. It looks like one of those quaint bridges that arch in the middle, seemingly making the journey more arduous. Only, from this bridge, should you look down midpoint, you'd see the earth below, much diminished, a child's toy globe. And around it, arrayed, the multitude of stars, paying it homage. On the bridge, Quicksilver stands, his mouth open, his face pale, his expression horrified.

W*hat was Proteus about?* Quicksilver thought. *Where was he headed that required the bridge of air?*

Then Quicksilver felt the emanations of eternal justice and dark flowing power washing over the bridge.

Straining his eyes to see the other end, he saw the dark castle and, above the castle, the standard flying, showing the Hunter with his hunting horn.

The Hunter.

By the hell and damnation of mortals, Proteus had gone to the Hunter.

Why? To sell his immortal soul for enough power to murder Quicksilver?

Quicksilver's heart skipped a beat, and his feet, as if possessed of thoughts and fears of their own, took a step back upon the bridge.

In that moment, for a breath, he thought he heard, behind him, the clopping of horse's hooves.

He looked over his shoulder and saw nothing save the bridge of shining light and the starry darkness below.

Quicksilver followed Proteus slowly, wondering at Proteus's complete absorption in his errand that ignored the feeling of Quicksilver's magic behind him.

Midway up the bridge, at the highest point of its curved expanse, with the earth but a marble beneath, and the spheres of stars arrayed at his feet, Quicksilver glimpsed the other end with more certainty, and his breath caught, frozen upon his throat.

Never in land of mortal or of fairy had Quicksilver glimpsed such a weird landscape, such rock frozen in an upheaval of waves, such trees so tall as though they'd been standing since land first emerged from the deep.

Then he saw the castle and his heart seized, for such a dark and ominous castle, one that flew the flag of the Hunter, could mean only that Proteus intended to revive war against Quicksilver's enforced truce.

Aye me, Quicksilver thought. *Ariel and Malachite have installed themselves upon my brain and think their misgivings through my thoughts.*

Ahead of him, Proteus had reached the forest of immense, dark trees, at the edge of the wave-tormented ground.

Coming to meet him, hands extended, a comely young girl advanced. Or rather, one of her hands was extended, while the other held on to a large book.

Who was this woman—no, this child on the edge of womanhood—with her spun-silk hair, her well-cut green clothing?

Quicksilver smiled to himself. Malachite's dire warnings of treason, Ariel's disturbed dreams, all came to this. For this had he been frightened at the sight of the black castle.

Foolish Ariel, suspicious Malachite. And fool Quicksilver, for listening to them. For all of Proteus's plotting was no more than this—that he was in love with this comely beauty.

But who was she that lived here with the Hunter, and who had attracted heartbroken Proteus from such a distance?

Quicksilver inched forward upon the bridge, wishing to uncover the mystery, yet not willing to violate the lovers' confidences.

Let Proteus preserve his privacy.

Quicksilver marked how the young elves laughed, how they smiled, how they touched, how they stood near each other.

Both were in love, Quicksilver judged, love as desperate as is the love of all the young.

He could tell the woman was an adolescent and comely and of elven race. He knew no more.

He advanced, fighting the feeling that behind him, step on step, hooves were carefully positioned on the light-woven pavement of the bridge.

I am imagining hooves, he thought. He remembered the centaurs gathered for the execution. *I have centaurs of the brain,* he thought. *I am a fool.*

He looked at the girl once more. Why would a child of elven race be living here? Why would an elf entrust his child to the Hunter, of all creatures on earth? Why give a child to the dark creature?

Or was this girl the child of a visiting elf, a potentate from a faraway land and not consigned to the Hunter's desolate landscape?

No.

The Hunter accepted no visitors, nor did he play congenial host to elven nobility.

Furthermore, the way this young woman stood, the way she moved, all had the look of one in her accustomed place. And then, Quicksilver thought, feeling her elf power flare around her as some emotion spiked high—and then, if she were a foreign potentate, she'd be a princess, at least a princess, to have such power.

And he'd have heard of such a one.

Perhaps the Hunter had had a romance with a female elf long ago, and from it this single girl had descended, this single, graceful creature.

But something bothered him all the same. The way the girl moved, and the way she walked, and the way she cocked her head sideways waiting for a reply, all reminded him of someone.

But she was so blond and so small, so graceful and so obviously female, that it took a while before Quicksilver's mind and feelings met upon the puzzle.

Then the girl smiled, and held both hands out to Proteus, and in that gesture, Quicksilver recognized a smile, a gesture he'd seen himself, often, before his mirror.

The girl reminded Quicksilver of himself, or rather of Lady Silver, who was sometimes the best part of himself.

But Quicksilver had no children. There were no children in his family. None, save only—

Save only his brother's daughter, the long-lost Miranda, Princess of Elvenland. Now Quicksilver remembered what he'd gone a long ways to forget.

His brother's only daughter, an infant, had been in her crib when Quicksilver had met and challenged Sylvanus for one last time.

And as Quicksilver won leadership of the hill and Sylvanus was collected by the Hunter for his many and terrifying crimes, Sylvanus—already transformed, already hunched into the shape of one of the Hunter's dogs—had picked his daughter up between his jaws, and with her had plunged into the midst of the Hunter's pack of dogs.

Now Sylvanus was dead, but his daughter . . . Could this be his daughter? This the lost Miranda?

Hair prickled at the back of Quicksilver's neck and he felt as though a cold finger ran down his spine.

This was her, then, Sylvanus's daughter, princess and heir to Quicksilver's own throne.

With suspicious eye, Quicksilver watched, remembering Sylvanus's treasons and Sylvanus's crimes, he watched Sylvanus's daughter and wondered what hid beneath that small face, that flying blond hair, those bright blue eyes that sparkled with such love.

Oh, let it be only love for Proteus and nothing more. Let it mean no more than two young people in love.

Then could Quicksilver have the two of them joined in matrimony and, thus unifying all the claims to his throne in one house, watch over them and their marriage with paternal joy.

Oh, then, thrice welcome long-lost Miranda.

And yet there was something else, some other feeling. The feeling of power flying all around these two.

He thought they did some magic. A viewing spell? Quicksilver was too far away to see what it truly was.

It was the power that scared Quicksilver. Without stepping off the bridge of air, he leaned closer, and saw the girl open the book she'd carried.

The power of the book flowed from it when she touched it, as it had not when in Proteus's hands.

The girl raised her arm, started reciting a spell.

What spell was this? What did it mean? The currents of power flowed from it strong and white and clear.

It was not, Quicksilver thought, a love spell. Nor was it, perforce, an attack spell. It felt harmless enough. Or did it not?

Tendrils from the spell stretched over Fairyland and reached for the mortal world and picked—

Quicksilver recognized the dark curls, the golden eyes. Will, he thought. Only it was not Will, but a child, Will's son, Hamnet.

What could this girl want with Hamnet?

He threw his power at the spell, trying to stop it, but it howled on, like a madman who would not listen.

Quicksilver felt within it the dark coils of a power stronger and older than his own.

Older than his own? How could it be?

And why would it meddle with Hamnet?

Before Quicksilver could think of any reason, he felt the vortex—a dark counterpart of the bridge of air—open, and through it, the child come hurtling, screaming.

Quicksilver had time to realize, in a momentary panic, where the child was being sent. He threw himself into the vortex, willed himself to follow the child. He yelled at the girl to stop, but he didn't expect to be obeyed.

Oh, Ariel's dark divining had been true, after all, in fact if not in detail.

By a dark castle had Quicksilver met his doom.

The child was Will's darling, Will's only son. Quicksilver would not allow Fairyland to steal him from Will.

Scene 11

☙❧

Proteus and Miranda stand amazed, in the landscape that looks too quiet, too glossy, filled with a drowned light, like a scene cast in glass or seen through the filter of softening memory. Slowly, Proteus's face shifts to an expression of anger. Caliban, sitting nearby, moves closer, to huddle near Miranda, like a protecting dog at his mistress's heel.

"Luckless girl," Proteus said. His voice came out strangled and slow, as though he'd forgotten how to speak or as though the remaining magic in the air made him witless. "Luckless girl. What have you done?"

What had she done?

Miranda would gladly have answered the question, but she knew not. She had done the spell. She had done it, as it wished—commanded—to be done. Had she not?

Those two voices in her mind, the sense of her father—her adopted father—so near, had it been real?

As she tried to remember what she had done, the memories and thoughts shifted and twisted just as the words had writhed upon the page, and she could not fix her mind to any certain thing.

It had seemed to her—it was passing strange—but it had seemed to her—she could swear it—that someone else had intruded upon the spell, that someone had touched her power with a greater power.

Quicksilver? The thought came to her, but she didn't know how to express it, nor even if it was possible. "Did Quicksilver—" she started.

Proteus looked on her with cold eyes—hard-pebble eyes, black and opaque. He took a deep breath.

"Quicksilver," he said. "Came quicker than we expected. I should have known the tyrant, the despot, was following me. Yes, Quicksilver was here, but for a moment and in that twinkling he jumped into the stream of power carrying that child—do you know where your spell has carried the child?" He crossed his arms on his chest and looked remote and distant, a superhuman judge, trying her for her crimes that she couldn't remember.

Miranda shook her head and lowered her gaze.

"You've sent the child to the crux," Proteus said, his voice assured and full of strength as though making a final, triumphant argument.

"The crux?" Miranda repeated like a child reading by rote, not knowing what the word meant.

Proteus's eyes opened wide in surprise, his mouth twisted in disapproval. "Oh, what are you that don't know what the crux is? The crux is the center of all magic, Miranda. It was once the world, or all the worlds. It enveloped all, was all, a part and parcel of the great egg from which the universe hatched, entire, all the spheres, the arrayed worlds.

"But magic has shrunk as these, our corrupted times, wound the world away from the force of creation.

"Now, the crux is nothing but an island, an island of magic in the ocean of unmagic. But there it is strong and there it is central to life, and from it magic comes to every world. Without the crux there would be no magic, none, in any of the worlds, mortal or elven."

Miranda swallowed. She imagined the crux as a sphere at the center of all the worlds. An egg within an egg. "I sent the child there?"

Oh, luckless. Amid such power, how could a human child survive?

"You've sent him there, through some grievous error."

"But I followed the spell, I made all—"

"Worse yet, you've sent your uncle there, also. In that center of magic, what might Quicksilver not do? For that land was not made for man or elf and there the presence of any thinking being can wound the delicate balance of the crux, the balance of all magic. Wishes are truths in the crux and there the very thoughts have blade-sharp wings, which cut as they fly. He might perhaps destroy the crux so that, with it, he can destroy all magic and us.

"You must send me there, Miranda. You must send me and my friends after the tyrant and the mortal boy. You must. There I can kill him, and then can I return to you."

She turned her head to look as the sound of hooves announced riders. "Your friends?"

She blinked as the riders approached for their magnificent stallions seemed headless, as from where the neck of the horse should be there rose the rider's torso, tanned and nude. Above the torsos, broad faces, surrounded by dark hair, showed concerned expressions.

"We almost caught him," the one upon the black horse said.

"Alas that he escaped," spoke the rider of the roan.

They had thick accents and in Miranda's mind their appearance and the accent fell together.

Centaurs. These were centaurs, the inhuman monsters who'd almost destroyed the glittering human civilization of ancient Greece in its crib.

These were Proteus's friends?

She looked at her lord, unsure what to think.

He smiled at her, a tender, wounded smile. "You made a mistake, Miranda, and now I must correct it. My friends are here to help me."

For a moment, chastised, her lips trembling, her eyes full of tears at having caused Proteus's anger, Proteus's vexation, an heretical thought that perhaps she didn't want him to return to her crossed Miranda's mind.

But then she looked at his perfect face, his dark eyes, his golden hair, and she sighed. She wanted him to return to her. But she was not sure she wanted him to go. "Will it be dangerous?" she asked. "In the crux?"

"It will be dangerous," Proteus said, and composed his face to manly courage. "But I will return to you."

She swallowed a lump of fear in her throat and opened the book. She raised her hands for the spell and stared at the words that slipped and twisted beneath her gaze.

And stopped.

She didn't want Proteus to risk himself without her.

Too many times, in these months that he'd courted her, she'd seen him leave and known that he was about to face some great challenge, some battle that might wither his soul or kill his body.

And now, must she again stand and watch him go into that dark vortex, that weird place from which he might not return?

Must she let him go to face the monster alone?

Raising her hands, she recited the words that twisted and writhed beneath her gaze. She called to her each of the centawes he'd indicated, and slipped the noose of the spell around Proteus's beloved neck.

And then she stood, hands raised, ready to close the spell.

She was doing the spell. She was closing it.

How could Proteus prevent her from going with them?

She pulled the spell around herself, and said, "So let it be," closing the spell.

The vortex opened and she dropped through it, shivering and breathless.

Proteus's scream—"Miranda!"—echoed in her ears.

She felt the book drop from her numb hands as the whirlwind swallowed her.

Scene 12

ᘓᘔ

A fine sand beach, white and unmarked by footsteps. The dark vortex of magic opens over it. As though the vortex brought forth wind to this timeless, undisturbed space, wind and sand and sea respond, agitating in sudden storm. Quicksilver drops from a man's height above the beach onto the sand, and rolls. Around him, sand blows in a raging wind and—though he can see no ocean—there is a feeling of the ocean nearby, a feeling of raging waves, of something crashing on this formerly undisturbed shore.

Quicksilver fell onto the sand. The force of his fall jarred him, addling his senses.

For a moment he didn't know where he was.

Where had this spell brought him?

Fine sand under him prickled the tender skin of his hands, scoured his face where it had touched the ground. The velvet of his doublet had ripped.

Wind howled around him, violent and sand laden, scouring his flesh and insinuating itself through the rip in his doublet and past the fine mesh of his shirt.

He opened his mouth to scream and breathed sand.

Raising his head, pushing himself up on his hands, he tried to look around through half-shut eyes—protectively closed against the sand.

He'd expected to see the boy nearby, his small body huddled, possibly hurt by the fall.

But there was no one else in sight, no living thing save a fringe of trees a little ways away. Quicksilver crawled on his hands and knees, searching the sand with his hands, as though the boy's body might be there, under the sand.

He felt nothing but more sand. Where was the boy? Where was Will's son, who had no part or parcel in Fairyland disputes? What had Proteus wanted with the child? Who was it whose power had intervened in the spell? Such an old power, so dark, so indifferent, could not belong to Miranda, Quicksilver's young niece. Nor to Proteus, his rebellious cousin.

Why would an unknown spell maker interfere in the girl's spell? Where would such a one have transported them all?

A loud howling, as of unleashed wind, made him look above. The black vortex spun faster, seeming to multiply tendrils as it spun, like a monstrous spider stretching its many arms.

Where could the boy have gone?

If the same spell had brought them both here, shouldn't they have landed in the same place?

Like a man, still drowsy, retelling to himself the dream from which he'd just awakened, Quicksilver thought about the last second before he'd fallen into the magic vortex. He'd reached for the boy. Faith, reached for the boy and almost caught him.

His fingers had as near as brushed the boy's dark curls.

He'd seen the child's eyes—so like Will's that thinking on it disturbed Quicksilver—so wide and so intent as they stared at Quicksilver in a silent appeal for help.

Quicksilver had tried to respond to that appeal. He had tried.

He'd been dropped here, and the boy had gone on. But gone on where?

And where was Quicksilver?

Clawing at the sand with his aching fingers, pushing against pressure as though he were submerged at a great depth, inch by inch and little by little, he managed to get up.

The wind seemed to press against him more, filling his cloak like a ship's sail. It pushed on his body, yes, but his mind and his soul also, till Quicksilver felt as though he stood, body, mind, and soul—battered and frozen—fighting with all his strength to remain standing.

No ordinary wind could do this to the King of Elvenland.

Only magic. Magic.

Quicksilver forced himself, step by step, to move upon the sand. Each of his movements multiplied the howling of the outraged wind.

His mind took halting steps, as his body did, seeking to get its bearings in this land.

There was only one place—only one—where magic was that rampant that the very wind, the very sand, was full of it.

And that was one place where no elf had ever stepped, a place that, until this moment, Quicksilver would have sworn didn't exist.

For this land was to him as Fairyland to mortals, a story told by his nursemaid and learned very early, but too fantastical and full of nonsense to be real.

Standing against the push of the wind, he shielded his eyes with his hand against the assault of the sand, and tried to see past the wind that the sand made amber-colored and almost opaque.

Around him, as far he could see, the sandy beach stretched, and it seemed to curve slowly, as though he were on a small island.

Inland from the beach, as though the beach wrapped around it, a wooded center stretched, woods so thick they looked like a single tree, immense and overgrown.

The clump writhed as if alive. Perhaps it just moved in the wind.

On the other side, the beach ended in something that seemed like the sea, but yet was not.

In that same space where, in a normal beach, the sea would be, something rose and fell, to rise and fall again in stormy grey waves.

But the feeling of it was not that of water.

The roar of water had never echoed thus in Quicksilver's ears, nor had the nearness of water disturbed him thus.

Quicksilver walked toward the *sea*, forcing his feet to move against the wind, against the sand, against a wave of fear that rose within him and set his hair on end.

From that space came such a wave of force, like the feel of a lightning strike, very near.

Only this was not the natural electric feel of thunder, but a force that insinuated itself in Quicksilver's mind and made him feel the quickening of pulse, the loosening of tongue, the deceitful, dangerous euphoria of wine.

It crept through his senses like a thief. Reaching the core within him that was his link to the magic of the hill, the power and souls of all his subjects, it slid in and it—

"No," Quicksilver screamed as he closed all his magical defenses and his shields around himself.

All his shields barely held, feeling insufficient and flimsy, like a threadbare cloak around his soul.

Through them, he still felt the pull and push of those waves so near. Those waves of magic.

It was *magic*. The thought startled him, like a sudden blow dealt by a stranger. Raw magic. An ocean of it.

Had it reached into Quicksilver, had it truly tapped his link to the hill, it would have ignited all of magic, all of the hill, till every elf in it were consumed and burned into nothing—magic and energy and nothing more, as everything had been at creation.

It would be like setting fire to a taper of bacon grease.

Stepping away from the ocean of magic, step by step, Quicksilver felt hot and cold by degrees, as the reality of where he was, the magnitude of his problem, sank in.

I am in the crux of all magic, he thought, and struggled to contain his panic.

He'd heard of this land first at Great Titania's knee. His nursemaid, she who'd given Quicksilver suckle, and who'd been a Princess of Fairyland, had told him of it too, as he grew older.

Of the land like an egg, at the center of all the known worlds, where magic enveloped all and moved in all.

That land, like a compass, kept magic centered and all magic alive in all other worlds. A change to that world and all magic—maybe all life—might well be lost.

No elf in living memory had ever told of being there, but Quicksilver remembered the tales he had been told, of the strange rules of this primeval place.

Legends spoke of the magical rules that went withal. The rule of threes, for instance. Three sunsets in the crux and you'd never leave. Magic would so permeate your being and replace your substance, that you'd become a part of this world, like the magic ocean.

Then there was the rule of paying for leaving the crux. A mortal could never leave the crux, once he'd entered it, unless he left something of himself behind.

And any mortal who made magic in the crux would always and forever be a little magic, a little like the elves, living between worlds.

Yet, if this were the crux—and Quicksilver's mind recoiled from the thought, for it was impossible, it should be impossible—if it were the crux, then everything here would be magic.

Everything. The sun, the wind, the sand, the least particle of air.

And everything that happened here would affect all the magic in all the worlds.

And the crux was not an island but an egg.

He looked up at the sky above him and realized, with a shiver, that it was more magic, of the sort he'd almost touched in the *ocean* before. If he touched the sky, he would be burned as surely as if he swam in the sea.

The wind, he realized, was no wind, but a pressing dislocation of magic, a magical storm.

The storm, then, was the protest of magic at an invasion, the screams of magical power against the intrusion of creatures, mortal and almost immortal—flesh and blood and weak cravings—into the world of eternal, incorruptible power.

Where could the boy be?

Forcing his eyes to remain open against the lashing of the sand, Quicksilver looked above the forest, where a tall peak rose past the green tops of the forest like a volcano from a frothy sea. This peak was white, glimmering white, and upon it a white castle sat, the exact, but white, twin of the Hunter's castle in the outer world.

If the boy were anywhere, Quicksilver thought, as the legends he'd drunk with his nursemaid's milk rounded in his head, he would be in that castle upon that hill.

Quicksilver couldn't feel his presence through the maelstrom of magic and loosened, irate power. But he knew the boy would be there.

For where else to keep a captive, by tradition and lore, but in the castle in the center of Fairyland . . . Or the crux?

Well, and if the boy was there, there must Quicksilver go.

Straightening against the power in the wind, Quicksilver tugged on his black doublet, trying to make it look severe and elegant once more, despite his tumble and the sand-laden wind.

He'd won a war. He could surely rescue a mere mortal boy from the center of the crux.

Yet if the crux truly gave power to humans . . .

Would the boy be a great mage? And how would he take Quicksilver's intrusion?

Quicksilver shook his head. No matter. The only reason any elf could have kidnaped the boy would have been to inflict pain upon Will and, through Will, upon Quicksilver.

Quicksilver didn't know why he still felt pain at the thought of Will's being hurt. But he did feel pain and that foolish fondness from which he cringed had made Will's son the target of this plot.

So the fault was Quicksilver's, and Quicksilver must pay the debt.

Having thus wrought Hamnet's doom, he must retrieve him from it.

He'd never yet shirked responsibility. He'd fought for his hill, his people, his kingdom. He'd put almost his last relative to death for the sake of his responsibility.

As he thought of this, Quicksilver felt very tired and all but tottered upon his feet.

Yet he must go to the castle. It was his duty to Will.

Just as he walked toward the forest, which seemed to sense his approach and grow thicker and greener and darker as he drew near it, someone fell in front of Quicksilver, in a splash of sand and a renewed fretting of the disturbed magical winds.

Turning, through the haze of sand, Quicksilver beheld William Shakespeare.

Scene 13

ᘓᘖᘔ

The same beach, as Will lands, and Quicksilver stands, amazed, staring at Will. Around them, the sand-laden wind howls, and the magical sea roars in their ears so loudly that Will's scream on landing on the sand is lost amid the fury of wind and sea.

Will landed on his stomach on the fine, white sand.

Where was he?

He pushed himself up on his elbows.

His hair, shorter than it had been in the past, yet was too long for this wind. It whipped into his face and gave him but a broken view of Quicksilver, interrupted by strands of darkness, as though the darkness of Quicksilver's own heart were thus translated to Will's view of him.

"Where is my son?" Will asked, and his mouth filled with sand as he asked it.

Quicksilver looked bewildered, shaking his head, his eyes all wide and innocent.

He looked still, Will noted, as he had fourteen years ago, when Will had first met him, in Arden Wood.

The elf looked young, like a mortal of twenty, no more. His blond hair, whipped by the wind, might be shining, molten silver. His features also, smooth and untelling of time, were perfect with that perfection that mortal man can't reach.

Only his eyes looked different, older—perhaps wearier.

Moss green and wide open as if in surprise, they strained to make Will believe that Quicksilver knew nothing of Hamnet's location, that Quicksilver had not kidnaped Will's son, that Quicksilver was innocent as the newborn babe or the fawn taking his first steps upon the forest floor.

Will could not, would not, believe it.

How could he believe Quicksilver innocent, when he knew the creature better than the creature—dual and deceiving as he was—knew himself?

Will pushed up on his arms and unfolded to stand against air that seemed to weigh upon him like water.

"Where is my son?" he asked again. "What have you done with him?"

In what strange land did Quicksilver mean to imprison Hamnet? What did the King of Fairyland want with Will's boy?

Or meant he to take the boy and, for his love, control the father whom Quicksilver had never managed to ensnare fully?

Quicksilver opened his hands as if to display his lack of weapons, the kind of weapons mankind must use.

But creatures such as this needed no weapons. They had treacherous magic at their call, and sudden wounding in the grasp of their unholy power.

Will clenched his fists tight and took a step toward the king of elves.

Either because of the expression on Will's face, or because he knew his own guilt, Quicksilver stepped back.

Step on step Will advanced on Quicksilver thus, and step on step Quicksilver retreated.

Oh, the elf was guilty enough, Will would wager. Else, why would he retreat before Will's advance?

Bold advance and foolhardy confidence—force!—befit Quicksilver better than such hasty retreat.

The first time he'd met Quicksilver, Quicksilver had worn his other aspect, that of dark, seductive Lady Silver.

In that aspect had he seduced Will, seduced him and led him like a babe through the forest of desire. The lust had been a blind, though, a mere deceit, and no love hid beneath the lady's blandishments.

Instead, she'd used her pale body, her dark hair, and the delights of immortal love to lure Will to kill the king of fairies. Which, if Will had done it, would have proven fatal not just to Will but to his whole family.

Will, who had been only nineteen untried and gullible, had barely escaped the lady's coil.

How could he believe such a being innocent?

Quicksilver opened his hands wide, and said, "I don't know. I don't know where your son is, Will. I followed him here, true, but . . ."

He'd *followed* Hamnet here? Was Will to believe that Quicksilver, king of elves, sovereign of fairies, Lord of the Realms Above the Air and Beneath the Hills of Avalon, didn't know the boy had been kidnaped? Didn't know when a mortal had been pulled into Fairyland?

Again, Will stepped forward and again Quicksilver stepped back, each of them moving step on step as though locked in the steps of an arcane dance.

The second time Will's and Quicksilver's paths had crossed, Quicksilver had callously allowed Kit Marlowe to go to his death to give back to Quicksilver the throne of Fairyland.

Thus had the greatest poet in the world died. Thus had Kit Marlowe's flame of life and poetry been extinguished, to keep Quicksilver upon an immaterial throne, in a land most illusory.

For this had Will been saddled with Marlowe's ghost, Will's words forever tainted with Marlowe's immortal whisperings upon Will's mortal ear.

Will's rage pounded in his mind, blinded him to all but the need to hurt this creature who looked yet young while Will had started aging and declining onto his inevitable grave.

This heartless creature, this cold being, who would remain young and unchanged centuries after Will had become dust amid the dust of his ancestors.

Quicksilver's youth as much as his deceit tempted Will to raging fury. With raging fury, Will leapt. He found his hands wrapped around the smooth flesh, the pale neck, of the sovereign of Fairyland.

"Where is my son, you cursed thing?" Will screamed as his hands squeezed Quicksilver's neck. "Where is my son, you spawn of darkness, you being of deceit, you tormenter of mortals?"

His hands around Quicksilver's neck made as if to squeeze the magical life from the creature's body.

But Quicksilver's hands came up, endowed with the greater strength of his estate. His hands, though slim and delicate looking, had the strength of iron binds as they pried at Will's fingers, loosening them from Quicksilver's throat.

Yet Quicksilver's voice flowed hoarsely through his lips as he said, "Cease this madness. You gain nothing by killing me. I do not know where your son is, and it was to save him that I came from my throne and safe court in Fairyland to this, the magical crux, the most dangerous part of all the magical world."

"Liar," Will screamed, his rage still streaming through him as a flooding river will stream through its bed, ravaging the banks. "Liar."

For who would have kidnaped Hamnet but with Quicksilver's consent, nay, by his order?

In Will's mind, filled with rage and tormented by the continuous howling of the magical wind, Quicksilver was guilty.

Yet Quicksilver opened his hands, and opening his hands, showed them void of weapons and clean of that magic sparkle that could, unawares, throw such fury into the world of mortals. "Will, forebear," he said. He spoke slowly, like a man who contains his anger beneath a net of propriety and, thus containing it, like a man who for a moment has fought a raging lion to a standstill keeps for a second at bay the disaster that is sure to follow. "Will, forebear.

For the sake of the love I once bore you, for the sake of the love you once said—"

"Love?" Will looked around as though somewhere, mid the howling wind, the rising waves, someone might lurk who knew what the elf spoke of, or who guessed in Quicksilver's words their true meaning. Someone who knew that, in Lady Silver's form, Quicksilver had ensnared Will in the thrall of lust and come close to ensnaring him in the thrall of love.

Knowing the truth of that almost-love, the soft vulnerability of such feelings that he had, once, allowed to trap his heart, Will spit out the word as though it were foul, a venom absorbed into his body and contravened only by divine grace. "Love! You talk of love? Know this, then, that the love I bear you can afford no better term than this: Thou art a villain."

Quicksilver blinked at the insult, his face reflecting something like true surprise.

But what was true and what were lies with these creatures of illusion?

Will blinked at the hurt in the moss-green eyes of his foe, at his foe's sudden paling, at Quicksilver's injured look, like that of a child punished for no reason.

He blinked in surprise and, feeling the first softening of sympathy, willed himself to see Quicksilver as he was, all poison and self-interest, all darkness and conniving.

Yet Quicksilver resisted Will's desires and stood there—untouched, beautiful, just as he had been in that youth that, to Will, seemed like something long-ago, a dream had by someone else, in which Will had been but a supporting character, an unperfect actor upon the stage.

Quicksilver looked like what he had been—hair of spun silver, pale skin like marble, now coloring on the high cheekbones after the paleness that had followed Will's insult.

Quicksilver's lips yet remained pale, but when those pale lips opened, the voice that came from them was controlled, exact. In its controlled, exact measure, neither low nor loud, it yet obscured the voice of the wind, the howling of the sand-laden storm. "Will, the reason that I have to love you, the very great gift loving you was to me once, doth much excuse the appertaining rage to such an insult. Villain I'm not. Therefore fare you well. I see thou knowest me not. Get you out of here. You belong not in the crux. Go. I'll bring your son to you."

Thus speaking, Quicksilver raised his hands, moving them through the air in precise movements that Will had long ago learned meant invoking magic. Fairykind magic, invoked at need and with almost no price, save a small depletion of the whole of magic in the hill.

Normally, when Quicksilver did this, sparks of magic flew between his fingers, the fatuous-fire of magic and of power that foretold the effect that magic would have on the natural world.

Now Will saw no magic, did not feel it. How could that be?

Quicksilver was the king of the hill and had at his disposal such strength and force, such power and might, that all he had to do was express a desire and it would come true.

Thinking this, knowing that what Quicksilver wished was Will out of here, out of his sight, out of this magical place where yet the elves planned to ensnare Hamnet, Will jumped.

Jumping, he landed on Quicksilver, and to his surprise, Quicksilver fell beneath his weight, and thumped to the hard sand with a most human noise of injured flesh. A most human grunt escaped between his immortal lips.

Will again felt confused. What he expected to happen turned out very different from his expectation. Yet was that not the nature of these creatures? Did they not cast their veil of illusion around hapless mortals and make a mockery and a shadowland of what had been rational expectation and reasoned reality?

"Oh, villain, this shall not excuse the injuries that thou hast done me." Will raised his fist above Quicksilver's still, pale face. Why did the King of Elvenland look so cold, so dispirited—nay, so scared, like a child lost in the night who knows not what to do?

Were those tears that trembled on those moss-green eyes, giving them the look of forest lakes, or yet of a forest submerged, an Atlantis lost?

Will brought his fist down and, instead, took his hands to Quicksilver's doublet, and grabbed him by the padded shoulders, and shook him, now hitting him against the hard, packed sand, now lifting him from it.

Quicksilver felt unresisting in Will's grasp, his weight no more than the weight of a few dried leaves on the forest floor, a wisp of windblown sand.

Will thought how, in the legends, fairy gold often turned out to be some dried leaves, a handful of trash from the forest floor, and shivered.

Was Quicksilver himself that immaterial? Was he a thing of cobwebs and dreams?

But if so, what gave him such power, to kidnap Will's son, to disrupt Will's life, to threaten Will's family, to reach for Will's heart?

Will looked at the green eyes and found them fixed on him with no resentment, nothing but a vague hurt, a pained pity. He shook the King of Fairyland again. "Fight, fight, why don't you fight? This shall not excuse the injuries that you have done me."

Quicksilver drew breath, noisily, loudly enough to be heard over the howling wind. "I do protest I never injured you, but love you better than you can devise." He lifted his hands and again he showed them to Will, empty of weapons and devoid of magic. "I am here, Will, to deliver your son from the clutches of this land, as though it were my own son, kidnaped. I'm here to protect your name and family. Go, good Will. Go and be satisfied. Be satisfied."

Satisfied? Will stared down at the King of Fairyland. Quicksilver could crush Will with a word, could he not? Quicksilver could crush Will with his own strength, his physical strength that was elf-given and full of that fire of Fairyland that blew the very engines of creation.

And yet, he lay there, still and meek.

"Please, allow me to send you back to your books and your rooms, your city and your human occupation, and I will bring you your son—I give my word in bond. I will bring you your son by night's fall. Listen, good Will, only listen to me." The voice of the princely elf rose in a high, desperate keening, the sound of a child trying to wheedle agreement from his powerful parents. "Listen to me." And now the voice had an edge of unmanly crying, and tears rolled from the moss-green eyes, down the marble-pale face of the King of Elvenland.

Will jumped up and stood well way from Quicksilver, who remained sitting and who but lifted a hand to wipe away his tears.

"Oh, calm, dishonorable, vile submission," Will said, wiping his own hands to his pants, as if by doing so he could wipe away Quicksilver's touch, Quicksilver's contagion, and all the feelings, good and bad, passionate and hurtful, that lay between them.

And staring down at the king, Will trembled, for who the king was, for what this meant. For if the king was weak, if he cried, meant it that Quicksilver was not truly guilty?

And then, who was? Who'd done this outrage? To whom should Will appeal for the return of his son?

And could he trust Quicksilver?

Or did the lady Silver's passions now control Quicksilver's behavior? Did she still love Will?

If so, would that accursed love have led her to stealing Hamnet?

Why did Quicksilver cry?

Once, Silver had seduced Will as much with her tears as with her slim form and the rounded softness of her bosom.

What did Quicksilver seek with these tears of his?

His own voice came out trembling, shocked. "What is this? What mean you by it? What do you want with me?"

Quicksilver dragged himself to his knees, in slow movements, like a bruised mortal, like a suffering penitent, and on his knees, turned to look at Will. "What is this you ask? A game is afoot that neither of us chose to play, Will. Your son was kidnaped by an enemy of mine own—nay, by my nearest relative, and yet an enemy. And therein lies the fall for you and I, both, that my heir kidnaped your heir and brought both of us here. Do you know where we are, good Will? Oh, can you scope it?"

Will shook his head and took a step back, and Quicksilver took a step forward, still on his knees.

This position of the king, this submissive, abased position, scared Will more than had Quicksilver strode about shouting commands and commanding thunderbolts.

Quicksilver's paleness scared him too, and Quicksilver's tears, and Quicksilver's trembling lips.

If the strong trembled so, if the one who had made this plan was this scared, what would not befall those without power, Will himself and—Hamnet?

Once more, Will tried to conjure an image of his son as he had seen him, six months—or was it eight months?—ago.

A fair child, with golden-brown hair and yellow-gold falcon eyes, a miniature of Will himself, and as such, deserving of all love. For who could help but love himself? Who could help but wish the best for himself?

And into that image of himself, Will had vested the best part of his heart, the kindest part of his soul.

And now Hamnet was endangered by the same creature who'd once led his father astray. His father's past would mar Hamnet's future.

Yet there the plotter knelt, seeking, in the guise of a lamb, to hide his lion heart.

Will sought for words, for insults, but could find neither.

And Quicksilver, as though taking Will's silence for interested attention, said, "We are in the crux, Will, the crux of magic. Faith, I didn't know it existed until now. But I'd heard of it, legends, told by elf mother to elf child, just like legends of Fairyland are told to human children." Seeming to find this funny, he smiled, or at least attempted to smile, a ghastly stretching of his too-pale lips. "At my mother's knee I heard it, and from my nurse, who was a High Princess of Fairyland, I begged stories and legends about it.

"The crux, it is said, was blown from the very heart of the universe, and fiery and full of magic, it sped a different way from the world of elves and the world of mortals.

"It went deeper, and it burned stronger, than any other world, and thus—full of magic and fiery power—it became the beating heart of all worlds.

"From the crux comes all magic and all strength, the force of life and the joy of spring. Yet this very land, strong though it is, is dangerous. It is as dangerous, faith, as holding fire in your hand. In this island of magic, where we now find ourselves, everything is different from what it should be. There is brawling love, and loving hate, and you see yourself wholly, without disguise. Even those without power at all are full of force, and in this magic land, thus, one cannot step but falsely, as magical quicksand twists and writhes beneath our every footfall."

Having thus spoken, Quicksilver looked up at Will, like a petitioner might look onto a sacred image, pinning all his hopes of justice and redemption upon its still, unmovable face.

Yet Will felt his face move, his features contort, displaying bewilderment.

But he must not be bewildered, he must not hesitate. This creature was so powerful, and the depths of his cunning so unfathomable, that Will could not afford to show his naked face to the creature's conniving.

He saw Quicksilver's lips move, as though the king of elves searched for yet another way to tell what must be lies—surely these must be lies, for how could they be true? How could Quicksilver be truly weak, truly devoid of schemes and hopes?

"Be still," Will yelled.

And as he spoke, Quicksilver stopped all movement, though his eyes showed the frantic hope, the frantic need to speak.

"I wish your lying mouth were stilled, that you could no more utter a sound," Will said bitterly.

Quicksilver's mouth opened as though to scream and his lips formed "Stop," but no sound emerged.

Only the wind howled, the storm raged, and Will felt a bitter anger burn within his chest. Quicksilver would mock him now? He would mock Will by pretending to be mute?

Yet he felt something—something like a cobweb—catch at his hands.

It was invisible, but he could feel it, tacky and soft to the senses.

The creature was trying his magic tricks.

"Why should I believe your lies, oh lying King? Why should I believe you'd save my son? Did not your kind once steal my wife, my wife *and* daughter both? Did not you, yourself, plot my destruction?"

Quicksilver's lips formed words, rapidly, eagerly, but their movements were as unreadable to Will as words in a book to a man who doesn't know the mysteries of the alphabet and the secrets of phonetics.

"Oh, cease your mockery," Will said, and raised his closed fist and sped it through the air. A good ways away from the elf—as far away as he could be and still speak to the elf and hear him through the maelstrom that surrounded them—Will punched the air and wished that the punch were directed at the elf's face and that Quicksilver could feel the strength of Will's wrath, the force of his hatred.

As he wished it, as his fist wounded the wind, so did Quicksilver's head rock upon his neck, so did the king trip back as though the punch had hit him full on the face.

This much could be mockery and mimicry, but—before the seeming mockery inflamed Will's anger yet anew—Will saw Quicksilver's lips bloom in blood, as though blood had burst forth through the pale skin under impact.

Quicksilver opened his wounded lips and screamed—Will was sure it was a true scream—though no sound emerged.

What magic was here? What mystery?

Will remembered how Quicksilver had said that here, in the crux, in this strange land, those who had no power in the world of men were full of power.

Will had desired Quicksilver to shut up. And lo, Quicksilver could not speak though he wished it. Will had desired Quicksilver to be hurt, and there, the king of elves, kneeling on the sand, had been struck by the magical equivalent of Will's fist and the raging anger that impelled it.

Will stood, amazed, watching as Quicksilver regained his knees and wiped his sleeve across his mouth—leaving his face stained with a streak of sparkling red elven blood.

Quicksilver opened his mouth, then closed it, looking as though not sure, not assured enough to speak, not certain of his matter, not commanding his strength.

And Will, feeling dread fill him as never before—for if Quicksilver were truly powerless and Will powerful, the world had turned upside down, and in a world turned upside down, how could a man find footing?—spoke, his voice slow and dripping with the dread of a man faced with the impossible. "Speak, oh King," he said. "Regain your voice, and speak true, how this may be, that I perform magic and you have none."

"It is the crux," Quicksilver said. His voice was softer than ever, meeker, a mere whisper like that of a lost soul upon the wind that whistles past the graves in an ancient graveyard.

"I have magic. But yours is stronger and I cannot protect myself from it. It is the property of the crux, the matter of my discourse. This is the crux of magic, the blessed and cursed land where every time and every magic current crosses. It makes the powerless powerful, the powerful powerless. It twists and winds around us all, and by us being here, we endanger with our thoughts and actions, crux and magic, and Fairyland, all." Quicksilver took in breath through his wounded lips, a quick breath snagged upon grief, somewhere between a hiccup and a sob. "We should leave. All of us should leave."

And now Will believed him, and now he stood amazed, and stepped back, more fearful than ever, not of what Quicksilver might do to him, but of what he himself might do to Quicksilver. Afraid of this magic he didn't know he possessed, of this unwanted power coursing through his veins.

He looked at his hands as though they were strangers, through which such strong magic might flow without his knowing. He closed firmly lips which, suddenly, could weave strange and abiding spells.

Yet, he watched blood flow down Quicksilver's face, from his injured lips—rivulets of suffering that didn't belong on the immortal face. Will felt himself go pale and his eyes open in horror at what he'd done.

Quicksilver again wiped his mouth to his black velvet doublet. Already the wound was healing by Quicksilver's magic or the virtue of his immortal flesh. "You do not know how to do it, and you might, beyond the attempts you make, cause more injury, and besides . . ." Quicksilver shook his head. "And besides, having done magic in the crux, having tapped into the strength and might of ancient fire, you will already, on earth, when you return to it, have some magical power. The more magic you do, the more power you'll have. Who knows what use might not wake in you? A creature divided, neither elf nor human . . ." Quicksilver frowned, as if a new thought had occurred to him. "I am, myself, a creature divided, my loyalties and hopes, my desires, my very self sundered in twain. I would not wish it upon you . . ."

Quicksilver would not wish it upon Will. Was that kindness? Fear? Will opened his mouth to speak, but stilled it again, afraid of what his words might do.

And yet he wanted to order Quicksilver to tell the truth, the whole truth. Had Quicksilver truly not commanded any of this? Had Hamnet disappeared without Quicksilver's knowledge or against Quicksilver's wishes? And if so, what could Will do? Should Will truly leave? Leave now, before the crux changed him forever? Leave now, and trust this powerless king, no matter how well intentioned, to bring Hamnet back to Will from this land of miracles and terrors?

Before Will could speak again, the black vortex, which had faded above them, came back in a howling of wind, a breath of thunder.

It was a many-fingered vortex, reaching to the beach and the forest and who knew where else?

Through the blowing sand, Will felt more than saw two bodies hit the beach.

And as the howling calmed and the vortex vanished, a voice called from behind them, "Get away from the villain, mortal, for we'd not hurt you."

The voice was that of a young girl, but gifted with immortal music, with harmonies such as befit the voices of angels.

Will turned around and, shocked, stared at the face that matched the voice.

The girl—an elf—stood at the edge of the beach and pointed at them with a trembling finger.

She was an angel, woven of light and gracile in stature and face. Her delicate features, her spun-light hair, made her look like God's very messenger descended from above. Her light green dress floated about a figure perhaps a little small, a little slight, caught between childhood slimness and the strength of adulthood.

She would be beautiful when she grew fully, Will thought, more beautiful than any woman he'd ever seen.

And caught between her present beauty and the certainty of her future wonder, Will felt his mind dazzle, his mouth go slack, and his eyes grow round in shock as the young woman pointed her finger at him.

Behind her, still on the ground, still looking stunned, a young man lay. Nay, a young elf, judging from his perfect and delicate features. Like her, he had blond hair, but as he shook his head and sought to raise himself on his elbows, the eyes that looked with dumb rancor at Will and Quicksilver were black as night.

"You, villain," the girl said. "You, traitor, get away from the mortal, if you prize him, for in our wrath we might well injure him as we punish you."

Will, too shocked to be offended, raised his hand to his chest and asked, "I? A villain?" And glancing back over his shoulder at the kneeling Quicksilver and back again, "And him? Mortal?"

Scene 14

ᖭᖯ

The same beach, on the same shores of a magical ocean, the same wind roaring loud and afflicted, like a mother mourning a child's loss. Quicksilver starts to stand up, as Will stands, his back to him, staring at the intruders Miranda and Proteus.

Miranda couldn't understand her uncle's question.

Why was he so surprised? Didn't he know himself for a villain?

She knew what was right and what wasn't. Oh, sure, she'd been raised in an isolated castle, by a creature not human. But she'd had the long memory of mankind and elvenkind, both, available to her through the legends and stories in the Hunter's library. She knew what was right and what was wrong, and who was good and who was a villain.

Nor had she any trouble recognizing the tyrant on sight. He was the ugly one.

Behind her, she was aware of Proteus's efforts to stand up. He must have been dropped from higher up onto the sand.

She wished he'd recover quickly and back her up, for these two meant to mock her, perhaps thinking her ignorant.

And that she was not.

Why, every book, every story, every page she'd ever read in search of escape from the immutable landscape at the end of reality, had told her the same thing.

Villains were ugly, with contorted features, decayed bodies, wasted—eaten by their own venom inside and out.

So when she and Proteus had landed on this beach, in the very crux of magic at the heart of all, she knew very well who the two men who fought on the sand were.

One of them, the blond one, with the face of an angel and a beauty that dwarfed Proteus's own, must be the mortal.

Oh, mortals were supposed to be second in beauty to elves and already Miranda's sense of proportion was offended by this breach in the hull of reality. But all the same, this mortal was good, or at least not bad.

There was no poison in him, no evil that could taint his features and twist his body. And he was beautiful enough to have attracted the heart of the King of Fairyland.

And cunning enough to see the evil of the tyrant's love, if their brawl was witness.

And surely, that villain, that mean creature who had killed her own parents and Proteus's too, must be the dark-haired, coarse creature, whose hair had deserted the front of his head, leaving his forehead an immense expanse, towering above his sun-burned face, where, at the corner of lips and mouth, small wrinkles had started to crease his dry skin.

Yet this creature turned surprised eyes toward her and questioned, "Who, me? A villain?"

There was sincere shock in his golden falcon-like eyes, sincere questioning in his bewildered voice.

But would the villain not be a great actor? Would the villain not be a great deceiver? He'd kept the hill in his thrall, believing his goodness despite it all, had he not?

"You. You, who murdered my parents, you who—"

A sound like a high, disordered laugh stopped her. It came from the blond mortal. He'd been on his knees, but now he stood, a hand over his mouth, as though repressing further laughter. His bright, moss-green eyes managed to look both grieved and amused, both shocked and disdainful.

As Miranda looked toward him, he lowered the hand that hid his mouth, and showed his lips stained with sparkling bright red blood. "Your quarrel is with me, fair maiden, with me, who am of your blood and your extraction. It is not with this chance, happen-met mortal caught in the currents of elven grief."

The creature's diction was perfect, his voice as harmonious as Proteus's own. He was a vision speaking and yet . . .

She tried to think of what he was saying. It didn't make sense, for he seemed to be claiming for himself elven blood and Miranda's own enmity.

She opened her mouth to protest, but she could not, for the creature took a step toward her and spoke, in his calm voice that yet seemed to command the attention of the very raging winds, the howling, moving landscape. "I am your uncle, fair maiden, or at least so I assume if you're the star-crossed daughter of that iniquitous Sylvanus who once ruled the hill and Fairyland. For I was his brother and I sit on the throne he disgraced."

Thus speaking, he walked toward her, his hands at his sides, looking meek and fond.

But what he said couldn't be true. He was beautiful. Even with his injured, bloodied lips, he was more beautiful than Proteus, more perfect than anyone Miranda had ever seen, save the Hunter himself.

Only the Hunter's beauty was a cold thing, a removed thing, dark and full of dread, while this elf's beauty was full of gentle appeal and caring kindness and something else—warm passion and fiery intensity, seeming repressed and for all that the more powerful.

If he was an elf. But how could he be an elf? Only one elf should be here, and that her wicked uncle, full of evil and darkness. In every tale, didn't evil make the evildoer appear heinous?

She could believe her eyes and this fair creature's voice, or she could believe the books she had read. The books must be true, while this creature . . .

Faith, she thought, feeling suddenly released from her dilemma. Faith, he was lying. Lying to protect the elf whom he loved. Proteus had said nothing about the mortal loving the elf, only about the elf loving the mortal, but surely—elven glamour taken into account—the mortal loved the elf, too. And out of his love, he wished to protect Quicksilver.

"Your intentions are good," Miranda said, looking on the gentle creature with softened gaze. "But you should leave this fight to the immortals and stand aside, good man."

This time, the smile in the bruised lips was unmistakable, but the green eyes still showed a mix of pity and amusement.

"I am not a mortal, kind Princess," the creature spoke. "My name is Quicksilver, King of Fairyland in the lands of Avalon, and I'm your uncle. I know not why you think I should be different, but this is the truth. And the truth is that your father tried to ensnare me and steal my throne and the Hunter, who is the avenger of injustice, took—"

"Stop, stop, foul liar," Proteus screamed. Running past Miranda, he jumped on the . . . mortal? King of Elvenland?

Miranda stared in horror as her love attacked this creature who looked even better than Proteus and therefore must be better or more righteous.

He must, or else were all tales false, all writers liars.

Proteus slammed into the other person, and the other person withstood his charge.

The dark-haired, ugly creature who stood nearer Miranda turned also to watch and, looking scared, put his hands to his mouth, covering it with both of them as though afraid that an unthought word or an incautious breath should escape it.

Proteus punched the—mortal?

Miranda grabbed the creature's arm, so hard that she could feel his flesh through the padded velvet of the sleeve. "Stop them," she said. "Stop them. Oh, can't you stop them?"

The creature looked . . . terrified.

His golden eyes stared at Miranda in unremitting misery. He shook his head hard.

Yet Proteus was throwing his punches with all his strength, attempting to scratch and claw at the blond person.

The blond withstood it, but did not try to hurt Proteus in revenge.

They must both be elves, mustn't they? For how could a mortal withstand the strength of Fairyland?

The other one, the defender—Quicksilver?—returned every move with a faster, stronger one, holding now on to Proteus's wrist and preventing the younger elf's punches from reaching their destination, and now stepping out of Proteus's misguided charges and allowing the young elf to fall.

No human could ever oppose an elf with greater strength, with more agility. Even among elves, only a better-born one or an older, more experienced one could do it.

But then the blond, with the face of an angel, the speed of a king, the strength of the best of elves, must be her wicked uncle, Quicksilver.

As the obscene certainty of what should be impossibility dawned upon Miranda's amazed mind, she turned startled eyes to the man beside her, the mortal, the human.

"He is the king of elves, is he not?" she asked, words dripping from her mouth almost unmeant. "That blond man is an elf, and the king, isn't he? And you're the mortal he once loved."

The man let his hands fall from in front of his face, and his mouth opened as though he'd protest, but he said not a word. His eyes reflected fear as though his mind were a measure that fear had filled till no more would fit. He pressed his lips together and nodded, looking afraid that even this gesture would have ill effect.

"Stop," the stranger elf—Quicksilver—said. "Stop, noble Proteus. The anger that fills you is justified, nay, righteous, in your circumstances. But it is misguided."

Miranda turned in time to see the stranger parry a knife thrust with his arm—did Proteus truly have a knife out? Had he unsheathed to fight an unarmed man?

The knife sliced through the fabric and skin and drops of immortal blood fell, glittering, to the sand of the crux which, as though injured, whirled in greater fury and howled in greater grief at the intrusion.

"Stop," Quicksilver yelled. "I did what I had to do, only what I had to do. How could I tolerate rebels in the hill? Your noble father would not swear fealty, and for it he had to die. But my quarrel is not with you. Noble Proteus, you are the only heir I'm likely to have. Marry this Princess of Fairyland." While stepping aside from a vicious thrust, Quicksilver gestured toward Miranda. "Marry her and be blessed, and only give me a little time and I shall step aside and leave the two of you to reign undisturbed in Fairyland. I am tired. The war has broken me. Take my throne and all honor with it." Quicksilver stepped just out of reach of the weaving dagger that Proteus wielded with fast-striking anger. "Take it, for I do not want it."

It seemed to Miranda the offer was more than fair, the justice more than just. If her uncle lied not—and every one of her senses, every fiber of her being, every instinct of the royal blood of Fairyland, told her that Quicksilver told the truth—then this offer was justice in itself, and they'd already achieved what they wanted from this daring sortie, this unequaled attempt on the throne of Fairyland.

But Proteus only clenched his teeth tight, and muttered through them, in a voice scarcely harder than a whisper, in a tone scarcely more human than a dog's growl, "I want the throne after your death and only your blood will slake the thirst for vengeance in my heart." Thus speaking, he threw himself at Quicksilver, yelling, "So die all tyrants."

But Quicksilver stepped out of the way, and held on to Proteus's knife-yielding wrist, even as Proteus's other hand scratched, in a fury, at Quicksilver's face, attempting to injure the king's eyes.

"Yield to reason. Listen to what I say," Quicksilver said. "And if you still need my death, I'll be contented to die, only not in the crux, where my death might cause magical storms that would swallow all. Only listen to me, noble Proteus."

"You will die now, dog," Proteus screamed. "Arise, black vengeance, from thy hollow cell!"

With renewed fury, he kicked at the King of Fairyland, hitting him between the legs and bringing him down to his knees, face contorted.

Quicksilver got his hands up, just in time, to deviate the dagger aimed at his heart.

Miranda screamed and ran in, but, close to the two fighters, didn't know whom to help. For she loved Proteus, but Proteus was attacking a man who did not defend himself. Even if that man were a tyrant—and had a tyrant ever behaved thus? In a fury of terror and despair, she scratched at her silken skirt and clawed at her own sleeves, her sweat-sleek hands searching for something she could do. "No, no, no," she screamed into the indifferent, hollow wind, the indifferent, fighting elves.

"Only stop him, maiden, stop him from killing me here, and elsewhere can you take satisfaction for any wrongs you believe I might—" Quicksilver said.

Quicksilver's dagger hung at his waist, undisturbed in its sheath.

Miranda didn't know what to think, what to do. Her whole world had turned upside down in moments.

Was Proteus not good, who looked so fair? But Quicksilver was fair also, and behold, he defended himself—defended himself only—from Proteus's vicious attacks, without retaliating, without inflicting the injury he could.

Was not Quicksilver evil and a murderer?

Oh, had she been mistaken? In Proteus's fair face, did a monster hide, like a dragon in a flowering cave?

Yet every poem, every story, every legend, human and elven both, said that virtue and beauty went hand in hand.

Again, Quicksilver interposed his hand, between him and the stab that would kill him.

His lips were healed, but his hand, arm, and shoulder bled in persistent rivulets.

And now Proteus reached in his jacket, for the net that would deprive Quicksilver of all magical power and allow him to bleed and die as a mortal would.

Miranda could save Quicksilver. She could pull back Proteus or deal an unexpected, stunning blow to her lover.

But he was her lover, was he not? Did she not love him well?

Oh, her mind was like one of those models of the spheres, which went round and round a fixed point and never arrived anywhere.

For she knew that Proteus was good—he had been kind to her.

Yet here was Quicksilver, whom Proteus had said was a villain, and the King of Fairyland was sparing Proteus, holding back his superior strength, his superior speed, his sheathed weapon.

Miranda could feel that strength in Quicksilver that could have reduced the young elf to nothing with a glancing blow.

Why didn't Quicksilver do it? Who'd ever heard of a villain who held back from causing harm?

Could Proteus be wrong, and Quicksilver not be evil, after all?

But if it was so, then Proteus's father had been evil and Proteus's own bend on revenge must make him evil.

Proteus brought forth the glittering net from his jacket.

Miranda heard a scream emerge from her throat, ripping it raw as it erupted between her lips.

The mortal turned to stare at her, and for a moment, the two combatant elves stopped—Proteus holding his bloody knife in one hand and the net in the other—like some statue in a long-ago monument, where models of long dead men carry on the form of a fight that future generations have forgotten.

The net dangled from Proteus's hand, and Quicksilver spared it but a glance, before staring at Miranda, stunned, worried.

He put his hand out to Miranda, as though he'd give her strength, as though he'd help *her*.

Miranda could understand none of it.

For so long she'd dreamed of living with Proteus and ruling in Fairyland, yet when offered that dream, when offered that chance, on a silver platter, Proteus clamored for blood and vengeance.

And when offered vengeance deferred, he clamored for it now.

Was her lord then so hot, his thirst for blood and death so great?

Was he then her lord?

She didn't know and she couldn't think, with the magical storm roaring around her and howling in her mind. She couldn't think, she couldn't look upon the two combatants.

If she could go away, then she could think—

Diving in, close to the combatants, she reached for Proteus's hand that held the net, and pulled it from his fingers.

It felt cold and burning in her hand, cold and burning both.

She saw Proteus's look of outrage. Would he come for her now? But before she could decide whether the look she saw was anger or just offense, her feet, reasoning before her head, carried her running, away from the howling sand and wind, away from the combatants, away from her doubts and fears.

Away into the forest, with the magical net.

Scene 15

ை

The same howling sand, the same beach, the sound of magic waves that beat upon a magical shore, and the two combatants frozen midfight, and Will staring at the elf maiden as she runs inland, toward the green fringe of woodland.

Pinned to the sand, beneath Proteus's fury-strong arms, Quicksilver struggled, as the girl elf—Miranda?—ran into the forest.

"Miranda," he called as Proteus let go of Quicksilver and stared after the girl and the magical object she carried.

Quicksilver had felt the magical strength, the dread power, of that object. What had Proteus planned to do?

While Proteus was thus distracted, Quicksilver shoved him away, struggled to his feet.

When Proteus turned back, Quicksilver was on his feet and danced back from Proteus's reach.

He felt blood drip from his arm, but it was nothing. Scratches, nothing more.

He looked on Proteus's furious face, his contorted features, his clenched teeth, and felt only pity.

Oh, how the young elf must smart, how his injuries must hurt for him to rebel thus, to take a young human from his family, to make use of a young maiden who had been brought up in seclusion in a land beyond Fairyland.

"She loves you, Proteus," Quicksilver said as he danced away from his cousin's reach. "She loves you, Proteus, and you're a fool if you don't thank the gods for the blessing."

But Proteus's teeth stayed clenched, and his face contorted as he lurched and launched toward Quicksilver.

His blood leapt, eager for Quicksilver's blood.

"She was the one who did the spell, was she not?" Quicksilver asked, this time parrying the stab with his arm. He should bring his dagger out. But his mind reminded him of other times when he had not meant to kill and yet had ended killing.

Once the dagger was in his hand, who could say what would happen and who would suffer for it?

And he'd not kill Proteus. He'd not.

Proteus was almost his last relative. Only the girl, Sylvanus's daughter, was closer. Only the girl. And the girl loved Proteus, and for the sake of her tender, young heart, Quicksilver would spare Proteus, no matter what Proteus's crimes.

Aye, Quicksilver would spare him were his crimes ten times worse, his heart ten times blacker. "You made her kidnap the young mortal, did you not?" Quicksilver asked. "And it was her inexperience that took him to the crux."

He spoke, trying to distract Proteus. Yet Proteus, teeth clenched, stabbed and stabbed and stabbed, hot-breathing vengeance behind his mad strength. His need to kill Quicksilver glimmered from his eyes like holy fire.

"Poor girl, what will she do when she finds that you marred her power and twisted her magic," Quicksilver said. "What will she do when she finds that you've endangered us all and all of magic besides? Go to her, Proteus. Go to her. If we get out of the crux, then I shall, in rightness and by my honor and by this dread oath I swear on the darkness of the Hunter and his dark vengeance, allow you to kill me and ensure you don't suffer the vengeance of Fairyland. I'll make you king of the hill first. Only spare my queen, the fair Ariel, and do with me as you will."

Just when Quicksilver thought his words fell on deaf ears, he saw that Will, standing just behind Proteus, had been riveted by them, and now ran, out in the same direction the girl first had run.

Too late, Quicksilver realized that Will thought the girl, having got them here, would know how to get them out of the crux, how to get young Hamnet home safe.

"Will, stop," Quicksilver yelled and, momentarily distracted, felt searing pain and terrible coldness upon his shoulder, where Proteus's dagger had entered to the hilt.

Quicksilver felt his blood rush out, following the blade. He felt cold. Cold, as though eternal ice had come into his flesh from the blade. His love for the mortal had brought him ill luck, he thought, his vision blurring.

Faith, it had almost killed him.

Oh, curse the luck and mortals and love too, that made Quicksilver such a fool and all of them, all such vulnerable creatures.

"Curse you," he said, and reaching for his shoulder, he pulled out the dagger Proteus had left there.

Something of his fury, of the madness he felt, must have shown in his eyes, for Proteus stepped back as Quicksilver dropped the dagger to the sand.

The magical blood that rushed from Quicksilver's shoulder fell onto the sand and each drop increased the force of the storm. The storm blew and grew around Proteus.

Proteus screamed, blinded, impotent.

Quicksilver ran into the forest, or what he hoped was into the forest, following the girl and the human, hoping to find them.

His thought of giving Proteus the throne now seemed sacrilege. How could he entrust the hill to such an untrustworthy elf?

Away from the shore, the wind died down.

He stepped into the forest, and it was like stepping into another world. Suddenly, there was green calm, and green filtered light, and the moist smell of growing plants all around.

Above him a canopy of leaves grew and entwined. The air felt warm and so moist that sweat ran in rivulets to soak his hair and course down his back.

He put his hand to his shoulder wound and pressed, willing the blood to stop flowing. Were he in Fairyland, it would have stopped instantly.

But even here, even in the crux, how bad could it be? For was Quicksilver not an elf and of that blessed race which can be killed by nothing save cold iron?

Yet it seemed to him—and perhaps it was because of his blood loss—that the sounds around him were remote and distant. The rustling of leaves, the howling of the wind on the beach, all of it seemed to recede to afar, as will the sounds of the waking world upon the ears of the sleeper.

And from this distance, nothing seemed to reach him—nothing.

Was his vision growing dim, or had a fog sprung up all around him, perhaps in response to the drops of his blood falling on the soft ground underfoot?

Fallen leaves and the remnants of other seasons' leaves cushioned his steps and drank most eagerly of the blood of elven royalty. It seemed to him as though, beneath him, a thousand mouths sprang up to drink his magical strength, his power.

Through the fog, he saw as though a fractured landscape: now the trunk of a tree and now large, luscious leaves reaching out for him with fleshy eagerness.

The caresses of leaves felt like so many fingers, fondling him as he passed.

He stepped between them and around them, hoping, guessing, imagining that he followed the path the girl and Will had taken.

Had Will even taken the same path as the girl?

Oh, fools that they were to have allowed themselves to be trapped in the crux. Fools they were who, with each step, took themselves deeper into this unpredictable magical land.

Fools.

Yet Will had gone and Quicksilver must go, and make sure no harm came to the human to whom so much harm had already come from Fairyland.

Quicksilver must go and find the child, Will's son, and restore him to father and family.

He remembered legends that said that each day in the crux was like a year in the mortal world, and he hoped it wasn't true.

Would Will age a year in a day? Or would he find, once he rescued his son, that his son was a man and didn't recognize him?

The boy would be in the castle in the center of the crux, the magical point, the nexus of power and magic. Would the effect of the crux be stronger there?

Would the child age faster?

Quicksilver shook his head, his mind as fogged as his vision.

There were no answers to his questions and nothing to do but find the people who had preceded him into this green fog, this confusion of leaves and green light.

A root made him trip. How weak he was. His vision seemed more fogged, or else, ahead of him, a pink mist rose, all pale and soft.

He leaned against a tree and felt his shoulder, and he would swear blood had stopped dripping. The soaked fabric didn't seem to be getting any more wet, nor did the wet patch seem to extend.

Or perhaps Quicksilver's sense of touch misgave him as much as his other senses.

It seemed to him as though, at the edge of his hearing, horses galloped. Horses in the crux? He must be mad.

He took a gulp of the too-moist air and wished he could find Miranda. If the girl had brought the child, and herself, and Proteus too, to the crux, she must have power of an extraordinary kind, power that would make her a natural ruler of Fairyland.

Happily would he give *her* the throne, happily, happily hand over the crown of a kingdom that more and more seemed to resemble a family quarrel with ill-defined borders.

And if she would be kind, then he would go, through the world, like a beggar or a mortal, taking upon him only that much power that would keep him from craving death and feeding on suffering and becoming one of the dark spirits that tormented men.

Oh, let him go. Let him go and be glad of it.

He felt cold and his teeth chattered. It seemed to him that his energy was leaving with the blood dripping from his arm.

He remembered, long ago, a friend dying of a seemingly harmless wound inflicted by an iron weapon.

But he must find the girl. And then he had to purchase his healing, his freedom and life from her, at whatever dear price.

He let go of the tree and, on unsteady feet, stepped into the pink mist ahead.

It seemed to him, for just a moment, that amid the obfuscation of fog and diffuse light, a woman moved, or something like a woman.

There was an impression of a long skirt, a green dress, and gracile, feminine movements.

"Miranda," Quicksilver called. "Gentle maiden."

But she didn't answer him.

Scene 16

ɔ⃝ɔ

A clearing in the green forest. Miranda sits beneath an overspreading tree, her head in her hands, in the position of a saddened child or one who doesn't understand the events around her and who needs guidance from somewhere or from someone. Into the clearing, Will emerges, running. Miranda gets up and Will checks his step.

Miranda sat beneath the tree and sobbed. She'd dropped somewhere in the thick of the forest the net that Proteus had acquired at such dear cost to himself.

She didn't think she could find it now if she so wished, and she didn't know if she wished it.

She couldn't tell. Her mind held, impressed upon it, the image of Proteus's ungallant behavior, his pressing close an unarmed adversary, his pushing for the blood of one who would gladly have surrendered all to Proteus's claims.

"Proteus," she sobbed. "Ah, Proteus. Beautiful tyrant. Fiend angelical. Dove-feathered raven. Wolvish-ravening lamb. Despised substance of divinest show. Just opposite to what you justly seemed. A damned saint, an honorable villain. Oh, nature. What had you to do in hell when you did bower the spirit of a fiend in almost immortal paradise of such sweet flesh?"

And yet, was this right? For perhaps Proteus had held back, perhaps Proteus didn't take the offered throne and power and magic and all for he knew it not to be offered in earnest.

Perhaps he knew the only way to stop Quicksilver was to murder the king.

And yet—how did she know the king was evil? How, but that Proteus had told her?

And how did she know Proteus was right, but that he was lovely?

And yet, wasn't there more to it? Proteus loved her. She'd known Proteus long.

Proteus said Quicksilver was a villain and Proteus was an honorable elf.

"Blistered be my tongue for my words. He was not born to shame. Upon his brow shame is ashamed to sit. Proteus is perfect and his brow is a throne where honor may be crowned sole monarch of universal earth. Oh, what a beast was I to chide him."

Some small sound called her attention, and looking up, she saw the other creature, the creature that wasn't an elf.

His coarse face was fixed in some anxiety, his skin gone the color of tallow candles.

How could Quicksilver love such a one? Did he truly?

He did if Proteus didn't lie, and Miranda had decided that Proteus told truth. But then Quicksilver was mad. Not a villain so much as turned from his wits.

For how could elf, perfect and true, love this creature where already the signs of death showed in the shedding hair, the drying skin, the dull eyes?

The creature stood, feet together, and stared at Miranda as a petitioner who would speak but is afraid.

He cleared his throat and doffed his cap and bowed his head, then looked up, his eye just spying to see whether she noticed his deference.

She grew impatient with it all. No one had ever showed her this deference except Caliban, and even Caliban had never been this obsequious.

She stood in a leap and wiped her tears with her hand, while her other hand attempted to smooth her hair. She wondered if she looked at all as a princess should look to this creature.

But what did this creature know of princesses? "Speak," she said, and heard her own voice crack and willed it to great decision as she ordered again, "Speak, mortal. Who are you? And what want you with me?"

Again the man looked up without straightening his head, which remained bowed. "Milady, my name is Will Shakespeare, and I believe you know who I am right enough. Or at least I knew you in that dim and distant infancy no man remembers, and perhaps no elf. To speak plain, I knew you when you were but a baby."

"A baby?"

He looked up now fully and some memory softened his gaze, as his lips tugged upward into an almost smile. "Aye, a babe you were, but months old, when my wife was kidnaped by your—" Will stopped. "My wife was kidnaped by Fairyland, to be your nursemaid. My daughter Susannah, who is much your age, was taken with her, and for a time, the two of you slept side by side in a single crib."

Miranda stared at the man in disbelief. His wife? A coarse, mortal woman had been her nurse?

How could this be?

It was as if she'd had a whole other life of which she remembered nothing.

"Your wife?" she asked. "She was my nursemaid?" It had to be a lie. She shook her head.

"My wife, Nan," Will said.

She frowned. How could it be that all these people knew her? Proteus and Quicksilver and now this mortal? They all knew her, but she knew nothing of them, nor could she guess whom to trust.

"I don't remember," she said. She spoke as a child speaks of a lost toy.

The mortal smiled, a smile at the edge of laughter.

What was so amusing about Miranda's lack of memory? Why did it please him? She stared at him out of the corner of her eye. Was he lying to her?

"You wouldn't remember," he said. "For it was but a week that Nan was your nursemaid and that so long ago that you were but a little fool. Yet you were the prettiest babe I ever saw."

"I was?" she asked, and almost smiled at this because, for once, this accorded with what Proteus had told her—that she was the most beautiful, the most royal of all elves. "I was? But why did your wife leave, then?" For if she were that pretty, wouldn't mortals have been in her thrall? She straightened her hair with her hand.

"Your . . ." Will hesitated. "She was taken against her will," he said. "And she pined for me and for our home, and thus, with the help of Quicksilver, your . . . your uncle, I rescued her."

"Quicksilver?" she asked. "My uncle? He helped you? Was that when he had my father killed and, treacherously, usurped his throne?"

She had never thought the confirmation of such a truth would come to her in this strange place.

But the mortal didn't seem to think she was telling the truth. He started, as though slapped, and shook his head.

"Your father was not killed by Quicksilver," he said. "Nor did your uncle take the throne unlawfully. He was the true heir, you see, by law and custom of Fairyland."

Miranda blinked. Quicksilver the true heir? No. No. This did not accord with what Proteus had told her. "Was Quicksilver the younger?" she asked. "For among us it is the contrary to the laws of mankind. It is the youngest or the woman that inherits. Only the youngest or the woman."

The mortal nodded. "Yes, Quicksilver is younger than your father was, younger by thousands of years."

"Oh," Miranda said. "But then . . ." She shook her head. It couldn't be true. It just couldn't. "But then my uncle was always the rightful heir, the rightful king. But then my father must—" She stopped, and her mouth dropped open. No. The mortal had to be confused.

Slowly, she raised her gaze to meet his. She felt as though around her the whole world were crumbling. Facts and certainties came crashing down.

For if the mortal were right, then Proteus was a villain, seeking to turn her against her uncle, the rightful King of Fairyland.

But if that were true, then was all of reality subverted. Fair was foul and foul was fair and everything was that which it wasn't.

And the mortal, so ugly, was good, and Proteus, so beautiful, was evil, and the world had turned so far from the course of legends that Miranda, deceived, would never find her way.

"Milady," the mortal said, and looked scared. "Milady? Are you stricken?"

"Aye," she heard her own voice. "Aye, I am stricken. I am spent. Who can help me? For I'm lost in a fog with no direction. Proteus looks like an angel. Can he be other? Proteus told me that my father was right and noble and honorable. He told me I was a Princess of Fairyland, daughter of the just, the true King of Fairyland. He told me my uncle was a tyrant who had held the throne by evil and over the bodies of those he subjugated."

She advanced toward the mortal, like a blind woman seeking sight. "You must tell me the truth, kind stranger. You must tell me what the truth is, how my father came to die, and how I came to grow up with the Hunter, the dread avatar of vengeance, the very body of final justice for both men and elves."

She felt magic crackling around her as she spoke, magic empowering her words, so that her command to the mortal was a compelling spell.

The magic crackled and shone around her, tendrils forming and reaching out for the mortal.

His eyes bugged out. He opened his mouth as though to scream, and took a step back, as if he'd bolt.

But he ran not. "My lady," he said, his voice small and strangled. "My kind lady." He stepped back from her crackling power, her radiating force. His eyes looked as if he'd rather run, but couldn't.

"Speak," she said. "Tell me the truth."

Sweat dripped from the creature's forehead. "Find another to tell you, for I cannot."

She shook her head. "What other? My uncle? But Proteus says my uncle is a villain. But then if my uncle isn't a villain, Proteus lies." She felt tears fall down her cheeks, hot and scalding, and her voice issue plaintive from her lips. "You must tell me the truth and tell me right, of who my father was and how I came by this weird life, being the adopted daughter of the Hunter."

"Your father . . . Aye, lady, your father was a villain or misguided, so possessed by his ambition, so overruled by his need for power, that he'd killed his parents to inherit."

"His parents?"

"Titania and Oberon they were called, and with a charmed knife he had them stabbed." The mortal bit his lip, and his eyes darted sideways, as though his lips wished to say more, but he prevented them.

The girl stopped in her tracks and said, "Oh."

More tears rolled down her face and she felt as though the world spun around her, as though she were the earth encircled by the sun. "Oh. Did the Hunter, then, take my father? Is my father one of the dread dogs with whom I grew up in ignorance?"

She thought of the dark, slavering creatures who jumped and fought and slept on the floor of the Hunter, ignored by him save for the occasional kick, the occasional summons.

They smelled, and looked vile and felt strange and cold to the touch. Miranda had avoided them as much as she could. Now she ran their low muzzles, their terrible fanged mouths, through her memory, trying to think which of them might hold the soul of her father: dark Malice, cold Unkindness, dread Envy.

Their muzzles looked all the same to her, as did their narrowed, glittering red eyes.

And she was descended from such a one?

The mortal shook his head. "No, lady. It is true the Hunter took your father as one of his dogs when the tangled skein of your father's treasons unraveled for all to see his guilt. It is true he took him, and your father, heartless villain that he was, in his last moment of freedom, took you with him into that dread captivity.

"Innocent and pure that you were, Quicksilver told us you could not become one of the dogs, nor be seduced by the evil that surrounded you. You must be raised in inviolate kindness, in some distant castle, untouched by man or elf, until you reached your maturity, when the kiss and true love of a true prince might release you. This Quicksilver told us was the legend and lore of fairykind . . ."

"And my uncle, Quicksilver, then he did not kill my father? What became of my father?" Her tears slowed, but she wasn't sure that she was well. It seemed to her that her heart had ceased beating and seized, in pain and anguish, within her chest.

"Oh, your father, lady. His immortal ambition would not rest, so he wrested power from the Hunter himself and ran, a plague upon the world. Quicksilver, who considered himself responsible, came to him, but he could not stop him, and upon London, the great city of mankind's Queen, your father descended, a predator feeding on suffering.

"There, a man, a . . . friend of mine lost his life and your uncle seemed on the verge of losing his throne and the world its freedom before, through my agency, by luck the Hunter brought your father to ground . . ."

"You killed my father?" Miranda asked, staring at him, reading between the lines and feeling the dread horror of facing her father's true murderer.

So, the legends were right. The evil were evil-looking. For killing her father must the mortal have become this twisted, aged creature. "You killed my father," she said. "You . . . villain."

Proteus had been right, right all along. And she'd stolen his weapon and left him alone on the beach, with no defense against the cunning tyrant Quicksilver.

Miranda must go back to him. This mortal, this . . . creature, she would deal with later.

She ran out of the clearing.

Behind her, the mortal yelled, "But . . . my son?"

Miranda ignored him. She hadn't decided what to do about the mortal boy yet.

For if his father was guilty, would it be proper to give the boy to a murderer?

Scene 17

ೲ

The enchanted forest, wreathed all in pink mist that obscures the tops of the tall trees and makes the overhanging ivy look like rent lace. Through this landscape, Quicksilver stumbles, looking dazed and scared.

What place was this?

Quicksilver had grown up with legends of the crux and the magic there, but nothing had prepared him for this.

It seemed that while he advanced, the pink-mist fog went with him, writhing and twisting about him and the surrounding trees like a living thing.

The woman whom Quicksilver had glimpsed ahead of him had disappeared now, or else it had been a dream, a delusion spun by this place of dreams and shadows.

Oh, this must be what the mortal hell was like, Quicksilver thought, to forever wander in a cold, desolate landscape in search of something he could never find.

In that moment, creature of magic and cold fire that he was, immune both to the terrors of hell and the hope for heaven to which mortals were prey, Quicksilver felt, nonetheless, cold and fearful. His shoulder had stopped bleeding, but it hurt with a steady, burning pain.

For was not his life nearly immortal, was not his nature nearly endless?

What if he wandered here forever, starving and cold but undying, looking for the girl elf that had disappeared into this mist and for the mortal with her?

He almost stopped walking, but the thought that Will, also, was lost in this morass woke him up, like a spray of cold water in his drowsy, discouraged face.

Will was lost in this, and how much more unprepared he was for such trek, for such search through the dark magical forests.

And he was here in search of his son. Childless—unable, perhaps, to have progeny—Quicksilver wondered about this paternal love that would bring Will careening from London to get involved in a magical battle once more.

Will, who hated magic. Will, to whom all magic was anathema.

Thinking of this, Quicksilver couldn't help remembering when he'd first met Will how enthralled and scared, both, the mortal had been of Silver and her magical might.

And thinking on it, quick upon such thoughts, other, tenderer thoughts came.

Silver was not Quicksilver anymore. Though no part of the king retained the soft gentleness that had once been Silver, nor Silver's high humor, nor Silver's contriving ways, yet Quicksilver remembered being Silver.

He remembered Silver's love for Will.

He tripped on a root the fog had hidden.

From the fog, a high, chilling laughter echoed, the laughter of unnatural children.

He shook his head. A dream. A dream, nothing more. A dream like this fog. An illusion.

If he could not follow the princess, then there was only one thing he must do. He must go the castle that he'd first glimpsed, before the crux—disturbed—had responded with storm and wind and sand. That castle was the center of this place, and in that castle, Hamnet Shakespeare would be. To that castle would Will Shakespeare eventually arrive, for one thing that could be said for Will was that he'd never leave his son here.

Well did Quicksilver remember Will's determination, so many years ago, when his wife and firstborn child had been stolen by Fairyland.

Through Silver's softened eyes, through his memory of Silver's feelings—for Silver had dearly loved this mortal, as dearly as elf ever could love mortal or elf or any other creature—he saw Will as he then had been: a rawboned boy with sparse beard and the eager, voluble features of youth.

Those eyes of his, falcon-yellow and falcon-intent, had burned a path to Lady Silver's heart, overcoming her natural reluctance at being involved with a mortal, a base creature.

Remembering Silver's love, in this place of naught and fog, Quicksilver trembled.

Silver had loved Will with immortal passion, with strength and force and magic beyond the reach of any other heart, mortal or immortal.

How she'd loved Will. And the love for Will had given her . . . the love for Will had given him, Quicksilver, the strength and magic to claim the hill. The strength from that love had made Quicksilver king.

At the thought, Quicksilver stopped amid the shading trees, in the pink and green gloom, because, like a man remembering a dream, he remembered loving Will. Truly, loving, not just feeling loyalty or care or friendship for him.

It was a thought he'd tried to forget, a memory he'd almost succeeded in erasing.

He'd loved Will. Not just Silver had loved, but himself, also. Or perhaps, the Silver side of himself had loved Will, but rooted in the same soul, sharing the same heart, Quicksilver had felt that love just as intensely.

He remembered, as he hadn't allowed himself to do in years—in three years, at least—the joys of mortal love, the touch of the mortals that Silver—he—had loved.

There was Marlowe, whom Quicksilver had fancied, whom Silver had seduced.

Marlowe had been very young when the magical being had first come across him—seventeen, maybe less, a shy divinity student, with auburn hair and broad, almond-shaped grey eyes.

How shy he'd been and, shyness once conquered, how fiery-bold. How his lust had surged and his love burned, so that its indiscriminate fires scared even Quicksilver, even the daring Silver.

For a moment here, in this land of loneliness, threatened and fearful, with his kingdom at risk, Quicksilver felt as if Marlowe's lips, soft as youth and warm as passion, had brushed his own.

But Marlowe was dead. Dead of that Fairyland love, or of the madness that came with it.

For Silver's love had stripped Marlowe of the frail religious faith that had stood as a protective shell between himself and his fiery nature. And, the shell gone, Marlowe had burned, living a life of danger, of spying, of hidden betrayal and secret intrigue, in the theater, in the secret service, in foreign wars and private vendettas.

And Marlowe's very nature, his tainted, betrayed goodness, had allowed Marlowe to fall prey to Sylvanus, the once King of Fairyland who had become the dark dog of the Hunter.

From that had Marlowe perished, from that, as much as from the dagger that, driven into his eye, had punctured his brain and stilled forever its maddening rush.

Quicksilver opened his eyes.

To the distortion of the fog upon the landscape was added a trembling of tears in his eyes.

If he could, if it were up to him, he would uncall that summer of madness in which, unbidden, he'd stripped Marlowe of mortal faith and youthful innocence. If he could uncall that mistake to which his own hot blood had led him, he would.

But nothing could bring a mortal back once his heart had stilled.

And this thought, this sobering thought, brought Quicksilver back to

Will, to Will's involvement in this, which, like Marlowe's, had started with Silver's intemperate blood, with Quicksilver's intemperate passions.

Had he not craved Will, in those days when Will was but little more than a boy, little less than a man?

Had he not craved Will and, with that craving, allowed the youth to get far more involved in Fairyland than he ever should have?

Had he not, by extension, exposed Will both to his doomed brother's fury and to Proteus's plans of revenge?

Wasn't it Quicksilver's own fault that Proteus was even alive to wreak vengeance and seek to ensnare poor, hapless mortals in his plans?

Did not the fault that Hamnet was here rest as much on the broad and unbending shoulders of the King of Fairyland, as on Proteus's narrow, grief-addled shoulders?

Oh, curse Quicksilver and his lusts.

Even now, thinking of Will, he couldn't help but feel that the man Will had become—tired looking, his hair receding—looked as fiery-gentle as the Will of yore had.

Soft, was that lust within the heart of the King of Fairyland? Did he truly still crave Will's touch, still long for the creature's presence, the creature's notice, the creature's . . . love?

The thought broke Quicksilver in two, denuded him.

He saw himself as he wished he'd never seen himself, he saw himself as he was, but didn't wish to be.

It was as though a ghost had pursued him all these years, the ghost of his lost love, his lost self.

From that ghost he'd run and, to avoid that ghost, to avoid the shameful softness that made him so vulnerable to this mortal, Will, he'd become something he was not.

Like a man who runs headlong into the night and stumbles helplessly, Quicksilver had stumbled into a darkness where, instead of being Silver, or

Quicksilver, or anything of what he truly was—that true self so helplessly in thrall to a lowly mortal—Quicksilver had stilled himself and armored himself, and become nothing but a king.

The king of the hill. Nothing else, but the king, dread and hollow, himself a dread shell for power, a head to carry the circlet of power upon.

Nothing else. No. Never, and nothing.

He'd been afraid of not being king enough, and in reaction, he'd been a king, a king in fact, but nothing else.

It was, Quicksilver thought, as he seemingly caught the glimpse of a soft green dress ahead of himself, it was as if instead of Quicksilver becoming the king, the king had possessed Quicksilver.

The spirit of kingship had found Quicksilver willing to be hollowed and emptied, a vessel, an empty thing ready to carry kingship within.

And into that form, kingship had poured itself, till Quicksilver was no more a person, and had no more thoughts or independent power than the crown that he wore upon his brow.

How strange it was now, to look on it, his fourteen years as a king, his ruling presence from the high throne.

Had Quicksilver's heart ever been in it? Had Quicksilver ever felt anything toward kingship?

No. Quicksilver hadn't existed. He'd not loved, not hated. Only judged.

Quicksilver caught another glimpse of the dress vanishing fast, fast, into the thick pink fog, as though the creature wearing it ran ahead of him.

In response he ran also, blindly, seeing trees only just before he ran into them, and tripping upon roots and steadying himself, his eyes fixed on the mirage that, ahead of him, like a reflection upon a hidden mirror, seemed to vanish and reappear and reappear and vanish again, always too far ahead of his reach.

It was like pursuing a rainbow, like trying to reach for the tail of tomorrow, yet Quicksilver rushed in pursuit of it.

Too long, too long, he'd done only what was rational. Too long, he'd been king and king alone, authority and voice of the ancient hill. Nothing more.

Now he'd be himself, now he'd reach for what was ahead of him as he should have reached for himself in his years as king.

Who knew? Had the rebellion happened because Quicksilver had ruled without heart, ruled as a king who knew no human bounds, no, nor elven bounds either, no boundaries or edges to his immense power?

Had revolution come because he'd been unbending and, unbending, had he been—not harsh, not cruel—simply empty?

Oh, Vargmar had rebelled because of his ambition, his envy of Quicksilver, his need to be king.

But the ones who'd joined him, the big, the small, the malcontents, the discontented, the disaffected . . . had they rebelled because they didn't find in Quicksilver that something to which loyalty and devotion must attach as they'd never attach to simple kingship, to the empty trappings of royalty?

Quicksilver ran, out of breath, weak from loss of blood, from expenditure of magic.

Oh, he had to know. He had to see. Was the war his fault? Had he killed his self, and Silver with it, more than his enemies could ever have? Had he hollowed himself so, to fill himself with kingship and power that he felt not? Could he not find the path back to whom he used to be?

Oh, if so, let him, let him be, let him become Quicksilver once more. Aye, and Silver too.

On that thought, as though the thought commanded the event, the pink fog lifted.

It lifted like a creature withdrawing, like a bird taking flight. It rose above Quicksilver's head in one swift swoop, then, taking flight over the tops of trees, headed toward the white castle upon the hill.

Quicksilver found himself in a clearing among the rank, overgrown forest.

It was a pretty clearing, or it would have been in another forest, in a world of less dreary magic. A pretty clearing, encircled by flowers, with a pink and green pond in the middle, the water seeming to change color with the reflection of the landscape above.

That it was not true water but pure magic didn't change its beauty.

The air, filled with cloying perfumes and floral effluvium, filled Quicksilver's nostrils and brought to his heart memories of being too young and far too intemperate, ready to pursue his lust—his love—anywhere.

The air brought with it a memory of Marlowe's kisses, the feeling of Will's innocent embrace.

In this clearing, were it in Fairyland, the great dances would be held, in which the creatures of magic would move and sway to the unseen rhythm of the season, to the imperative of their kind.

But this was not Fairyland, and something to the perfect landscape, something to the warm, perfumed air gave Quicksilver a terrible feeling of dread and emptiness.

His eyes stung with tears, as if he were near crying upon some great tragedy, some just discovered loss.

Not knowing whence this feeling came, not knowing what he felt or why, not owning himself, not in possession of his feelings, Quicksilver stumbled toward the pond, whose waters moved and changed and looked like a great egg about to hatch something.

Whether something beautiful or something horrible, Quicksilver could neither hazard nor guess.

Blindly he stumbled, blindly, thinking to take a closer look at the waters and minding himself all the ancient legends on looking on one's reflection upon a pond.

For had not Narcissus, looking upon his own, lovely face, been thus captured and condemned to stare at his own face, consumed by lethal self-love until he wasted away to nothing?

And had not Hylas, Hercules's servant, gone to the fountain for water, by the nymphs been seized and pulled in?

Oh, Quicksilver minded himself the danger, but approached the pond nonetheless, led by some indominable need, some irresistible imperative.

But on the waters of the pond he saw . . . not himself.

The face that looked back at him from the pink-green depths was pale, yes, as his own, and with his own shared many features.

But where his chin angled in manly square, where his nose rose, noble and aquiline, the face reflected upon the pond had a gentle, impish triangular chin, a small nose with the slightest tilt, and large, large silver eyes that seemed to reflect more light than fell upon them, and hair dark and long and unashamedly free, framing her face.

"Silver!" Quicksilver said in shock, for he'd never beheld Silver but in a mirror and only when he himself was transformed.

In a frenzy, he took his hands to his face, and felt the square chin, the manly nose, the stubble of blond hair upon his cheeks, and stared at the reflection of Lady Silver as it rose from the waters of the lake.

It rose like a woman lifting out of the water, like a creature being formed from those watery mists and insalubrious spirits that hung over ponds and rivers.

It rose and assembled and joined, becoming solid all so fast that Quicksilver scant had time to draw breath, before she stood in front of him, wan and lovely, in a pale green dress that he now recognized as the very fabric he'd been chasing through the enchanted forest.

"Silver," he said again, and it was not so much calling her name as a whisper, an affirmation to himself that she stood there, in front of him.

This part of himself, always cherished, this part that since birth naught had ever separated, was now another thing, a thing not self, a woman who stood, mist and shadow, over a pond and stared at him with sad silver eyes.

Quicksilver felt cold run up his neck, making all the little hairs there stand on end.

"Silver," he said again. "How come you here?" he asked. "How came we two, thus divided?"

Scene 18

ဢ

Quicksilver stands in the clearing, in front of Lady Silver, who rises above a lake.

How beautiful she is, Quicksilver thought. The thought shocked him. He'd never thought of Silver as beautiful even when, spying through her silver eyes, he'd watched her practice her seductive poses and smiles before his mirror.

He'd never thought of Silver as anything much but another part of himself. She had always been there, always immutable. Her face had changed from infant to child, from child to woman. He'd thought nothing of her looks. She was simply Silver.

Yet here she was, standing before him, silk-black hair whipping around in the cold, magic-laden wind, and broad silver eyes staring out at him with a pleading look.

Here she stood, so beautiful that he felt an ache in his heart as if it would break with delight at the sight of her, with pain at having lost her for aye.

Here she was, her high breasts rounded and looking large above a ridiculously small waist. Beneath the green skirt that the wind played with, long white legs stretched—creamy white, velvet soft. Quicksilver could remember touching the legs, with those pale hands at the end of the lady's pale arms. He remembered feeling both the touch and the touching—velvet on velvet, a softness like newly opened rose petals, and the joy of touching.

She was a stranger and, as a stranger, beautiful. How odd it felt, seeing her like that. Like being one in two and two in one, and yet none. Yes, now must he be none. For who was Quicksilver if not half of Silver?

She stood in front of him, apart from him, a pale, bodied ghost.

The lady was not him now and he not the lady.

He remembered the touch of her hands upon her skin, the feel of that black hair spilling down his back over his breasts—her breasts—and the thoughts felt like going mad—like a memory of the impossible.

He looked into her wide silver eyes, confused, divided.

She was so lovely. A loveliness that went beyond her looks, the contrast between her pale skin and her black hair, the eery beauty of her reflective eyes. Her beauty resonated with a grace that Quicksilver could remember only in her steps, but could not recover in this, his heavier body.

Her fascination, woven of charm and magic and echoing mystery, filled him with awe.

No wonder Christopher Marlowe had fallen at the sight of her and that even Will, honest Will, wedded to his wife and faithful to his word, had fallen abed with Silver as sure as a stricken bird fell when the hunter's arrow found its heart.

Yet for all her wondrous beauty, she looked cold. She looked infinitely sad, the lady Silver.

Like staring upon a mirror that reflected only feelings, Quicksilver saw in Silver's eyes his own pain, his own stricken division. He wanted to be whole again. He longed for the feeling of the two of them conjoined.

Tears blurred his vision.

Tears filled her eyes and dropped down the gentle slope of her face, and Quicksilver felt the echo of those tears rolling down his face, hot and moist, to drip from his masculine, bearded cheek onto the frayed collar above his black doublet.

Without meaning to, needing to feel her presence, he stretched toward her small, soft hand his calloused, masculine hand, used to battle and wielding the heavy magical sword that now depended from his waist. The sword weighed down his belt like a stone—like the memory of past sins upon the stricken soul.

When their hands met, he recoiled, shocked. He'd expected that she'd be a vision, a passing phantom, an illusion of his overstretched mind, his breaking heart. He expected a feeling of coldness, a cold fog where his hand reached.

Instead, he touched silky skin upon Silver's perfect hand.

Silver's tears redoubled at his touch, as though springing from an inner force that his hand had woken.

In that springing, his own grief found expression and loosened the pressure of tears behind his eyes, making the tears fall faster, a fountain of water sprung from grief and fear and terrible wonder. It rolled, uncontrollable, down his face.

He lifted his hand to her cheek. Her hands, soft and small and yielding, both came up to envelope his hand that touched her face.

Her hands were warm and gentle and full of tenderness. Their touch was like velvet, their warmth like the fire of a mortal cottage, late at night, when it was raining outside and the mortal had tired himself in a long day's work.

A smell of lilacs, strong and intoxicating, surrounded Quicksilver. The smell of magic, the smell of fairykind love.

In his memory, it was a summer night, and Quicksilver walked, through it, free and careless, to his first assignation, Silver's first love.

He remembered that night well, and the freedom, the youth, the speeding heartbeat, the warm, dry air, the excitement and anxiety of the moment that came with it. In his mind, now all of it, fear and excitement and the smell of summer, on remembering became aching nostalgia, the missing of the youth he'd never again be, of the maiden innocence that Silver would never again recapture.

His heart ached with longing and memory.

He reached for her, and her hands met his.

Had Silver moved closer?

How had she come so near?

He hadn't noticed Silver moving closer, nor yet his moving closer to her, but she was there in his arms, her body soft and yielding, warm in his arms, pliant against his body.

She pushed against him, her body warm, warm, through his jacket and shirt, pressing against his body limb for limb. Warming her, he felt himself warmer, their bodies' touch recalling their natural union.

Her breasts pressed against his hard, battle-scarred chest, where the magical swords of the enemy had more than once done their worst and where only the great ability and magical strength of elven healers had stopped death from cutting short the days of the King of Fairyland.

For the moment Quicksilver had forgotten he was king, forgotten all but this lady in his arms—this warm, enveloping body against his.

His body, and not his, hers and yet not hers only.

He could feel her breath as she breathed. Breath by breath, it was his own breath, flavored with the same scent of Fairyland—the spices of the Indies, the heat of the sun. His heart and her heart beat one on one, each beat one beat and two beats and then three beats together, a drumbeat speeding up, closer and closer, chasing its own echoes, as it climbed a slope of misguided passion.

His free hand squeezed her sleeve and caressed her silky hair, and slid, with knowing, exact need down the slope of her low-cut dress to cup her full breast.

He remembered what it felt like, having a hand on her breast. He knew the tingle and pressure as the nipple tightened. He guessed at the moist rush below.

He knew what her sharp intake of breath meant, why she suddenly straightened up and reached for him—her eyes half closed and her lips half parted, the tip of her pink tongue peeking between.

The hunger in her lips that searched for his with blind, eager need was his hunger. The craving in the tongue that searched her mouth was her craving.

He knew her desire as she knew the need that now surged through his veins and made him crave more than he ever had.

Oh, he needed her body and his body, both bodies conjoined, both knowing with each movement what the other felt. Together again, together at last.

Both of his pleasures, his and hers, would feed his pleasure. He needed those joined pleasures for his comfort. Without her, he was lonely and divided. He craved the mingling of his divided self.

He was married, and he'd promised Ariel fidelity forever, a rare enough vow in Fairyland.

Forever stretched out of sight into the nearly endless span of elvenkind lives. Alone, without Silver, forever seemed to Quicksilver like death, like unending punishment. His body echoed with loneliness as though it were a resounding palace built for a large court, through whose vast halls and monumental rooms he walked alone and exiled.

And how could you be unfaithful with yourself?

Silver's lips were salty with the salt of his tears and her tongue that searched his tongue was the incarnation of his own desperate desire.

He sucked at her lips and moaned at her pleasure, and searched for the ties of her dress that he knew as well as the fastenings of his own, masculine clothes.

The knots felt unaccustomed from this position, from outside, and he remembered this was how they had all fumbled—Kit and Will and the others, the many others who, through Quicksilver's wild and free adolescence, had served the lady's pleasure.

He undressed her, pursuing his pleasure, paying little mind to her own hands undressing him.

His craving, his need, resided upon her naked body and sprang from her flesh. He needed to view again that white, unbroken skin that he knew like his own—that had been his. Unable to step into Silver's skin, to be Silver, he wanted Silver as close as she could be—as near as he could hold her, till the texture of her skin, the taste of her, was part of him again, inextricable, inseparable.

If he joined with her, wouldn't it all be solved? Wouldn't their bodies slip together and become one again, like the wayfarer who, on returning home, becomes again at ease with his routine?

Wouldn't he be Quicksilver—Quicksilver again, as he had been before the horrible war?

He sucked at her nipples, and ran his hands along her slim, naked waist. She tasted of sweat and sugar-sweet dew upon newly opened roses.

His hands lingered upon her, trying to absorb the skin that felt like velvet beneath his hands—the skin that by rights was his own, as well as hers.

His own—his own—how could they live apart?

Her hands, which played along his arms, his chest, his neck, his buttocks, were the unneeded kindling to his flaming passion.

He laid her down upon the surface of the magical lake, taking care to set down a spell first, so that neither of them touched the magic beneath. By the power and virtue of Fairyland, a bed of fogs and mist supported them both.

A smell of lilac writhed around them both, a living fog hot with their desire, moist with their tears, frantic like their passion, touching their skin all over, more intimate than even the other's reach.

Upon the mists he joined her, his body in hers, her passion echoing in his cries.

Together they climbed this passion that could not be tamed, ascending need on need and craving on craving—his hands in her hair, her nails raking the length of his already scarred back—till there was no pinnacle to climb and nowhere to go. There, pausing for a moment of wondrous pleasure, with a scream they released passion like a fleeting bird to the magical skies of the crux.

Time stopped, then resumed.

Spent, exhausted, Quicksilver lay on Silver.

First came breath, returning to his lips like life returning to a body it had fled.

He breathed in small, hungry gasps, and felt a great sadness, a great fear, a great anger come over him, blinding him.

He didn't know why or whence the anger came, yet he saw it in her eyes: in the tears forming, the disappointed, immense loss that made her lips tremble and her whole face sag, like wax too near a candle flame.

He bit his tongue to prevent the same tears from forming in his eyes. He felt his lips tremble.

His anger, his disappointment, his heartbreak, gathered into words.

Alas, I am betrayed, he thought. But betrayed by whom?

He could not answer. He could get no nearer to it than this feeling that both he and Silver had been grossly abused.

This joining had been no less—no more—than his many encounters with elf and mortal alike.

How could you make love to your other half and feel no more than when you joined with a stranger?

Looking down on Silver, he knew her no more and no less than he had known his mortal lovers, or his other elf couplings.

There was her face, filled with disappointment, like the face of a child who feels eternal loss. He could guess that she, like him, felt grief at union denied.

But her thoughts remained locked behind the wall of otherness that kept him out.

She was not him. She might never be him again.

This union, rushed, craved, had served only to underline their separation, their awful, aching separation.

He saw her hands go to her breasts and cover them in belated modesty, while they remained joined, and he still above her.

He saw her hands touch her breasts, but he could not feel what those hands felt, or those breasts, when her hands covered them.

He was bereft. Yet something in him—he was sure of it—had resisted their reunion.

But what?

When had it happened and why had she fled? When had she left his body and his soul, ripping herself from him like new cloth from an unsound old patch?

Was it the death of Vargmar, when Quicksilver had felt as though a long-held cord broke within him?

Was it the death of Vargmar that had expelled the lady for good from Quicksilver's being?

But how could it be when the lady, like Quicksilver, knew the need for defense and blood and death in that defense? And yet perhaps she didn't see it thus. Though neither of them had sought the kingship that had fallen upon their conjoined shoulders like a mantle of lead, Quicksilver had understood the need for serving kingship.

Yet Silver had thought kingship should serve them.

And thus, divided, over tradition as over their own nature, they had started their painful separation.

Thinking on the crown that he wore only for ceremonies of state, it seemed to Quicksilver that he could still feel its weight—old and accustomed, heavy gold and spells woven through all the centuries in which it had symbolized the responsibility and power of Fairyland.

As the keeper of the power and souls of elves and fairies and those grosser, inferior races—trolls and centaurs and mountain dwarves—Quicksilver would always feel the crown upon his brow.

But Silver had felt it not, nor did she see any reason to conform to the tradition of the kings before them. As though Quicksilver alone could create a better system a sounder realm than what his ancestors had devised over countless generations.

It had started with the crown, Quicksilver thought. And their disagreement over how a king should behave.

Refusing to concede, Silver had distanced herself, and Quicksilver had remained alone to wear the crown and sit in audience and receive guests, and be King Quicksilver, not the Lady Silver with her flirtatious ways, her carefree laughter, her caprices, her loves . . . her love for Will.

He thought of how she loved Will, and he flinched, as a wounded man will flinch from touching raw flesh.

It had started like that, thus. Now it wasn't convenient and then it wasn't proper, and then again they disagreed. Silver had bled away from within him like a man's life leaving through an open vein that he heeds not.

Little by little she'd trickled away, and he'd never felt it till they were divided, separated.

How could a man be so oblivious to his own self, to the currents of his own soul?

How could an elf reign who knew himself so little?

Quicksilver looked down at the perfect face of Lady Silver, crumpled in grief, her eyes overflowing with woe.

He lowered his own face to hers and kissed her gently, tasting the salt of her tears.

She cried still.

Had the loss of her brought about his other woes?

Was it his lack of her that had brought about the war, the hill deaths, the destruction? Would Silver's irreverent, experimental approach to kingship have worked better?

He'd been an elf divided, who knew not himself. Little by little, trickle by trickle. He'd lost Silver, and then his soul appeared to have fled after her. When was the last time he had felt alive? When was the last time he'd laughed?

Fair Ariel had seen him as though dead. And she'd been right. He'd become naught but the crown on his head that crushed all thought and stopped all feeling.

He'd become a king, a king and nothing more, and as a king, he'd ruled heavily, his hand resting in crushing weight upon the hills of Fairyland.

There had been no dissent allowed, and no jokes, and no one could mention that the king was two and could become, at will, Queen Silver of Fairyland.

Fairyland, Quicksilver had determined, would have only one queen and one king—and those in different bodies.

And in that decision, how humorless he'd become, quenching jest and flirting as though they were crimes, and allowing no elf to speak his mind, unless his mind met with Quicksilver's own.

There, there, Vargmar's treason had found fodder.

Alone, Vargmar would not have been able to rebel.

His early attempt at killing Quicksilver would have ended as it did end, in a midnight discovery with everyone watching.

But his attempt at raising an army would have died 'ere it began, were it not that Quicksilver had long nurtured discontent amid the ranks and squelched the voice of the little ones of elfland, till the little ones rose against him like a tide, like an unstoppable storm. The odd ones, those who didn't fit in—trolls and centaurs, pucks and brownies—had Quicksilver allowed himself to be who he truly was, would he have understood them better?

Had he shown himself for what he truly was—an impetuous, imperfect shapechanger—would they have loved him better?

He looked at Silver's crying face, and felt her sobs.

It was too late now. He'd shown himself a perfect, unassailable, cold king and they'd turned their hearts from him and wholeheartedly served Vargmar.

Oh, Vargmar had been guilty and deserved death.

But then, what of Quicksilver, who'd encouraged and created the division as much as Vargmar ever had? The division that had led to the war, for which the youth of Fairyland had bled?

If Vargmar had earned death, what had Quicksilver earned?

He saw, in Silver's eyes, that her thought, traveling the like path, had arrived at a similar destination.

He saw her small hands clench into fists, and the fists lift to pound upon his battle-scarred chest.

Had he not earned it?

He had killed her, had he not? He'd pulled her from him, and in Fairyland she could not appear and had no expression.

Only here, in the crux, where magic was free and rampant, could he see her.

No more would the lady Silver's laughter echo in the glades and circles of Fairyland. No more would she dance, graceful and happy, in the ceremonies of her people.

No more would she jest and smile and joke and with her cheering encourage all around her—inspire them to courage, show them the way of love.

No more would her white body, her beautiful face, her joyous love, lend itself to those her heart inclined to—in the Fairyland palace and in the rooms of humankind.

No more would her joy be Quicksilver's joy, her love make him regard mortal and elf with less than disdain and more than hauteur.

He needed and craved her, yet he could not allow her to become part of him. They were so different.

Her eyes were sad, her features shocked, afraid.

He reached for her as she pushed him away, kissed her as her small fists pummeled his chest and shoulders.

What should have died together was separate. The world was broken and Quicksilver could not mend it.

Getting up, he ran blindly into the forest.

Scene 19

೦೪೨

Will walks through the forest, looking tired and bedraggled.

Never so tired. Never so in woe. Will could no further crawl, no further go. The fog around him, like a living thing, grew tendrils and fingers that reached for him and pulled him now in this direction, now in that, like a wanton child playing with a doll.

Trees swayed around him and, in swaying, made sounds that echoed a familiar voice. "Stay," the voice said. "Stay, stay, stay."

That one voice spoke in the carefully cultivated tones of Kit Marlowe as though, from beyond death, the shoemaker's son still attempted to affect the manner of speech of the cultured elites.

"Stay, Will," Marlowe whispered from Will's left.

A succession of mournful echoes repeated, "Stay, Will." The echoes, like sad bells, went chasing through the tree tops, sighing through the underbrush, till they died in the distance.

"He's lost," the voice whimpered from his right. "Quicksilver grieves. He shall presently die."

"Die" was a sigh, turning to despairing moan.

Will flailed at the trees around him, trying to stop Marlowe's voice.

Why had Marlowe's ghost followed him here, to this accursed land?

What terror had brought so low that spirit that had once aspired to the stars? Having left the earthly plane in so untimely a manner, why did he pursue Will? Why did he not head for the freedom of the great spheres above?

Will remembered what Marlowe had said about doing a good deed and about the scales of good and evil being too exactly balanced. But why must Will be the recipient of Marlowe's misguided charity?

"You have my poetry," Marlowe said. "I must follow you."

"Oh, be still," Will said, his voice little more than a hoarse whisper. "Be still." He couldn't remember exorcisms or incantations to keep the creature away. He must be content with this. "Be still."

"Will, you must go to him," Marlowe said, and the tops of the trees swayed in agitation and each leaf was an eager, echoing tongue. "You must bring them back together."

Them? "I don't know of what you speak. I am here for my son. Leave me alone and return to your grave."

Will kicked aside a root that twisted toward his ankle like a monstrous snake. This was no place for humans.

"Go," he told Marlowe. "Why don't you go? You do not need to follow your poetry here. I'll not be writing."

But he remembered Marlowe's eye, the sad, tender look in it when speaking of Quicksilver. Marlowe said he was tied to Will by his poetry, yet Will suspected that it was Quicksilver's presence that kept the ghost here. What an illness this love was that not even death could cure it.

He glimpsed Marlowe just ahead of him, standing between two trees, a translucent Marlowe, his body seemingly distorted, now stretched this way, now that by breezes that blew through him. Marlowe's remaining eye filled with urgent concern.

"Come," Marlowe's voice said. "Come."

Will shook his head. "I will go nowhere but in search of my son," he said.

And where could his son be? He wished he knew. He'd seen the castle and, knowing his fairy tales, suspected the captive Hamnet of being there.

But captive how? And what manner of monster guarded him? Will had started on a path that should have led to the castle. But then there was the fog and the roots that twisted beneath his feet. He suspected the path itself was magical and changed to keep the unwary from their destination.

"Quicksilver will help you find your son," Marlowe said. "But you must go to him."

"I am no servant of elf."

"He is dying."

The words were so sad, so serious, tolling with such unrelieved certainty, that for a moment Will saw Quicksilver lying dead, and his breath caught. But then he thought that Quicksilver, somehow, was guilty of bringing Hamnet here, guilty of bringing Will from his safe world.

"Let him die. Let him die." Will stopped, lacking the breath for both walking and talking at the same time. "Let him die. He stole my son. He ensnared—"

"Hush," the ghost voice whispered. Will felt Marlowe's half-ethereal hand upon his own, pulling him.

"Hush," Marlowe said. "He ensnared no one, but is himself ensnared."

"You believe him," Will said, his voice tolling with withering scorn. "You believe him yet."

Marlowe smiled. For a moment he became visible, flickering and translucent like a candle's flame against the green jungle. His sad smile and his bleeding eye warred with each other. It looked as though he wept blood and smiled at doing it.

"I've gone beyond doubt," Marlowe said. His voice sounded remote, echoing from a great distance. "Doubt was my living self's only faith. But now, being a spirit, I am nowhere and everywhere, and as a spirit, I have seen the bloody war in the elven kingdom. It came not from Quicksilver, but from his kinsmen, who longed for his crown and his throne and thought Quicksilver weak and frail.

"I do not say that Quicksilver is blameless, but he did fight fair and bravely, and with great wisdom."

"But my son—"

"His enemies, not himself, stole your son. He came here only to rescue Hamnet and return him to you and thus spare you grief."

While he spoke, he pulled Will and Will stepped after that forceful, half-solid hand. It tugged him on an erratic path between trees and round misty ponds.

"There was a war in Elvenland?" Will asked, for it had never crossed his mind that such ethereal kingdoms could fight with swords and hot-blooded armies.

Oh, he knew elves dueled now and then. But . . . a war? He tried to picture armies of magical beings, fighting and dying in the moonlit harvest fields, dying and killing amid mortal homes, and in homey mortal gardens, invisible to all mortals but mages and Sunday children.

He shivered.

"A war that tore the hills of Avalon apart and spilled the blood of the noblest families," Marlowe said. "Quicksilver's kinsmen rebelled against him and formed an army of like malcontents. With it, they almost destroyed Elvenland, almost won the throne from Quicksilver. Quicksilver's victory in the end might have cost him his soul."

On the last sentence, Marlowe's voice descended, descended, till it was, once more, indistinguishable from the persistent murmur of the trees agitated by a lilac-scented breeze.

Marlowe's image, likewise, flickered and dissolved—pale face, auburn hair, grey eye, coming unglued and floating in the wind like great bits of color and finally melting into the landscape, as though it had never been.

"Marlowe?" Will asked, and turned around and around. He saw nothing.

The whisper of the trees sounded now no more ominous than the sound of any wind-disturbed leaves.

"Marlowe?"

What madness was this? Had Will just slumbered here, while these visions did appear?

"Marlowe?"

No sound answered his call save a soft rustling and somewhere—to his left?—a gentle sobbing sound.

Sob? Who sobbed here, in this inhuman land?

The sounds were human—or elven—and, Will would say, feminine.

"My lady?" he called, thinking of the young elf girl.

Young she was, no older than his Susannah, and how could she be expected to bear this barren desolation with fortitude?

She had run from him when he'd told her what she did not wish to hear about her father. He'd ripped the veil of her filial illusion and made her face the truth without pretense. Truth had scared older beings and steadier minds.

He stumbled toward the sobbing. "Lady?" he asked.

A frisson of fear ran up his spine. He felt cold sweat trickle down his back. Why answered she not?

He remembered her power crackling around him, the way she'd forced him to tell her the truth. He shivered. And she had such power while Quicksilver was impotent. Even the crux could not drain her of all her magic.

So much power and so ill controlled. She knew herself no more than Susannah knew herself—and was no more proficient with her magic than Susannah with her mending needle.

Yet he must go to her, for the girl was young, and therefore pliable. She'd brought Hamnet here and she'd know how to find the path to the castle, the path to Hamnet.

This thought hurried his feet. Cold and tired, he could think only of reaching Hamnet, of taking his son in his arms, of pulling him, with Will—by the witch's magic and virtue that Will himself didn't fully understand—to the safe world of men.

Then would Will take Hamnet to Nan, and calm Nan's fears. For Nan must be worrying over her boy even now. She must wonder where he was.

How long had Will and Hamnet been absent?

Was Will's Nan sick with worry? Had Lord Chamberlain's men starved or dispersed for lack of the revenue from Will's overdue play?

In these magical places, time was ever relative, and unraveled other than in the world of men. Will had heard stories of people who danced away one night in the fairy hill and came home to find that all their relatives were dead, their village gone, and themselves no more than a half-believed legend.

He shivered and hurried forward, toward the girl who could take him to Hamnet, who could get him out of the crux as soon as possible.

The trees ended abruptly in a circular clearing. There, sitting on what appeared to be a small pond, a woman sat crying.

Will stopped, startled. The woman was not the elf princess, but Silver, the female aspect of the king of elves.

His breath caught in his throat. She was naked and, in the white, flat light of the crux, yet managed to look irresistible. Light glimmered upon her pale skin and made her hair seem darker and softer.

So it was true. Will's worst suspicions must be true. He took a step back. The deceitful Quicksilver creature was seeking once more to catch Will in the net of her passions and, to that end, had assumed this form to which he knew Will to be most vulnerable and most yielding.

Anger gave Will his breath back and blinded him to the lady's seductive beauty.

"Quicksilver," Will said and, forgetting for the moment his tiredness, stalked into the clearing, fists clenched.

The woman looked up. Her face was pale and tear-ravaged and her naked flesh showed red marks, as though rude hands had grasped her unceremoniously here and there—on her pale breasts, her hips, her legs.

She saw Will and stared, as though she didn't recognize him, or could not understand what he was doing there.

Her eyes widened in shock, her eyebrows rose. She whispered, "Will."

Yet Quicksilver knew well that Will was there. They'd brawled on the beach. Had the elf already forgotten that?

"Do not play the fool, Quicksilver," Will said. "You'll not catch me with your tricks."

The woman shook her head, she swallowed. "There is no Quicksilver here," she said. "Only Silver."

Will heard something much like a growl of frustration leave his lips. "Where Silver is, there Quicksilver lies, waiting but his opportunity to emerge."

To his surprise, Silver stopped crying. The hands that had half hid her face lowered. They hesitated in front of her breasts. Her face twisted in an unreadable rictus. Her hands tightened in fists, they pounded her own thighs, while she threw her head back and laughed like a madwoman.

Half scared, not understanding this at all, Will stared at her, unable to move.

Laughter slowed, then stopped, and the face that Silver turned toward him showed not a hint of mirth. "Oh, Quicksilver was here," she said and pointed with trembling finger to a fine velvet suit, somewhat the worse for the wear that lay all in a pile upon the ground near Will's feet.

"Quicksilver was here, and here he left. Here has he left me, forsaken."

Will looked at the suit, then at Silver. Ever before, when Will had watched the elf change aspects, Quicksilver had changed his clothes with his body.

Was this one more cunning trap than Quicksilver had thought? Or was it the truth? But for a truth, it was a strange truth, for a trap a *very* strange trap.

He thought of Marlowe's ghost, his plaintive complaint that *they* were separate, *they* were now apart, and apart *they* would die.

Were Quicksilver and Silver the *they* to whom Marlowe had referred?

But how could that be?

"You are one," Will said. "How can you speak of being separated? How can this be? You are one."

The lady Silver stood, unfolding gracefully from her sitting position.

Standing above the water of the pond, naked, with her well-proportioned rounded body, her long black hair, she looked like one of those ancient goddesses that in olden times visited poets in their dreams.

Her body was white and pale, her skin so even that it appeared to shimmer with the subdued glimmer of pure silk. Her oval face and within it symmetrically arranged generous red lips, a small nose and expressive, metallic silver eyes—all looked exquisite.

Even the ravages of tears had done nothing to erase the beauty of her high cheekbones, the gentle appeal of her eyes. Around the face, framing it and falling down the lady's back, black hair like a rich velvet curtain hid some of her charms but none of the important.

Her soft, rounded breasts rose and fell with her every breath.

"We were one," she said. "One was our birth, one our conception.

"But Quicksilver thought that I injured his chances to reign in Fairyland, and as such, he pushed me further and further from reality, till I existed as no more than a dream, a feeling within his mind. At last, through the hard years of the war he pushed me out entirely, so that now it is only here, in the magic-filled crux, that I can find existence and a voice to speak.

"Yet, even here, he rejects me."

With that, she put her head down again and cried once more, in loud, inconsolable sobs.

Will had almost loved this creature once and even now, weary and old as he felt, he looked on her and couldn't help his heart's softening toward her plight.

"Lady," he said. "Go to him. Find a way to become one with him once more. Or if not, become that which you are, you, yourself alone, and be free."

She looked up and shook her head, strewing her tears about in the wind. "I've tried to merge with him, but he will not allow it. For he believes he cannot be a king while I am half of him. The core of him resists me and wishes itself rid of my soft passion. I cannot live without him, nor do I think that he can live without me. His was the stronger aspect, though, and I do not think he has yet noticed his own lack." She cried. "But he will, and when he does, it will be too late."

Will sighed. He stepped toward the lady. He opened his arms. Her nude form fit itself within them, warm against his cold body.

He longed for her—for who could avoid longing for this creature of perfection?

But he knew where that slope led, and how slippery it could be. He knew she was not human, no matter how much she resembled one. Her silvery eyes were only the external and smaller mark of her oddity. The strangest thing, the thing that could not be changed and that made her not human, was her elven heart.

Not that she didn't love. He'd seen the lady love him, he knew the lady had loved him true, her lust and her love mingled and conjoined like two fires burning together, inextricable.

He looked at her tear-filled silver eyes, turned to him in adoration, and he thought that perhaps she loved him yet, perhaps she loved him still.

But all her love was nothing to that love that Will's wife, his Nan, felt for him. Nan's love was a steady fire, forged and tempered in the certainty of its own ephemeral nature, in the specter of death that would end both their lives.

How could a creature know love who knew not death?

And Lady Silver, even now, even dying, was a creature who did not understand death.

Death could not be compassed within the mind of an elf who could not age.

Fourteen years ago Will had made love to her, and yet here she was, here she remained, with no sign of aging, no sign of dissolution to her sweet features, her dark hair.

How could such a creature understand death that crept on humans white hair by white hair and wrinkle by wrinkle?

No. His lips searched for hers, and they kissed, but it was the chaste kiss of siblings, and with it, Will realized how different a creature she was from humans.

He wondered where that other elf girl was, who'd brought Hamnet here. Had she gone in search of Quicksilver to avenge herself on him?

And if so, would she find him?

Scene 20

cy6y

A path in the forest, fog writhing in tendrils around trees and around the figure of Quicksilver who, looking addled, walks amid the trees— not in the path—completely naked, his long blond hair his only covering.

Quicksilver stumbled, and his feet hit hard against a root that made his toe bleed.

He stared, uncomprehending, at the magical blood, the sparkling blood of Fairyland, dripping out to soak the rude root.

He and his body seemed as divided as he was from Silver. He felt numb, and distant and strange, as though his pain reached him at a remove, traveling a long distance.

Staring at his foot, he waved his hand to stop the blood, yet he wondered why he should.

Let the blood flow. Let it all flow.

Why should not Quicksilver die, now, painlessly, who'd already lost half of himself? Or why—why—could he not go home, to his palace and his wife, his home and his safety?

Quicksilver had determined this land was a trap for him. In his resentment, Proteus wished to murder Quicksilver. Therefore, why stay?

No other King of Fairyland would have done so.

But here, Quicksilver found he was not like other Kings of Fairyland. Though he'd pushed Silver away, though he'd given up a half of himself, yet he had certain responsibilities and certain feelings that would not be ignored.

Will's face appeared in his mind: a Will who looked anxious and harried, puzzled by this one more intrusion of the supernatural into his ordered life.

Will, in whose life Quicksilver had intruded twice, once led by lust and once by need for help.

Will, who hated fairykind and did not wish to become enmeshed in the elves' plots of love and faceless treason, but whom the elves could not leave alone.

In this trap, Will had fallen also, and here he would remain till he found his son.

Quicksilver, whose actions had led to the revolt that had made Proteus commit this folly, could not wash his hands of Will's fate and walk away from it all.

As he was the King of Elvenland, it might be his duty to preserve his throne and his life, so that the many that on him relied would not be left bereft. But as he was guilty of causing this snare in Will's fate, it should be his penance to clear it.

He'd find the boy, he thought to himself, while stumbling naked amid the strange wood, and give him to his father, and then send both mortals to their proper sphere. And then could he judge who was guilty and who should be punished in Elvenland. And if in himself he found the greater guilt, could he perhaps leave, exiled from the hill.

Save only that he had misgivings about Proteus's ability to reign in his stead—indeed, to reign at all.

"All infections that the sun sucks up, from bogs, fens, flats, on Proteus fall," a rumbling voice said from beyond the trees and the fog in front of Quicksilver.

Quicksilver jumped, surprised. Looking whence the voice came, it seemed to him that amid green tendrils, tall trees and bubbling fog, he saw a movement, a thing . . . a man?

"And make him by inch meal a disease," the voice growled from the bush. "For this land where he hath transported my lady and me, it breathes with spirits and boils with strange events. His spirits hear me, and yet I needs must curse: but they'll nor pinch, fright me with urchin shows, pitch me in the mire, nor lead me, like a firebrand in the dark, out of my way, unless he bid them."

Amazed, Quicksilver watched, till the creature emerged out of the fog and the surrounding vegetation—a rough creature with the general shape of a man, but as much resemblance to a dog as to a human, and to neither enough likeness that either race could call him a brother.

For though his face looked furry and canine, this hair grew hirsute around brown eyes that owed nothing to the faithful devotion of a dog's look, but were all human in their bitterness. And his mouth, where it closed, with black, lipless fissure, showed only powerful canines that overhung his chin like the promise of cruel death.

His arms were thick and likewise his torso, and the legs with which he advanced, step on step, heavily, upon the root-covered ground, were bent permanently backward, so that he slouched.

Quicksilver knew these looks well. This was a troll, like the ones who'd been his enemies in the just-ended war.

And he spoke of Proteus. Had Proteus then not severed all his connections with the treasonous trolls of the northern mountains?

A smell came from the beast, like the smell of wet dog fur. And he muttered under his breath, his voice more growl than human speech. "For every trifle are they set upon me, sometime like apes, that mome and chatter at me, and after, bite me. Then like hedgehogs which lie tumbling in my barefoot way, and mount their pricks at my footfall. Sometime am I all wound with adders, who with cloven tongues do hiss me into madness."

He stopped, having reached the path and seen Quicksilver.

Quicksilver cleared his throat.

The troll opened his mouth, as if to cry out or mutter, and Quicksilver took two steps back hastily.

Trolls were vile creatures, at the fringe of Fairyland, and this example looked not like the most civilized of the trolls Quicksilver had ever encountered. And though their magic was but curses all, it could be powerful and withal change the fair to foul and foul—rarely—to fair.

But the creature gave Quicksilver the weather eye, and with lowered brow stared upon him, while he raised his hairy hands to heavens in disapproval. "Here comes a spirit of his, and to torment me, I doubt not. For it has the look of the elf around it, and it must be one of Proteus's faithless companions who helped Proteus land my mistress in this."

Quicksilver breathed shallowly. Who was this strange troll who seemed to despise Proteus? And how had he come to the crux?

Caught in the puzzle of who this creature might be, Quicksilver wondered how would a troll get to the crux? And why did he speak of Proteus? They were pack creatures, and of low magic. Who was the mistress of whom he thus spoke?

Quicksilver opened both hands wide in a sign of peace.

"Peace, creature, what are you? I *am* none of Proteus, and do not do his bidding."

The troll stared for so long that for a moment Quicksilver imagined that the troll didn't understand speech and that the words the creature had said were like the words of the parrot—learned and spoken, but with no true meaning behind them.

Then, his eyes wide, the creature fell upon his thick knees and cried out, "Do not torment me, pr'ythee. I'll do anything you want."

Speaking thus, he put his head down and moaned.

And Quicksilver, half curious, half pitying, advanced on him, and the creature cowered further into himself, forming himself into a ball, as like onto a furry hedgehog.

Yet, Quicksilver guessed, long knowing the instinct and proclivities of this race, had the troll quills, he would, gladly enough, sting the King of Fairyland.

The king.

Quicksilver's dignity told him to get away from this creature. What had he with such as this monster?

Of old, traditionally, the King of Fairyland had not dealt with trolls, nor with those more unclean spirits of the woods—the pucks who snagged maiden's hair and, deluding horses, made them run mad, or soured milk, or converted everything to ill that was good, till humans despaired of their livelihood and the creatures' tricks. Or the centaurs—strange, hot-blooded creatures who remained aliens in Elvenland, though they'd lived there almost as long as elves.

In horrible wars, before pacification, in times so far away that men were but one small band upon the vastness of the earth, trolls had flung themselves at the well-guarded precincts of the hill and been mercilessly mowed down by elves' greater magic.

Quicksilver had heard stories of trolls' heads displayed in front of the hill palace, their corruption and gore magnifying the high, clear wall of elven might.

Now were trolls a naught, a people of little account, who neither influenced the politics of Elvenland nor deserved the attention of Elvenland's monarch.

Yet looking on the troll, Quicksilver felt uneasy and for the first time wondered if the policies of his ancestors toward trolls might not be wrong.

For though the trolls, like all other feyfolk, contributed their magic to the king of elves, yet they got naught in return: no protection, no care in their illnesses, not even defense from other kingdoms of trolls.

Would that not cause trolls to be viler than nature had made them, and less disposed to mild civilization?

Vargmar had tapped into the trolls' discontent, and—his arming the halfwitted mountain hordes with crude stone axes—their unfettered rage had loosened the worst plague ever to take on the fairy kingdom of Avalon.

It had been those axes and trolls, those malicious canines, that had put the scars down Quicksilver's left shoulder, rending the tender, magical skin with magic-poisoned sharpness that would, ever, leave a scar even when, by dint of potions and healing spells, it did heal.

It seemed to Quicksilver that his scars tingled now anew, as if a memory of past pain made him suffer. And the wound on his shoulder, still not healed, was another magical wound that would leave a permanent scar. It trickled a little fresh blood as he thought of the trolls.

As for his head, it pounded with aching sharpness. Were his ancestors wrong? How could they be, when their policies had held the hill in prosperous peace so many years?

How dared Quicksilver, a shapechanger, imperfect spawn that he was, to doubt the elven kings of yore?

And trolls were low beings. Just look at them, furry and dim-witted, living in packs and never having aspired to art or architecture or the works of civilization.

How could they be included as equals in the same court as the higher races?

Quicksilver looked at the sharp canines, the dim-witted hatred in this troll's dull eyes, and he knew that the King of Fairyland should leave here now.

But Quicksilver paused and restrained himself from doing what he knew was proper. Quicksilver and not the King of Fairyland should operate here. That was, he thought with tears stinging his eyes, what Silver would have told him. And perhaps Silver was right.

Perhaps admitting trolls into equality with the other races of the hill was not the best thing. And yet perhaps it was, for if no race were left out, where would the next rebellion find malcontents to feed its angry ranks?

Perhaps mild mercy would serve where strength had not, and kind caring reach where the power of elf law had remained defeated.

Forcing himself to look friendly, Quicksilver bent down, and touching the creature with his hand—the coarse slickness of the fur disgusting upon his fingers—he said, "Get up, for I am no spirit, nor do I wish you ill. My name is Quicksilver and I am an elf, the ruler of Fairyland."

The creature looked at him just a moment, out of a rolling terrified eye. "If you are such, then I worship you." He knelt. His slobbery lips touched Quicksilver's naked foot. "But would the King of Fairyland go naked? I thought he had velvets and silks, great furs and warm wool, and other good fabrics to cushion his flesh against the harsh world."

Quicksilver forced his mouth to smile, despite the creature's smell, the creature's proximity, the repugnant memory of his touch upon Quicksilver's foot. "I had an encounter in the bush which rendered me naked. But I warrant you, I am the king."

Or the king was him, he thought, which might better describe this condition by which Quicksilver had been sucked into kingship and the weight of the crown had become the essence and fact of Quicksilver.

The creature looked at Quicksilver, this time with both eyes wide open, both eyes seeming very dark and as unreflective as the eyes of the dead. "Oh, but then you must have power enough to clothe yourself and to make a fire, by which we can escape this dank dampness—and power to get Caliban some food and some drink, too, like the victuals conjured up at the table of the King of Fairyland."

Quicksilver opened his mouth to say he would not squander his magic in such futile endeavors. Besides, he was none too sure he could reach beyond the crux and get solid substances from the outer space, from Fairyland, or earth, or elsewhere. And all he could make with his own unaided magic, like most other powers of Fairyland, was illusion and a trick of the light.

Cold and tired and hungry, he took a breath and tried to reach for magic of which he could not be sure. Yet he might as well try. Uncertain as the outcome was, he knew that this cold, dreary tiredness would find no other comfort but what he could conjure.

The creature looked expectantly at him. Quicksilver waved his hand in cabalistic passes and wished for the clothes that, nightly, lay upon his bed waiting for him to change for the dance in the palace.

It would be his dark suit tonight—dark in mourning for Vargmar, who, though a traitor, had been Quicksilver's nearest living relative.

But it would be splendid too, in lace and rich velvet, for tonight would be a victory dance.

Quicksilver, feeling the nip of the magic-laden wind of the crux upon his bare body, longed for this suit, longed to be covered, to feel like himself again.

Only the fear of facing Silver—with her grief, her undeniable separate identity—kept him from going back and claiming his other clothes.

As he called up magic and reached for the hill palace, he could almost feel the warmth of his suit upon his flesh.

He felt his extended magical power snag upon something on the other side—past the barriers of magical force that were the shell of the crux.

The something was soft and inert. He tugged on it. Soon, he'd be clothed.

Instead, he found himself holding a green, light blanket, the covering of his bed.

He tried to look as though he'd intended this and, wrapping the blanket around himself, further tried to command food from his palace kitchens.

Upon the soft sand of the path, in succession there landed four bottles of wine and a very large cauldron, which only missed smashing the bottles because Caliban had snatched them away. Into the cauldron banged, one after the other, a large hunk of bleeding venison, a mess of vegetables, and a container of oil.

Caliban, watching it all with rounded amazed eyes, stared at Quicksilver with something like admiration.

Quicksilver wondered what was wrong with his power and his strength that this should happen thus, for he wanted the food cooked, the venison readied.

But Caliban, sipping from a bottle, said, "You're a brave god and bear celestial liquor. I'll bow to you. I'll swear upon this bottle to be your true subject, and kiss your foot." Again he crept forward, and again he slobbered upon Quicksilver's foot, while Quicksilver disciplined himself not to shy from the ignoble touch.

"I'll cook our meal, milord, my King," Caliban said, and crept away carrying with him both bottle and cauldron with its contents. "I know me where water runs. I'll lay some wood by, if only you'd touch it with your grace and thereupon make fire."

And thus speaking, the creature scurried, hither and thither, bringing half-rotted wood and hollowed trunks, which he lay in a rough pile. Then he returned, the cauldron filled with pond water. Did Caliban know that what seemed like water was naught but liquid magic?

Quicksilver stared the pile of wood into flame and then the creature, with great industry, set about filling the cauldron, which soon bubbled and put forth savory enough odors.

But what happened to meat submerged in magic?

Though Quicksilver's stomach growled in hunger, the king was none too sure he could eat the food.

Upon a dank log, the King of Fairyland sat, and looked at the fire and at this strange servant he'd acquired, and dreamed of being not the king, but what he'd been while his parents were yet alive and himself young and irresponsible.

He dreamed of being free to be who he truly was. He fantasized about being whole, a dual creature. That dual nature he'd often cursed he now craved, and wished—wished—he could be Quicksilver and Silver both, and nothing more.

Scene 21

❧

The beach where all this started. Proteus sits on the sand, dazzled, look-ing lost. Miranda emerges from the forest. As she runs toward him, he lifts his head and, with joy shining in his eyes, extends both hands to her.

Oh, how could she have abandoned him?

As Miranda walked upon the cold shifting sand of the beach and saw Proteus sitting on the sand, looking sad and deserted, she couldn't compre-hend her own thought.

Grey waves still pounded the shore, but the magical wind no longer howled. The crux, having absorbed its invaders, had calmed its magical fury. Only the beating of ghostly waves, unseen, upon the grey edge of the beach gave the impression of continuing tempest.

How tired Proteus looked. How wan his complexion. How his shoulders sagged in despondence.

Had Miranda's desertion hurt him so?

And how ragged his clothing looked, how ill his whole aspect. Had his uncle then fought back, after Miranda ran? Had his uncle hurt him so?

Proteus looked tired and ragged and destroyed by the encounter with his uncle, by Miranda's desertion.

His hair was disheveled, having escaped the leather bind with which he normally confined it. In a blond mess, it surrounded his face, making him look wild, barely civilized.

Blood that had trickled from his nose had dried upon his skin, marring its smooth whiteness.

When she first arrived upon the beach, he turned at the sound of her steps. On seeing her there, his eyes seemed to fill with the joy of a man seeing paradise.

He stood up, but his attempt at rushing was betrayed by his left leg, which gave out under him as he stood and caused him to grimace in pain and steady himself upon the other leg.

Miranda's heart misgave at that grimace and she hurried to him and offered him both her hands, feeling guilty that she'd ever deserted him. For he was her Proteus, a hurt Proteus, a miserable and bedraggled Proteus, but hers nonetheless, her lord and her love.

"Milord," she said as her hands met his cold, too-dry hands.

Had Quicksilver, then, hurt him so much? Was Quicksilver, perhaps, one of those villains who held their temper a little but, when aroused, did more damage than any other?

But she would not think on it.

Had she not seen Quicksilver hold still while Proteus attacked him?

The matter was too complex for her mind, and she'd not judge Quicksilver yet. Nor Proteus.

If Quicksilver had defended himself, he'd done no more than any elf would, stopping the knife that would slay him, the hand that would hurt him.

If he'd hurt Proteus, maybe Proteus deserved it.

Yet need he have hurt Proteus so badly?

Proteus squeezed her hands, hard, and said in a voice scarcely louder than a whisper, "Do you forgive me, then? Does Miranda speak yet to her misguided Proteus?"

"Misguided?" Miranda said. His voice was so sad, so full of remorse, that she had no trouble at all calling a smile upon her face. "How can Proteus be misguided when he loves Miranda? Isn't loving Miranda the fact and essence of sanity, the measure of good taste, the exactness of fashion?"

Proteus smiled in answer to her smile, but his smile was wan and half-hearted, the sickly wince of a patient who tries to forget his pain. "Oh, how kind my lady, who yet saw her lord act worse than any villain and attack, again and again, a man who sought to do him no harm.

"Look here, these wounds." He moved the tattered bits of his suit, to uncover a red gash upon his leg, and yet another upon his arm. "These wounds I got when I tempted that poor king, my cousin, beyond his endurance." Tears appeared in Proteus's eyes, making them shine brightly with something like a light of remorse. "He, who could have killed me where I stood, only did this harm to me and no more."

Miranda, her heart clenching at the sight of those piteous wounds, those tears upon Proteus's fair, smooth skin, thought that Quicksilver might very well have forborne from inflicting even those wounds upon her love.

"You've changed your mind about my uncle, then?" she said. "You do not wish to kill him?"

Proteus shook his head. "Aye me, no. Long life and prosperity to the King of Fairyland." He squeezed her hands hard. "I'm not saying he always acted right, but the quarrel was between him and my father. And my father being dead, who I am to carry it forth? If Quicksilver would not kill me—me, who had attacked him—even while I lay unconscious upon the sand of this super-natural place, then surely, surely, he cannot be evil. All will be understood when I speak to him, for I'm sure he meant no ill to me. Know you where my cousin Quicksilver lies, that I might be reconciled?"

Miranda shook her head and congratulated herself on Proteus's excellent head, his great mind that he was already ready to forgive Quicksilver, to believe the best of him.

And if Miranda now doubted Quicksilver's peaceful intentions—if she thought that perhaps, just perhaps, the villain had faked peaceful behavior for the sake of winning Miranda's support away from Proteus—if she doubted Quicksilver, yet it was good that Proteus was willing to consider all angles of this.

It was good that rage no longer blinded her lord.

Proteus had an excellent wit, she decided, and their life would be such as fairy legends promised at their end—a happy ever after for the whole of eternity.

"I know not where my uncle is," she said. "But I have thought myself on a greater responsibility."

Proteus frowned on her, puzzled. "Responsibility?" he asked.

"That child," she said. "Whom we—"

"Of course," Proteus said and his eyes softened with eager gentleness. "That child, that poor creature of mankind that we lured to the crux with our black arts. He must be allowed from hence, to his mother's side, where he'll be safe. We must go," he said, and picked up her hand and pulled her toward the forest. "We must go to the castle at the center of the crux. Can you feel the true path? I cannot. The fight with my cousin and the exhaustion from it have blurred my mind," he said. He put his free hand on his forehead as though cooling a raging fever. "My ill-conceived attack on my cousin and his just response have left me too tired to find the magical feeling of the true path."

"The path is this way," Miranda said. "And I will guide you if you desire it of me." What sort of an attack could Quicksilver have inflicted on him that would make him blind to the feel of the path? She looked at Proteus's pale face and felt dull resentment at Quicksilver.

Justice need not be reckless.

Holding his hand, she led him, tenderly, to the edge of the forest and set Proteus's feet upon the path that would take them both to the heart of Fairyland, the castle in the crux.

She looked back and saw his smile and smiled at it.

"Where is that net that you took from me?" Proteus asked. "The magical net?"

Miranda's smile faltered. Why did he ask about the ill-omened object? What did he mean to do with it?

And how would he react when Miranda told him it was wholly lost?

Scene 22

ᗡᗡ

The misty clearing where Will stands before the lady Silver who, naked and unashamed, looks at him.

"Do this one thing for me, Will," the lady asked, her voice soft and gentle. "If ever my love meant aught to you, do this one thing for me and I shall never ask another."

He felt too sorry for her, in whose voice there still echoed the remnants of tears so recently cried, to tell her no. Yet knowing the creature, he could not say yes before she told him what the favor was that she requested.

For it might well be his love, or his attention, or his lifelong faithfulness.

Silver smiled on him, an apologetic smile, as though guessing his hesitation and forgiving it. "If you see my lord, Quicksilver—my brother, my spouse, the other half of my soul born with me in a single birth—tell him that I crave his company, I crave being whole with him once again.

"But he kept us apart when I would have rejoined him, and now it is he who must accept me, call me back. It is he who must want me to be a part of him once more—want it with every fiber of his body. And he must call to me, and tell me so.

"Then will I come back to him and, reunited, shall our flesh be one once more, shall we be saved . . ." She looked at Will and sighed, and fresh tears rose to the nascent of her glimmering eyes. "But I fear it is all for nothing and he won't wish it intensely enough, he won't truly want me to be part of him again. At least not before the division is irreversible, both halves of the soul scarred over where they split, each one lonely and on its own forever."

Will shook his head, bewildered. "If I see him, I'll tell him, but why should the king of elves listen to me?"

Silver smiled, revealing a row of small and very sharp teeth, which made her look, for a moment, wholly feral and all without mercy. "The king of elves listens to no one," she said. "It was to stop listening to me that he divided us. He wanted his attention given only to cheerless duty and aching toil and all must be done according to the way of his revered ancestors. Nothing more." She sighed again. "And yet, if he listens to someone, it will be to you, whom he loves despite his own wishes."

"But how will I overtake him, lady? I know not where he's gone. And more yet, I came here to rescue my son that was trapped by an elf—who, I neither know nor care. I want to rescue my son and nothing more.

"If I chance upon Quicksilver, I will tell him your message, but surely my first duty is to my son."

Here the lady smiled, a tear-streaked, weak, tremulous smile. "Aye, Will, but so will Quicksilver also view it as his duty to rescue your son. He'll see it as his duty as a king, his duty as the elf who first introduced you to Fairyland, to rescue your son and restore him to you. So in rescuing your son shall your paths meet. Only you try to find your son and sooner or later you shall find Quicksilver."

"And how to find my son, lady?" Will asked. He remembered his lonesome walk out there, in the shifting path, amid the tree roots. "How to find my son in this land where even the trees have thinking life and all shifts and changes beneath my feet at every moment?"

Silver frowned, not a frown of disapproval, but a frown of thinking, the expression of someone remembering long-ago heard lore. "There is a path," she said. "A true path. There always is one through magical forests.

"Could I but go with you, I would gladly lead you. But you see that I am this ethereal creature, chained to this point of great magic for my only existence, now that Quicksilver has cut me loose from his magic and the magic of the hill."

She frowned more intensely. Her small, pale fingers drummed upon her white, naked thigh, a gesture that would have looked natural were she drumming upon the silk of a court dress.

"Take you a twig," she said, pointing at a tree nearby. "Cut one from that tree, and bring it here."

Will stepped toward the tree, and reached his hand up for the thinnest twig.

A scream, like a wounded child's, sounded, growing till it seemed to fill the whole isle. Will froze, quivering, his hand half raised toward the tree.

"Take it," the lady said. She sounded tired, forceful, like an adult controlling a child's foolishness. "It will no more hurt it than paring your nails hurts you. It is being a coward and quaking only at what it doesn't know. The trees in the crux have never been broken or put to the ax, and thus they fear what they have never felt." She sighed. "As I fear eternal separation and all-engrossing death."

Gingerly Will reached for the twig at the end of the branch nearest him, a twig to which only two leaves and one bud clung.

He took hold of it and, in a single movement, broke it from the tree.

The tree shrieked.

Shimmering sap sprang from it, like water pouring from a living fountain. It felt hot and sticky on Will's fingers.

The shriek ended in the whimper of an injured child.

Will, feeling cold down his spine, tried to ignore the scream still echoing in the air and the sap like blood pouring from the stick.

Quicksilver had told Will that everything Will did in the crux—everything—would have an effect on the world of magic and that other world of men—beyond the crux.

What had Will done just now? Had he perhaps pruned a family tree, taken a son from his mother? A baby from his cradle?

He thought of the witch's baby in its humble cradle.

He closed his eyes and took deep breaths, and told himself he would not think on it, but he must have looked guilty as he handed the stick to Silver, for she smiled and said, "Think not on it. You have done no wrong. I promise you that much."

But what was her promise worth? She'd deceived him before.

And if he had done harm, what could he do to remedy it now? It was a necessary evil, was it not? Helping him find his kidnaped son.

Silver now looked at the stick and a mist formed all along its brown length. She stared intently at it and the mist swirled round and round it.

She handed it back to Will. The wood felt cold and trembled in his hand. "Go now," she said. "The stick will pull your feet onto the path. Only, do not forget to tell Quicksilver of my request."

Will nodded.

The twig pulled on him, pulled him out of the clearing.

As he walked away, he heard Silver call, "Will, wait."

He turned to look at her.

"The love I bear you," she said, "demands that I warn you. Your son might not look as you expect when you find him."

Will ignored the pull of the stick and held still, staring back at Silver.

How would Hamnet not look like himself? Was she warning him of those illusions which had been used against him these many years past, when he'd rescued his Nan?

By the power of elves, she'd been seemingly shifted onto fire and serpent and other things, but none of them meant much more than the illusions the witch had cast on Will some days ago.

"I understand illusions," he said calmly. "I will not be frighted."

The lady shook her head. Her intent eyes were full of inexpressible sadness. "It won't be an illusion." She took a deep breath. "Your son, Will, might be fully grown. A man. For the time in the castle at the heart of the crux, where doubtless your son is, passes a thousand times faster than time here. More than three years does every day count, and most of a day have we already passed."

Most of a day. Hamnet had been eleven. Will tried to imagine Hamnet at fourteen.

The twig in his hand pulled him impatiently toward a path he couldn't see, but that would lead him, insensibly, toward a magical castle where his son was held captive.

Would his son recognize him? Who had been looking after Hamnet this while? What creature, in this land of dread magic, had served in place of Will in his duty of raising Hamnet? Or had Hamnet, alone in the dread castle, spent his days in solitude?

And how would Hamnet receive his father?

Scene 23

ᘉ

Night is falling over the crux—a strange night that descends in dark blue tendrils, blown about by a lilac-scented wind. In the forest, beside a path, Miranda and Proteus stop and she sits on a large rock.

Miranda felt tired. Cold crept from her feet to her limbs as though the cold magic of the crux were overtaking her from the soles up. She looked at Proteus, who bustled about making fire.

What did he think, and why did he seem so deeply immersed in his thoughts that he was not aware of her?

As a night such as she'd never seen descended from the sky like the fingers of an evil giant, she thought of her father.

Not of her elf father, whom she'd never known and who—Proteus still said—had been a just and fair gentleman. Much as Miranda wished to believe Proteus's opinion of the late King of Fairyland, it was of her adopted father she thought—nay, her real father—the immortal Hunter.

For how much more real could a father be than one who'd raised her with love, though she was no kin of his?

When he'd come home to his castle and not found her, what had he thought? What had he thought of his errant daughter? Oh, how could she have returned such loving care with such disobedience?

And where was Caliban, whom she'd transported to this place? Where were the centaurs, Proteus's companions? Had they also been transported? And if so, where were they? In the castle with the boy? Or had their nature, not as innocent as the human boy's, prevented their access to it?

She looked up at the blue sky, remembering what Proteus had said about only three nights in the crux making one unable to ever leave it, and she trembled.

Proteus's strong arms surrounded her, Proteus's gentle embrace held her up. "Fair love, you faint with wandering in the woods," Proteus said. "We'll rest us, Miranda, if you think it good, and tarry for the comfort of the day."

Miranda started to shake her head but, faith, she could hardly keep her eyes open. And Proteus's arms around her felt warm, as though they restored some of the vital warmth that this evil land, this cold landscape, had stolen from her.

Oh, every fairy tale spoke of trials before one reached the castle where the captive pined. But Miranda had never imagined the trial to be just walking through a landscape where no mortal, no immortal, could ever find his way but by magic. Guiding Proteus and herself, both by magic, had consumed her remaining strength.

Of late, her ears, deceiving her, had given her sounds like hooves stepping cautiously through the undergrowth, the brush, the leaves and mulch on the forest ground—just out of sight. But the only hooved thing here would be centaurs, and those were Proteus's friends and would have shown themselves.

"Be it so, Proteus," she said and, leaning into him, yet attempted to push him away with her hand, as modesty required, as they stood. She stumbled over to a pile of leaves.

"Find you a bed." She attempted to droop onto the moss-and-leaves-covered ground at her feet. "For I, in this bank, will rest my head."

But Proteus prevented her from lying down, his arms around her as tightly as if their bodies were already conjoined in marital union. "One turf shall serve as a pillow for us both," he said. "One heart, one bed, two bosoms, and one troth."

Speaking thus, he set his warm lips on her cold ones and, with infinite tenderness, coaxed a kiss from her.

He felt so warm. She was so cold. And faith, his love was real. She could feel his tenderness for her in the way his lips traveled, pressing to her cheek, her neck, her shoulder—for which purpose he pulled away the lace and silk of her dress, and reached behind her to unhook the fastenings that held her dress closed.

They could lie together through the night, and in this strange land they could find comfort, their heads upon one patch of ground, their bodies entwined as their hearts already were.

For a moment, just a moment, between heartbeat and heartbeat, she leaned into his embrace and savored the touch of his warm lips upon her cold flesh.

Then she thought of the Hunter, the Hunter who was in rights and truth her father and who deserved, from her, obedience. The Hunter who must give consent for her marriage, her having no other relative living save Proteus— and that King of Fairyland that Proteus now said was innocent, but of whose good intentions she was by no means sure.

Quicksilver had hurt Proteus. Faith, hurt him beyond need.

Could she trust such a one? Could she ask him blessing? No. When they left the crux with the human boy, she would tell Proteus to take the throne and exile the cruel tyrant, Quicksilver. Send Quicksilver right away to where he could not hurt them.

Therefore, the Hunter remained the only one who could bless her union with Proteus. And the Hunter would know if Proteus and Miranda had taken their pleasure of each other before marriage.

He would know it with a look.

Already having stolen the magical book from her father, already having run from his judgment, Miranda didn't know how to face the look that would cloud his eyes if she also, without his consent, lay with her chosen partner.

Besides, she remembered how Proteus had attacked Quicksilver upon the beach. Some of her doubts about him awakened now. How could she trust herself to him without defense when he, but so short a while ago, had behaved as a violent stranger and attacked an unarmed man?

"Nay, good Proteus," she said, and feebly pushed him away. "For my sake, my dear, lie further off yet, do not lie so near."

But Proteus, who had unhooked the top of her dress, now cupped her small breast in his eager, warm hand. "Oh, take the sense, sweet, of my innocence. Love takes the meaning in love's conference. I mean that my heart unto yours is knit, so that but one heart we can make of it." Fervently, he kissed her neck, her hair. "Two bosoms interchained with an oath, so, then, two bosoms and a single troth. Then by your side, no bedroom me deny, for, lying so, Miranda, I do not lie."

The cascade of his words woke Miranda. In this strange land, her beliefs, her opinions, her certainties had been so challenged that now she suspected everything and, knowing her suspicions baseless and, ashamed of them, yet she could not help suspecting.

Opening her eyes fully, she pushed harder at Proteus, who stepped back, surprised. His face, she thought, betrayed no eagerness for lovemaking. *That* she could have understood.

But this, his narrowed eyes, his mouth set determinately, all of them spoke of planning—plotting?

Plotting of what and against whom, and what part could lovemaking have in such schemes?

Oh, she would go mad. She was already mad for even thinking of this. For what could Proteus be plotting that involved her favors?

She forced a smile onto a face that wanted to strain in aching disbelief. "Proteus riddles very prettily. Now so much beshrew my manners and my pride, if Miranda meant to say Proteus lied." She grinned at him, trying to make herself look impish, innocent.

His eyes remained narrowed.

She put her hand on his chest, pushing him gently away. "But, gentle friend, for love and courtesy, lie further off; in elven modesty, such separation as, may well be said, becomes a virtuous bachelor and a maid: so far be distant and good night, sweet friend. Thy love never alter, till thy sweet life end." As she spoke, she reached behind her and hooked her dress closed again.

Proteus shook his head. He straightened himself, like a man who shakes off unworthy thoughts. He pulled at his doublet and ran his hand back over his disarrayed hair. A smile, though small and hesitant, painted itself upon his lips. "Amen," he said. "Amen to that fair prayer say I. And then, end life when end loyalty."

He stepped away from her to a moss patch beneath a stately oak. "Here is my bed." He extended his hand toward her, a gesture like a blessing. "Sleep give you all rest."

Miranda let herself down onto her own patch of moss and leaves. It felt cushiony and warm beneath her. "With half that wish, the wisher's eyes be pressed."

She could barely finish the sentence, as tiredness pushed her to sleep.

She hadn't eaten since leaving her home, and she could not remember feeling this tired.

This sleep, this prostration, had come over her this last half-hour's walk through the forest.

Before that, she'd been herself, but of a sudden, she could think on nothing but sleep, and it seemed to her that her tiredness circled her head like a bird of prey, waiting only for her to lie down, so it could descend upon her.

It felt, she thought, as when she'd been very young and some sickness kept her awake and crying through the night.

Then had the Hunter, out of paternal concern, used a sleeping spell on her little head, till she drooped, of sudden, with tiredness and, laying her head upon her small bed, presently slept the sickness away.

A sleep spell. This felt like a sleep spell.

Frightening herself with her thought, Miranda opened her eyes, scaring sleep away.

Overhead the sky was dark blue rayed through with lighter blue, the whole swirling around like water in a whirlpool.

She stared at it, and wished for stars, for the familiar stars of her home where something would show her the way. But this was a land of mysteries, and she was blind.

Who would put a spell on her?

She sat up. Proteus, lying on his moss patch, looked sound asleep and as innocent as a newborn babe.

Oh, she was mad, she was unworthy, to suspect her love as she did.

This was just her tiredness and her hunger combined, knitting her brain in a monstrous knot even as her body craved sleep. She forced herself to lie down on the moss and leaves and determinedly closed her eyes.

But though tiredness wrapped itself around her like a blanket, it seemed to her that, beyond the nearest trees, hooves clopped and someone whispered.

And if not a sleep spell, then what Miranda felt was very strange—to feel so like sleeping, while one's mind seethed.

If she slept . . .

If she slept, by virtue of a sleep spell, what might the spell caster not do during her rest?

She must go and look. She had to find out what hid there, or she'd not sleep tonight.

Scene 24

❧

The true path, where Will walks. He holds the stick the lady gave him in his hand and it pulls him impatiently, like a child pulling an adult by the hand. Night closes in on all sides, and he is tired. He looks longingly toward piles of moss and leaves.

Will felt as though he could not walk anymore. Each of his steps was dearly purchased in effort.

He took a step, and then he thought of Hamnet—alone, who knew alone for how long?—and he took another. Again he thought of Hamnet, and wondered if the lady was right. If she were right, who had been raising Hamnet these many years? He stepped forward again.

The path—a sandy way that meandered amid trees and beyond groves—felt hard beneath his feet. His weary muscles complained over the effort of every step.

Sometime ago his stomach, complaining of long neglect, had joined its laments to the rest of his body's woes.

Now and then it seemed to him he heard the sound of hooves in the woods, and now and again the sound of a voice complaining. He did not look. He did not tarry. Perhaps Marlowe's ghost pursued Will. Perhaps it had commandeered a pale ghost horse.

Or perhaps the Hunter . . .

Will closed his mind against any thought of the immortal justicer. He had reason enough to fear without thinking of new ones.

By a high mound of leaves, he felt as though he could walk no more, and stopping, he whispered to himself, "O, weary night. O, long and tedious night. Abate thy hours: shine comforts from the east, that I may get to the castle and free Hamnet. My legs can keep no pace with my intent. Here will I rest me, till the break of day. And sleep, that sometimes shuts up sorrow's eye, steal me a while from mine own company."

Putting the magic rod—which still strained to find the magic path and follow it—within his doublet, where it pulsed and pushed like a small child begging for a sweet, Will lay himself down upon the mossy ground, his head on a mound of leaves.

He closed his eyes, and for a moment, he was back at Stratford, with his wife, Nan. He sat at the broad kitchen table, and Nan had just put a bowl of soup in front of him. Across from him, Susannah and Judith sat, both miniatures of their mother, though Susannah already showed a woman's form—as yet a shy womanhood, as reticent and unsure of itself as Miranda's.

But there, at the broad, scrubbed kitchen table, in the small, rustic kitchen in the house at Henley street, sat Hamnet—a different Hamnet, grown and matured, looking much as Will liked to think Will had looked in his prime: with golden eyes and soft dark curls, and the first blossoming of a beard upon his chin.

Hamnet wore a bright blue velvet doublet and looked regal and full of confidence as his father had never felt yet.

Will looked at his son, and smiled, happy that Will had gone to London, and slaved away his days and wasted his nights away from Nan and the girls. He had made Hamnet a gentleman out of it, hadn't he? A gentleman who'd never need to be humble to any person.

But then, in the way of dreams, Will felt disturbed, and his heart misgave him that he had forgotten something or misapprehended something. Something was wrong. His plan for Hamnet had not worked as intended.

"Wish us joy," Hamnet said. "Wish us joy, Father."

He lifted his hand that held another's hand. Turning his head, Will beheld—sitting beside Hamnet on the long bench in the humble kitchen—the elf girl that he'd met in the crux earlier this day.

She was blond and slim and more beautiful than any human girl could ever be. She was a Princess of Fairyland.

Now, in Will's dream, Nan leaned over him, her warm body against his, and whispered in his ear, "I always knew it would be thus, ever since I nursed her. I always knew she'd be our daughter."

Marlowe's ghost stood, half leaning against the wall of the kitchen, near the hearth hung with shining pans. One of his legs was raised and half bent, his foot resting flat against the wall.

He crossed his arms on his chest, much the same way he'd been represented in his portrait, limned while he was at Cambridge.

But one of the eyes that gazed so ironically out of the portrait that hung in the buttery at Cambridge was now punctured and dripping gore.

And Marlowe was a ghost, dead for his Fairyland love.

Will looked on Hamnet, who held the elf princess's hand. Hamnet said again, "Wish us joy."

Will stood up. He yelled, "No."

Fairyland would not steal his son from him. Will would see his son successful and be able to be proud of Hamnet in the world of men. This was his son, and not Quicksilver's to steal.

Marlowe threw back his head and laughed a high, uncontrolled laughter like a drunk man.

"Stop," Will yelled. "Stop." He reached for the bowl of soup and threw it, over Hamnet's head, at the laughing ghost. "Stop."

But the laughter went on and on and on.

Will woke up, his heart beating fast, so fast it seemed about to crack his ribs and escape his chest.

The dream gone, Will found himself lying on the ground, atop moss and leaves. A leaf stuck to his face, where sweat from his dream had dripped.

But the laughter remained—high—coming from just past the nearest trees. There a light moved, trippingly, like a lantern carried by someone who was none too sober.

And a woman's voice screamed, high and faltering, "Help. Oh, help me."

Scene 25

✸

The campsite where Quicksilver and Caliban sit companionably on either side of the blazing fire and eat ill-cooked meat. Caliban sits with a bottle in his hand and three others at his feet.

Quicksilver eyed Caliban, while Caliban ate in fierce, growling bites, all the while making sounds as though he muttered to himself beneath the chewing.

Quicksilver picked desultorily at the slice of venison resting on a large leaf upon his knees.

The venison had cooked unevenly, in water that was really magic, as was the ocean of the crux—pure magic, under the aspect of water.

Quicksilver was thirsty but hesitated to ask the troll to drink from the one open bottle into which the creature had been slobbering.

And yet, who was Quicksilver to call any being a monster? What right had he, who'd been born double and was now single, to call less than an equal to anyone?

He looked across the fire at Caliban, and the troll grinned at him, showing his sharp fangs encrusted with bits of meat, most of it raw.

Quicksilver looked away and set aside the venison, upon which a spark of magic force seemed to run, sizzling upon the tongue, hot to the fingers.

Quicksilver wiped the tips of his fingers to the covering of his bed, which he'd wrapped around himself like an uneven toga. He cleared his throat, looking at the troll. "You're from the northern mountains, then?"

For a while it looked as though Caliban wouldn't answer, but then he growled once, twice. He held his dinner by the bone that ran through the piece of meat, and with each of his bites, he scraped the meat off and cut two swaths into the bone beneath.

He swallowed with another growl, then looked sideways at Quicksilver. "I was born in the mountains, but I didn't stay there long enough to know them. The Hunter, the creature of the night who takes those who break the ancient laws, came to my den and took me away, while I was no more than a cub."

Caliban looked away from Quicksilver and into the distance. For a moment his dark eyes softened, acquired an almost human expression. Quicksilver would swear they had filled with tears that caused them to shine in the firelight.

Did trolls cry?

"I remember my dam," Caliban said, and a catch of tears seemed to stop his voice from coming out fully. It caught upon itself in the creature's throat, seeming to thin as it squeezed past a lump of emotion. "She was a brave one, standing up to the Lord of the Night, and growling at him, and yelling that I was but a cub, a little one, and didn't deserve damnation."

Caliban blinked, and fat tears fell down his muzzle, water rolling over the orange fur before seeping slowly into it. "Faith, I remember her well, her moist tongue, her long fur. I was her favorite from the litter, and she gave me the tit first. She tried to keep me. She tried. But the Lord of the Night said he wasn't taking me for my crimes, but for his needs. He said he needed a servant and playmate for his daughter, and he'd return me to my tribe and my clan, my den and my mother, when his need was past."

Caliban looked down at the gnawed-clean bone in his hand and gave a growl, low upon his throat. He flung the bone violently into the fire, raising a shower of sparks. "That was almost fourteen years ago, and sometimes I wonder how my mother and my clan fare in the northern mountains."

Quicksilver wondered also. So many clans of trolls had fought beside Vargmar, so many been decimated root and branch, the caves they inhabited blocked with trunks and leaves and set on fire—every creature, mother and father, adult and warrior, cub and babe alike, dead.

Thinking on it now, on that ruthless strategy, Quicksilver wondered how he'd found the heart to do it. Though, faith, his heart had little to do with it. The elves had not fought with their heart but with their brain—with cunning and decision and strategy. With tradition and knowledge and duty.

Quicksilver had fulfilled his dynastic duty. He'd fought the ancient enemies, just as the other Kings of Elvenland had—Quicksilver's father, Oberon, and before him, Oberon's father.

Caliban took another sip from the bottle. He watched Quicksilver through narrowed eyes, as though knowing what scenes passed behind Quicksilver's tired gaze, as though he knew that he might not have a clan to return to and that the guilt for their destruction would rest on Quicksilver's shoulders.

Quicksilver looked away, feeling remorse for actions that he'd never before even questioned. He felt his throat close from thirst, thirst and hunger together—the hunger he could not slake, not on this venison that was more rare than cooked and cooked more by magic than by fire. He could not stomach it.

As for thirst . . .

From everywhere, nearby, came the sound of running water, the sound of water dripping. But it was an illusory sound.

Quicksilver remembered the pond where he'd met the lady Silver, remembered the feel of it. That was not water, but living, liquid magic. A drink of it and, force, he'd burn alive.

He cleared his throat again. "Kind Caliban," he said, "may I have a drink?"

Caliban looked surprised, and well he might, since the wine was, by rights, Quicksilver's, by him transported from the palace in Fairyland.

To his credit, he made no protest, but smiled, showing his overgrown canine fangs, as he passed the bottle to the King of Fairyland.

Quicksilver took a deep draught and told himself that he only imagined the slightly foul taste in the wine.

He tried not to think of the creature's lips touching the bottle neck.

The wine was wet and—faith—wet was all Quicksilver required now.

He wondered if even now this wine would be flowing freely in Fairyland, to commemorate the victory he'd obtained.

What would Malachite, what would fair Ariel, think of Quicksilver's disappearance? How long had he been gone?

He stared into the fire and saw in it patterns and shapes of monstrous import—armies in battle, creatures meeting each other in a field where neither love nor reason mattered, and only duty counted. Each one's duty, differently arrayed, called in an opposite direction till only one race, one point of view, emerged victorious—the other, perforce, dead.

"And you?" Caliban asked. "Who are you, oh King? Why came you here?"

Quicksilver opened his hands. He couldn't—nor did he wish to—tell the troll about Will and Will's child, and Quicksilver's feelings for Will and Will's suspicions of Quicksilver. "I am the uncle of your mistress," he said.

The troll smiled. "Ah, you're Proteus's enemy."

Quicksilver inclined his head. "You could say as much."

"Oh, how I crave vengeance on Proteus," Caliban said. "He has magicked my mistress with a magic more potent than any philter. He's made her fall in love with his false ways and her innocent maiden heart has he deceived with tales strange and wondrous." He paused. "He's made her believe you are *her* enemy."

"And you believe it not?" Quicksilver asked, wondering what the monster would say if he knew Quicksilver's inner thoughts and Quicksilver's sins and how long Quicksilver had fought against his trollish kin.

Caliban shook his great, matted head. "Proteus is too smooth, his tongue too glib. He loves not my mistress, nor could he, for all his heart is taken up with himself. He is too smooth and gentle to be true, and he knows those manners of men and elves that I cannot muster—but lord, we trolls have some memory from our species, and some things we know without being told. With that memory, thus older than myself, I know when an elf is true and when he's not. This elf is not."

Something vibrated in Caliban's voice—a hint of tears, a touch of affronted feelings. Of a sudden, Quicksilver saw it, and his eyes widened in shock.

Caliban loved Miranda. The troll, with his inhuman looks, his glimmering fangs, loved delicate Miranda, highborn princess, the daughter of the late King of Fairyland.

Oh, what a wondrous thing this was, for did not each creature love after his own kind?

To trolls was not troll fur and a gentle, moist canine tongue more important than the fine features, the long hair of humans or elves?

And yet, Quicksilver was sure of it, sure he heard the tremolo of love in the creature's harsh voice.

Caliban might possess the memories of his ancestors in some things. He might have the sense and feel of how the world worked. He might not trust all he heard and all he saw and he might know truth beyond the reach of his young eyes.

Yet he remained an innocent, a tender young fool.

Caliban didn't know troll females. Coming of age beside fair Miranda, he'd made her the pattern and plate of his affection until his love had slipped from the adoration of playmate, almost brother, to something quite different.

Quicksilver wondered if Caliban knew it.

He stared at Caliban and felt moisture come to his own eyes, moisture he could scarcely spare. For here had nature arranged a snarl, where elf loved human and troll loved elf, and none of them, neither elf nor troll—nor perhaps human—had the least chance of fulfilling their desire or gaining their happiness.

Quicksilver finished his bottle and his body slipped down to curl on the ground. He fell asleep upon moss and leaves, wrapped in his bed cover.

In the moment between sleep and wakening he heard the tinkling of glass, the beast's footsteps upon the leafy ground, and he knew the troll had besought himself some privacy for crying—carrying his bottles of wine with him.

He knew then that Caliban was aware of being in love with Miranda, and that Caliban knew his dreams would never come true.

Scene 26

❦

Miranda, lying on the ground, with Proteus a few steps from her. Moving no more than necessary, she lifts her hand. Someone watching from above would see little sparks of magic flying from her fingers toward Proteus's head. But no one is watching. Proteus's eyes are closed, either in sleep or a good imitation of it.

Lying on the cold ground, on a pile of leaves and moss, Miranda thought about the spells her father had used to put her to sleep when she was very little.

Leaves poked through her dress and something that might be an insect squirmed beneath her. Miranda ignored such things, recalled those spells.

How could one cast the like spell? Miranda didn't remember the words her father had said, but it seemed to her that spells were about feeling. The words simply anchored the magic, but the magic itself, wild and unfettered, streamed across the magical being's mind and imposed itself on reality—aided by the words, but never tied to them.

And Miranda's father had once told her that her magic was such that she'd soon outgrow the crutch of words.

She should not need the words.

Miranda lifted her hand and bethought her on the feel of the spell and, her hand raised, wished magic to go and close Proteus's eyes and put him to sleep, a sleep as sound as that which had been wished upon her.

Had Proteus wished it? Or someone else?

She did not know, nor, she thought, should she care.

If Proteus had sought to put her to sleep, then she would see what he'd tried to hide from her.

And if Proteus was innocent, and someone else, some creature—her uncle, perhaps—had wished her to sleep, then perhaps, perhaps, this creature threatened them both. Perhaps she would save Proteus's life.

Again, fantasies of being the heroine of the hill, as well as the queen and Proteus's wife, beguiled Miranda into sweet dreaming.

She cut them short, for such imagination was but a lullaby leading to sleep and oblivion while—what treason went on beyond her sleeping eyes?

She thought on the spell and with all her might wished magic to fly from her fingers to Proteus.

The tingle of magic ran burning down her arm and sparkled from her fingers.

Opening one eye, she caught the last reflection of magical light shining upon Proteus's bright hair.

With her eye still open, she spied her lover. Was he asleep? Truly asleep?

Or had he expected this spell and, perhaps, in the manner of elves more experienced in the world, protected himself?

She spied with her one open eye, and she didn't see Proteus move.

Rather it seemed to her as though he relaxed further into his leafy bed, as though the breath coming between his lips were more even, the rise and fall of his chest more spaced.

She took a deep breath. Either Proteus was asleep, or so dissembling that his heart had rotted even as his exterior remained fair and dazzling.

She would now get up and, if he were asleep, then let him go on sleeping. And if he were not asleep—if he were a traitor—she was ready for him and curse her breaking heart.

She stood up. He moved not.

He is asleep, she thought, and smiled to herself. Faith, he was innocent of plotting and dark deeds, and everything she'd suspected for the last few hours.

Her suspicions were mad, his love steady.

She would now go and see what threatened them both and plotted against their happiness.

She indulged in a look at her sleeping love. How beautiful he looked, his lips set in an almost smile, his golden hair framing his oval face. Let him sleep. Oh, let him sleep and dream only of her.

Standing up, she shook the leaves from her dress and tiptoed in the direction of the swaying light, from which also came the sound of hooves, the sound of voices.

She glimpsed through the trees the shapes of men on horseback and blinked. Something was odd. The men sat too far forward. She shook her head. Oh, these were not men on horseback, but centaurs.

These were Proteus's companions, Hylas, Chiron, and Eurytion. The one with the body of a black stallion, and the one with the dappled black and white body, and the brown one.

All three looked tired and a little angry as they stood in the clearing, talking in loud, brisk voices.

Though their accent put an odd sound in it, they spoke the common language of elves of Avalon, close enough to the English of humans that it could be understood by humans and elves alike. The two races, living side by side, had likewise learned each other's speech, each other's ways.

Hylas, the dark one, glanced at the trees behind which Miranda stood. But his gaze rested not on her. "He comes not. The traitorous dog comes not."

The traitorous dog . . . Did they mean Quicksilver? Why would Quicksilver be meeting the centaurs? Were not the centaurs Proteus's allies?

Her heart sped up. She caught her breath in a pitch of panic, trying to subdue it but feeling it rise within her against her best efforts.

Did this mean that the centaurs, Proteus's supposed allies, actually served Quicksilver? Oh, had Proteus been double-crossed all along, been led in a fool's paradise, knowing it not?

Catching her breath, subduing her impatience, she watched as the brown-bodied centaur danced impatiently, his hooves pounding on the ground, his broad, golden features set in impatience. Clutching his large hands into fists, he waved them midair. "Curse the cur. He told us he would be here to finalize the plan. Is he then so weak livered?"

The dappled one snorted. He had a smaller face than the others and looked more delicate. His arms and chest were not so massive, and black hair covered his human chest more sparsely as though he were younger. A young centaur just past adolescence. "Weak livered as he's ever been, shirking battle, ever looking to evade that most fearful of contests in which death is meted," he said. "But I didn't know him an outright coward."

The black one held an oil lantern in his other hand at the end of a stick. He lifted it high as if its light would reveal someone hiding in the under-growth and snorted. "If he were not a coward, why would he have invented this whole plot? A coward's plot it is and a foolish one at that. Only a coward who knows he has no rights to what he holds and what he craves would squander his opportunities thus."

A coward who had no rights to what he held. Oh. They *were* talking about Quicksilver then, that unworthy King of Fairyland who'd stolen the throne from his brother, Miranda's true father.

The other version, what the mortal had told her, must be a delusion or an outright lie.

Or else, nothing made sense.

She thought on the mortal, the way he looked, with sparse hair and sun burnt skin. No.

It was all clear. The story the mortal told was a lie. For someone ugly as that must have, in his heart, some dark crime, some twisted vice. Lying would come easily to him.

Which still didn't explain, she thought uncomfortably, how beautiful her uncle looked, if he were a villain.

But then, perhaps that beauty was an illusion. In many stories, did not the villain—ill-favored witch or ungainly mage—buy with his soul the power to make himself appear lissome and attractive?

Yes, that had to be it.

Quicksilver, the traitor, the criminal, must have purchased a lie for his appearance.

She wondered what that must have cost while another being, no more than a shadow, lumbered into the clearing. As the creature stopped and stared, dumbfounded, at the centaurs, the centaur with the lantern turned, throwing light on the intruder, and Miranda saw a stooped creature, covered in reddish fur, his features a mix of the human and the canine.

She stifled a scream. Caliban. So, he had indeed come to the island, as had Proteus's companions.

But why was he here? What was he doing here alone in the middle of the night? And why did he carry, in his many-fingered hands, three dark, glistening bottles of the type used to store wine?

Caliban stopped, looking at the centaurs as though surprised at seeing them.

The centaurs, in turn, seemed shocked, almost frightened. The brown one cantered nervously about. "What's the matter?" he said. "Have we devils here? Do you put tricks upon's with savages and men of Inde, ha? I have not scaped the weird whirlwind to be afraid now of this creature. As proper a man as ever went on four legs cannot make him give ground: and it shall be said so again, while Chiron breathes at nostrils."

Caliban looked scared. "Pray," he said. "Pray, do not torment me, for I've done nothing." Visibly scared by the huge half-horse beings, he stepped back, step by step, as though trying to efface himself.

The dappled one laughed, a high, nervous laughter. "This is some monster of this isle, with two legs yet not an elf nor a human, who hath got, as I take it, an ague. Where the devil should he learn our language? I will give him some relief, if but for that. If I can recover him and keep him and get back to New Thessalony with him, he's a present for any emperor that ever trod on horseshoe."

But the black one scowled. "He's a troll, you fools. I'd have thought you saw enough of them in the damned war. He's the girl's troll. The elf girl Proteus craves."

"Ah, the girl," said the dappled one. "As fine a piece of elf body as ever crossed my path, and I had my way she would cross more than path."

"Yet, what have we here?" the black centaur said. "Why should a troll carry bottles? For trolls neither make wine nor consume it." He bent at an awkward angle and reached down for one of the bottles that Caliban held. "Give us the loot you've stolen, beast."

With a whimper, Caliban let the bottle be pulled away. His eyes were wide, his mouth foamy. He looked as though he'd like to cower into himself.

The dark centaur, Hylas, held the bottle to the lantern and whooped. "Liquor. Fine liquor, by Zeus."

He cackled, a high cackle, as he galloped to a tree and broke the bottle's neck upon the trunk. "Elf liquor," he said, tasting it. "Such as no mortal could make. Why, it is distilled moonbeams and wild summer nights and the girls, with their tresses undone, under August moon."

His poetry went unheeded. Already, the other centaurs were getting wine bottles from Caliban who, terrified, tried to run out of the clearing.

But he could not run, because a visibly inebriated Hylas—though Hylas had only just tasted the wine—galloped in circles around him, cutting his escape.

Hylas looked quite changed. His handsome dark features seemed coarser. His nostrils flared and his eyes flashed. A smell of human sweat, and horse sweat, mingled, rolled off him, filling the clearing.

His dark, Greek-dreaming eyes ignited with something animal, something uncontrollable. He flared his nostrils and blew through them, like a horse that smells the hay, and galloped around Caliban, and laughed. "I smell your terror, troll," he said. "I smell your fear. Trolls are ever cowardly when alone, and only great bands of them dare to attack what crosses their path. But alone, they run from a cat and pay obeyance to a dog. Indeed, they're like rats in that way."

The brown one and the dappled one had broken the necks of their bottles, and were drinking them now. "Leave him alone, Hylas," the brown one said. He grinned at Caliban. "That's a brave god, and he bears celestial liquor. I will kneel to him." And thus speaking, he joined action to words and went down on his front knees before Caliban, who shrieked in fright.

The black one laughed and reached for Caliban, and held him aloft, his hands under Caliban's arms. "He's but a small one. Still a cub. Tender, sure. In the days of yore did our fathers roast just such who lived in the caves of the isles. We've not eaten for a day and every creature in this cursed isle is damned with magic. I say we make him our dinner."

Caliban shrieked again. His legs kicked maniacally but hit nothing. The centaurs laughed. Caliban's eyes rolled into his head, and he foamed at the mouth over his great canines, his huge fangs that bit at the air *in* his fury. "I wish me," he said. "I wish I'd never left my mother's cave. Curse the Hunter that took me so from my litter mates and from my mother with her warm fur and her soft tongue and her bountiful tit."

Miranda, her heart beating with terror, her breath coming in short gasps, looked about her for a weapon.

These were Proteus's allies, were they not? How then could they be such savages?

But then, had they not planned to sell Proteus to the cursed, unrighteous King of Fairyland?

And if they had, what did it mean? How could Proteus be so foolish that he knew not with whom he dealt?

But then, had centaurs not always been dual? Had they not, at their start, been gentle creatures who lived among men? And yet alcohol turned them to raging animals. When their kind got drunk at the marriage of Pirithous and Hippodamia, had they not, tasting human wine for the first time, become violent and brutal and tried to violate the bride at her own feast?

And had that not led to the war between centaur and Lapithae, which almost extinguished both races?

It was so, for Miranda's father had taught her so, as he had taught her that some of the remnants of the centaurs' decimated population had then immigrated to the South of Avalon and there become a permanent focus of rebellion, a permanent thorn on the side of the sovereign of Fairyland.

And the Hunter did not lie.

"I say we skin him with my hunting knife," the brown Chiron said. Speaking, he pulled a long knife from his belt, while his friend held Caliban, Caliban's arms back and held together, Caliban's fierce horned toes kicking at the air, Caliban's canines ineffectively snapping at nothing.

They might be joking. A coarse joke.

But they'd tasted wine.

Miranda dared not risk it. She pulled at the branch of a tree and broke it and, as the centaurs turned toward the sound, leapt into the clearing, screaming, "He is my servant. How dare you offend him?"

"Oh, better prey is afoot," Hylas screamed, and dropped Caliban, then leapt over the moaning, prostrate troll toward Miranda. "Better prey. I smell her, her hot female smell."

The other centaurs hooted.

They surrounded Miranda. A pair of indelicate hands reached for her shoulders, more daring ones touched her breasts.

She lay about her with her stick, blindly hitting this one's knees, the other one's elbow.

She saw Caliban scurry away into the forest while the Centaurs yelped in pain from her blows and remained confused at her sudden attack.

She ran. She ran away into the forest, the sound of hooves fast upon her steps.

Even running she knew that they would catch her, for they ran like horses, faster than any elf.

"Help, oh, help me," she screamed, hoping in vain that someone would hear and respond. But who could help her? Her father was in another world and knew not where she was. In this strange world, this island in a sea of magic, she had only a mortal whom she did not trust, a treacherous king who probably sought her death, and Proteus, upon whom she had laid a sleep charm. Would he wake at her voice? She feared not.

The centaurs neared and she could feel the hands of the foremost one upon her shoulders. She tried to pull away, she struggled, but the centaur was stronger than her and lifted her, as though she were a rag doll. He laughed at her distress.

"Oh, help me," she screamed, but feared no one would.

Scene 27

⤫

Will, sitting up. The stick, struggling beneath his shirt, looks like an additional, impatient heart. He sits up in the dark, swirling night of the crux, and sees a lantern moving beyond the trees, and hears a woman scream.

Will thought it was Silver who screamed. The voice had Silver's timbre, Silver's tones.

His first impulse was to think that Silver had caused a distraction to scare him, to tempt him into coming to her.

But he thought of the lady as she'd been—nude, scared, afraid of her own shadow, afraid of a death that her almost-immortal mind could not understand but of which her halving felt like a prologue.

She could have had him back in that clearing. All it needed was a little more crying, a little more show of helpless grief, and Will would have been hers, faith, hers as he'd ever been.

But she'd not done it, and even as their lips touched, even as he'd tasted her intoxicating mouth of sweet wine, she'd stayed well apart from him—a sister, or a sweet friend from the days of childhood.

He'd wanted her, wanted her with an aching, physical desire, and any encouragement on her part would have given *him* to *her*.

But she'd not encouraged.

And there, Will thought, sitting in the clearing, rubbing sleep from his foggy eyes, there was the rub, for perhaps the lady no longer wanted Will— Will with his receding hairline, his tired eyes.

But then, why was she screaming?

"Oh, help me," the lady's voice echoed.

Will stumbled to his feet and brushed away leaves that had stuck to his face and hair. He must look like a demon from the woods, he thought as, sleep-befuddled, he stumbled toward the light.

There was a woman. He could see that in the light of the swaying lantern held by a creature that was half horse, half man.

Half horse, half man. Three of them. Centaurs. Three centaurs and one woman, and one of the centaurs held the woman with his powerful arms, while the other tore her green dress, exposing her soft body.

But the woman was no woman. Scarcely a woman. A girl at the edge of womanhood, the same age as Will's Susannah at home.

Small breasts, narrow hips, innocent eyes, and fragile shoulders.

Miranda, the Princess of Fairyland, Will thought. This was the girl who'd run from him when he'd tried to tell her the truth about her father.

And now she faced much worse prospects than the truth.

For the centaur who'd torn her dress off was feeling her white body with large, careless hands—huge hands, larger than any human's, than any elf's hands, and so unfeeling that they left red marks on her soft skin wherever they touched.

To Will's brain it was as though they were offering violence to his own daughter.

Madness overtook him, madness and that desperation of a righteous man facing evil he can't understand.

"Spawn of a forgotten monster," he said, stepping from between the trees. "Let the girl go."

His anger spoke through his voice, his anger filled his voice with power. Magic. He'd forgotten that here he had magical power and was too irate to stop himself from using it.

The very air crackled with magic, like the living air before a storm. He felt magical power, generated within his mind, crackle between him and his enemies.

Magical power hit the centaurs like a wave. They recoiled from the force that slammed them, and they stepped all out of order and almost fell.

They stepped back and put up magical shields.

Will could feel their shields go up, he could feel their power blocking his power.

Oh, but their power was no match for his *anger*. And they were drunk. He could smell it in their breath and in their presence, a revolting smell of liquor mingled with the stink of horse sweat and horse hair.

"Back," he said, and threw all the power of his anger into the word. "Back, you dark stallions of the night, you nightmares who gallop in flesh and blood through a maiden's fears."

Each of his words seemed to push them back, each of his words seemed to impel them further away, toward the fringe of trees and the darkness beyond.

The black one, who held the lantern, screamed, "How can you have such power, you who are mere mortal?"

How could he? Was he still a mere mortal? Where was the line, invisibly drawn, in the scales of the universe, the measure of the crux? At what point would he cease being Will, a mortal playwright, earning his living in London through the honest labor of his ink-stained hands? When would magic cling to him like a plague, cutting him off from the world of mortals and the heaven he could hope for hereafter?

At another time he would have panicked, but now it didn't matter.

The girl, dropped by the centaurs, stood where they had dropped her, pale and scared looking, the marks of their hands still standing out too vividly upon her smooth skin.

"Back, vermin, back, and never bring your coarse desires near this maiden more. Go away."

At his words, the centaurs went, dropping all pretense of civilized retreat and stumbling one over the other as they galloped into the forest.

Will was left alone with the elf maiden.

He looked at her and marked her chalk-white face, her wide-open, unseeing eyes, her hands slowly covering her small breasts.

"Lady," he said. "Lady, are you well?"

She shook her head, looking bewildered. In that movement was more than Will wanted to know, more than Will wanted to think about.

For despite her narrow waist and her high breasts and her beauty such that it could break the human heart, this elf girl was just that—a girl, a child, a little one lost and far away from her home.

The violence had taken her by surprise, shocked her as violence can shock only those whose life has been protected and coddled from birth.

"They are all gone," Will said, in the same voice in which he used to reassure Hamnet after Hamnet's episodic nightmares. "They are all gone. You are safe, lady."

His hands, as gentle as his voice, pulled up her ripped dress, careful to touch only the fabric not the soft flesh beneath.

Holding her dress up in front of her, he willed it knit again in a single piece as though it had never been split.

"You are safe, lady."

Now she turned to him wide, scared eyes, more scared than they'd been when the centaurs had her in their rude grip.

She opened her eyes wide and fixed, and a small wrinkle of incomprehension divided her forehead. "Safe?" She asked. "But safe how, when it is all a lie?"

"A lie?" Will asked.

She nodded. "A lie. Every word, every legend has been a lie. Fair is not good, and foul is not evil. I am lost in a world with no clear signs, and I know not which way to turn."

Faint moonlight-silvery tears chased down her pale face. She looked more like a child than ever.

Oh, what mattered if she were elven or human? She was a child and Will would protect her.

Scene 28

❦

The same clearing. Miranda looks at Will, bewildered.

Miranda read in the mortal's face—in his blank eyes, his half frown—that he understood her not at all.

How could he not? Knew he not the legends, where the good were always beautiful?

She looked at the mortal with his wrinkled, ugly face. Why didn't he *understand* her?

He was good. He'd been good to her and rescued her from the foul centaurs. He'd done this by using magic despite his terror at the very thought of being magical—that terror she'd first seen on his face at the beach.

Why had he done it, but for love of her?

And why for love of her when she'd so cruelly turned her back on him when he'd tried to get her to help him—and had manipulated him with magic, too, and made him tell her that which he didn't wish to say.

Therefore, the mortal was good and—look at him—his wrinkling skin, his faded curls, already receding from the broad forehead. Look at his stature, so much smaller, less imposing than either Proteus or Quicksilver. Look at his shoulders, half folded in upon themselves.

How could he be good?

Were this a story, his looks alone would make him the villain. Yet, he was kind and good. Why were stories written if they lied so?

How could Miranda, who'd been raised in solitude and knew naught of the world but through stories and legends, know what to do, what to think?

"Beshrew the stories I heard," Miranda said. "Beshrew my soul and my heart, for I know not what to think."

"What do you mean?" the mortal asked. He looked solicitous, concerned. His expression reminded Miranda of the Hunter when he bent anxiously over her, worrying about a skinned knee, a childhood tear.

Shocking. Strange. How could this weak mortal resemble the eternal Hunter?

Yet it was true. She saw in the man's gentle eye, in his softened features, the look of her adopted father. His gaze had the same kindness and concern.

And how could she doubt the one thing she'd always known for love?

Feeling tears wet her face, the pressure of her confusion and her anger wearing away at her composure, Miranda tried to act as a princess should. "How I may thank you for my rescue?"

Will hesitated. "You may tell me you wish me to call you, milady."

Miranda sniffled, dangerously close to losing all her poise. "Miranda."

And that was as far as her composure held. Looking on him, seeing his expression of mingled pity and affection, she threw herself in the mortal's arms. Unlike the Hunter, he smelled warm and dusty, of leaves and decayed moss, where her nose pressed against his doublet.

He hesitated too. It was moments before he embraced her.

But his arms were comforting as they surrounded her, and his hand soft as it patted her hair. And his voice, though nothing like the thunderous sounds of the immortal Hunter, echoed with the same reassurance. "There, lady, there," he said. "There, fair Miranda. Nothing for you to lament. They are gone and your virtue is saved. Cry no more."

Only then did Miranda realize that she was sobbing, small, afflicted sobs. Her flood of tears soaked through Will's jacket.

Why was she crying? What foolishness was this? Had the mortal not rescued her, then there would have been reason enough to cry. But now, why did tears fall, hot, down her cheeks?

Oh, stop, foolish tears, she thought. She dried her face with the back of her hand, and smiling up at Will through her tears, she stepped out of his embrace and put her hands on his shoulders.

She'd been walking alone through this dreadful land of shadow and deception. Oh, not alone, for she had Proteus. But even Proteus seemed to have become shifting and deceiving. She'd been alone a day and a half in the crux, knowing not whom to trust nor whence to expect kindness or sudden violence.

Like a ship, rudderless in a storm, she'd been buffeted and swayed by inconstant winds.

Now, in this mortal she had finally found an anchor. In his unassuming being, reflected, she saw the love and kindness of the Hunter—her father, her protector.

Therefore, why should she cry? Why did her tears, like a river bursting a dam that long has held it at bay, flow unstoppable down her shamed face?

If she could trust the mortal—and she had to believe she could—then mayhap this tangled knot could yet be undone.

"Tell me, mortal," she said. "Tell me true—is my uncle, truly, the rightful King of Fairyland? And did my father commit such dark crimes as you claimed?

"Or did your partiality for my uncle lead you to paint him in rosier tints than truth deserved?"

The mortal's ruddy face became redder—a dark blush peeking at his cheeks. "I have no partiality for your uncle, lady," he said. "Rather I owe him having thrown into my life, many times, such grief as other men know not. He claims to love me, or at least half of him claims to love me." Will looked up at the dark sky of the crux, now swirling in lighter rays of blue as morning approached. "But his love is a curse, without which I'd never have known this desolate place and I would not now be in fear for my son.

"Had his love not, again and again, pulled me from my ordered existence, would I, like other mortal men, be blissfully unaware of this shadow kingdom that twines our land and makes all men dance to tunes most can't hear." He shook his head. "Say not I love your uncle. Did you not see us fighting on the beach?"

Miranda nodded, remembering. But the memory seemed odd to her, because—she realized, thinking of it now—there had been more fear than hatred in the mortal's anger. And even now, speaking of that fighting, she thought that his brow furrowed and his eyes squinted as though the brawling memory brought him only pain.

She blinked as a further shocking understanding pierced the order of her education.

She understood of a sudden that creatures, even good and noble creatures as this mortal was, sometimes lied, not only to others but to themselves also, about their feelings, their deeds, and their memories.

For where Will's mouth blamed Quicksilver, his features spoke of diffident tenderness.

Oh, how could the stories not lie, if men lied to themselves in their thoughts?

What insane world was this for which she found herself so ill prepared?

Yet, she told herself, the facts about her birth father could not be so changed by the creature's affections as to be reversed. If her father had never been captured by the Hunter, then it would take more than hatred or love for the mortal to imagine it.

And of one thing Miranda was sure as she looked at those golden eyes. Will would never lie deliberately, and—even to himself—if he lied, it was unknowingly.

"Aye," she said, speaking slowly. "I saw you fight. But what you said of my father . . . the late King of Elvenland? Was that true? Was he so evil that the

Hunter seized him? And did you see it with your own eyes, or were you told about it?"

"Aye. Aye, I saw it, and he was so seized, as I live and breathe," the mortal said. He stepped back and looked scared.

Miranda swallowed. It was true then. And then, perforce, Proteus had lied. But she thought of Proteus's features and his gentle words, she thought of how she had loved him at first sight. Could her own heart be so wrong in flying to him on winged feelings?

Perhaps Proteus himself was deceived as she thought the mortal had been. Perhaps he knew few facts, and his father had lied to him.

Yet someone had tried to cast a sleep spell on her this very night. Either Proteus had cast it, or else, Proteus too had been under the same spell— which her spell had only reinforced.

She thought of the centaurs speaking of someone else, someone who was a coward.

"Would you call my uncle a coward?" Miranda asked Will.

Will looked startled. His eyes and mouth both opened wide at once. Then he closed his mouth and frowned. "No. Not ever. Rather hot-tempered and often led astray by that temper of his. But never a coward."

Then of whom did the centaurs speak? Who could have deceived both her and Proteus? If what Will said about Miranda's birth father was true—and how could she doubt his word on this?—then her uncle was brave and had never done aught wrong. He'd done only what he needed to do, defending his rights against all usurpers.

Would such a man resort to sleep spells and alliances with such vile creatures as those centaurs?

She thought not.

Who else was on the island, who might have commanded this evil? There was Caliban, poor Caliban, who couldn't keep even himself safe. And there were the centaurs—their evil an unreasoning one, born of drink, and therefore unsuited to plotting and strategy.

And there were Will and Quicksilver, herself and the child.

None among these could be a powerful and magical manipulator of old, setting Proteus's mind against his king, and laying sleep spells on Miranda.

Yet something or someone resided in the crux. That much was clear from the magical castle and from the way Miranda's transport spell had fallen apart into many branches when they'd landed here.

Another magical power reigned here.

The mortal, looking concerned, patted her shoulder. "Lady, I told you true, your father was a villain. But evil is seldom inherited. You need not concern yourself. You're not a villain."

"No," Miranda said. Such had never occurred to her. "And yet there's something more in this," she said. "I was wrong. The stories were wrong. At least they were wrong about mortals, who can be ugly and still be good and generous as you are," she said, smiling at him. It seemed to her that the creature flinched at her statement, but occupied with her own thoughts, pursuing the thread of her own reason, she ignored it.

Surely he knew he was ugly. The truth could never offend.

She took a deep breath. "But among elves, I still think the rule applies, that the beautiful must be virtuous. Else, why would all the stories insist on it? Why would all who tell stories make them lies? No. It must be that elven stories tell the truth as it is in Elvenland and that, therefore, both must have solid virtue and right between them."

The mortal opened his mouth, as though to speak, but she raised her hand, commanding silence.

"And since you say that my uncle is innocent and I know that my love must be, that means that someone else has been playing upon Proteus's mind and making him imagine what isn't so.

"Perhaps his father didn't really die, but brought us here and here keeps your son captive, and here plays with our thoughts like a child with marbles."

The mortal looked doubtful, and opened his mouth again, but then closed it. What meant he to say? And what did it matter? He was only a mortal. What could he truly understand of the affairs of elves?

"Be still," Miranda said. "For I must think through this. This is matter for elf, not for mortal. Give me leave to reason."

The mortal frowned at her words, then smiled, and his lips formed the word *children*.

She ignored him. There was a greater riddle that she must solve. But how?

She thought of her father. How would the Hunter solve this riddle?

In her mind, it seemed to Miranda she heard the Hunter encouraging her to practice the art of scrying—both the art of looking into the future for that which would almost surely happen and the art of looking far away with eyes not of the body.

From a very young age, Miranda had been able to scry, an ability the Hunter had taught her to cultivate, saying that such scrying, such reaching into the future, was a gift of the gods and not to be disdained.

To scry she'd need a pool of water, but those seemed abundant enough in the clearings around this strange forest.

"Come," she said to the mortal and, reaching for his sleeve, pulled him unceremoniously. "Come, we'll get to the bottom of this yet, and find the reason for all."

"But—" the human said.

"No. No. Mark what I do. We'll find the truth."

The human sighed, but walked after her obediently.

Following gurgling water, she came to a pond fed by a small fountain, and yet calm enough and reflective enough to see her face in the still surface.

She raised her hands and desired to see the interior of the castle.

The pool sparkled and shone beneath her hands and Miranda jumped back scared.

What she'd believed was water was truly magic. Liquid magic. That which was but thought and invisible emanation on Earth was here concentrated, made liquid, a physical form of a power more often guessed at than understood even by those that wielded it.

Scared, she gaped at the water.

The pool seemed to move, agitate, like a whirlpool forming, and swirling. Then it stopped and fogged over, like a summer morning, early, before the sun burned off the low vapors of the riverside.

Upon the fog a face formed, and for a moment, Miranda frowned at it, for it seemed to her to be the reflection of Will's face.

But then the face defined itself and she saw—her breath arrested upon her throat.

A very young man appeared upon the surface of the lake. He looked like Will and yet different.

He had the same golden falcon eyes, the same dark curls.

But where Will's dark curls had receded from his forehead, this youth's framed a pale face in perfect proportion. And his skin was white and as smooth as Miranda's own.

His shoulders were broader than Will's. He wore a velvet suit of good cut—of elven cut, more exacting than any mortal's.

There was more to it, though Miranda could not articulate it. It danced in her thoughts, in images and feelings, suspended just beyond the reach of encompassing words.

There was pride in the golden eyes, certainty, and joy. It was, she thought, the look of a king gazing over his domain.

The young man stood at the white ramparts and looked out over the crux.

Miranda's heart jumped within her, fluttering like a bird first longing to take wing, and her mind, foolishly, stopped being able to think at all, much less think clearly.

If this was her villain, oh, then let her die steeped in his plots.

"Who is he?" she asked, but didn't wait for a reply.

The scene upon the pond was coming into sharper focus, the surroundings of the young man becoming more defined.

Upon the ramparts of the white castle the young man leaned over the white stone and looked out, his eyes clear and dreamy, as though he could see Miranda through all the fogs and fens, through all the greenery and dense forest intervening.

But Miranda gasped and blanched. Fear and surprise, joy and anguish commingled in her mind and heart, and gave her the sudden sense of being dropped, head first, into an abyss.

On the ramparts, a dark red flag fluttered, and upon it, delineated in midnight black stood the figure of a horse-mounted hunter, lifting up a horn to his lips.

Miranda knew this standard as she knew herself, as she knew the home of her raising, as she knew that the sun rose in the east and set in the west.

"Father," she said, feeling surprise and almost joy. But in saying it, she froze.

For what being could have laid the trap upon the crux and taken over her magic, and done it all better than the all-powerful Hunter could? Who better than the Hunter could deceive Proteus about the history of elvenkind? Who better could make Proteus hate his cousin?

What being, better than the one who knew the guilt and ambition in every heart, could have arranged to have them all trapped in the crux?

And what being could better manipulate magic to divide them all ere they fell to the crux, sending Miranda and the others to the beach, the centaurs and Caliban to the deep forest, and the child to the secret seclusion of the castle?

Miranda had felt the Hunter's magic in her spelling, before they'd all come here.

Yet how could she accept that her father, the only father she'd ever known, had set this trap for her and for her love?

How could she expect evil where she'd known only love?

Scene 29

ᏬᎦ

Quicksilver on the ground of the clearing. Caliban enters, running, and starts shaking him.

"Master, awake," someone said. "Awake, master."

His mind overtaken with wine, his body collapsing with tiredness, Quicksilver had been dreaming that he lay in his bed in the palace, with his wife beside him.

He stretched his hand toward Ariel's side of the bed and touched—leaves? He sat up, struggling to open his eyes against an unforgiving weight on his eyelids.

"Malachite?" he asked, confused at the voice screaming in his ears, at the rude, strong hands shaking him.

Beneath him there were rude leaves and moss. His fogged brain thought perhaps he was, after all, at the battle front. Perhaps this was Malachite waking him to fight. But Malachite's voice had never sounded like a growl, and Malachite's breath didn't smell like decayed meat and dank moss.

By an effort of will, Quicksilver opened his eyes.

And saw a troll's dull, unreflective eyes staring at him.

He jumped up, and his hand reached for his dagger.

The troll screamed and tried to escape. "Not me, master, not me . . ." he screamed. "I'm not the enemy."

Something about the troll looked familiar. The orange fur, the scared face, the canines, the . . .

"Caliban?" Quicksilver asked, sheathing the dagger again. "Caliban, what do you do here?"

"It's them, master," Caliban said. "They are coming. I thought I must wake you."

"Who is coming?" Quicksilver asked. His head spun and a fog obscured his vision. He was still confused by sleep, by too much wine, by this strange land. "Who?"

The monster looked terrified. Even his dark lipless mouth looked pale. "Centaurs. They would eat me, if my mistress hadn't distracted them." He shook Quicksilver. "They would have made me into a meal. And my mistress, sir, my mistress, they pursued her, they offered her violence."

"Your mistress?" Was Miranda in danger? Quicksilver felt a quickening of apprehension and woke fully. Had something happened to Miranda?

Even as he felt it, he wondered at his own concern. How could he love a creature he didn't even know? How, so quickly, could he feel a protective, fatherly love for this elf girl?

And yet what he'd glimpsed of her had been pleasing, bespeaking a tenderer heart, a gentler upbringing than he could expect of Sylvanus's daughter, or of the adopted daughter of the Hunter.

And Quicksilver *wished* to love her as his daughter, the daughter he likely would never sire for his nature seemed to be as sterile as it was mutable.

If he loved not the girl, then he loved his dream of a daughter, the daughter she could be to him.

But . . . "Centaurs?" Centaurs upon the crux? How? "Centaurs?"

Caliban didn't answer. He opened his mouth as if to speak, but made only a strangled sound, like a man so terrified that he cannot find the strength to scream. He looked at Quicksilver and covered his mouth with his hairy hands.

"What? What is this?"

Something—a cold something—a web, a net, fell over Quicksilver's head and extended to engulf his whole body, covering him, whole, from head to toe.

With it came a coolness, a cold, cold, icy dankness that was, as it were, death traveling through a mortal body and advancing its army and its pale standard.

His strength gone, his breath a shallow mockery of life, Quicksilver fell to the ground.

Yet his mind remained clear, and he knew, moment by moment, what happened to him.

The troll covered his own mouth, his eyes wide, looking in horror at Quicksilver.

Did the troll's mouth shape *forgive me,* or was that an illusion of Quicksilver's fright and the creature's odd features?

Meanwhile, the centaurs rode into the clearing, a black one and a dappled one. "The net that your silly niece threw away was easy enough to find, its power calling to us from the undergrowth. It is from our region, and it was for many years kept under centaur guard. It is woven from such material that it will remove all magic from whomsoever it covers. Now are you without power, now are you defanged." Hylas—Quicksilver remembered the dark centaur's name—grinned. "I could kill you with a spell, or with my dagger. But I fear me the protections of the hill are not yet neutralized. Unworthy though you are—" He kicked at Quicksilver's chest, inflicting a sharp pain. "You are the king. To stop the hill's vengeance, we'll need Proteus's strumpet, or at least her power—either willingly given upon the bed of love, or else taken by a force spell. That was the reason he sought her out and courted her and got her involved in this plan. And she's so infatuated by him that he controls all her thought. Surely her power shall be his in time also. Meanwhile, your free life is gone. From now on it falls to us to drag your carcass to the meeting point, where you shall die."

The centaur looked at Caliban and grinned. "Well played, troll, keeping him busy while we sneaked into the clearing. For a moment I thought you played me false, for you did wake him, but now I understand it was but a precaution against his waking with the sound of our hooves." He grinned at Caliban. "For this we'll forgive all your past insolence, and we'll forgo feasting on your flesh."

Quicksilver looked at the troll.

Caliban looked away, his eyes half closed. Caliban could not be read.

To be truthful, trolls were slow creatures and Caliban probably had trouble understanding language itself. Maybe he didn't know what he had done.

Yet Quicksilver didn't believe it. Despite his extravagant and strange behavior upon meeting Quicksilver—a behavior perhaps born of panic—the night before Caliban had proven himself a rational being. As rational as most elves, if not as well mannered.

No, there was no other explanation but that Caliban had betrayed him. Quicksilver had, for the first time in the history of the kings of the hill, taken a soft, compassionate stand toward one of the lower races, and see how he was repaid!

He shook his head at his own folly. Maybe he should be glad he'd lost Silver. For what was she but that erratic softness, that reckless spirit that led him to such traps?

Scene 30

⚙

The clearing where Miranda has done the scrying. Will stands beside her, gone very pale, shaking.

"Hamnet!" Will said, and turning to the girl, said, by way of explanation, "That's my son. My son, who was but a child. How he's grown. Sixteen? Seventeen? He's no more my child."

Will felt a great sense of loss—a grief afraid to own itself. For Hamnet was alive and he should be happy. Yet Hamnet was no more Hamnet.

The girl met his startled glance with a panicked one of her own. "That's my father's standard," she said. "That's my father's banner that flies beside the youth, my father's own flag on the ramparts of that white, magical castle. What plot is this? And why would my father plot against me?"

She lifted her hand to her throat.

"Your father?" Will felt as though his blood had turned to ice in his veins. "Sylvanus?"

She shook her head, her disheveled hair though matted and twisted still shining like moonlight in the dark of night. "The Hunter. My true father. My father who raised me."

She looked cold as she said it and Will wondered what coldness, what harsh loneliness, she might not have learned, living with the Hunter all these years. He remembered his own brief encounter with the creature of shadow and midnight, of dark chases and unforgiving slaughter.

He gazed at the small pale face that looked cold and wan like the face of a child who has lost her way. "Lady," he said softly, in such a tone as he might have said *child*. "Lady, why would the Hunter conspire against anyone? Is he not a creature of greater power than I, mere mortal, can dream, or even you, semi-immortal though you are, can conceive? Could he not crush all of us with a look, or kill us with a thought?"

She nodded, then shook her head, then shrugged. Her lips, which looked colorless, opened in a round "O" and shaped a sigh. "I'd have thought so, but I, his daughter, was disobedient and perhaps my disobedience hardened his heart against me. Does not his paternal duty include the duty to discipline me?"

Will sighed. He had some experience with the other side of this. He knew it was his duty to discipline his children. He'd always known it. But ever since Susannah, the eldest, had walked into trouble with her one-year-old feet, and reached for trouble with her little pudgy hands, he'd found himself more inclined to tell her stories and by example show the folly of her ways.

"The good book," he said, and then realizing she might not know what that meant, he explained, "The sacred book of humans in my land says that you should not spare the rod, lest you spoil the child." He looked around him, at the dark turbulent skies, the dark turbulent trees, the agitated landscape. "But truth, sending a child to the crux as a punishment seems well beyond a touch of the rod, a scolding, or even a whipping. Why would your father take it upon himself to do something so cruel to his only child?"

And even as he said it, Will thought he couldn't say such thing. How could he know what the Hunter felt as a father? How did he know how the Hunter felt about this creature he'd adopted, this creature who was no true kin of his?

Did he feel toward Miranda as Will did toward his own children? Or as Will felt toward Nan's irascible black and white cat—beloved, perforce, for he was Nan's pet—but not beloved like one of the children. And what would they not do if the cat betrayed them?

The elf princess shook her head. Tears shone in her eyes, and trembled at the edge of falling down her cheeks. "I don't know," she said. "I don't know. He was ever gentle and kind, watching over me with a concern more than fatherly—the concern of a mother anxious for her cub. He saw to my needs and my wants, and indulged my tantrums with a smile. But now . . ."

Strangely, in Will's mind, a picture formed: the Hunter as doting a father as he knew himself to be during his visits to Stratford. He could see the Hunter bending his immortal heart to accommodate this small, fragile charge, guiding her, step by step, to adulthood.

Knowing what kind of a father the Hunter had been, he knew that such a father, being as he was, could never turn upon his own child in this way.

He shook his head to the girl's worry and, ever so gently, set his hand upon her shoulder. "Do not cry," he said. "And do not fear, for I'm sure such a father would not change suddenly, nor torment his child in this way."

"But then—" The girl looked at Will and her lip trembled. "But then who could have lured us here and trapped your son upon the castle, and played with Proteus's mind so that he thought the King of Fairyland was evil? Who could have arranged to meet with the centaurs?" she asked. She spoke the last word as though it stung her lips. "Who could have betrayed me thus? And why does the tower fly my father's standard?"

Will would dearly love to have the answer to that last question himself, but he knew he stood no chance of finding out till the powerful immortal desired to reveal it.

So he spoke to the other questions. "There are others who might have done it, I think. Having been raised by an immortal, always truthful father, perhaps you trust too much. And perhaps you should not assume that beauty always equals virtue, even in elves."

Miranda sighed and rolled her eyes—a gesture so much like Susannah's fits of rebellion that Will couldn't help smiling.

His smile made the girl frown and stomp her foot. "Oh, you know nothing of elves."

Will sighed in turn. "I know of males, elf and human alike," he said. "I know beauty is no sign of goodness and that fair elves, like fair humans, can and do lie."

She stared at him, and her eyes went wide, and again, the slightest bit of suspicion entered their blue expanse. But she shook her head. "If you mean Proteus, that cannot be true, for he loves me, and loving me, he's kind and joyous and smiling."

"Ah," Will said. "Ah, but a man may smile and smile and be a villain."

She shook her head. She sighed. She closed her hands, one upon the other, their grip strong upon each other, as though by one hand holding the other both could be saved of falling into the abyss and Miranda with them.

She set her lips in a straight line. She shook her head. "Nay," she said. "Nay. Proteus is good. You do not know him as I do. He's good. Deceived perhaps, but good. And I hold a duty to him, having left him sleeping under a spell. I must go find him, wake him." And then, raising her eyebrows with sudden memory. "Aye me, there's Caliban also. I've forgotten Caliban. I must go to him, and make sure he's well and safe. For he's but a poor creature, none too bright, my servant and my responsibility since we were infants together."

She started to walk away from Will, then returned, and offering both hands to him, suffered them to be enclosed in his rough, calloused hands.

"Thank you," she said. "For I was blind to truth, but you have revealed to me that ugliness and evil aren't always conjoined."

Will smiled. He'd become used to the idea that this beautiful, dainty elf princess thought him horribly ugly. And well she might, having been raised in the Hunter's world of perfection where such people as Will could never exist.

Yet he cautioned her, with weary voice, "Neither is beauty always married to goodness."

She nodded and smiled.

He knew she didn't listen.

"I wish you good luck in finding your son," she said. "I wish that you may get out of the crux well, for you belong not here nor should you have been caught in this net of elven discord."

Will nodded. He couldn't agree more with that, and as he parted with Miranda, he felt the stick thump, thump beneath his shirt like a second heart, anxious to find and follow the true path.

He wondered if he'd be the only one walking it, though, the only one walking toward the castle—the prize, the place of reckoning and victory.

For Quicksilver and Silver were divided and—if Silver spoke true—both were dying.

Will must get Quicksilver to Silver. But where would he find Quicksilver, save where Quicksilver would go to rescue Hamnet—at the castle. And Miranda was doubling back upon her own steps to find Proteus, about whom Will's heart misgave him. Proteus, Will suspected, would be going to the castle, to try once more to entrap Quicksilver.

He wished he could have told Miranda more, warned her of what might happen.

But he suspected anything he said would fall upon deaf ears.

Too well did he remember his first love, a girl his age, named Katherine Hamlet.

Will had been sixteen and mad in love. His mother and father had warned him about her, told him she went with other men and boys, though remaining chaste with Will. But he'd not believed them, never believed them until she drowned herself, pregnant by one of the local gentry.

Like his mother's and his father's pleas, would any warning he gave the girl be heard? For it was true that one's first love was often a disease that must run its course, the poison spreading through the body and ruling it wholly before it subsided and diminished its influence upon the afflicted limbs and presently retreated to a memory that made one smile or cry and nothing more.

So Will leaned his head and spoke in the voice of a man who knows his own limitations, "And fare you well, kind lady. Flocks of angels watch over your progress and keep you ever free from harm."

She shot him a curious look but she smiled, and nodded—and she walked away.

Was her gait slower? Was her gracefulness somewhat more controlled? Had the episode to which her impetuous goodwill had led her put some more thought into her actions? Having learned the evil of centaurs, was she now on guard?

Will couldn't tell. As with any child, he could only hope that she'd learned a lesson and would not do it again.

And then he realized, with a shock, that he was thinking of Miranda as one of his own children. Remembering his dream, he grinned at the foolishness of it all.

But the rage he had felt in his dream no longer haunted him. Miranda was like one of his own daughters. Elf, perhaps, but no longer fearsome.

He shook his head and, taking the twig out of his shirt, allowed it to tug him onto the right path.

How foolish could a man who had adopted an elf be?

He remembered how Nan had told him that she'd once considered doing just that—leaving Fairyland with both babes and raising them together as sisters.

He wondered what Miranda would be like if she'd been raised in Henley Street, in Stratford-upon-Avon, as the daughter of a struggling playwright.

Humbler, he thought as his feet found the true path and his stick pulled him on and on. As graceful, as beautiful as she now was, but humbler and quieter. More modest. Not that the Princess of Elvenland was boastful, but even while crying on Will's shoulder, she had been regal.

Regal, he thought, seizing upon the word. That was how Hamnet had looked in that image of him upon the pond.

Thus Will thought of what he didn't want to think: Hamnet much older, standing on the ramparts of the white castle.

Had it been an illusion? He remembered what Quicksilver had said about the different rates of time in the crux.

Had Hamnet truly grown that fast in a few days? Had years passed for him? And who had raised Hamnet those years?

How could Will take Hamnet back to Stratford and explain how he had grown in just a few days? Who would believe him?

Worse, if they did, would he be tried for witchcraft? Would enough magic remain to Will, from his use of magic in the crux, that all would believe him a dark mage?

Oh, let it not be so.

And what about Hamnet? Would Hamnet be magic?

Who was this son that Will was trying to rescue? He recalled the haughty air, the impeccable clothing.

A son of Will's? By whose fiat?

Who was this prince that, having originated in Will's humble loins in a night of passion with Nan in Stratford-upon-Avon, had now become quite something else?

He didn't know and he couldn't think on it, nor how he would explain his son's sudden growth and superior demeanor to Nan, to the neighbors, to the family in Stratford.

But he did know this land was dangerous. Already once, the sun had set on their stay here. Any longer and they'd be trapped here forever. And this, also, was no place for Hamnet.

Only let Will get to the castle where Hamnet was captive, and ransom him, and take him safe to the earth whence they'd come.

All the rest would solve itself upon the ripeness of time.

For the sake of the son he could no longer call his, Will held on to his stick and wearily walked the path.

Scene 31

ႲႥჂ

Quicksilver, lying on the ground, covered in the magical net that steals his powers. Hylas stands near by and a terrified Caliban, a few feet off, covers his lipless mouth with his trembling paws.

Quicksilver hurt. His chest hurt where Hylas had kicked him, and his shoulder, where the wound from Proteus's blade still smarted and where the cruel hooves had brought forth blood anew.

Something about the crux made Quicksilver less than invulnerable and slower healing. Or perhaps something about his separation from Silver, Quicksilver thought.

And thinking it, he felt the now familiar pain of the separation.

Hylas laughed, an easy laugh. He stood beside Quicksilver and laughed, at Quicksilver's helplessness or perhaps at his look of pain. He trotted in place, giving his movement the look of a victory dance.

"Now is the King of Fairyland brought low," he said, and laughed.

Aching, bleeding, his face in the dirt, breathing in the bracken scent of moldy leaf and old moss, his power sapped by the cruel net, Quicksilver found voice to whisper. What he whispered surprised himself.

"Why do you hate me?" he asked.

His voice, raspy and pained, barely rose above the rustling of wind upon the trees.

But it was heard by all and hung upon the cool air of the crux and upon Quicksilver's mind.

For it was a mad question. Rebellious centaurs had always hated the elven kings.

There was nothing to know.

Hylas stopped his dance and was silent a moment. Then, in a voice that rose aggressively, he said, "Why do I hate you? Oh, I hate you as I hate death and pain and all elves. Your infant race—like the race of men—clambered upon our ancient, ordered world and took it from us.

"With your ideas of a proper life, of right government, you sullied our nation-states. You destroyed our loves, our rhymes, our heroic wars, our hunting bands, our academies.

"You took the meadows where we ran free and fenced them in parcels so small there was scarcely space to get up to a trot. Our forests you turned into plowed fields, where the hoof can catch and the ankle break. In our sacred glades you built haughty palaces, from which we—half animal, you said— were excluded." He spit in Quicksilver's face.

His spit, warm and smelling of wine, landed on Quicksilver's eyelid, making Quicksilver's eye smart.

"All this we withstood, in patient calm, till humanity invented wine. Tasting it unlocked our rage and our hurt. Then, over a private brawl and minor damage—such as humans do daily to each other—did the Lapithae almost destroy our race.

"And when the sad remnants of that race asked for asylum and help in your land, were we told we had to surrender all our power and magic to the king of elves.

"In return we got nothing, not even that magic that all other subjects of the hill can access. Rather we were kept at bay and kept down, feared and despised at once."

Hylas pawed at the ground with irate hoof. "For the lack of healing magic, our young foals die. Because we lack the use of our own magic, let alone the magic of the hill, we're unable to catch animals in the woods and amid the houses of mankind. Our people starve, oh King, while you dance in your palace.

"Again and again, have our people rebelled and tried to improve their lot and have use, at least, of their own magic. Time and again, elves have killed our best stallions on the field of battle—and given us nothing."

Hylas stopped talking.

For a while, only the sound of wind on the trees, the sound of the centaurs' breathing—all three of them in unison—broke the perfect silence of the crux.

"And you ask why I hate you?" Hylas said.

"But I have not done this myself," Quicksilver said. "I've only reigned for fourteen years. How can you accuse me of centuries of injustice."

"You knew of it," Hylas said. "You perpetuated the injustice and so all the injustice is yours."

"But Proteus would be no better king than I," Quicksilver said.

Hylas laughed. "Did I say we want Proteus for our king?" Turning half away from Quicksilver, Hylas grinned at Caliban. "You, beast, serve me true, or you shall be our meal. Watch this *king* while we go hunting. Something in this land must be edible, and I've seen some deer over yonder."

Together, the centaurs galloped out of the clearing.

Caliban lowered his hands slowly and looked at Quicksilver—an unreadable look.

Lying on the ground, cold, empty of magic, and trembling in fear, Quicksilver boiled with rage that he'd been unable to express. Why was he blamed for the evils of all his race? How could he defend himself from such all-encompassing charges?

As soon as he judged safe—hooves sounded nowhere, and the voices of the centaurs had receded in the distance—he spoke. "Caliban, remove the net from me."

Quicksilver must go rescue Miranda. He must go back to the hill and surround himself with those who didn't accuse him of crimes he could not ever mend.

Caliban looked at him. His eyes were dark and reflected nothing. If eyes were the mirror of the soul, then Caliban's soul remained unreflected.

Perhaps he had no soul.

Caliban shook his head. "I can't," he said. "I'll not risk my life for your sake."

"Remove the net," Quicksilver said. "And then I'll be able to do magic and I'll set it all to rights. And then, when we return to Fairyland, shall I make you a courtier, one of my honored ministers."

"Your cave in the mountains shall be transformed by my might and magic to a palace, and your mother shall be honored above all mothers in Elvenland."

Now did Caliban stare harder at Quicksilver. He squinted, his eyes narrowing, without showing any more expression than before.

"He's told me the truth," Caliban said. "Hylas has. When they caught me again, they said I must help them, and they told me the truth. Trolls fought on *his* side in the great elven war. And your side killed countless trolls."

"Hylas told me how, once, you and your servants blocked the entrance of a cave with burning branches, and there suffocated a whole clan of trolls, male and female, infants and children."

His eyes looked, if possible, more opaque and more expressionless. "That might have been my clan."

Quicksilver swallowed. What he'd been afraid the monster would find out, the monster had indeed found out.

Lying on the ground, staring at the creature's great, gnarled feet, with their huge, hard claws like horns, Quicksilver wondered what would happen if

e claws rending him, tearing into him. He remem-
ws, of troll teeth, of the immense strength of trolls
they gnawed on his shoulder.

Had Malachite not come then, Quicksilver would have been dead. Dead and eaten by trolls.

But how could Quicksilver explain this to the creature who, in many ways, whether he believed it or not, was as innocent as the little fairy princess?

"It was a war," he said, and to himself, his voice sounded teeny and false. "When the gods cry havoc and let slip the dogs of war, what can elf or man— or troll—do, but fight and do his duty till his duty is done and victory or defeat reaped from the bitter harvest of fighting?"

Caliban shook his head. "That might have been my clan," he said. "And man and elf *can* think. So can troll."

"And yet," Quicksilver said, "I could still make it all better. I could give you honors, riches. I could protect your mistress, whom you prize." Quicksilver strained against the threads of the net, fine as spiderweb, which seemed to cut into him and freeze him to the heart.

Caliban glared at him out of the corner of his black eyes. "Even you, oh, King, cannot restore life to the dead, nor can you undo your injustice with honors." He grinned at Quicksilver, showing his sharp fangs, his yellowed teeth. A smell of putrefaction floated from his breath. "The net remains, till the centaurs come back. And till they finish their job and kill you. And you'll kill no more trolls, oh, King of Elves."

Scene 32

❧

Miranda, walking through the forest, meets Proteus. They run toward each other.

O h, how Miranda had missed Proteus.

Seeing him now, amid the swaying greenery, was like seeing an old friend among strangers, like knowing your home from a long distance, looking through sheets of dreary rain.

"Proteus," she said.

"Miranda," he said, and ran toward her, graceful and swift, skipping over roots of trees and jumping over low branches, till he met her, with open arms, and in his arms, he encircled her and twirled her. "Miranda. I was worried—I feared— The gods know what I've feared. But you're here. You're well. You're well, my love." Thus speaking, he set her down and ran his hands up and down her arms, caressing her arms and shoulders. "My love, my Miranda."

She smiled and cried, and crying, she smiled through her tears, like a spring day when rain dims sunshine and sun shines through rain.

Her voice came out, high, strangled, telling him of the centaurs, how the centaurs had tormented Caliban and how they'd insulted her and how the little mortal—the ugly little mortal whom she'd assumed was evil because he was ugly—had come to her rescue.

Proteus held her in his arms and exclaimed at her tale, and kissed her tears as they fell, sparkling and hot, down her face.

She cried, and her breath coming in gasps, she said, "And he was so kind. So kind, Proteus, and he says you have it all wrong. He says that my father *was* a villain and taken by the Hunter as the Hunter's own dog and that it was when the Hunter took him that my father, craven and heartless, delivered me to the Hunter also."

"What father would do that, Proteus? How *could* you think him good when he did that?"

Proteus's kisses stopped. His arms still around her, he straightened. "How can I explain the mortal's delusions, Miranda? How would I know what he thinks? Faith, they think little at all, being but little more intelligent than your pet monster, your Caliban."

Miranda opened her mouth. She looked up and into Proteus's eyes. In them she found uncaring amusement.

How could he speak like that of the mortal who had saved her? How could he speak like that of the troll whom his erstwhile allies had so frightfully tormented?

How could Proteus smile thus at her, so unconcerned after all she'd revealed to him? Why was he not exclaiming over her hurt? Why was he not hurt on her behalf? Why did he not vow to hunt down the centaurs and avenge their offense toward her?

Through her mind, the mortal's words echoed: *A man may smile and smile and be a villain.*

She'd been about to tell him of the flag on the castle, the emblem of the Hunter upon it. She'd been about to tell him of the boy, Hamnet, and the strange feelings he had awakened in her.

For it was as though she'd met the boy long ago, or in a dream. She knew his golden falcon eyes, his features, his regal bearing. It was as though she'd waited all her life to meet him.

She'd never felt this way about anyone.

All this she was going to tell Proteus, all this reveal, and in all this ask for her love's comfort and his wisdom.

But that bright, uncaring smile, that disdainful way of referring to the creature who'd saved her, it seemed to stop every thought within her head, every word upon her lips.

"But you're well," Proteus said and grinned. "And that's what counts. All these questions of guilt, all these ancient, blood-soaked feuds can wait. For now, we'll go to the castle, along the true path, and there find the boy and restore him to his father." He winked at her. "And then the two of us will go to Fairyland, where all might meet you and admire your beauty. And there, by peaceful means or not, I'll crown you queen."

Miranda looked at him, at his blithely happy face. *By peaceful means or not?*

Something there was, behind his smile, his easygoing expression, like a shadow behind a curtain, hiding the window that would let in the blessed day.

Like a shadow, this patch of darkness hid, who knew what? What thoughts did Proteus have and not share? If he loved Miranda, why hide his mind and heart from her?

Oh, Miranda hated suspecting her lord so, but she did. The words of the mortal came back to haunt her. If ugliness did not mean evil, indeed, why should beauty mean goodness?

What a fool she'd been, what a besotted fool!

All of a sudden, Proteus felt wrong, different, separate from her.

It was as though, both being in love, they'd lain side by side in the same bed but, upon waking, didn't recognize each other. When they'd lain together, they'd been lovers, but the ringing, pale morn found them strangers to each other.

"From Fairyland I'll conjure us food and water, for this water is not safe to drink. And then we'll set out," Proteus said. "Soon, my lady, soon, all this strife will be over. We'll be married, and you'll be my queen."

Miranda nodded and forced herself to smile.

Why did his words put a shiver down her spine?

Scene 33

꧁꧂

Will, walking along the true path alone. He looks ready to drop—the color of tallow, bedraggled, with dark circles round his golden eyes.

How tired Will was. How far he'd come, with no food, nor drink. Nothing but his longing for Hamnet could have got him to do it, his love for his son, his love for his wife, his daughters—his need to restore his family to what it had been.

He walked along the winding path, while branches flogged him and leaves tugged at his coat, like beggars attempting to detain him.

The stick in his hand pulled on while, tired and confused, Will kept holding on to it.

Thirst and hunger warred within him. It was all he could do to walk on.

Suddenly, as though out of nowhere, he heard voices again, as he'd heard them before, in the night.

He slowed his step, and stowing the stick beneath his shirt, where it beat and pulled like a living creature, he walked cautiously, amid the trees, over tree roots, keeping himself hidden.

Ahead, in a clearing, men were talking—or perhaps not men, but those creatures that Will had met before, for these had the same accent, the same haughty tones, the same foreign intonation.

Cautious, Will stepped forward.

The dappled horse-body and the black one sat by a fire upon which a hunk of still-bleeding meat roasted.

Whence that meat?

Will felt uneasy over Caliban, Miranda's troll, the one Miranda had said narrowly escaped being eaten.

But then he spied the monster sitting by the spit, turning it, while the meat roasted. And the meat looked like a deer carcass. Behind Caliban—

Hola. What was here?

A bundle lay on the ground behind Caliban, and for a moment, it looked to Will like a bundle of green cloth—a large blanket or a roll of cloth.

Then he saw the moonlight-bright hair and, looking harder, spied Quicksilver's pale, severely beautiful face beneath the hair.

Was Quicksilver alive? Was he dead?

Forgetting himself, Will stepped further forward, till only a few branches, a few sparse leaves, stood between him and the centaurs. Such was his anxiety over the King of Fairyland that Will's breath came short and shallow.

Many years ago, Will himself had unjustly imprisoned Quicksilver. He'd wrapped him in iron, almost killing him.

Quicksilver had looked like that, then—drained and pale, his moss-green eyes dull, his lips bled of color.

The then-Prince of Fairyland had forgiven Will for imprisoning him, for almost killing him. He'd taken no revenge. He'd forgotten all.

Will thought suddenly, startled by the thought as though it were an alien intrusion in his mind, that Quicksilver had as much reason to resent him as he had to resent Quicksilver.

Had Will not, once upon a time, ambushed Quicksilver and wrapped him in cold iron, almost killing him?

Hadn't Will's father, while Will was still a youth, beguiled by Sylvanus's evil schemes, helped murder Quicksilver's own parents?

Hadn't Will, in London, spurned Quicksilver so that the hill and London, aye, and the world entire, had almost been lost to the dark Sylvanus?

And yet, did Quicksilver complain of mortals? Did he fear the mortal world and refuse to face it? Did he tell Will to go elsewhere, to apply for help from some other supernatural being? Did he tell Will to go beguile another elf with his facile mortal lies, his mortal problems?

No. No. Quicksilver's devotion was still such that when Will's son was kidnaped, Quicksilver followed without thinking.

Will was here because Hamnet was his son.

But why was Quicksilver here, if not to rescue Hamnet and spare Will the grief of losing a son?

And yet—without this being Quicksilver's strife—how Quicksilver suffered for it, captive, on the ground, wrapped in something. Iron? He looked tired, almost dead.

He could be in his hill, with his retainers, pampered and coddled but for Will's sake he was here, in the dangers of the crux, captured by centaurs, brought low by his enemies.

It was only by staring intently that Will could discern the minute rise and fall of Quicksilver's chest.

A great relief flooded Will at seeing that movement.

Alive. Oh. Quicksilver was still alive. But for how long?

Slowly, slowly, trying not to snap a twig beneath unwary feet, trying not to set his foot wrong, Will walked around the clearing.

The centaurs talked, and Will listened with half a mind, noting only that they talked as people do who do not know they're watched.

"So, we'll see him tonight?" the brown one said.

"Tonight as it ever was, if he manages to give the shrew the slip."

"Is the meat not done yet, worthless creature?" the brown one said, and aimed a kick at Caliban.

Caliban stepped out of the way in time and turned the spit faster.

"And tomorrow will be the end of that haughty creature," the black one said. "That tyrant king for whom so many have been killed."

Will crept forward silently, holding on to the trunks of trees to avoid accidental falls that would lead to noise.

He had a very clear idea what to do.

Reach Quicksilver and free him, of course, from the net or the iron, or whatever it was that held him captive.

But how to do it and in what way, he couldn't imagine, as he didn't know the true nature of what constrained Quicksilver.

Whatever it was must dampen Quicksilver's magic, for Will had seen, on the beach, that Quicksilver's magic was more than a match to everyone else's here. Except his.

Walking stealthily was difficult, and every time one of the centaurs moved, Will was afraid he'd somehow see Will through the foliage around.

Will could use magic to free Quicksilver.

That alien thought, too, made Will stop. Magic!

It was true. He *could* use magic. He'd proven his gift in rescuing Miranda.

But if he used magic, then Will would be, as Quicksilver had said it, neither elf nor human. A human who could do magic, unleashed upon the unmagical world. A mage who'd scare his neighbors. Perhaps scare them enough that they would kill him.

Even if magic weren't evil in itself, what business had Will with magic? What would he do with it? He'd never been taught to use it, nor did he wish to learn, and if he performed magic, would he not make mistakes and cause himself to suffer?

Or bring death on himself and his family.

Once, Will had imagined imprisoning Quicksilver in the mortal world and seen how awful a situation that would be.

Now, Will pictured *himself* in the mortal world as a magic user.

Marlowe would have liked that and the secret power that came with it. But

Will was ever saner than Marlowe, and perhaps, for all of Marlowe's flaunted cynicism, it was Will who trusted less in the goodness of mankind.

He knew that his being special or having a special power would only bring him the envy and resentment of his neighbors.

Besides, Will didn't trust himself at all.

Yet if Will had a power no one else did, how long till Will felt that he must abuse it, and impinge on others with his force that they couldn't counteract.

How long until all mortals, men and women like him, hated him and killed him?

No. No. He'd stay without magic. No matter what it took.

He crept around the clearing, staying within the covering of the trees.

Near Quicksilver, he stopped.

Quicksilver's chest still moved only the slightest bit, like a man in a sleep so deep that he might never wake up.

He was pale and cold, cold and pale.

Will crept up on him, keeping close to the ground.

The brown centaur and the black one had their backs turned, and only Caliban stared at him, his face betraying nothing, as trolls' faces ever did.

"Quicksilver," Will whispered.

Quicksilver's gaze turned to Will, and then stared frantically over Will's shoulder.

"Look out," Quicksilver rasped.

Will turned his head.

He'd forgotten about the dappled centaur, or assumed he was out somewhere, hunting or answering a call of nature.

But there the centaur stood, hand raised and a thick branch grasped in it.

Will tried to run out of the way, but the centaur's other hand grabbed him.

And then the branch descended upon Will's skull.

A moment of pain, and then there was darkness.

Scene 34

ᙦᙣ

Miranda and Proteus, stopping in a clearing, while the night of the crux swirls above in streaks of black and dark, dark blue. Around them, the forest rustles. It sounds as if the shadows, lengthening beneath every bush, are animated with purposes of their own. The night smells of frost and fear.

"Let us rest here, and proceed apace," Proteus said. "And here shall I con- jure food to slake your hunger, water to quench your thirst."

Miranda nodded. She'd talked but little the whole day. She felt that Proteus was not being truthful with her and she shied from talk in which he might tell her untruths.

As of yet, she could not decide whether Proteus had lied to deceive her or lied because he had deceived himself.

The world outside fairy tales and legends was more complex than she'd ever dreamed.

Now she watched as, standing in the middle of the clearing, he made arcane gestures and strange passes and called to him the food from the elves' tables in Avalon.

He'd told her that elves sometimes did this, and stole the food from the tables of humans, leaving only shadows and illusions in its place, things that could not feed the mortals, nor fulfill their physical needs.

Yet the illusion remained and humans didn't know themselves duped.

Looking at Proteus doing the summoning, Miranda wondered if she, also, had been taken in by a shadow and an illusion.

Was fair Proteus that which she'd imagined, the creature with whom she'd believed she'd spend her whole life?

Or had he lied to her?

Proteus, midsummoning, looked at her and smiled, a gentle, kind smile.

Oh, unworthy thoughts. Oh, cursed doubts.

Miranda smiled back. He loved her. How could she doubt it? He had told her he loved her. And look, the fond looks he bestowed on her. Unworthy Miranda doubting Proteus.

Yet a man may smile and smile and be a villain.

Proteus brought forth flat cakes, cooked in the kitchen of the hill, and warm, savory roasted meat, and ale in a foaming pitcher.

Miranda ate the cakes but only tasted the meat.

It seemed to her that if it were Proteus who had tried to lay the sleep spell on her the night before, then he might try something different today.

In fact, whoever her enemy was, he might try something else today. The spell to make her sleep having been detected and failed, whoever had tried that might now set a sleeping potion on the ale or meat and make Miranda sleep thus—in a way her magic training could not detect.

And while she slept, what would happen?

Had she slept last night, Caliban would have been eaten. Had the mortal slept, she would have been—she shrank from thinking on it. Up in her mind came an image of herself, surrounded by the wild centaurs.

"Give me of your ale," she told Proteus. He had conjured thick ceramic mugs and poured ale for each of them in separate mugs.

He looked at her, gently puzzled, and creased his eyebrows in wonder over his dark eyes. "You have your own, love," he said, and gently touched the side of her mug with his finger.

"I want yours," Miranda said, seeking to put into her voice just the right caprice, the right careless command to sound like a spoiled girl playing with her lover. She smiled on him, what she hoped was her most radiant smile. "For all that your lips touch is sacred to me, fair Proteus."

He wrinkled his brow. He looked puzzled. He smiled and sighed at once, as though accepting the inevitable. "Far be it from me," he said, "to disobey my lady's command."

He offered her his mug. He took her own.

Taking it to his lips and tasting it, he made a face, then looked at the mug and chuckled. "How came this blade of grass onto my mug?" He poured the ale out, gave himself a new portion from the pitcher.

Miranda sipped her ale.

There were leaves and moss aplenty here, but no grass in sight. How not to suspect ill when so many reasons for suspicion were at hand? How not to fear? How not to plot and plan?

She slaked her thirst on that one mug of ale. When Proteus poured her a second, she noted how his hand lingered over the mug, and how it seemed that some dust fell from his sleeve onto the drink.

She pretended to drink it, but when he turned, she poured it into the ground behind her.

Then she faked sleepiness, and she covered her mouth with her hand while she yawned. "Oh," she said. "What is it with me all of a sudden, that my eyes close and my head droops."

If she were wrong, she was doing Proteus an injustice. But what would Proteus know of it, if she were wrong? How would it affect Proteus if her suspicions of him were unfounded?

He would know she looked sleepy, and then nothing more. He wouldn't know of the night she'd spent, vigilant, upon the hard ground, spying on him.

And their life, and their love, would go on unaffected. Their joys would erase her shaky suspicions. Thirty years from now, she might tell him and then would they laugh on it, together, in their palace.

But first she must be sure, and to be sure she must stay awake.

"I am so sleepy, my lord, that I can scant see your beloved face, and my eyelids, weighted like two stones, pull me down to the bottom of the lake of sleep."

Proteus smiled again, his smile perhaps just a little too satisfied. Satisfied at her calling him her lord? Or did he have darker reasons for satisfaction?

"Let yourself sink into sleep then, Miranda, and upon this clearing, let us call the day farewell. Tomorrow is the last day we may spend in the crux without forever becoming a part of it. Let us, tomorrow, finish our journey to the castle and free the small, innocent prisoner. Then we shall return to the hill and make terms with your uncle, who might be truly more sinned against than a sinner."

Scene 35

✩

Miranda and Proteus lying on the leaf-cushioned ground. From afar they look indistinguishable—two people-shaped mounds, each coiled upon itself. But then one of them moves, and rises. It is Proteus. The other one—Miranda—coils tighter upon herself. There's vigilance in the tilt of her head but not so much that it would be noticed by someone who doesn't know her to be awake.

Miranda heard Proteus get up and, without changing her position, half opened her eyes, spying through her golden lashes as Proteus stood up.

He looked handsome still, even in the dark, even in the dread light of her suspicions. His slim body glided with graceful secretiveness. His hair sparkled in the scant light. And the smile that half twisted his lips made them look riper and more appetizing.

How could she not love him when she saw him thus and, seeing him thus, not love him so wholly?

Yet he was up, while she—as he thought—lay sleeping.

Why was he up? Suspicion, wakening, stood beside love and held it in check. Silently, he brushed leaves from his suit and headed toward the fringe of trees, as though following a prearranged path.

Oh, traitor. How could he? How could he have deceived her so? With what grace had he been blessed, and all to throw it away on such dishonorable dealings.

She bit her lip. Yet she judged too fast. Had she not, just the night before, set a sleep spell on Proteus and, with it, made sure Proteus could not follow her when she got up?

And yet she loved him well and she was true to him.

Perhaps he, also, suspected a great, unnamed enemy. Perhaps he now proposed to find that enemy and keep them both safe. Perhaps for that reason he'd tried to make sure that Miranda was asleep that she might not interfere, nor risk herself.

And perhaps Miranda was wrong to suspect him.

In the dark of night, in the solitude of her suspicious heart, Miranda felt so remorseful for suspecting Proteus that she almost stood up and fell on her knees before him, almost begged him for forgiveness and explained that she, too, had suspicions and asked if, perhaps, together they could find their mutual enemy.

Could it be her father?

But—her birth father, or her true one? On this thought, her heart clenched as though it had transformed to a block of the purest ice, and from it, cold flowed out to freeze her limbs.

Could it be her true father, the Hunter, who thus plotted against her? How could she bear it if it were?

But how could she bear it if it were Proteus?

Which would she rather suspect: Proteus or the Hunter?

Oh, cursed choice, and she could not choose, but in the indecision of her fears she would suspect both and believe neither guilty. She lay awake as Proteus tiptoed into the forest.

Then, heartsick and hating herself, she stood and followed her love into the dense growth, looking to find what he went to do.

She saw him advance into the trees, and she saw, in the distance, a lantern carried erratically, like the beacon of a drunken firefly.

The centaurs! That must be whom Proteus had gone to seek out. Proteus would discover them now and know for sure their treachery, their horrible treachery.

She was sure that was what he meant to do tonight—avenge the insult they'd offered Miranda.

Her heart beating so hard that she fancied Proteus would hear it and turn around to look at her, she followed Proteus with cautious feet, careful not to step on the brittle twig or the rustling leaf.

There.

The centaurs were within her view—surely also, within Proteus's view—and Proteus's stride acquired a greater confidence. He would now lay waste their treasons and their dark plans. He would avenge his lady's honor. Watch how he tilted his head up in angered pride. Watch how he lengthened his stride. Watch how confidently he called forth, "Hola!"

She almost called to him. Almost. Almost offered to fight by his side.

But in the glimmering beacon of the lantern, she saw in the clearing not only the three centaurs but someone else whose presence so surprised her, she all but lost her power of speech.

For amid the centaurs, Caliban sat. A sullen and bedraggled Caliban, to be sure—a Caliban hunched upon the ground in the pose he assumed when he'd been denied some treat that he craved.

But it was Caliban, nonetheless, and how could Caliban thus consort with his mortal enemies?

With those who, but yesterday, had sought to eat him?

Oh, Miranda would go insane. She felt as though the whole world spun around her in drunken revelry, doing the improbable and glorying in the impossible.

Oh, she understood neither mortal, nor elf, nor troll. Was all the world but herself mad?

And on the ground, near Caliban, two bundles lay, trussed and immobile. One of them—her heart leapt in shock at the sight—was her uncle, covered in the net that she'd taken from Proteus. The magical net she'd thrown away the first day at the crux. The magical net she'd thought was well lost.

And the other . . . The other was Will, the mortal who but yesterday had saved Miranda from harm. He was tied, hands and feet together, and his mouth covered with a cloth. No doubt to keep Will from invoking that devastating magic with which, just yesterday, he'd laid waste to more magical creatures.

Oh, the centaurs had truly overreached, mistaken their power, and now Proteus would—

Proteus stepped into the clearing, into the light of the lantern.

The dark centaur, Hylas, turned toward him and smiled, a broad smile. "Ah, now comes our laggard friend to us, who yesterday left us to do all the work by ourselves." He gestured a broad hand, glimmering with brass bracelets, toward the trussed-up figures and Caliban. "And what thinks noble Proteus of our work?"

Proteus smiled. How different his smile was from the kind ones Miranda had seen before. This smile was sharp as a drawn knife and just as cruel.

"You did well," Proteus said. He said it like a king, like a commander rewarding his troops' bloodiest deeds. "I'd all set to come yesternight, but the Hunter's hag felt it and somehow deflected it, somehow put upon *me* a spell of sleep."

The hag? Could he be referring to her? He could not, could he? Miranda blinked, in shock.

The world swam before Miranda's eyes, and she put out a hand to the nearest tree trunk, to keep herself from falling, faint with distress.

And yet Proteus remained fair and limber. Oh, the stories had lied indeed.

"But today put I a cunning potion in her ale, and with it I lulled her to angel sleep, that I might walk abroad unfettered and do my work." Proteus grinned.

Oh, had a fair grin in Proteus's handsome face ever been so foul?

"And now I find that you have done my work for me, or almost done it, for something remains to be accomplished and that needs my direction and the shrew's subduing. Therefore, brave friends, hear you me.

"We'll toward the castle tonight, as we should—it's easy enough for me to get the shrew there, as she thinks we're going to rescue the mortal cub. Thus, fooled, can I lead her where I wish. For knew she the truth, she might make my life difficult—being of greater power and more royal blood than my own.

"Once we approach the castle, shall I, with my more schooled power, ever so subtly, set a spell upon her that will make her more willingly obey my will than does that misguided love that I've implanted upon her maiden heart and that she—being a fool—is tricked into believing." He grinned wider. His eyes glimmered with hard-set pride. "Then shall I command her to use her magic—for she is a Princess of Fairyland—to remove from her uncle the great protections of hill power."

"I thought," Hylas said, "that you were going to break her maiden knot and get control of her power thereby."

Proteus blushed and pouted. "I thought I would, but alas, for power to be transferred through lovemaking, the lovemaking must be willing, and she'll have none."

Eurytion laughed. "Poor Proteus. Even the one he courts will not give him love."

Proteus gave Eurytion a cold, cutting look. "I'd still have tried again, except that some centaurs, while drunk, soured her on all physical expression of love."

The centaurs quieted, looking at Proteus, as though knowing that beyond this controlled anger there was another, stronger and deadlier one.

But Proteus shrugged.

"It matters not," Proteus said. "For she's untrained, though she be very magical. Chances are I can blind her with love and magic and make her willingly interpose her body and her power between me and the punishment of the hill.

Thus acting as a shield, she can save us from the deadly retribution that waits those who attack the ruler of Fairyland. But if not, I can control her, and make her protect me anyway. And then I can kill him impunely." Proteus smiled toward the elf with blond hair who, tied up and lying on the floor, writhed at the words, as if by writhing he could evade the net's magical prison. "And then, if she be still alive before we leave for Fairyland shall we take her, the princess, and kill her also. For my kingdom shall have only one master, and no mistress."

He grinned.

"But won't death in the crux bring about such a storm of magic that the crux shall be laid waste and, exploding, set the worlds of elves and men—and indeed, all possible worlds and all spheres—clashing like inharmonious cymbals till all be destroyed?" Hylas asked.

Proteus's smile faltered only for a moment. Then it returned to full luminescence, and he shrugged. "Oh, my kind cos, Quicksilver, would tell you so. But then, what lies would he not tell, to avoid death?" He turned a gloating gaze on the writhing King of Fairyland. "For we all know he's but a cowardly wretch without his armies."

The centaurs hooted.

Miranda felt dizzy. That smile seemed to her the baring of teeth of a hungry tiger, or a lion's glittering ivory menace, and he'd willingly kill her also. He'd kill them for his own sake and he cared not if with it he destroyed the crux, and the world of humans and elves. His ambition, voracious, would gladly devour all life. Oh, what a fool she'd been.

"And the mortal?" Hylas asked. "And the mortal's son?"

"Oh, we'll take the mortal to the castle with us, lest he can think up something to do that would undo us. Even fools and children can, by luck, wreck the best laid of plans.

"But he is unimportant. When we kill Quicksilver and Miranda, we'll leave the mortal trussed up as he is. As for his son—who knows what has become of him? For all we know, he is already dead, of hunger and thirst or magical fire, within the castle walls.

"If alive, both of them can remain in the crux and be consumed by the crux magic that devours all."

Miranda bit her tongue to keep from crying out. She'd been in love with an illusion and now, like a widow, would bewail the loss of the elf she'd loved.

But he'd never existed and the reality beneath Proteus's protests of love, his kind smiles, was as cruel as the grave, as sharp as the serpent's tooth.

She would swoon from fear and heartbreak and the loss of what had, after all, never been hers—that fair dream she had but imagined.

But she must not swoon, she thought, as her vision seemed to darken.

Others, her uncle, and Will and that human youth she had but glimpsed once needed her help to get out of the crux alive.

Oh, that she could die here. Now. Oh, that she could end, cease her breathing and with it her griefs. Oh, that all rushing thought would end and with it sad Miranda's sorrows.

Oh, that she'd not live to serve this traitor's plans. Oh, but for a dagger to still her heart and bid breath return to her body no more.

For she, a Princess of Fairyland, the adopted daughter of the Hunter, had as surely been deceived as a peasant lass, a girl with neither sense, nor wit, who follows the first fair-faced knave to come a-courting.

But her deceiving had graver consequences than the loss of her maidenhead had for a village maiden.

For her foolish love, Miranda had allowed all these others to be ensnared into a lethal trap.

Mortals whom she'd never before seen would now die in the crux because of her.

She thought of kind Will and of his son who, in the castle, had grown to resemble a Prince of Fairyland, and she felt as if a band of iron constricted her heart.

Therefore, even as her despair whispered in her ear of the sweetness of ending all strife, something rose in her—something deep and angry and as swirling-dark as the night above, painting the sky of the crux tomb-black.

How dared Proteus deceive her? How dared he toy with her feelings? How dared he cross the daughter of the justicer, the daughter of the Lord of Night and Justice and Punishment?

Her anger swirled within her like strands of darkness.

Looking on Proteus—hearing him ask Hylas, "And the beast, how got you him to follow our scheme?"—she felt her anger plunge sharp fangs into her heart.

And hearing Hylas reply, "Oh, he only wants but to have the shrew once, for he has craved her since they grew up together," Miranda's blood rose with impetuous anger.

They would, craven cowards, give her as reward to her servant troll. And Caliban, whom she'd always thought was hers to protect, had harbored such thoughts about her? Her anger beat a mad rhythm on her temples and put a red veil upon her sight.

She was the Hunter's daughter, he her true father—regardless of whose spawn she'd been before the Lord of Night had taken her to his dreary, cold, loving, comforting heart. The Hunter had raised her in his dark castle. He had molded into her a nature as steely as his own. In her anger and pride, she would not stand this.

She would free the King of Fairyland—who was so humble as to love a mortal—and the mortal, too, that the king loved and who had proved, in his righteous gentleness, to be worthy of all love. She would free them, she would avenge herself. The centaurs, Caliban, dreadful Proteus—them she would deliver to her father's kind mercies.

And then would she ask the Hunter's pardon and, a dutiful daughter, live in nun-like seclusion in his palace, caring on nothing but making her father happy and looking after his house exactingly. Thus would she spend her remaining days, singing vestal hymns to the fruitless moon.

Not for her the love of elf and mortal. For they were all mad and she could never love a creature that was out of his right mind.

But first, she must go back to the clearing and pretend to remain asleep. She must go back and pretend to be the simpleton that Proteus believed her to be. And she must deceive him tomorrow and still pretend her love while protecting herself against the compulsion he wished to lay upon her.

It wouldn't be easy, but she could do it.

For in her anger, she had found a cool, clean place within herself—an acceptance of her own guilt, a hope for forgiveness. It was like the dark forest and the pursuing Hunter, the moon shining overhead and the smell of pine and cold. She knew right from wrong again and her mind, logically arrayed, allowed no phantoms of love, no shadows of care to deceive her.

No doubt remained, for *a man may smile and smile and be a villain.*

Faith, so could an elf. The stories had led her astray and storytellers lied. Proteus was a villain as were the centaurs and even—in his small, nasty way—Caliban.

Their enemies would therefore be her rightful allies.

This decision so soothed her mind that it was like balm upon her torn heart. It was like being in her father's arms and comforted and reassured it would all turn out well.

Scene 36

಄

It is the dawn of the third day in the crux. The clearing where the cen-
taurs, Caliban, Will, and Quicksilver spent the night. Day breaks above
and all is still.

Quicksilver himself looks asleep. But Will is awake and frowns at a
moving shadow by the fire, a moving shadow that slowly takes human form.

Will had awakened and been surprised that he'd slept thus, lying upon
the hard ground, his hands tied together behind his back, his feet tied
together, his mouth bound with a kerchief.

But he must have, for now he wakened from a sleep barren of all dreams,
but which nonetheless left within Will a sense of sadness and calm hopeless-
ness. The sense that all was lost, the world already destroyed, and there was
nothing he could do to change it.

He sagged within his binds.

Quicksilver was asleep, or perhaps dead, though Will would assume
asleep, since he'd heard the vile elf—Proteus—yesterday expounding on the
objective of all this, his desire to kill Quicksilver.

If Quicksilver were already dead, Proteus would have felt it, and he'd have
killed the elf princess and left, abandoning Will and Hamnet to their fate.

So Quicksilver was alive yet, and Will must find a way to keep him so, and to thwart Proteus in his evil plans. Looking at Quicksilver, Will remembered how he'd hated and dreaded the elf.

He could not remember why.

Was it Quicksilver's gracefulness he had hated? The capacity for moving like music made flesh? Or the glimmering moonlight hair? The gentle voice?

Faced with the likely death of all of those qualities in that one being that embodied all, Will could but think how all of them were, after all, like a blessing on a harsh world.

Was the world not a better place for Quicksilver's handsomeness? For Silver's gentle seductiveness?

Hadn't the world been better for having them in it? Wouldn't it be a cold, barren place when they were dead?

Will looked at Quicksilver and felt a tear slide, warm and moist, down his cold face.

Had he truly ever been afraid of elves and magic—or afraid of not being afraid?

Had he been afraid of loving the lady Silver too much, of loving the lady who was also Quicksilver with his moonlight hair? Ah, but which of them scared him the most?

Two loves have I, he thought. *Of comfort and despair, which like two spirits do suggest me still. The better angel is a man right fair, the worser spirit a woman colored ill.*

Oh, it was not love like his love for Nan, but must he—a poet—not allow space in his heart for more fanciful love, more dreamlike fantasy?

For all Will had—so often, so desperately—wished to hate Quicksilver, now, staring at the inanimate features of the King of Fairyland, he could summon nothing but affection and sad, desperate fondness, like longing for a lost love, the glimmer of an extinguished dream.

Quicksilver still remained beautiful and composed, but Will couldn't bring himself to envy him for it. For what was Quicksilver's life but a constant wrestling between what he was—his fractured person—and the dark turmoil of his conniving relatives?

How could such a creature be happy? And what would almost eternal life mean to one such as Quicksilver? Oh, Quicksilver was safe from old age and disease, but treason slept at his feet and snarled at his ankles, and ate from his board every day of his life.

And yet he remained beautiful and good. Good? How could an elf be good? The very thought surprised Will, raised on legends of the heathen, supernatural creatures. And yet, if an elf were good, it would be Quicksilver. Had he not restored Nan and Susannah to Will? Had he not come here for Hamnet?

"Will," a voice said, a voice Will knew. "Will, you must help him or he *will* die, and with him, all the worlds die. You must free him. You must tell him to accept Silver back into himself."

The voice was Marlowe's and it echoed, assured and clear, over the cool morning air, near as breath, real as a speeding heart.

No one else moved. Not Quicksilver, not Caliban, not even the centaurs who, their legs tucked under, their human torsos weirdly coiled, slept together in a large heap upon the forest floor.

Yet the voice was loud enough to wake the dead.

Marlowe's laughter echoed in Will's ears and now, by the side of the extinct fire, where the dinner had been cooked that Will had not been allowed to eat, Marlowe's spirit took shape and form—an elegant form, an easy shape.

This was Marlowe at his best—a young man in a velvet suit and white lace shirt. His russet hair, tied back, framed his too-delicate features. Both his eyes looked intact and Will asked himself why.

Was it the magic of the crux restoring Marlowe to what he once was?

"No," Marlowe said, answering Will's thought. "It is my son," Marlowe said, and smiled. "Since I tried to save you and, thereby, paid my debt to exacting heaven, I can hear my son calling me heavenward. His voice makes me remember who I was, and what I could have been. But his voice is not enough to draw me away while yet my lot remains divided. So you must listen to me. I must save you. I must know that Quicksilver is saved and Silver with him. Silver would make an uncomfortable ghost, crawling between earth and heaven. And without her, Quicksilver is less than half of himself. You must free him from this vile imprisonment. You must save him that she can return to him."

Will raised his eyebrows. It was all he could do. Marlowe had ever been unmindful of human limitations, or for that matter of social limitations on his mad schemes. But this passed all. For couldn't even Marlowe's undead perception see that Will was tied up, that he was gagged, that he could not speak, much less perform magic.

Marlowe smiled. "Ah, but do you want to perform magic?" he asked. "For you see, Will, if you do, then all these binds are nothing. Magic is not words but intent. And did you but wish it, that gag would fall, and you would be able to speak words that would reform the world." The smile died down and Marlowe looked grave, serious, almost sad. "But you do not want it. You've ever been thus—a would-be poet, but at heart a burgher, attached to your own safety, unable to cross the line that divides your safe existence from danger unbound. Thus, you look at danger from the other side of a great river but stay on your side of the river, watching the river of life run by you, while on the bank, you remain dry and unaffected, thinking of nothing but your own safety."

Marlowe sighed. "Perhaps you were right. My habit of jumping in and doing what the gods fear and the angels tremble to attempt got me early death and no more. And yet now, Will, now, if you remain as you've always been, you'll lose all, while if you *dare*, all can yet be saved. All. You and Quicksilver and that son you claim to prize above yourself and, alas, also me."

On those words the ghost vanished as if he'd never been.

Had Kit been there, or had Will dreamed him? And if he'd been there, had he told the truth? Was magic a matter of Will's belief and not his words?

Had he told the truth? Was it a matter of Will's believing and magic would be done? Was it a matter of his willpower, not his knowledge, not his power?

Will thought on this as the centaurs awakened. He thought on it as, still bound, he was thrown over the back of the dappled stallion and Quicksilver over the back of the brown one. With Caliban trotting behind, they set off down the true path to the castle.

Could Will make his gag fall by wishing it?

He looked at Quicksilver, who appeared half dead, and tried to wish his gag away with all his mind.

He visualized his gag untying, falling off. He thought that he felt the cloth give, loosen upon his face.

Then Will thought of Quicksilver telling him that if he performed magic in the crux, then he would—forever—be magic even in the world of men.

Is this true? Will thought, and the fear of that, the fear of that unwanted magic tainting his everyday existence, like a cold blade upon his neck, like a strangled fear at his throat, stopped his ability to concentrate.

He tried to move his lips, but the cloth was tight as ever over them.

Was he a coward?

Faith, he didn't know, but he feared that he and Quicksilver and Hamnet and all would be lost, and Will would never test the limits of his courage, the bounds of his ability.

Oh, he wished that Quicksilver could hear his thoughts, as Marlowe's ghost could.

And in wishing so, in screaming *Quicksilver* within his mind, he found that something happened.

It was as if the thought pushed on a barrier that, turning into a door, swung inward.

Quicksilver raised his head, looked at Will. Quicksilver's eyes opened fully, their moss-green depths trained on Will.

And his pale lips shaped, "Will?"

Scene 37

⚭

Quicksilver, slung over the back of the brown centaur, jarred and jostled by the pace of the creature as it trots down the true path.

Quicksilver heard Will call out to him and, opening his eyes, found Will's gaze trained on him, those odd golden eyes that looked still as in Will's youth, but now filled with such shock that it made Quicksilver want to laugh despite it all.

You heard me, Will's mind-voice echoed in Quicksilver's mind.

Quicksilver smiled, nodded. How odd it felt—Will's voice in his mind. How far he'd come that Will's small attention, Will's agreement to speak to him, even to mind-speak, made him so grateful that his eyes tingled with tears.

Oh, Silver had loved this mortal desperately.

But then, why did *Quicksilver* still feel this gentle enchantment toward the mortal with the falcon eyes, the receding hair, the fear of all things magical?

Marlowe says you must accept Silver, or you'll both die, Will said.

Marlowe? Quicksilver thought, raising his eyebrows in surprise. What did Will mean?

He didn't know if Will heard his thought, or just read his expression.

Will's golden eyes became intent, fixed, and Will's mind-voice, hesitant and unpracticed, whispered in Quicksilver's thoughts, *Marlowe's ghost. I've been seeing him for days now. He says he gave me his poetry and, with such a bequest or the good thereof, came his inability to go on towards heaven or hell. Now he wants to save us that he might be freed and join his son in heaven.*

Will frowned, and his eyes showed doubt of what he himself said. *At least,* he thought, *that's what he claims, but faith, I believe that he still loves . . . you.*

Quicksilver laughed at this, for here was the wonder.

In her life, Silver had loved no one but Will. In his life, even Quicksilver's love for his wife paled in comparison to this affection he'd caught from Silver like a catching sickness. And yet Will spoke of love for either aspect of Quicksilver as a strange thing, incomprehensible, to be pondered and thought of and not fully believed.

Will, staid, sane Will, could never love an elf, much less a divided elf and half of it a male.

And Marlowe, whom Silver had used for her pleasure, whom Quicksilver had used for his plaything, had loved Quicksilver so truly that, having died for that love, he still did not consider it enough.

He says, Will said, *that unless you can become Silver again, become one with her, you will die. This seems to pain him.*

"Die," Quicksilver whispered. "Die? What can I do but die?" *For Proteus will kill me today. He will kill all of us.*

Lifting his head at an awkward angle, he saw the white castle at the center of the crux moving ever closer as the centaurs trotted toward it.

Its white, tall towers defied even the best elf architecture.

Quicksilver had heard the conversation between Proteus and the centaurs yesterday. He knew what would happen when they got there, when they joined Proteus and Miranda there.

Proteus would use Miranda to protect himself from the vengeance of the hill and with one murder rid himself of all rival claimants to the throne of Fairyland. And there was nothing Quicksilver could do to stop him.

After a night of writhing and trying to think his way out of this cunning trap, Quicksilver had found that perfect despair that was like calm at the eye of a storm.

Miranda was powerful enough, faith, to shield Proteus from the results of killing a king of the hill. Though chances were she would die from it.

And if not . . . if not, Proteus intended to kill her, that he could reign alone.

Oh, the poor besotted girl. Quicksilver pitied her most heartily, for he knew what it was like to love in vain. But he knew not what he could do about it. Not while he was wrapped in this net that suppressed all his magical powers.

He watched the centaurs talk to each other, even as they galloped on the smooth road, ignoring the captives on their backs.

He thought they would not ignore Silver thus, and felt a momentary relief that Silver had not fallen to their crude mercies, for hot-blooded centaurs always craved human or elf female flesh.

But on the heels of that very relief, a contrary thought crept. For Silver would get them to remove the net. Quicksilver would wager on it.

Centaurs had ever had an eye for elven beauty. If only Quicksilver could change into Silver perhaps, confuse the centaurs with the change—did they know he could change? He hadn't changed in the last ten years, never in public—perhaps he could convince them that Quicksilver had escaped and left a beautiful girl elf in his place.

Then, perhaps, the centaurs would be stupid enough to free Silver. Oh, they would free her only to rape her, or so the legends said, although they all spoke of inebriated centaurs and these were sober.

But if they freed Silver, Quicksilver's magic would be enough to oppose them.

Oh, if only Quicksilver could change into Silver . . .

He reached inside him for the memories of Silver, for Silver's warm affections, and tried to shape her from the effluvium she'd left behind.

Scene 38

❧

Proteus and Miranda walking down the true road, toward the white castle at the center of the crux.

As Miranda and Proteus walked the true road, drawing nearer the castle, Miranda tried to discern her father's standard upon the towers, but the flagpole over the castle was empty. And try as she might, she could not see—upon the ramparts—even a trace of brown curls, or the glimmer of those broad shoulders: of the mortal raised as prince of elfland, as the Hunter's own pupil.

Had she imagined it? Had she imagined all?

Her dread, her grief, her anger, beat within her like warring tides, and made her wonder about her sanity.

Still she smiled, and kept her voice even and low.

And tried to slow Proteus down.

For though she was sure of being prepared, though she was sure of being sure of her power, she feared that her death was waiting by those white ramparts.

"Wait awhile, love," she said to Proteus as he strode ahead of her. "Wait awhile. For my feet hurt and I'm all out of breath."

"Miranda, there is not time to wait," Proteus said. As he spoke, he pressed on in broad strides, at an almost canter. "Miranda, we must press on, for the day is short and after this day will we forever be part of the crux, bonded to it by magic and unable to live as ourselves. If you prize me and our future happiness, we must press on."

Miranda sighed and pressed on, for what could she do? What could she say that would justify her dread and not give away what she knew of him?

Yet as the castle drew near, she felt something falling over her—a heaviness, like a blanket that muffled her thoughts and sensations and made her feel as though she were walking, asleep, through a dreary, sleeping world.

Had she not heard the conversation the night before, she'd have thought she was tired.

But as it was, she knew her disease for its symptoms—a compulsion upon her. She pushed at it with her will and held it at bay with her anger.

She wondered if Proteus could feel her resistance.

It seemed to Miranda that—now and then—he stared at her doubtfully, out of the corner of his eye.

She would gladly have told him what she thought of him and ended this deadly charade.

She was tired, she was hungry, she was scared. The world in which she'd longed to live, the world that had seemed so enticing in her solitude, had proven bewildering and passing strange. It was but an unknowable land, populated by people that belied all tales.

How could anyone, human or elf, find her way amid these beings that deceived with their very appearance and lied even to themselves?

But she was all that stood between Proteus and sure death for all his captives, sure death for the unending worlds.

She had to stay free. She had to muster all her strength for the duel that she would have to fight.

For now that her uncle was captive, of all of Proteus's intended victims, only she had the power to oppose him.

Scene 39

⚬

Quicksilver, bouncing on the back of the centaur.

Quicksilver abstracted himself from surrounding reality, from the approaching castle where he'd meet his death, from the centaurs and their stink of hot, sweaty horse.

He thought of Silver as he never had, as a part of himself as inextricable, as true as Quicksilver.

Had he ever wished himself rid of Quicksilver? No, for that would have been madness.

Then why had he thought he could be rid of Silver? How had he thought he could survive without her?

Yet, from his first conscious thought, from his first moment of realizing that he was not like his brother, his parents, or the other elves around him, he'd wanted to be just Quicksilver—and not Silver.

And how strange it was—Quicksilver thought now—that Silver had never wished to be rid of Quicksilver. The thought had never crossed her mind.

How strange, Quicksilver thought.

He pondered Silver. He looked at Will and remembered Silver's love for

Will and how, even now, Silver couldn't help but think Will attractive. For Silver loved more than Will's body.

In the timorous mortal, she loved the glimmer of unbound genius, the hope of a soul too large to be contained in any time or place. It wasn't yet true. Will was now small and self-contained, keeping himself within narrow, safe boundaries. But to elf sight it was obvious how large the soul loomed within—how brightly it could shine if it were allowed.

He thought of Silver, naked, crying by the pool of magic.

All he could think, all he could feel of her, he imagined in his mind in exquisite detail.

Then he attempted to slip into the memory as though it were a dress, a favorite suit.

The net that, upon him, prevented any magic could not prevent his change. He knew that. Silver was not some magical transformation but another side of him, and it should be as easy to become her as it was to breathe or smile or talk. Even when, before, he'd been deprived of his magic, he'd always been able to change.

Though he'd wished not to. Oh, what a fool he'd been.

But now Silver's aspect felt unaccustomed like a tight dress that no longer fits.

It was as though—in a featureless plane—Quicksilver pursued the fleeing Silver, calling after her, while she, a beloved phantom, ran ahead of him—ever ahead, ever out of his reach.

She'd not listen to him.

He thought back on Vargmar's execution, when she'd severed herself from him. It seemed to him that on remembering it, he heard her voice in his mind, calling, "Wait, wait. Don't give the defeated a martyr around whom they might hatch fresh plots. Exile him, rather, disgrace him, and then shall he be nobody."

If her voice had thus been in his mind, he'd ignored her.

And what a fool he'd been. Her solution, unorthodox and against the cannon of the Kings of Fairyland, might have worked. His had surely failed.

How he wished he'd listened to her.

As he thought this, it seemed to him that Silver's phantom in his mind turned and stopped running, and smiled at him.

He remembered all the times that Silver had led him astray, every time Silver had played him false and dashed Quicksilver's planning on the shores of her uncontrollable behavior.

Yet if Silver was himself—as she must be—it was Quicksilver who'd gone astray himself.

And just as many times, she'd served him well.

Why—did a man whose hand dropped a coin blame the hand and forthwith punish it? Nay, he knew his hand was but part of himself. It was madness to think of it as separate.

And so it was with Quicksilver and the lady Silver. For Silver was himself. But he must change. He must.

Thus thinking, he forced himself into the shape of his memories of Silver.

For a while nothing happened and then it seemed to Quicksilver that something ripped, some resistance broke.

He felt his form change within the net.

Taking a deep breath, Silver let her voice erupt, high and harmonious, from her lips. "Oh, help. Help me."

The centaurs stopped.

Will, across the centaur next to Silver's, opened his eyes almost to splitting.

Silver smiled at him. How beautiful Will's eyes were, and how scared he looked.

She would swear that beneath the kerchief that bound his mouth, Will attempted to grin.

A dreadful longing for Will filled her. Oh, what she'd not give to touch his face and kiss his lips one more time. One last time?

"Lady, who are you?" the centaur over whose back Silver was lain asked, turning back his broad, barbaric face.

Silver smiled at him. She made her voice small, shaky, and as full of fear as it wished to be. "I don't know. I am but a common elf, and of a sudden snatched from my palace of delights, I found myself here. I don't know how this happened, how this came to be."

"It's a trick," said the dappled centaur. "He's changed his aspect."

But the brown centaur looked back, derision in his voice, "How could he when he has the net of Circe upon him?"

His fellow shook his head. "And yet he did."

"He did not."

Silver felt Quicksilver's anxious fear climbing within her.

The centaurs are suspicious, Quicksilver thought. *This won't go well.*

Hush, she thought, and she tried to calm him while she said aloud, "I know not of whom you talk, nor what this awful device is on which I find myself imprisoned. Oh, free me that I might go in peace."

The dappled centaur turned around, and reached with eager hands for the lady. His fingers felt rough and hot and eager on Silver's shoulders, clawing at the net.

But his friend moved out of the way, pulling Silver from him. "No. Do not. How could he transport himself and substitute another with Circe's net upon him? Think. Do not do what he wishes you to, do not. Or all will be lost."

"Please, let me go," Silver screamed.

Inside her mind, Quicksilver whispered, *They never will, we'll all die here. How ineffective you are. Why did I want you back? Oh, that I'd been a single being.*

"Please free me," Silver said, her desperation betraying itself in her voice.

"Do not," the centaur said. "I don't know why, but I know it's him, the old tyrant who has kept our people pining and rotting under his dark rule. If we free her, we free him, and then we shall all die—stallion and mare and tender foal. His vengeance will fall upon our people and make no distinction of guilty or innocent."

It is not my fault, Quicksilver protested. *Why are they attacking me for this?*

Oppressed? Why, they are foreigners, and they live as they ever have. They must have someone civilized keeping them under control for they are, themselves, brutish and unruly.

"And for this he will kill us if he gets free. Be not a fool, Chiron."

"Please, let me go," Silver said, and cried now. The centaurs' and Quicksilver's foolish prattle filled her with fear and despondence.

But the centaurs looked at her tears and were not moved, and Quicksilver's anger fought within her, and she felt herself being pushed away, pushed, while Quicksilver shoved in to take her place.

Quicksilver lay, exhausted, atop the horse, the net enclosing him in its lethal embrace. Sweat ran down his back in freezing rivulets. He'd accomplished nothing.

Chiron laughed. "See? I told you it was the old tyrant."

Why did they call him a tyrant? He'd done nothing other sovereigns of the hill hadn't. He'd been no more, no less, than the king of the hill.

Tears sprang to his eyes at the centaurs' coarse laughter.

Had this role of king into which he'd fitted himself, like water into an empty vessel, been unworthy?

Would he have done better with his flawed, double nature, than in the diamond perfection of the king's role?

How could that be?

It could not, he told himself, closing his tear-stung eyes. It could not be true that Quicksilver's ancestors were unworthy and that flawed Quicksilver and Silver, conjoined, would have made a better king.

Else, all the legends of elf were false. Else, all history was a lie. How could he doubt all that he'd been taught? How could he dare start afresh, as though all his ancestors had been as—or more—unworthy than he knew himself to be?

Scene 40

∽⃝∽

The smooth, arched oak door of the white castle is closed. Miranda sits on the steps leading up to it, Proteus stands next to her. To the right of her, a pond of pure magic lays, undisturbed and flat. Galloping down the road comes the party of centaurs, and Caliban with Will and Quicksilver.

"What is this?" Miranda asked, standing, feigning surprise. "What does this mean?"

Down the road, at a gallop, in a cloud of dust, came the strange party—the galloping centaurs, their tied-up victims, and Caliban.

What did Caliban think he was doing? Was it true that he intended to violate his mistress?

Had their childhood friendship meant nothing? Had he always resented his subservient position? But he was a troll . . .

Yet, what did that mean? Was Caliban not as good a troll as Miranda was an elf? And yet, Miranda had always treated him as a servant, a monster, unworthy.

Feeling cold and scared, Miranda spoke in a thread of voice. "What is the meaning of this?"

Proteus smiled at her but his smile was not the kind light of days gone by, but a hard, cold display of teeth. "Ask not what it is, Miranda, for you know well. I don't know how you found out, but I know you did. Doubtless you spied upon me, as remorselessly as you stole from the Hunter. Yet I love you well. Now will we kill the tyrant, and you'll shield my poor self from the death that waits those that kill the sovereigns of the hill. And then shall we be married and reign in Elvenland."

Miranda looked at Proteus and wondered, were she besotted yet, would she have mistaken this for a call of love, for an appeal to her loyalty?

She remembered how, at his suggestion, she had stolen her father's book. He'd only mentioned it, and she'd hastened to obey the implied command.

Now forewarned, she stood and willed herself encased in magic, protected from a powerful enemy.

The centaurs arrived at the foot of the stairway.

And Proteus laughed at Miranda's use of magic. Even as she tried to hold her power close, he tugged on it.

"So you know the truth," he said. "So much the better. Now lend me your magic, for I'll shield myself with it."

He wrapped his power around her magic with crude, magical feelers, and seemed about to tear that living power from her body.

But Miranda was angry and—her anger overpowering her fear—she found within her that place of strength that was like holding the Hunter's power to herself.

"No," she yelled, and with the cold force of the Hunter, held the villain at bay, and hugged her power to her. "No. You leave me be."

They stared at each other across the stone step.

Proteus's face was chiseled in anger and tight with determination. He reached for her power and she pushed him back, and back and forth they went, in a deadly tug of war.

Sparks of magic flew around them, as a smell of lilacs rose.

All of Miranda's unschooled power was just enough to keep Proteus's smaller but well-schooled power at bay.

He projected images around her, of the Hunter's infernal dogs, gathering, opening their maws in hatred of her.

But Miranda could see these were not the real dogs, who from her tenderest childhood, had peopled her nightmares.

The dogs' smell, horrible and sweet like the reek of the grave, was absent. As was their emanation of freezing cold.

They were only the incarnation of Proteus's hatred.

Closing her heart, she reached for those images around her and willed the illusory dogs back against him, blood-red tongues lolling, teeth gleaming, rough throats growling.

He stepped back, looking confused, but as they closed in, he waved his hand.

They vanished.

A bolt of blazing fire flew at Miranda.

Miranda held it at bay, suspended in midair between them. Proteus pushed harder. She quaked, but she held firm.

Should she be distracted, should she fear, Proteus would have her power and her self. She could not allow that.

Locked in this duel, afraid to look away, she was only half aware of the centaurs' dropping their bundles upon the dusty ground, galloping toward her.

She felt Proteus reach for the centaurs' power and, with that ancient power, so different from elves, patch up his own power and augment his force. With his greater force he pushed against her defenses, and she pushed back as hard as she could.

Yet the power of the centaurs was little, she remembered. The king of elves held almost all of it.

The ball of fire drew nearer and nearer.

She sweated and grunted and felt she could not hold on long. Their power, smaller though it was, was better aimed and more intent.

Oh, why wasn't her uncle free? Why could he not help her? Let him help her, for she couldn't do it alone.

Yet why should he help her when it had been she who'd brought them both to this trap?

Panic rose in Miranda as she felt her power give under the push of the centaurs and Proteus combined.

The ball of fire, near, singed at her hair and made her skin smart with the heat.

"Leave her be," Caliban's voice said.

And Caliban, a fury of fur and unbound fangs, threw himself in front of Miranda, nipping at the horse legs of the centaurs and growling at Proteus.

Proteus jumped back and—for a moment—Miranda found such respite as she'd been seeking. With all her mind, she extinguished the ball of flame.

"Foul thing," Proteus said. "I thought you were loyal to us."

"Loyal to you, corruption?" Caliban asked. His voice sounded more human and less encumbered than usual. "Toads, beetles, bats light on you." He ran in and nipped and ran back from the centaurs' kicking hooves.

"Thou most lying slave," Proteus said. "Whom I offered thy whole heart's desire, your love, your mistress to do with as you please."

"As I please . . ." Caliban stopped his run and stood, his mouth half open. A sob tore through the lipless fissure. And now, the beast's voice echoed with human tears. "As I please, you say. But what I please is to let her be, to let her be herself and to me, nothing. For if she loved me, oh, if she loved me, what I would have done. I would people the world with Calibans, a strong tribe, a fierce people. But she loves me not. Her desire was for you, you low, smooth-tongued villain."

Caliban stood, as though stricken by the truth, the awful truth of this idea. He didn't notice Hylas's charge nor the hoof aimed at his head.

"Caliban," Miranda screamed, and in her anxiety for him, for a moment, she forgot her defense, her magical shield, and reached toward him.

The ball of fire enveloped Miranda. It didn't burn her skin, though it stung. But it seemed to burn away at that place of calm and resolute anger that was her right as the Hunter's daughter.

The hoof descended and hit Caliban's head with a sound like a stone hitting a melon.

Caliban whimpered and fell, his fur all blood, his eyes wide open and fixed, staring.

She knelt beside him, cradling his gross, blood-spattered head. "Poor creature," she said, and looking up, flung with hatred, "And yet he's worth a hundred of Proteus."

She felt Proteus's power pressing her all about, trying to force her to do what he wished.

The leash of his controlling power closed about her magic. She could not now oppose him, nor attack him. But something she could still do to prevent herself from following his commands and being used as a shield between him and his most foul crime.

She closed her eyes and wished herself to sleep, as she had slept when she'd been very young, in her little bed, while the Hunter crooned a thunderous lullaby.

Scene 41

ۄۄ

Quicksilver is carried forth to lie next to the insensible Miranda. The two centaurs carrying him joke and laugh.

Quicksilver didn't know what to think. He'd seen the troll, Caliban, then Miranda also collapse.

Caliban—what a tangle of deception he'd woven—had been a loyal friend all along, trying to protect his mistress, and for the sake of that, Quicksilver would gladly forgive him any offenses toward himself.

But now Quicksilver and Will were left alone and defenseless.

"The fool thought to trick us," Hylas said, and laughed coarsely as he dropped Quicksilver to the hard ground. "By changing to the aspect of a female and in that aspect entreating us let him go."

Proteus raised his eyebrows and smiled. He'd drawn a knife from his belt. "Aye, the fool. The cursed fool. That's an old, accustomed trick of his."

The knife was dark onyx and sparkled. It was the same knife, Quicksilver knew, that had inflicted the wound that still smarted upon his shoulder. It must be magical and now it would sever his life.

"What will you use for shield," Hylas said, "if she won't do it and would rather collapse than serve you in this?"

Proteus laughed. "Oh, she'll help easily enough. One of you, revive her."

And while the brown stallion knelt by Miranda and patted her face, and reached for her with his power, forcing her awake, Proteus ordered, "Bring me the mortal."

The mortal within his reach, he lifted Will up, and put his knife to Will's neck.

"She'll help me for the love of him," he said.

Trembling, Quicksilver imagined Will's dear life severed here, before his eyes.

Quicksilver would have helped for the love of Will too. He closed his eyes. He would have killed himself for Will's love, also. But he could not move, nor use his magic. And he didn't wish to see Will die like that.

He didn't wish to think that, in seconds, all their misbegotten lives would be over. He might deserve it, but these others didn't. Silver had been right, Quicksilver wrong. Divided as Quicksilver was, he had proven at least as unworthy as any of the tyrants of old, who'd murdered trolls and oppressed centaurs—good and bad alike.

Silver, herself, would never judge anyone for his appearance. Oh, if only Quicksilver could be her again. He'd never realized she had been a true gift of the gods, of magic and of fate, designed to guide him, to make him a better king.

If only he could have accepted her and learned from her.

Within him, he felt Silver stirring, mourning her lover's life, and her lost life too.

But it was too late. He didn't know how to accept her. How he wished with all his mind, his power, all his heart, that he could be Lady Silver again, and be one with her.

Oh, what a tangled web Quicksilver's elven life had woven that fate found a way to kill his joys with love.

Scene 42

༄

Will stands next to Proteus, Proteus's left arm holding him up, Proteus's right hand holding a knife at his throat.

Will felt the knife at his throat and knew that this was the end—if not this way, then another, for the evil elf did not intend to let Will go.

Will, and Hamnet also, would die here, in this cursed land beyond imagination.

Oh, how far Will had come only to die, and yet not so far at all. His ambition had ever been tempered with fear, he thought. Marlowe's ghost had been too right.

For Will had wished to be a poet, but had borrowed his words from Marlowe and not dared to put down his own words, or bare his own soul upon the paper. He had never thought himself the like of those other poets who, with their university educations, had stormed the London stage.

Will had but a grammar school education. How could he be their equal? Everyone knew that university men had learned all about theater, and the proper way to construct a play.

He knew himself a fool even to dream on it, and thus had stayed within the safe boundaries of the artform as Marlowe had created it, blazingly alive, from Marlowe's fiery mind.

Will was nothing but an empty shell, a crow beautified with another's swan feathers. And for his pretensions without support, for his ambition that he was not willing to fight for, he would now die. He and Hamnet, his only son. Hamnet for whom he would gladly have given his own life—or at least he'd said so, but in the end, he'd been too timorous to attempt risking anything for Hamnet.

Oh, that he had it all to do again, Will would be braver and save his son. Even if Hamnet was now different and changed, even if Will could no longer claim him as his legitimate son and integrate him seamlessly into the world of men.

Even if Will had already lost his son as such, he wished he could restore this new Hamnet to freedom and the sane world of men.

To free Hamnet from here, to give him a chance at happiness, Will would gladly sacrifice himself.

Alas, he had already sacrificed himself in vain, without fighting.

The girl on the ground opened her eyes, and now Proteus hissed close to Will's ear, "Miranda, protect me, or the mortal dies."

The woman looked on him with uncomprehending blue eyes. "But he will die anyway," she said slowly as though speaking out of dreams. Then, with blazing fury, "You'll let him die. Kill him now, villain, kill him swiftly if you will, for I will not help you."

Will closed his eyes. He would die.

Upon the darkness of his closed eyes, Marlowe's ghost appeared and Marlowe's voice spoke clearly in Will's head. *You think, Will, that like Doctor Faustus, you shall trade your soul for magic. And yet, you need not. And yet, without magic is your soul forfeit as is that son you claim to love more than your own soul.*

This was said in mockery and Will *felt* Marlowe's doubt of Will's affection for Hamnet.

Will opened his eyes and saw Miranda, and Quicksilver, both helpless, lying side by side on the ground and staring up at him.

He felt the cold edge of Proteus's weapon, heard Proteus say, "I mock not, so trifle not with me. Obey me, or he dies."

Will thought of how desperate he, himself, had been when he'd tried the like gambit on the witch.

Would he have killed the woman? Perhaps not, but then Proteus was no Will.

Will knew he'd die if Will allowed this to go on.

But how to stop it?

There was only magic. Could Will, even if he dared, summon that magic he'd disdained till now? Would it damn his immortal soul if he did? Or if it didn't, would it prove that all Will had been taught was wrong?

At that moment, fearing to destroy his own beliefs, Will remembered what Miranda had believed and how, those beliefs had led her here, to this near death. Perhaps Will's beliefs were just as wrong. He must dare test them.

His fear, his fury, his love for his son—all in a bundle—pressed in on his brain, and with all his might he willed the gag to tear and give around his mouth.

The cloth ripped as though cut by a knife.

As the pieces fell away from around his mouth, Will spoke. "Back," he told Proteus. "Back, dread creature, and touch me not, nor dare harm these elves whom I protect."

Thus speaking, he stood before Quicksilver and Miranda. The assault of Proteus's power hit him like a harsh body slam—blow upon blow, as though Proteus and the centaurs were punching him, enough to fell a man in a tavern brawl. Such tavern brawl as poor Marlowe was rumored to have died in.

But Will, who'd never brawled in his life, stood under the blows, legs wide apart for balance, and threw back blow by blow and punch for punch, magically willing the villains to be crushed.

He saw his enemies flinch and duck.

But Proteus and the centaurs looked one at the other, as though coordinating their attack, and returned to the fray with redoubled force.

A magical punch, then quickly another fell on Will, punches so strong Will tasted his own blood in his mouth.

He stood, and defended himself as he could. And yet, he knew he couldn't hold on much longer.

Scene 43

ॐ

Quicksilver, staring from the ground, while light and power fly in a battle between Will and Proteus.

O h, what might Will has, what power, Quicksilver thought. No wonder Silver had loved him.

In that moment, he understood Silver's love. The guilt and shame Quicksilver hadn't even known he felt at her preference now fled from him. A mortal, Will might be, a lowly mortal. But how could anyone be ashamed of loving him?

For Will, mortal—and male—though he was, must be a rare creature, engendered from the womb of nature on a singular day. How he battled the magical ones, with no fear. With what strength he opposed what he didn't even understand.

Yet, Quicksilver, long an adept at these duels, knew that Will would lose, for the centaurs pressed in upon him also, increasing Proteus's might.

Will, unschooled in magic, could not stand the trained might of his enemies.

Quicksilver thought of the centaurs' just complaints against the king of Elvenland and felt guilty, but time was not for guilt. From his throne could he redress the foreigners' to complaints. Not now.

Now, must he help Will to save them all.

"Lady," he asked the girl who, on the ground beside him, sobbed like the child she was. "Lady, I know you fear me, but you must untie me, so that I can help the mortal and free us all."

Miranda looked at him, her eyes wide, and stared like a blind woman who, suddenly given sight, cannot interpret what she sees.

"Lady, you must help me," Quicksilver said. "And you can have my throne, or yet my life, or my riches or anything of mine you crave. Only let me save Will and all of us with him."

He looked at Miranda and wished her strength.

And he wished he could be Silver again. Her follies were his follies and together they were far less foolish than apart.

Scene 44

ʚϧɞ

The same scene seen through Miranda's eyes.

Now, what should she do, and whom to believe? Her uncle, whom she'd learned to consider evil, had asked her help.

Was he telling the truth? Did villains beg?

Miranda stared at him, her eyes wide.

"My kingdom," he said. "My life if you believe yourself wronged, all of mine is yours if only you will free me. For if you do not, then will my friend be killed, and you, and your troll also."

Should Miranda trust again, when she'd been most cruelly deceived?

Yet, if she trusted not . . .

She looked on Caliban who, after all, had not been a deceiver or not of her, but had lain in wait till he could avenge her. Was Caliban alive still?

Looking close at the furry body, it seemed to Miranda that she saw him breathe. His head upon her ankles still trickled blood.

She looked at the mortal, arms wide, sparks of magic flying, his hair—possessed of a life of its own—standing around his head.

If she said no, if she did not help her uncle, all this would be lost. Well she knew that neither she nor the mortal nor the both combined could oppose the might of these beings trained in magic.

Yet, if her uncle lied, what would he do? What could happen that was worse than what waited them already? Miranda would die, but *maybe* Caliban would be saved. And the mortal would be rescued, if Quicksilver had any say in the outcome of this.

She'd risk her life in saving Caliban because her uncle—like Proteus—might not wish to have competition for ruling in Elvenland. Once the game was won, he might have her killed.

Yet, her life was already forfeit if she didn't help Quicksilver.

Besides, was Miranda's life worth all that much?

She'd stolen from her father; she'd left her home, all in pursuit of a false, foolish love.

If she died now, redeeming the mortal and Caliban, what was she doing more than what she *must* do? Her duty was to redeem herself now and, in doing it, to save all these others.

Trembling, she sat up, afraid that Proteus would notice her and kill her with a magical blow, before she could free Quicksilver.

But Proteus and the centaurs, in close, hot battle with the mortal, looked not at her.

Trembling with nervousness and fatigue, Miranda reached for her uncle.

Gambling her life to save those she prized, she reached over and, with nimble fingers, pulled Circe's net away from Quicksilver and threw the net wide.

Scene 45

⟡

The scene through Will's eyes. Behind him, the door of the castle flies open.

Will felt the shoring up of another magic strengthening his shields, putting extra force in his punches. Had Quicksilver freed himself?

Turning to where he felt that magic, Will met the eye of—he opened his mouth in shock and, for a moment, almost lost control of his magic—Quicksilver, who stood free behind Will, but even as Will watched, Quicksilver melted and changed and the Lady Silver smiled at Will.

Naked as the day she'd seen light, she was pale and beautiful, cloaked only in her silken black hair. Her silver eyes shone impishly and she said, "You are gifted in magic use, Will, for a beginner."

And in saying it, she took hold of his newfound power and threw it at their enemy.

Will felt his stomach churn and his teeth rattle with the force of his own punch.

"I'm too old for this," he said, looking at the lady and at Miranda who, behind her, seemed to hesitate still.

But Silver grinned and said, "To me, my friend, you shall never be old."

Their gazes locked and Will realized with a shock that Silver did mean what she said. She didn't see him as old or unattractive.

He felt a blush of gratified pride warm his cheeks.

The lady loved him still, who had so adored him in his youth.

In her eyes, he saw himself as young, and dazzled by her affection, he failed to feel the magical punch from Proteus, which threw Will to the ground.

"Will," Silver screamed.

His face hurt. His eyes fogged in pain. Will said, "Care not for me, for you must defend us all."

Silver turned. Will felt her shield go up, but feared it would be too little too late. Then he felt yet another power join their conjoined powers.

This power was stronger than all of theirs, powerful and strong.

The door of the magical white castle flew wide.

"Father," a man's voice called.

Down the steps a man came running, a young man of maybe twenty attired in red and blue silk. It took Will a few seconds and a hasty breath to recognize Hamnet. But he could feel Hamnet's power touching his, shoring his, like soothing water upon abraded skin.

"Father," Hamnet said, and smiled at Will. Magical sparks flew around them. The centaurs neighed and screamed as fireballs singed their hair. The Lady Silver, naked and noble like a goddess of old, stood with hands raised and shaped the crackling magic to righteous assault of the unrighteous foe.

Now, Miranda also rose and, looking very oddly at Hamnet, drew herself to stand behind the lady, shoring Silver's magic with her own.

Under their conjoined command, flames of magic fire erupted round the centaurs' hooves.

Miranda, looking dazed, still held in her hand the net of Circe.

Proteus, pale, his lips white and trembling, stood his ground despite the flames that licked at his broad shoulders, his noble features. Hamnet threw himself in Will's open arms. "I've been raised by the Hunter these long years, but I knew you'd come and rescue me, I was sure of it."

Will felt his eyes burn with tears, but turned away. "Let us first be safe," he said. "And then, shall we talk of all the years wasted."

Speaking thus, he turned toward the enemy who, in a disarrayed group, stood facing them.

Hamnet's power, and—Will realized—Hamnet's knowledge of magic, had joined their collective force and given them victory.

The centaurs buckled and fell backward, whinnying and crying. Proteus alone stood, staring.

Madness burned in his eyes.

"Oh, I am betrayed," he said. "I am undone. I, who loved the Lady Miranda well, and loved her true."

Scene 46

⚉

The scene from Miranda's eyes, as she stares at Proteus.

How pale he looked and yet still handsome.
   Miranda felt the old accustomed softness toward him as he turned his dark, dark eyes toward her.

"Oh, Miranda," he said. "I loved you well. Yet you betrayed me."

The centaurs, behind him in disarray, looked on, their faces full of terror, their eyes rolling, as magical flames licked their tall legs and singed the ringlets of their human hair.

Miranda could sense that the power of the alliance, hers, her—uncle's? She looked at Lady Silver—and that of the two mortals, all of it did no more than keep the centaurs encircled in fire and neutralize Proteus's power so he could not attack them.

But they could not penetrate Proteus's defenses. The force of desperation strengthened his shields and put steel in his self-defense.

Unharmed, yet he looked ill and tired and miserable. "Miranda, you used to swear you loved me true. I know I've done you wrong." Proteus opened his hands, wide, in a gesture of appeasement. "But think you on my many wrongs. I lost your father, my beloved cousin, who would have advanced me in his realm. And then I lost my father.

"I might have done wrong, but can you fault me? It was only my angered heart that led me astray."

As he spoke, he approached her step by step, step on step closer. "You have the net, Miranda. Just throw it over Silver, she's but Quicksilver's female aspect. Stop her making magic. Then, together, we can be happy yet."

Proteus's presence, that near, as in the days of yore, was disturbing, but Miranda remembered what she'd heard him tell the centaurs when she'd hid herself in the forest.

Had that been naught but his intemperate, angry tongue? Had he truly meant naught by it?

She couldn't quite believe it, and yet his beautiful, stern face commanded belief and his black eyes shimmered with held-back tears.

"Miranda, please," he said.

"Mistress, don't," Caliban said from the ground.

Looking down, Miranda saw that Caliban had crawled toward her till he lay at her feet, his hand on her ankle.

"Mistress, don't, for he is but a villain and he'll kill you too. Those others— mistress, they might not be perfect. Indeed, the king has many crimes upon his tainted soul. But they'll not hurt you. That villain, Proteus, will. Oh, mistress, I care not what happens to me, just so you live."

"Listen not to the vile creature," Proteus screamed.

But Miranda looked down at Caliban's sad eyes and bloodied fur.

She heard a scream form in her throat, and she leapt forward past the Lady Silver.

Miranda flung the net, and it flew wide—a golden cobweb sparkling in the cold light of the crux.

It opened as it flew, like a bird taking wing.

Proteus stepped back, startled, but it was too late.

The net fell on him and stretched to envelop him.

He fell to the ground, wrapped in the coils of the very weapon he would have used against Quicksilver.

The centaurs, too, their power worn out by the magical flame that encircled them, collapsed to the ground, one atop the other.

Miranda, staring at Proteus, who writhed in the coils of the net, felt a human hand upon her arm.

Turning, she looked into the golden falcon-eyes of the creature who'd been the human child that she had kidnaped for the love of Proteus.

Now he was no child and his features, his demeanor looked like those of a Prince of Elvenland.

He smiled at her, and his gaze sparkled with something she didn't quite understand.

"You've done well, milady," he said.

Miranda's breath caught upon her throat and her hands trembled.

The odd sense of belonging together that she'd felt before at seeing him, upon the pond, was a hundred times magnified, and she realized suddenly she'd loved him since that first, magical glimpse.

Did I love before? she thought, and bewildered, glanced at Proteus who, writhing upon the sand, seemed insignificant, unimportant. A stranger for whom she cared not.

Heart, forswear its sight. For I ne'er saw true beauty till last night.

Scene 47

୧୨୧

The scene through Will's eyes. He looks, amazed, at Hamnet and Miranda, then gazes in wonder at Quicksilver, who has resumed his male aspect.

"Look you upon them," Quicksilver said and smiled at Will. "Have you ever seen sweet love so fast birthed?"

Will shook his head.

He remembered his lust for Lady Silver, but it seemed to him here something else blossomed. In the way the young people embraced, the way their gazes met, he read something else than lust.

Prodigious birth of love, so quickly grown, and she no more than fourteen.

Imagine there, he thought, a tragedy, where a fourteen-year-old girl falls for an enemy—a man of another house, another realm almost.

He shook his head. This was not a play.

There could be no tragedy here. But what else could it be, when Miranda was an elf and Hamnet a mortal?

"How can this be contrived?" Will asked Quicksilver in amazement. "How can they live together?"

Quicksilver smiled, and his eyes were soft. "I fear me you'll say I stole your son from you, to my shadowy realm of slippery magic. But only listen, Will, with thy consent . . .

"You cannot take your son back to the mortal world. He was raised by the Hunter and he is magical. He'll never fit amid mortal men. Give your consent and he'll a changeling be, a Prince of Elves, Miranda's bethroded, their union confirmed when she first shall reach the age of reason. They'll be my heirs when I the world depart, or when I am too tired to carry the burden of state." He looked at Will with a soft, pleasing gaze. "Thus shall our blood joined be. Say you'll allow it, and with that one word, secure so many people's happiness."

Will did not know what to say. Or perhaps he simply couldn't find the words to say it. So long he'd been afraid of magic. So hard, as he'd fought to keep magic from stealing part of his family.

And now, he'd let the dearest part of him go to Elvenland?

He looked on Hamnet and Miranda and would swear they'd not heard any of the conversation, their gazes lost in each other.

"Aye me," Miranda said, and glanced at Will and Quicksilver. "My only love sprang from my only hate."

Hamnet, his gaze on her, replied, "Prodigious birth of love, this is to me, that I must love whom I thought my enemy."

Will remembered his Nan and how he'd loved her in the first blush of love, how neither her age ten years more than his nor her reputation as a shrew could divide them.

Truth, he loved Nan still so well he would never part with her forever. Not willingly. How could he ask Hamnet to do that, and thus also reduce himself to a smaller world than he could attain?

Will forced a laugh and heard it echo, brittle, at the edge of tears. "You have my consent, friend," and in saying so, for the first time named Quicksilver thus. "I never thought for all my ambition that I'd sired a king."

Now, this the young people *had* heard, and turning, stared at Quicksilver, who smiled kindly on them.

"Then Hamnet as my gift, and thine own acquisition worthily purchased, take my niece. Sit and talk with her. Soon, we shall to the hill and there shall both of you be happy."

"Not so fast, sir," Miranda spoke. "My father's leave I crave, the Hunter's dispensation. And then there's these creatures." With her gesture she encompassed Proteus, who had sat up, looking dazzled, and the centaurs, who, looking scared, were regaining their senses. "They rightly fall to my father's justice."

Scene 48

ᗉᎶ᎒

In front of the castle steps, the centaurs start to revive and Proteus writhes upon the ground. Miranda and Hamnet gaze adoringly at each other. Will and Quicksilver look on the couple with bittersweet tenderness. They all start as the rumble of thunder echoes.

Quicksilver started. Thunder? In the crux? Could that be, when there was neither rain nor true sun here?

Then he saw the gigantic shadow leaving the white castle and taking on an almost human aspect as it approached. It was a hunter on a giant horse, who rode down the front steps, followed by snarling, dark dogs.

Miranda cried out and held Hamnet tight in her embrace, as tears ran down her face at her adopted father's approach.

Still on horseback, the Hunter stood a few paces from the group.

The centaurs attempted to rise, but could only fall again and whimper in fear.

Will jumped to stand in front of Miranda and Hamnet, his arms open wide as if to protect them.

And Quicksilver, feeling less than innocent here, feared the blood would drain from his heart as he faced the immortal Lord of Justice.

"How now?" the Hunter asked, his voice rumbling with the thunder of all the storms absent from the crux. "What have we here?" He looked at them, a smile of amusement in his inhumanely perfect features.

"It seems to me that all of you are guilty of crime, or action, or absent thought." He grinned. "So make confession and, mind, make it true. Some will be pardoned, the others punished. For never was there tale of greater woe than this you have enacted."

Quicksilver, rousing himself, looked at the perfect immortal face, then glanced back at his scared companions who lay upon the sand. He stepped forward.

He must take his punishment and protect everyone else. He could feel Silver's agreement within him.

Naked and vulnerable, his silvery blond hair his only covering, leaving bare the scars with which war had marked his flesh, he stepped forward and bowed to the Hunter.

"Lord of Night and Justice and Eternal Law, leave my companions and adversaries in peace, for I alone am guilty.

"By my own reasoning and upon my own head, I decided to suppress what I was and make myself into a perfect King of Fairyland.

"Thus became I inflexible and harsh and, with my stern rule, tempted my kinsmen to revolt." He waved toward Proteus. "By my ill thought did I also allow crimes against centaurs and trolls to continue, till those races erupted in fresh mutiny. Thus did I my crown and power abuse, till the reels of my misdids ensnared in their plots my friend, his son, your daughter.

"All here are innocent, save myself. I alone am guilty and you may punish me."

He knelt and waited and the Hunter looked on him.

Quicksilver's heart beat fast, fast. Would the Hunter kill him? Or make him one of the cursed dogs, who, even now, slavered and strained toward Quicksilver's flesh, lacking only the Hunter's word to let them fly?

The Hunter's loud, rumbling laugh erupted, and Quicksilver looked up, terrified.

"Oh, King, you are guilty indeed," the Hunter said. "Of folly and love. But if those were the crimes that I punished, there would scarce be a living being, human or elf, still alive on earth. Trust that Lady Silver who shares your soul, and mend your ways. You're not so guilty that you can, upon your shoulders, carry the burden of guilt of all these here."

Scene 49

ɷɷ

All stand or lie in front of the white palace. Quicksilver looks bewildered as he rises from his knees. The Hunter smiles. Miranda advances.

"It is my fault, Father," Miranda said. "I thought myself in love and disobeyed you."

"No, my fault, mine," Caliban said. "I loved her so much that, for her sake, I did not reveal her encounters with the traitor elf. And in seeking to save her, I allowed the centaurs to ensnare the mortal and the king."

"It is my fault," Will said. "For fear of magic did I refuse to think over it all till it was too late. And with my incautious temper did I rush here, where I was not needed and could only do harm."

But the Hunter laughed, waved his hand, and said, "Pardoned, the sorry lot of you." Then, turning to the centaurs, he said, "And you, creatures?"

"We're not guilty," Hylas said, managing to stand. "Our race has been kept—"

"Not guilty?" the Hunter thundered. "How not? The oppression of your race, however great, could not have caused you, as a centaur with a mind of his own, to offer violence to my daughter."

"It was the wine," Chiron said.

"That he gave us," Eurytion said, and pointed toward Caliban.

"Master—" Caliban started, squirming.

"It is my fault," Quicksilver said. "So the guilt is mine. Mine and only—"

"Be still, oh, King," the Hunter thundered. "I grow tired of your obsessive guilt." With fierce brow he turned to the centaurs. "But you and that pool of inequity." He pointed at Proteus. "You have committed crimes that naught can excuse.

"For your cold hearts and twisted souls, I call you guilty."

On that word, the Hunter's dogs rushed upon the centaurs who, summoning their strength, scrambled up and shambled away.

"Now, you," the Hunter said, pointing at Proteus.

The net vanished and Proteus stood.

"You'll be my dog, cur, for eternity," the Hunter said.

"You'll not win thus," Proteus said, and his body changing, fur growing upon it, he lopped in the direction of the pool in front of the magic castle. "I'll burn myself and Fairyland with me," Proteus yelled and leapt in.

Flame exploded.

Proteus's magic caught, and he burned like a living torch.

"Proteus," Miranda yelled, feeling keenly the horror of the moment.

Beside her, her uncle screamed.

In a flash, Miranda understood.

Quicksilver, as King of Fairyland, was still linked to Proteus, who was his subject and part of the hill magic. So when he burned, like a fuse, he'd set the whole hill aflame.

"Stop, Proteus," she screamed and, throwing her own power between the two, knew she'd be consumed.

For she must stand between her and those she loved. She must save Hamnet and Will and Quicksilver.

She felt flame engulf her, burn her. She would stop existing.

But then the smell of dark forests surrounded her. The Hunter. Her father's power, strong and icy, covered her, encased her.

She could see Proteus burn like a living candle, but it didn't hurt her. Quicksilver looked unhurt and puzzled.

Quicksilver stared at Proteus, who was all consumed. "How, how am I saved?"

"She saved you," the Hunter said.

"And he saved me," Miranda said, baffled. "My father saved me." She turned uncomprehending eyes to the Hunter. "Father," she said, then conscious of being unworthy of such a parent, she amended, "Sir, I am not worthy."

The Hunter smiled and looked kindly. "None of you are worthy, nor am I. But each of us must do what fits the time.

"Even I who am the Lord of justice have, upon this poor troll, committed grievous harm, dragging him from dam and cave, from den and pack. Caliban, your pack lives yet, and to them I'll restore you, making you and them both forget these years when you have been away."

Caliban shifted and dragged his nail on the ground. "But Lord of Night, I do not wish to forget." He regarded the Hunter with a jaundiced eye, looking him up and down and frowning. "These years—" He looked at Miranda. "Even the pain in them have shaped Caliban. Caliban is not a troll from the mountains, without experience of the world of elves. If you take that away you take a part of Caliban, as bad as taking Caliban from his dam and cave."

The Hunter looked surprised at being thus addressed and, for a moment, looked as though he would thunder his rage. Caliban shrank into himself, but kept looking up, kept looking at the Hunter, as though dutifully waiting an order.

The Hunter's face smoothed and he laughed suddenly. "Well put troll, and once more it proves that none are without guilt, for even in our well-intended moments we might violate the needs of another creature. Go then, oh, troll, back to your mountain home, and remember you this."

"No, wait," Quicksilver called out "Wait, be not so quick, good troll. To your own land go, and there gather your people. Too long have they been subjected to elven rule. Now I'll let you choose if you wish to remain in the hill or to be a faithful neighbor to us and friends of elves. And if you remain, in return for your magic shall you receive the same power that the elves derive from their submission to my rule."

Caliban bowed and mid-bow a tear in space appeared all around him. Through that tear one could glimpse craggy mountains. Caliban raised his head, sniffed the air, and took off running toward a distant peak, as the rent in the fabric of the world closed.

The Hunter laughed. "Was that the Lady Silver speaking there, milord?" he asked. He pointed to Quicksilver. "King, be both your halves and be not ashamed, for that shall you more the king be and less the fool."

As he pointed, Quicksilver vanished, though as he did, as though a door opened around him, the people in the crux saw a lavish bedroom and a blond woman, who ran to embrace Quicksilver.

"And you, Miranda, daughter, and you, Hamnet, my foster son." The Hunter took Miranda's hand in his cold one and, smiling, joined it with Hamnet's warm one.

"You have my blessing," he said. He grinned at Hamnet. "And you, you've been a son to me these long years. My daughter take of me, and make her happy."

He grinned at them, a smile most inhuman. "Now is the riddle solved and I have by this contrivance of bringing you all to the crux raised for my daughter a companion most worthy. Now shall I to my ancient occupations, and unlearn the cares of a human heart. Fare you well, and may you be blessed."

With his wave, Miranda felt as though the ground had opened beneath her.

She struggled to regain balance and found herself, still holding Hamnet's hand, in a sumptuous salon.

There, Quicksilver stood, dressed, wearing a crown and wrapped in a cloak. He smiled at them. Beside him were the blond woman and a serious-looking elf with dark hair and bright green eyes.

"Ariel, Malachite," Quicksilver said. "Here are my new son and daughter."

Scene 50

ॐ

Will and the Hunter, before the castle.

"And you, oh poet," the Hunter said. "What shall we do with you? The witch warned you that to leave the crux mortal man must pay in forfeit a part of himself."

From far off in the crux came the snarling of dogs and the screams of centaurs.

Will shivered. "I have lost my son," he said.

The Hunter chuckled. "Part of yourself? Poet, I think not. You scarce saw him from year to year, him in Stratford-upon-Avon and you in London."

Will hugged himself. Must he, indeed, lose even more to the crux? What could he give? His son had already left.

But no, it had to be something closer: some quality of mind, or sight or hearing, breath from the body or else years of life.

Quality of mind? Will thought and thought on the poetry that Marlowe had bequeathed him. He could leave that behind and then Marlowe would be free and Will, himself, free also.

But Will had made his fame, and not inconsiderable fortune, from Marlowe's words. What if alone Will could not write at all?

He felt his throat close in panic.

Did he want, truly, to be forever beautified with another's feathers? Did he, otherwise, wish to starve?

If he let it go, what of the people who depended on him? Ned Alleyn and Lord Chamberlain's men depended on Will's plays.

Could he let them down?

He felt the fog close about him. His throat constricted. Yet he must leave something behind.

Oh, let Marlowe's poetry stay here in the crux. Let it go. Will would succeed on his own words or not at all. And if Ned starved until he found another playwright, or until Will regained his footing Will would gladly divest his purse to keep his fellows alive.

And go back to Stratford and gladly be a glover, if that were what fate of him demanded, if he had no words of his own.

Let *him* pay the price alone and let Marlowe go to his reward.

He felt as though something invisible but attached to him broke off.

Suddenly, he breathed more freely. It was as though he'd carried a weight for years that was suddenly lifted from his back.

"You chose well, poet," the Hunter said. "Now let me return you to your work. Now that my plans are all overthrown and that strength I have is mine own—it is most strong. Be free, and fare you well."

On those words, Will found himself in his bare room in London. What strange events he had witnessed. He could hardly compass losing his son.

As for the words, well . . . he might never write again.

Yet letting go of Marlowe had been worth it. The ghost was gone, and it seemed to Will he remembered scenes and voices in a fog, as though something had happened in that heartbeat when Will had forsworn Marlowe's words. Something too quick for the human eye to perceive and yet crystal clear to Will's heart.

He remembered a fog, and a small boy running through a featureless landscape—a boy with auburn hair and wide grey eyes.

"Father, Father," the boy said.

"Imp," Marlowe cried out, and his ghost looking whole and unblemished, reached for the small ghost, and lifted him high, whirling him around in a rapture of joy. "Imp, I'm here at last."

"And now we'll truly be together forever?" Imp asked as Marlowe set him down. Imp raised his hand to meet his father's.

"Forever," Marlowe said.

Together they walked off, toward some bliss only they could see.

But all this seemed too metaphysical for Will's small, tidy, homey room. So did all of the crux.

It all seemed a dream.

Yet there was an idea Will had for a tragedy.

What was it now?

Ah, yes, young love and adverse houses. A parent who refused to let his child change and therefore would create a tragedy.

He sat himself down and began to write.

Scene 51

It is a week later, at night in Will's lodgings, and Will sits by candlelight before a completed manuscript, frowning down at a letter in his hands. From outside come the sounds of tavern shills and drinking songs, and the call of sellers hawking their wares.

Will read the letter three times. The handwriting was not Nan's—who couldn't write—but the small, perfect handwriting of Will's brother, Gilbert, a worthy Stratford merchant.

But the words were Nan's, and from the page leapt her distress and grief at the news she gave.

She said Hamnet had been found dead in the woods, and they'd buried him for, it being summer, they could not risk the corruption that would soon come.

She said Will would no more see his small son, only perhaps to pray at his humble grave.

And Will, knowing his son wasn't dead, that what they'd brought from the woods was a stock—a stick or twig enchanted to look and feel all like Hamnet's corpse—wondered whether to tell Nan. Would it multiply her grief or soothe it? Faith, he could not bear it if she hated him for having consented to the arrangement.

What else, though, could Will have done?

He closed his eyes, trying to decide. Either way, he must go to Stratford soon and console his wife, and his grieving daughters.

They were all he had now.

For though his son was alive, Will had lost him, perhaps as all fathers must lose their sons.

Hamnet, for whom Will had dared dream so much, had, after all, grown into a life that his father couldn't imagine.

In the kingdom of elves would his life be lived, a kingdom so different from his father's sphere as to defy Will's understanding.

And yet, Will thought, wasn't his own sphere of London and the theater a puzzle to his father, the provincial glover?

Someone knocked at the door and Will went to open it.

He found himself facing Ned. "You look hag ridden, still," Ned said. And anxiously, "Have you any play yet?"

Will smiled. He went to the desk and got his manuscript, and slowly set it in Ned's hands.

"Here is," he said. *"The Tragedy of Romeo and Juliet."*

"A tragedy?" Ned said. "Are you sure? And wasn't the name different you told me before? Rowena and . . . what was it?"

Will smiled. He felt serene confidence that this play, written with his own words and without Marlowe's, was the best thing he'd yet penned. "It is the tragedy of Romeo and Juliet."

Ned peered doubtfully at the first page. "Two households, both alike in dignity, In fair Verona, where we lay our scene, From ancient grudge break to new mutiny, Where civil blood makes civil hands unclean—" Ned read. He looked up and blinked. "This is like nothing you ever wrote before, Will."

"I know," Will said.

Ned peered back down on the paper. "From forth the fatal loins of these two foes, A pair of starcross'd lovers take their life; Whose misadventured piteous overthrows, do with their death bury their parents' strife. The fearful passage of their death-mark'd love, And the continuance of their parents' rage, Which, but their children's end, nought could remove, Is now the two hours' traffic of our stage." Ned looked up, and slowly, a rare smile curled his lips upward, erasing the marks of tension in his features. "Faith, Will, it is the best you've written."

Will grinned. "I know."

And it seemed to him, though it couldn't be true, that somewhere nearby Marlowe's ghost laughed.

Author's Note

ᘓᘔ

And again I attempted to give yet another explanation for Shakespeare's genius. This one, devoid of all artifice, blames it on those fractured memories, those lost afternoons of childhood, those collections of imperatives and impulses that make up each human being. That is, it blames it on Shakespeare himself and who he was.

Giving up the false crutch of Marlowe's words at the end, he relies on himself alone and so comes to know his own words and his own individual expression. Because genius, like all other human qualities, is ultimately inexplicable and a part of that small universe that is each of us.

I've found I was very bad about posting the bibliography on my website, preferring to write new work instead. The bibliography for this book is more or less coincidental with that for the first book. The bibliography for the second book I'll attempt to post at some time.

As usual, I apologize for taking liberties with William Shakespeare's words and biography, but I feel he would have wanted it so. Always a crafty borrower of others' plumes, a re-weaver of lusterless tales into his own sparkling concoctions, he might well forgive my borrowing of his diamonds to ornament my rags. And perhaps my lie, humble and contrived though it is, will hold some semblance of deeper truth within its pretend construction.

Sarah A. Hoyt
Colorado, 2003